Mary E. Pearce, a Lon... ...in the relative peace of Gloucestershire. She tackled various jobs – shop assistant, filing clerk, waitress, usherette – before settling down to write seriously in the 1960s. Her career began with the appearance of short stories in magazines and has led to the publication of nine highly successful novels which have been translated into Dutch, French, German, Italian, Japanese, Norwegian and Portuguese, as well as being bestsellers in America.

'A keen eye for beauty in everyday things' *Sunday Telegraph*

'Warm and vivid' *Publishers Weekly*

'About the human nature of people which is Mary Pearce's secret ... The dialogue both convinces and entertains' *Manchester Evening News*

'All the characters are drawn with warm understanding and humour' *Eastern Daily Press*

MARY E. PEARCE

THE OLD HOUSE AT RAILES

WARNER BOOKS

A *Warner* Book

First published in Great Britain in 1993
by Little, Brown and Company
This edition published by Warner Books in 1994
Reprinted 2000

A CIP catalogue record for this book is
available from the British Library.

ISBN 0 7515 0909 4

Printed in England by Clays Ltd, St Ives plc

Warner Books
A Division of
Little, Brown and Company (UK)
Brettenham House
Lancaster Place
London WC2E 7EN

In memory of

Arthur and Ellen Millest

CHAPTER

1

The early wealth of the Tarrant family, as of so many Gloucestershire families, had been founded on wool and the manufacture of fine cloth, and the manor house at Newton Railes had been built in 1565 by William Tarrant, who owned a number of fulling mills in and around the town of Chardwell, at the head of the Cullen Valley. William and his immediate descendents had invested their surplus profits in land until the Newton Railes estate, lying at the foot of Ox Knap, in this southern corner of the Cotswold Hills, comprised a thousand acres or more, divided into four farms. By then they had severed their connection with the woollen trade and had settled comfortably into the life of the typical country gentleman.

During the eighteenth century, however, there had been a steady decline, and successive members of the family, some from thriftlessness, some from bad luck, had seen their fortunes dwindle away until, by 1815, most of the estate had been sold and all that remained was the Home Farm. Later, during John Tarrant's time, even this had to be sold, which left only the house itself and the five hundred acres of parkland in which it stood. The Home Farm was now known as Old Manor Farm and its stock still grazed in the Newton Railes park, thus keeping the turf trim and bringing Tarrant some revenue.

His only other income came from a few investments: shares in the Cullen and Leame Canal; in the Turnpike Trust, threatened by the advent of the railways; and in the

District Railway itself. He also owned a number of cottages, some in Chardwell, some in the villages round about, but often spent more in repairing them than he got back in rent. So, by the year 1844, John Tarrant's income was barely enough – sometimes it was *not* enough – to cover the upkeep of the house and grounds; to enable him, in the winter months, to entertain a few friends now and then; and to keep half a dozen good horses in stables built to hold a score.

Over the main door of the house, the date of its building was carved in stone, together with the figure of a Cotswold sheep, now somewhat worn away by time, and William Tarrant's woolmark: a square, seriffed cross with his initials set twice in its four quarters. John Tarrant was proud of his origins and would point out the woolmark and the sheep to visitors from other districts.

"We were people of substance then, and all of it came from wool," he would say. "But we're not the men our forefathers were and money slips through our hands these days." And sometimes, in a teasing way, he would tell his children, a boy and two girls, that they must be sure and marry well, to repair the Tarrant family fortunes. "Though what I shall do without Kate, to manage the house and mind my affairs, is something I don't care to think about. And her suitor will have to be somebody special before I'll agree to let her go."

Katharine then was eighteen and the twins, Hugh and Ginny, were three years younger.

"And what about me?" Ginny asked. "Don't I deserve someone special, too?"

"If I can find him for you, my child, you shall have the noblest, handsomest husband in all England. And he'd better be the richest, too, for you don't have Kate's gift for making a little go a long way."

Ginny, fair-haired and blue-eyed, with the kind of prettiness so often seen in Romney's portraits, looked at her father with a mischievous smile.

"Have you got that gift yourself, Papa?"

"My own special gift, as you well know, is for robbing Peter to pay Paul, and as I've been practising it for thirty years—"

"What sort of wife will you find for Hugh?"

"Well, now, let me see!"

But here Hugh, looking up from his book, put in a word on his own behalf.

"I don't think I am cut out for marriage. It does so tie a fellow down. I think, if you don't mind, papa, I would prefer to stay as I am."

"And who will carry on our name?"

"Does it have to be carried on? We've had a good enough innings by now. Personally, I am quite content to go down in history as the last of my line." Then, in a deliberate way, he tilted his face towards the light, thus drawing attention to the mottled scar that disfigured his throat and part of his jaw: the result of a burn in early childhood when, due to a nursemaid's carelessness, a candle had set fire to his cot. "And who would wish to marry me, marked as I am in this ugly way? To say nothing of my unfortunate asthma."

"My dear boy!" Tarrant exclaimed. "Do you expect to go unloved simply because of a facial blemish? You underestimate womenfolk. They will see past that scar of yours—"

"You don't have to worry about it, you know. I never worry about it myself. Most of the time I forget it's there."

"Yes, well, and so do we. So, too, do all your friends. And so it will be, when the time comes, with whatever young woman you choose to marry. So let us not have foolish talk about being denied a happiness that is every man's expectation and hope."

Gravely, Hugh inclined his head.

"I shall in all my best obey thee, father. Behold me, chastened and contrite. But I hope, being barely fifteen, that I may perhaps be allowed to enjoy my freedom a while longer yet."

He returned to his book, his face quite tranquil, absorbed, content. It was not a defensive pose with him when he claimed to forget his disfigurement; it was, for the most part, true and sincere; for life, as Hugh Tarrant found it, offered such an unending variety of interest, amusements, and pleasures, that vanity had no place in it. What he looked like meant nothing to him. His mind was too full of other things. And when he did discuss his scar, it was in a philosophical way, with something of the whimsical humour already habitual to him.

"It's a good thing it happened to me and not Ginny. She could never have borne it so well as I." And once, regarding himself in the mirror, when Katharine had just cut his hair, he said: "It's just as well I'm marked like this. I should be too pretty otherwise."

The twins took after their dead mother in looks. They had the same corn-coloured hair, thick, with a light crisp curl to it, and the same vivid blue eyes. Both were somewhat short of stature, slightly built, with small delicate bones. Katharine, on the other hand, favoured her father's family. She had their height and their upright bearing; their look of unhurried serenity; and she had the Tarrant colouring: dark brown hair, smooth and straight, with a hint of burnished copper in it; clear grey eyes under shapely brows; and a skin that seemed always to glow from within. Though just eighteen, she appeared older, probably because, for the past five years, she had borne the responsibility of running her father's household; had been substitute mother to the twins; and, for the past eighteen months, had also been their governess.

For although John Tarrant often talked about the need for economy, it was only the practical Katharine, always diligent, always alert, who actually succeeded in saving him money. She it was who made sure that there was no wastage anywhere; who encouraged Jobe Roberts, the gardener, to grow enough fruit and vegetables to keep them supplied throughout the year; who had the old shabby carriage adapted so that one horse could pull it instead of two. It was she who, when Miss Sturdee retired, decided to teach the twins herself.

"Where should we be without Kate, and her talent for making shift?" Tarrant said. "It is she who keeps this household together and stops me from getting too badly in debt."

"I'm good at making shift, too, papa," Ginny said plaintively, "but you never seem to appreciate it."

"I know your shifts of old, that's why. You save a shilling repairing your hat and expect to get a new dress in return."

"I haven't had a new dress these three or four months past."

"And how long is it since Kate had a new dress?"

"Oh, Kate never seems to mind about clothes."

"She still manages," Tarrant said, "to look fine and elegant all the same, and you would do well to study her ways, first to achieve the same effect, second to avoid extravagance."

"Oh, papa!" Ginny exclaimed, shaking her head reproachfully. "That you should talk of extravagance when only three weeks ago you bought that rug to put down in the window-bay of the great hall. Why, I could have had twenty new dresses *and* as many new silk wraps, out of what you paid for that rug."

"And grown tired of them all in a twelvemonth, no doubt, whereas my Polonaise rug will delight all beholders for years to come, long after I'm dead and gone. It is the same with this house of ours. It takes an enormous amount of money - more than I can find sometimes – but would you have me neglect the place and leave it to tumble about our ears?"

"No," Ginny said, with a little sigh. "You know I wouldn't want that, papa."

The old house at Newton Railes was built of good Cotswold stone. It had stood for nearly three hundred years and would probably stand for three hundred more. But later additions, such as the end of the kitchen wing and the newer parts of the stable block, were already crumbling badly because, forty years before, they had been built with inferior stone, quarried on the estate itself.

All repairs to the stone-work at Railes were done by Rufus Cox, a local mason and quarryman, and that year he had been called in to renovate part of the stable walls and extend the groom's quarters over the coach-house. The work had taken a long time, for the only assistant Rufus had was his son, Martin, aged fifteen, and they had to bring the new stone down from Scurr Quarry, on Rutland Hill. But it was all finished now – only the tidying-up remained – and, as always with Cox's work, everything was well done.

Tarrant stood in the stable-court and surveyed the repairs with satisfaction. The only thing that irked him was the way the new rubblestone blocks stood out so very clean and pale, almost the colour of shortbread, against the old, rough-weathered stone, encrusted with lichen, silver-grey. But this, as he knew, would tone down in time, and the main thing was that the work was done; that the buildings surrounding the stable-court were all in good order again, just as they deserved to be.

Above the coach-house, with its wide entrances, there was a sun-dial carved in stone: a new block, newly engraved, the old one having crumbled away till its rays and its Roman numerals could only barely be discerned. The new dial could be read with ease, and the wrought iron style, casting its shadow, showed the time to be just after four. Tarrant, shielding his eyes from the sun, read the inscription newly carved above and below the rim of the dial: *I count the light hours only: Do thou likewise.*

Behind him, in the yard, Rufus Cox was clearing up. He had put his tools into his bag and now, with a small hand-brush, was sweeping the dust from the workbench, onto the cobblestones below. Tarrant went over to him.

"Your boy did an excellent job, carving that new sun-dial. It tells the time accurately and he's carved out the old saying exactly the way I wanted it."

"I should hope so, too," Rufus said. "It's his job to get things right. We should soon be out of work, him and me, if we didn't do as we get asked."

"Not much likelihood of that. Not with a man of your quality. And there's always more work for you here, to be done at some future date. Repairing the end of the kitchen wing – that's the next important job. But it will have to wait,

I'm afraid, until the day my ship comes in."

"H'mph!" Rufus said scornfully. "It's no good talking about repairs – not where that kitchen wing is concerned. That wing-end needs a lot more than repair, as I've told you time and time again. Your father had that extension built, and he thought to save himself money by getting the stone dug from his own quarry, so-called. And that won't do, Mr Tarrant, sir. That stone is all very well for field-walls, and the odd pig-cot here and there, but when it comes to important work, like part of a house, it's no good trying to do it cheap cos that always comes dearer in the end. Bad stone, badly laid. – That's what's wrong with the end of that wing. It needs to come down, the whole lot of it, and be built again new, from the footings up."

"Yes, I daresay", Tarrant said. "But where is the money to come from, eh? Tell me that and the job is yours – and you can start just as soon as you like. Meantime, I already owe you for three months' work, which will make a tidy sum, no doubt." Looking at Cox's grey-stubbled face, with its long straight nose and wedge-shaped jaw, he added in the same jocular way: "Don't be in too much of a hurry, sending in your account, will you, or I may have trouble paying it. Things are just a bit tight at present. These are hard times for men like me."

Rufus, having finished sweeping the workbench, put his hand-brush into his toolbag and took up a long-handled broom instead. He glanced at Tarrant once or twice from under lashes pale with dust.

"I know how it is, right enough. These are hard times for everyone. But you've never found me pressing you hard in the past, Mr Tarrant, and you won't find me pressing now. I'll send my account in due course and you can pay when it suits you to."

"Thank you, Cox. You're a good man. I knew you'd be sure to understand."

And Tarrant, having got that little matter out of the way, spoke again in praise of the work Cox and his son had just completed on the stable buildings surrounding the yard.

"Where is Martin, by the way? Has he gone home?"

"He's taken some bits and pieces of stone back home in the cart," Rufus said, "but he'll be back again directly, to take this bench and the rest of our stuff."

"He must be a great help to you, now that he is growing up. He works hard, I've noticed that, and he has the makings of a first class mason, like yourself."

While talking, Tarrant stooped and took a scroll of paper, dirty and dog-eared, from Cox's toolbag. He opened it out on the workbench. On it were notes, drawings, and measurements, relating to the work just done, and although there were some spelling mistakes, – "harness-rume" and "mountain block" – the writing was neat and disciplined, and the drawings and diagrams showed great skill.

"This is Martin's work, isn't it?"

"Yes, every bit."

"It's really very good, you know."

"Not bad, Mr Tarrant. Not bad, I'll allow."

"Come now, Cox! For a boy of fifteen? Don't be so grudging!" Tarrant said. "Or is it that you don't like to boast of your own son's cleverness?"

"Cleverness is all very well, but it isn't a lot of use by itself." Rufus stopped sweeping and leant on his broom. "I worry about that boy sometimes. I do, that's a fact. I've learnt him pretty well all I know, in the way of reading and writing and that, and of course I'm learning him mason's work, too, but—"

"Why, what's wrong with him?" Tarrant asked.

"He needs bringing out a bit," Rufus said. "He needs to mix with other folk."

"Not much chance of that, eh, stuck up at Scurr most of the time? It isn't much of a life, you know, for a young lad like him. Nor for your daughter, come to that."

"What my boy Martin needs is to mix with all manner of folk. People with something to say for themselves. People of learning, like yourself."

"You should have sent him to school," Tarrant said.

"Yes, well, maybe I should. But I needed the boy to help me. And schools, if they're to be any good, cost a whole lot of money, I believe."

"Damn it, Cox!" Tarrant exclaimed. "You're not so hard up as all that, I'm sure! An independent craftsman like you, well known as a first-class mason, working your own quarry at Scurr, which, as I've heard you boast all these years, yields the best freestone this side of the Cullen? – You can't be a pauper, I'll be bound!"

"No, not a pauper, I'm thankful to say. I never said I was that, Mr Tarrant, any more than you said it yourself when we was talking about your account. But – well, you've never sent your own boy to school, have you, Mr Tarrant, sir?"

"My boy is asthmatic, that's why, and the doctor says he's better at home. I'd have sent him to school, otherwise, even if it had taken every last penny I had."

"I'm sure you would, sir. I'm sure you would. So would I with Martin the same – if I had that last penny, whatever it was. But these are difficult times, as you say, not only for gentlemen like yourself but for all us other sorts as well. There isn't much building done these days, and that means there isn't much call for my stone, due to the present depression in trade. The newspapers say things are picking up, and I pray God they're right, but down there in Chardwell and all around, there's not much sign of it happening yet. But getting back to my boy Martin—"

"Yes, by all means," Tarrant said, and as it was perfectly obvious that Rufus wanted something from him, he now came straight to the point. "I'm not quite sure what you want him to learn but it seems to me that the best thing would be for you to let him come to us. I don't employ a governess now – we have to cut out expense where we can – and Katharine teaches the twins these days. So, if you'd like to send Martin along, we'll see what she can do for him."

"That's uncommonly good of you, sir. It is, that's a fact. And it may be just about the sort of thing I had in mind."

"Then I'm glad I thought of suggesting it."

"As to what the boy should learn, well, for one thing he needs chamfering."

"Chamfering?"

"Ah, that's right. He needs the edges taking off."

"Yes, I see," Tarrant said.

"General knowledge, that's what he needs, but also a few other things besides. I want him to know how to deal with folk … how to conduct himself, as they say … so that whatever sort of men he may meet, he need never think himself less than them."

"And how long can you spare him for, away from his ordinary day's work?"

"I dunno. That's hard to say. I'll have to think and figure that out."

"Well, send him on Monday at half past eight, and we shall see how he gets on. I'll have a word with my children about it and let Kate know what you have in mind. She will soon see for herself what he needs, I daresay, and you can be sure she'll do her very best for him, just as she does for her brother and sister."

"I know she will, sir. I know she will." Rufus pulled at the brim of his hat. "And Martin will do his best for her. Else, if he doesn't, I'll want to know why! Half past eight on Monday morning. I'll see he's there, sir, on the dot."

"Right you are, Cox. That's settled, then." And Tarrant turned away with an affable nod.

Smiling to himself at the roundabout way by which Rufus had struck a bargain with him, he entered the house by the back door and went upstairs to the schoolroom, knowing he would find his children at tea. It was something of a custom with him, to join them two or three times a week, to chat with them about their lessons and to take a cup of tea with them. Today, however, he was in a hurry, having an engagement elsewhere, and although he accepted a cup of tea, he drank it quickly, standing up, explaining the purpose of his visit at once.

"Kate, I've got a new pupil for you. – Rufus Cox's boy, Martin. It seems Rufus has got the idea that Martin's in need of some special schooling, to give him a better chance in life. I said you would take him in hand. I hope you have no objection to that?"

"No, I don't think so," Katharine said, "but when will he come?"

"Half past eight on Monday, then further arrangements will rest with you."

"And what am I to teach him?"

"Well, Rufus was rather vague about that, but I think what he really wants is for Martin to be given a little polish. It may be an uphill task, I'm afraid, but at least the boy is intelligent. And well worth helping, I think."

"Oh, yes, most certainly. I've spoken to him a number of times, about the work he's been doing for us, and I'd say he's very intelligent indeed."

"Excellent! Excellent!" Tarrant said, and, having finished his tea, he set the cup and saucer down on the tray. "I knew I could rely on you."

Ginny, having listened in silence so far, now spoke with some hauteur.

"You don't ask Hugh or me, papa, whether we mind having Martin Cox here."

"If you wish to please your father, my child, you will make it your business *not* to mind. The work Rufus has done for us is going to cost me a good deal of money and he has been good enough to say that he'll give me plenty of time of pay. So, one good turn deserves another, and helping Martin is our good turn."

"Will he come to us in his apron, papa, all covered in stone-dust and smelling of sweat?"

"However he comes," Tarrant said, "you will please be civil to him."

"The question is," Ginny said, "will the boy be civil to us?"

"I have always found him to be perfectly civil in every way."

"So have I," Katharine said.

"Well, *I've* never spoken to him," Ginny said.

Her brother Hugh gave a little snort.

"You may not have spoken to him, my girl, but you've found excuses often enough to walk through the yard when he's been there, and you have always made quite sure that he was bound to notice you, – flaunting yourself in your finery."

"That's not true!" Ginny exclaimed. "I went to see what work had been done."

"Is Ginny a flirt, then," Tarrant asked, "and she only just turned fifteen?" But his surprise was only pretence, for this youngest daughter of his had sought and secured admiration from the time she had first begun to talk. "God help the young men of our neighbourhood during the next few years!" he said. "There will be mischief done among them, now that this girl is growing up. – Beginning, it seems, with Martin Cox."

"Pooh!" Ginny said, disdainfully. "A stonemason's son? What's he to me?"

"Stonemason's son or not, he is rather a fine-looking boy, I think." And Tarrant, turning to his eldest daughter, said: "It will be up to you, Kate, to protect Martin as best you can from Ginny's wiles."

Katharine merely smiled at this but Hugh spoke up in reply.

"We'll see that he gets fair play, papa, though from the little I know of him, I would say he can take good care of himself."

"I think it's just as well," Tarrant said. "And now I really must be gone."

As soon as the door had closed behind him, Ginny burst out anew.

"It's all very well for our papa, bringing clodhoppers into the house, but it's we who will have to put up with him—"

"Only one clodhopper so far, if you must use such a word," Katharine said.

"And how will you manage to teach such a lout when he is so far behind us?"

"That I'll be able to judge better when he comes on Monday morning."

Outside, in the stable-court, Rufus had finished clearing up and was waiting impatiently for his son to return with the horse and cart. When the boy arrived at last, Rufus went forward at once, to take hold of the horse's bridle and bring him round carefully till the cart was backed close to the workbench.

"What kept you all this time? Been gossiping with your sister, I suppose."

"One of the lime-kilns was giving trouble cos part of the chimney had fallen in. I stayed and built it up again."

"Is it all right now?"

"I suppose it is."

"What do you mean, you suppose?"

"I mean it's as right as it was before, which means it still works, after a fashion, just like the other old kilns up there."

"H'mph!" Rufus said, with a sharp glance. "The answer was yes, then, wasn't it? Now give me a hand with shifting this bench, and not so much old rigmarole."

Together he and his young son lifted the big flat slab of stone that formed the top of the workbench and eased it carefully into the cart. Then they took up the smaller blocks that had formed the pillars supporting the bench and laid them on top of the slab. Rufus put in his bag of tools, climbed up onto the box, and took the reins. Martin got up beside him and they drove slowly out of the courtyard, each taking a last look round at the stable-block, especially the coach-house and harness-room, where the greater part of their work had been done.

"It looks a whole lot better now than it did when we started," Rufus said, "and that new stone we've just put in will last a lot longer than the stuff we took out."

"Yes," Martin said reflectively. "That's something I don't understand – that people owning a house like this should have added to it with such shoddy stone, when all the old part is so well built."

"They was people who thought they could cheat on the place, and they was wrong," Rufus said. "You can't cheat with stone. Not for long, anyway. If it don't find you out in your own lifetime, then it'll find you out in your son's. Cheap always comes dearer in the end, especially when you're building in stone."

They drove under the archway, out onto the carriage-road, and Martin, glancing up at the house, caught a movement at one of the windows, of a slight figure in a pale blue dress, drawing back and turning away. Brief though the glimpse had been, he knew who it was by her fair hair and by a certain flounce in her manner, and although she was no longer visible, he felt she was still watching him, secretly, from the shadows somewhere, probably with that lift of the chin he had noted in her at other times. Well, she might watch him if she liked, but he would not allow her to think that he cared about it one way or the other, and so he turned his face away, firmly resisting any impulse to glance up at the window again.

The long carriage-road at Newton Railes led, by a series of sweeping curves, gently downhill through the lush parkland where, just now, in the first summer warmth, the chestnut trees were in full flower, their branches borne down low by the weight. On reaching the first of these curves in the road, the boy allowed himself to look back, turning sideways in his seat so that he could see the house, now two hundred yards away, standing at the top of a gentle rise, and sheltered by the higher ground behind. Its grey stone walls and lichened roof had a warm mellow look in the afternoon sun, and its mullioned windows, where they faced south and west, gave off varied, glancing reflections, due to the small rectangular panes, which were set unevenly in their leads. Wisteria, with its pale mauve blossom, grew over the west porch, and Virginia creeper, now in full leaf, hung like a green rippling arras from top to bottom of one gable wall. And all through the gardens surrounding the house were the ornamental trees and shrubs; some exotic, like the cedar and the oleaster;

others homely, like the maple and beech; the honeysuckle, lilac, and sweet briar.

There were, Martin thought, many finer houses, larger and more imposing than this, to be found in the southern Cotswolds, – he could have named half a dozen at least – but there was something about Newton Railes that touched some deep chord of feeling in him. He could not explain what it was. Nor why he should feel like this. He only knew, as the cart drove away, that when the house became hidden by trees, he felt a tender ache in his heart, and a sense of loss.

"So that's goodbye to Railes," he said, facing forward in his seat. "At least for another year or so, until Mr Tarrant wants us again."

"It isn't goodbye for *you*," Rufus said, "because you're coming back on Monday morning to start having lessons in the schoolroom, along with Miss Ginny and Master Hugh, with Miss Katharine as your governess."

"Lessons? What lessons?" Martin said.

"Lessons to learn you a few things that'll be some use to you later on. Things that'll help you get on in life and make a place for yourself in the world. Just think of the Tarrants and what they are like ... Always so tarnal sure of themselves ... Never at a loss for the right word ... Never in doubt about what to do ... It's study and schooling does that for them, and they can pass it on to you."

Martin stared straight ahead, his brows drawn together in a deep frown, his lean-jawed face, with its high cheekbones, set in lines of rebelliousness. The prospect of returning to Railes, and the reason for it, had caused a conflict of feeling in him: first a quick jolt of excitement; then a cold, plunging fear. Nor, despite what his father said, did he fully understand the motive that lay behind the proposed arrangement.

"Shall you be paying for these lessons?"

"Indeed I shall not," Rufus said.

"It's a favour, then?"

"Yes, that's right."

"Well, I don't know that I want to go, – being beholden to

folk like that, – receiving charity at their hands."

"Beholden be damned!" Rufus said. "We've just done more than twelve weeks' work, making good those stables back there, and not a penny piece shall we get for another twelve weeks at least! And that's the way it always is. 'Don't be in too much of a hurry, Cox, sending in your bill-of-work. Things are difficult just at present.' Well, I was ready for him this time, and thought I'd get something back in return. So don't talk rubbish to me about being beholden to them, cos if there's any question of that, the boot is on the other foot!"

"Do you mean to tell me that we are not to be paid for our work, nor for the stone we've supplied, for so long as six months or more?" Martin's rebellious thoughts were now given extra fuel. "And how are we supposed to live while we wait so long to be paid?"

"Ah, now you're asking me something, my son! *We* have to live as best we can, by scrimping and saving and going short, and making what little I've managed to save go just about as far as it will. And that's why we have to watch out for a chance of getting something back, to make up for the way we're used."

"I'm damned if I want lessons from them! I'd sooner we was paid our dues so that we might live decently and have decent food on the table at home. Yes, and live in a decent house, instead of that shack we live in at Scurr! Oh, when I think what our lives are like, compared with people like them! Why, even their dogs are housed better than us! And yet they ask for time to pay what *we* have earnt by the sweat of our brow!"

"Yes, well, there you are," Rufus said. "That's how it is in this world of ours. The likes of us get trodden down. I'm just a simple mason, that's all, clever enough, working with stone, but got no proper schooling behind me, because of the way I've had to work. But you're only just fifteen and this is a chance for you to get on. – Get some learning into you, so that your life can be better than mine."

"But how will it help me, when I'm only a mason, too?"

"I don't know how, exactly, my son. A lot of that will depend on you. All I know about anything is that schooling is a valuable thing and this is your chance of getting it."

"And what about my proper work? We're due to begin on that new byre over at Dipsikes on Monday, first thing, and after that there's those repairs to the stove-house at Brink End."

"It'll only be in the mornings, that's all, as and when I can spare you. It'll mean some sacrifice on my part, but it's one I'm well prepared to make, to let you have your chance in life. And you must be sure and pay me back by making the most of it while you can."

"I still don't know that I want to go," Martin said in a deep growl, and he looked out over the parkland, stretching away on either side.

"You will do as I say, my son, and that's all-about-it," Rufus replied. Then, glancing at the boy's sullen face: "I should've thought you'd have *wanted* to learn. You've asked enough questions, all your life, on every subject under the sun, and I don't know how many times I've caught you reading one of those old books Parson Talbot gave you that time. Well, now you're to be given the chance of learning in the proper way, with people who know what they're about, and it seems to me the least you can do is show a bit of gratitude when I've taken such trouble on your behalf."

"But I shan't feel *easy* with folk of that sort! Not meeting them in the house itself."

"It'll be strange at first, I know, but the more you go among folk of that sort, the less strange it will be to you. It isn't only the stuff out of books – it's a whole lot more besides. You can learn useful things from the Tarrants and their kind, just by rubbing shoulders with them, and one of these days – who knows? – something worthwhile may come from it. So no more argument, if you please, cos it's settled whether you like it or not."

*

On leaving the grounds of Newton Railes, they turned to the right outside the gates and drove down the hill towards Chardwell. Before reaching the town itself, they crossed the bridge at Fordover and turned left into a lane that led up the side of Rutland Hill. A mile or so up the hill, the lane divided into two tracks, one turning right to Hey-Ho Farm, the other left into Scurr Quarry, carved out from the side of the hill.

The flat, open part of the quarry was like an arena, and because it faced southwards, the pale stone-dust that covered its floor glared blindingly in the sun, with the heat shimmering above it in waves. Around the quarry's inner side, the rock-face rose in rough terraces, the stone of the lower parts clean and new, where it had been most recently dug; that of the upper parts darkened by weather, its ledges sprouting wild grasses and plants. Below, on the floor of the open arena, five or six huge lumps of stone, quarried a few weeks before, lay in a row, drying out, waiting to be rough-hewn into blocks, and in front of these lumps stood a number of blocks already hewn, each of them roughly a yard square. A good distance away again, on either side of the working area, were ranged the endless reserves of stone, cut and shaped, ready for use, and stacked according to their style: pole-face, burr, and chisel-finish; rubblestone, kedge, and sawn ashlar.

Some of this stone they used themselves, and some they sold to other masons who also worked in a small way of business, in Chardwell and the district around. Recently these sales had been few but Rufus nevertheless insisted that the stocks be maintained and added to; and so, in any spare time they had, father and son worked in the quarry, breaking out the raw stone and reducing it to usable blocks. For work on farm buildings and cottages, rubblestone was mostly used, but for finer buildings, especially in towns, ashlar blocks were preferred, and often they had to be fine-dressed. Martin's sister did much of this, achieving a handsome patterned finish by drawing a strong steel comb to and fro over the surface while it was still soft and "green". Martin could not understand why they all had to work so hard and sometimes he grumbled about it.

"Why must we always be cutting stone when all we ever use or sell is scarcely a twentieth part of it?" And Rufus, shaking his head, would say: "Because one of these days our luck will change and when it does we must be prepared."

All round the outer edge of the quarry, where the ground fell away downhill, it was littered with the detritus of years: stone-dust and chippings and useless offcuts, swept away from the central area, together with those items of rubbish resulting from human habitation: old iron kettles and pots, eaten into holes by rust; fragments of yellow earthenware; ashes and soot and vegetable waste. For Rufus and his two children lived right in the quarry itself, in a lean-to cottage of rough weatherstone, built into the hillside, in a curving corner of the rock-face, well away from the quarry workings. Rufus had built this cottage himself, some thirty years before, when he had first come to the quarry as a young man of twenty-two. He had been a bachelor then and had built the cottage hurriedly, to suit a bachelor's simple requirements. It consisted of one narrow room, divided at night by a rough curtain, and cooking was done on its open hearth. When Rufus had married, at the age of thirty-four, he had added a small scullery, and this was the only improvement he had ever considered necessary.

In dry summer weather the cottage was hot – unbearably hot at certain times – but in wet weather it was quite the reverse, for the inner edge of the lean-to roof was only roughly jointed with mortar, and rain ran straight down the rock-face, which formed the inner wall of the cottage, to collect in puddles on the rough stone floor. In winter the place was always wet; even a good blazing fire on the hearth could do nothing to dry it out; and all through the summer months, even when the door and the window were open, the place still smelt of damp stone and earth, and still had a clamminess in the air, "like as if we lived in a cave," Martin would say to his sister sometimes.

On these fine hot summer days, Nan would fetch out all

the bedding and hang it over the line to air. She would lay
their pallets out in the sun; the pillows, the curtains, the
rushwork mats; and would turn them over, again and again.
But even when dried and aired like this, everything still had
a sour, musty smell; still felt clammy to the touch, soon after
being taken indoors.

"And always will have," Martin said, "so long as we live in
this hole of a place." The cottage filled him with disgust. "If
it weren't for you," he said to Nan, "doing so much to freshen
it up, we should all have taken the palsy by now, or be dead
of consumption like our mother."

"Oh, Martin, don't say that!" Nan's dark eyes were full of
fear. "Such a terrible death poor mother had! So much
suffering, so much pain! I often think of it when I'm alone.
Sometimes I can't get it out of my mind."

"I know, I know," Martin said, and inwardly he reviled
himself for having spoken so brutally. "But I didn't mean
what I said. We're a lot stronger than mother was. We take
after father. We're tough as oak."

"Yes, I think that's true," Nan said. "We're healthy enough,
the three of us. But this old cottage—" She gave a sigh. "What
wouldn't I give to live in a place that was dry and clean and
always smelt sweet. Down the hill at Fordover, or right in
Chardwell itself, perhaps. That's what I should like best of all
– a cottage right in Chardwell itself, where there were
neighbours all around, and something going on all the time."

"Got any particular place in mind?"

"Yes," Nan said, guiltily. "One of those cottages by the old
church ... with a bit of garden in the front ... I always stand
and look at them, whenever I go to tend mother's grave, and
that's where I'd live, if I had my way."

"With the church clock to keep you awake at night?"

"And the rooks cawing away in the elms!"

"Where the chapmen and hawkers come to the door ... "

"And it's not far to go to the pump on the green ... Oh, just
to think of living there!"

"What about the smell of the brook when Jervers Mill, or

Cranshaw, perhaps, empty their fulling-stocks into it?"

"Oh, I shouldn't mind that at all! I should just close the windows and door until it had blown away on the wind!" Nan gave a little tremulous laugh. "Oh, Martin," she said wistfully, "do you think it will ever come to pass? Father says it will one day. He says if we're patient and trust in him, we shall end by being as well-to-do as ever we could wish to be."

"Yes, but he never says how or when. 'All in good time.' – That's all he says. But you *shall* have a decent house one day! And yes, at Chardwell Church End, if you choose. Cos if father doesn't bring it about, I shall bring it about myself."

"How shall you?"

"I don't know. It seems I'm the same as father in that. But I'll do it somehow, come what may, and I'll swear to it on the Good Book if you like."

Martin and his sister were very close; they could always find something to talk about and were almost always in accord; and the bond between them was, at this time, their one and only source of comfort; the only thing that brightened their lives and gave rise to laughter now and then. Martin, although two years younger than Nan, felt strongly protective towards her, because her life was so drab and dull. He felt he was lucky compared with her, for at least his work took him out and about, down into the valley towns or out to the villages around. But the only change Nan ever had was her Friday morning walk into Chardwell to buy their meagre groceries. She rarely left the quarry at other times and when her father and brother were away, she saw not a single human soul from early morning, when they left, until they returned in the evening, and that, during the summer months, was often as late as ten o'clock. It was small wonder, then, that she should listen so eagerly to whatever they had to tell her, and, since Rufus despised idle chat, it fell to Martin to pass on to her whatever news he had gleaned in the day.

On that warm summer evening, however, on getting home from Newton Railes, Rufus himself was inclined to talk, dwelling with keen satisfaction on the arrangement he had made with John Tarrant.

"It may be the making of your brother," he said. "He's about as bright a boy as you could meet in a day's walk and he only needs the right chance to make him into the kind of man that'll carve out a place for himself in the world. It was a good idea of mine to mention the matter as I did, and Mr Tarrant took it up almost in the winking of an eye."

Martin had little to say on the subject and Nan could see that he had his doubts; and later, when they were alone for a while, she spoke to him about it.

"Don't you like the idea of going to Railes for lessons?"

"No. I do not."

"But you have said oftentimes that you wished you could have gone to school."

"School, yes," Martin said, "but not with people like *them*, in a place like Railes."

"But you like the family, surely? You've always spoken as though you did."

"Yes, well, maybe I have. But after what father told me today, about Mr Tarrant not paying us for another three months or more, I dunno that I feel the same. Why should people of that sort get us to work so hard for them and then keep us waiting for our money?"

"I don't know. But they always do. Father has said so many a time."

"That don't make it nearer right. Not while we have to live as we do, in a place like this, scarcely fit for pigs."

"Oh, Martin, don't talk like that! It's such a stroke of luck for you. If it was me, I'd be over the moon!"

"Yes," he said, "I reckon you would." And he looked at her in silence a while, touched by the fact that this sister of his, even while envying him, could still be so pleased on his behalf. "It's a pity you can't go instead."

"What you learn at Railes," Nan said, "you will be able to pass on to me."

"Yes. I hadn't thought of that."

"What are they like, Mr Tarrant's children? They have spoken to you and father, haven't they?"

"Miss Katharine has spoken to us a few times, about the work we've been doing there, and so has Master Hugh the same. But the other one, Miss Ginny she's called, she don't never speak to us. She just walks past with her nose in the air."

"And what about the house? Is it very fine?"

"It's not just fine, it's beautiful. And there's something else about it, besides … It's hard to say just what it is … but a feeling about it, that's special somehow."

"A happy feeling?"

"Yes, that's right. How did you know?"

"Because, whenever you speak of it, that is the feeling I get from you. – Of peacefulness and happiness. Of light and space in summertime, and comfort and warmth in winter. A feeling of safety and trustfulness … Isn't that how it makes you feel?"

"Yes. I don't know why I feel like that. I've never felt it anywhere else. And I haven't even been inside – only into the kitchen, that's all. But somehow I feel I know every room … I dunno why. I can't make it out."

"You're bound to like having lessons there, then. Surely you will?"

"But where will it lead me to, I wonder, and what will come of it in the end? That's something I can't figure out - just what father's got in mind."

"It's bound to lead you somewhere, I'm sure."

"Yes, but where?"

"Out of this cottage, for a start, I hope."

"Ah, well, if it does that …" A little gleam came into his eyes. "If only it gets us out of here … gives us a better life somehow … then it seems I must do as I'm told and be sure and make the most of it."

He went outside and across the quarry to where his father was already at work, chipping away with his scappling axe at one of the big raw lumps of stone. Martin took up his own axe and set to work on the next lump, chip-chip-chipping away, knocking off its protuberances, ... until one side of it began to be roughly straight and flat. This was easy, mechanical work, which left his mind free to roam, and, Nan having imparted some of her own bright optimism, his mind was less gloomy now and his thoughts were better company.

Just before half past eight on Monday morning, Martin arrived at Newton Railes. He had come a few minutes early, hoping to see Miss Katharine alone before his lessons actually began, but: – "Miss Katharine is busy just now," the maid said, as she took him upstairs to the schoolroom. "She will join you as soon as she can." So Martin, on entering the room, found the twins already there, sitting at a table in the window, conversing in French, with a map of France spread out before them. They broke off as he came in, but Ginny, looking him up and down, then made some remark in the same language, the nature of which was plainly derisive. He was dressed in his Sunday best: a brown serge suit, too small for him, and a new pair of boots, much too big; and as he stood inside the door, hindering the maid from closing it, he suddenly saw himself through their eyes: a gawky figure, ungainly and rough, with too many inches of scrawny wrist showing below his jacket sleeves. He had taken off his cap, and his thick straight brown hair, although Nan had trimmed it the night before, was falling untidily over his brows.

"Come in, Martin," Hugh said. "Hang your cap up on that hook and take a seat here with us. My sister Kate is not here yet. She's somewhere down in the domestic regions, dealing with some sort of contretemps."

"He won't know what *contretemps* is," Ginny said, and although she pretended to lower her voice, it was plain she intended Martin to hear.

"He will now," Hugh said, "and it will probably stick in his mind as the first new word he ever learnt on setting foot inside this room." Then, as Martin sat down at the table, he said: "We're studying the French Revolution at present and we were just discussing the fate of King Louis. My sister here feels nothing but loathing for the revolutionaries and what they did, but I was arguing, with Tremille, that the Bourbons brought it on themselves. What is your opinion, I wonder?"

"Who were the Bourbons?"

"The monarchy."

"Then I think you're in the right of it."

"Why do you?" Ginny demanded.

"Because of the way they treated the peasants, grinding them underfoot all those years."

"And what about the way they treated King Louis? Do you condone regicide, too?"

"I don't know about regicide. I only know they chopped off his head."

Brother and sister both laughed but Hugh's laughter, as always, was utterly innocent of spite. Martin recognized this and, although mortified by his blunder, found it possible, with Hugh, to speak about it comfortably.

"Seems I just learnt another new word – and my lessons haven't begun yet."

"I suppose you think," Ginny said, "that if you learn enough new words, that will make you a gentleman?"

Martin did not answer her but sat erect in his high-backed chair, his hands clasped together on the table. After a moment she spoke again.

"Isn't that why you've come here – so that you may acquire some polish? It seems a tall order to me and I don't envy my sister her task. But what good will it do, anyway, and what do you hope to gain by it?"

As Martin remained stubbornly silent, she turned to her twin.

"He'll never be a gentleman, will he, whatever he learns here with us?"

"That depends," Hugh said, "on what you mean by 'gentleman'."

"Now you're just being tiresome. Everyone knows what a gentleman is."

"What is it, then?"

"Well, it certainly isn't someone like *him*, who works for a living," Ginny said. "It isn't someone with rough, red hands and dirty, broken fingernails, who talks broad Gloucestershire and dresses in outlandish clothes."

Hugh, looking at Martin's face, saw the dark colour rising there.

"Don't be upset by what Ginny says. She's just showing off, that's all." Then, in his lazy way, he said: "What do *you* think a gentleman is? Have you any ideas on the subject?"

"Oh, I've got ideas, all right!"

"Out with them, then. I'm all ears."

"A gentleman," Martin said, speaking with angry emphasis, "is a man who can afford not to pay his bills."

Hugh threw back his head and laughed, but his twin sister was highly incensed.

"Oh, what a horrible thing to say! Just because our papa owes you for the work you've done! And what would become of people like you, it were not for people like us, always giving you work to do? You would very likely starve! Coming here, great hobbledehoy, asking to have lessons with us, and then saying a thing like that! It's nothing but impertinence—"

"I never asked to have lessons here."

"Your father did, on your behalf."

"Maybe he did, but that's not me. I wouldn't have asked. Not for anything. I'd sooner swallow a cake of soap."

"You could always leave. No one's stopping you."

"I will in a minute, if you don't watch out."

"A minute is just sixty seconds, so if I start counting now—"

"Ginny, stop it," Hugh said. "Papa will be sorely vexed with you if you drive Martin away."

At that moment Katharine came in, carrying some papers and books.

"Good morning, Martin. I'm sorry I'm late. I'm afraid you must think me very rude." She stood at the table, looking at him, noting the dark flush in his face and the way his lips were tightly compressed. "May I ask what's been going on?"

Martin, avoiding her gaze, mumbled an answer, inaudibly. Hugh spoke up on his behalf.

"We were having an argument. Ginny began it, needless to say, and Martin here, not knowing her, allowed himself to be provoked."

"If you had heard what he said—" Ginny began.

"I'd rather not hear it," Katharine said. "Schoolroom squabbles, whatever their cause, must be put aside once lessons begin, and as we are already late—"

"That's not our fault," Ginny said. "We've been here nearly half an hour."

"Precisely why I do not intend to waste any more time," Katharine said. She took two sheets of paper from the sheaf in her hand and placed them on the table, one in front of each of the twins. "Those are some points for you to study, on the aftermath of the Revolution, and how it affected the rest of Europe. We'll discuss them together in a little while. Meantime, Martin and I will adjourn to the music-room to discuss a programme of instruction for him."

"I wish you joy of it, I'm sure!"

"Get on with your work," Katharine said.

The music-room was next to the schoolroom, connected with it by double doors, and was furnished in much the same simple way, with the addition of an upright piano, a 'cello, a harp, and two music-stands. The table under the window was spread with a cloth of dark green velure and on it stood a tall vase filled with green ferns and white marguerites. Katharine moved the vase to one side and sat down at the table. She invited Martin to sit opposite and when, with some awkwardness, he did, they looked at each other in silence a while, Katharine's gaze openly searching, Martin's less steady, less frank, less sure. For although they had spoken together before, on many occasions over the years, and especially during the last three months, the circumstances were now changed, and each had a new assessment to make, a new relationship to form. And although Martin felt more at ease with this older girl, sensing her kindly interest, he was still in a state of resentment at the way the younger one had behaved; still painfully aware that among these people, so fine, so assured, he appeared ignorant, clumsy, uncouth. Katharine could see something of this; could read his feelings in his face; but she could not read the whole of his mind and something in his manner troubled her.

"Martin," she said, quietly, "are you here against your will?"

The question took him by surprise. He looked away in embarrassment.

"Not against my will, exactly. But it was my father's idea, not mine, and I don't think it'll work out."

"Why ever not?" Katharine asked.

"For one thing because I'm not wanted here."

"Have I made you feel like that?"

"No, not you, but your sister has. And I reckon she's in the right of it because I don't belong in a place like this. I'm like a toad that's got into the wine."

Katharine smiled.

"The toad will soon get used to the wine, so long as he's hard-headed enough, and *you* will soon get used to us."

"I'll still be a toad at the end of it."

"Not if you want to be something else."

There was a pause. He looked at her. Some of his stiffness was slipping away.

"Can you help me to be something else?"

"I think, before answering that, I need to know just what it is that your father has in mind for you."

"I dunno what he's got in mind. I wish I did. A chance to get on in the world, he says, but how and when is a mystery."

"Is that what *you* want? To get on in the world? It it that you're dissatisfied with being a mason and a quarryman?"

"No, I like my work well enough, but I wish—"

"Yes, what?"

"I wish I could feel it was all worthwhile. That we should get something out of it, better than we've had so far. The way we live up there at Scurr ... I should like something better than that ... a better life for my sister and me and ... a better chance for us to *grow*."

There was another, longer pause, and in the course of it Martin wondered if he had revealed too much of himself. But the young woman sitting opposite him, looking at him with her clear grey eyes, showed only interest and sympathy, and somehow he knew he was safe with her.

"You can't change my life, I know, but can you help me to change it myself? Can you put things into my head that'll help me to make the best of myself? Help me to know and understand what other folkses' lives are like, outside of the quarry, where I live?"

"Yes, I think I can do that. You've got a perfectly good brain. It's just a question of setting it to work along the most profitable lines."

"And shall you know where to begin?" he asked, with a touch of self-mockery.

"I shall have some better idea when you have done this task for me."

She put a sheet of paper before him, on which, in a clear hand, she had written a few questions. She gave him some sheets of blank paper, a pencil, a sharpener, an indiarubber, and an ebony ruler for drawing lines.

"I want you to answer these questions for me, using as many words as you choose, and taking just as long as you like. I'll look in again in an hour or so to see how you are getting on, but if you need me before that, I shall be next door with the twins."

In a moment he was alone, staring at his list of question, the first of which asked him: "What can you see from the window of this room?" From his chair he could see little but when he stood up he could see much more: a terraced area of the garden, giving way to flat parterres; a man and a boy at work there, weeding out the flower-beds; and a yew hedge with openings in it, leading to the greater garden beyond.

He sat down again and read through the rest of the

questions. There were four in all. "What can you see in this room?" was one and "What books have you read?" was another; and these were followed by: "State what you know about these people: Columbus; Dick Turpin; Alfred the Great; Lord Ashley; Lord Nelson; Robert the Bruce." He read the questions over again and looked around him, pondering.

Behind him, through the double doors, he could hear Miss Katharine's quiet voice as she talked to the twins in the next room; and through the window of his own room, the casements of which were open wide, he could hear the sound of small birds chirping and fluttering in the creepers outside. Never in his life before had he sat in such a room as this, so full of sunlight and sweet-scented air, with objects of such interest in it, and just for a while he was content to let the cool, quiet pleasure of it soak into him, through his pores.

But Miss Katharine's questions had to be answered. His alarm at the thought of making a mark on the first of these clean white sheets of paper had, somehow, to be overcome. "What can you see from the window of this room?" Quietly he moved his chair so that he could look out even while sitting down. He drew the pile of paper towards him, picked up the pencil, and began to write.

Lessons in the schoolroom at Railes were based on a firm but flexible pattern and consisted of an hour's formal instruction followed by an hour's debate. This pattern had been laid down by their governess, Miss Sturdee, and Katharine, taking over from her, had followed it faithfully ever since. Her transition from pupil to teacher, therefore, had not caused any great change, and the twins had accepted it with grace, according her the same respect they had accorded Miss Sturdee, though their manner to her, inevitably, was more casual and relaxed.

Having helped them with their lessons from an early age, she assumed her new rôle quote naturally, and as they were already well grounded and possessed lively, intelligent minds, teaching them was easy enough. But Martin Cox was a different matter; the only instruction he had received was rudimentary in the extreme; and when, at the end of an hour, she read his answers to her questions, she found, not unexpectedly, that the rules governing grammar, spelling, and punctuation, had yet to be disclosed to him. These, then, must be her prime concern, and would form the major part of his lessons for some little time to come.

But, uncertain though his grammar might be, his answers nevertheless showed that he had some feeling for words: an appreciation of them as tools and a certain zest in using them. This was in part explained by his list of the books he had read: *Life of Nelson*; *Life of Wren*; *Holy Bible* ("parts, that is"); *Robinson Crusoe*; *Ivanhoe*; and *The Pilgrim's Progress* ("three times"). Describing what he could see in the room, he had merely listed its contents, but, describing what he could see from the window, he had blossomed into sentences: "Gardiners talking instead of working"; "blackbirds bizzy feeding their yung, hopping about among the shrubs"; and "a spanyel has just cum on too the terris with three pupys and has now layed down with them, letten them crawl over her."

His general knowledge, too, although erratic, at least showed a bent for positive thought. Dick Turpin he briefly dismissed as "a High Way Man and a Thurrow Rogue" and Columbus as "a marriner who set out to prove the World was Round and discuvvered America to Boot." But he had written a whole page on Nelson and his death at Trafalgar; and half a page on Lord Ashley, ending with these words: "A good man even though he is a Lord whose done good things to help the Poor."

Katharine, having read this aloud, sat back in her chair and looked at him.

"It seems you have no high opinion of lords, even though Nelson was one."

Martin frowned.

"I didn't mean it to sound like that. What I really meant was, lords don't often help the poor, but this one did." And, after a pause, he said: "Words are contrary things sometimes. They don't always say what you want them to."

"They will do in time," Katharine said, "when we've had a few lessons together, and you have learnt a few simple rules; and it seems to me we can't do better than begin with those straight away."

While Katharine was giving Martin his lesson, Hugh and Ginny, in the schoolroom, were engaged in private study, but promptly at eleven o'clock Hugh put his head round the music-room door and announced that "bever" had arrived.

"Shall we bring it in here and have it with you?"

"Yes, do," Katharine said.

She moved books and papers aside, and the tray was set down in front of her. On it were biscuits and fruit cake, and a jug of freshly made lemonade with balm leaves floating in it. Katharine began cutting the cake, and Hugh poured the lemonade. Ginny, sitting down opposite Martin, fixed him with a bright blue stare.

"What have you learnt so far? A for apple pie, I suppose?"

"No," he said, looking away.

"What, then?" she asked.

"Never you mind."

"Oh, really!" Ginny exclaimed. "Making conversation with him is like trying to get blood from a stone."

"Conversation," Katharine said, "should not take the form of a catechism." She put a plate in front of the boy, on which was a large slice of cake. "But it *is* our custom here, Martin, to discuss the subject of our lessons together."

"Do I have to?" Martin asked.

"No. But I should like you to show the twins that our hour together has not been wasted."

"So!" Ginny said, returning to him. "What, then, have you learnt so far?"

"Verbs, mostly, and nouns," he said.

"What about adjectives?"

"Yes, them, too."

"And do you really know what they mean?"

"I reckon I do."

"Very well, let me try you out. What am I, for instance? – Noun, verb, or adjective?"

Martin looked at her stolidly.

"Seems to me you're all three of them."

"How can that be?"

"Well, biddy's a noun, isn't it? And saucy is an adjective. And if the biddy *teases* folk, the way you keep doing with me, well, then, I reckon that's a verb."

For an instant Ginny was speechless, her discomfiture made worse by the fact that her brother and sister, far from being sympathetic, were laughing openly at the way Martin had turned the tables on her.

"There! Are you satisfied?" Katharine asked.

"Do you mean to let this lout be just as rude to me as he likes?"

"I'm sure Martin will stop being rude when you are no longer rude to him. Now let us be peaceful together and enjoy our refreshments. Martin, you are not eating. Don't you like fruit cake?"

"Yes. I like it very well."

He picked up the large piece of cake and took two or three bites from it. He chewed for a while with bulging cheeks. Ginny watched him with distaste. She ate her own cake very daintily. Katharine, while talking to her three pupils, cut another piece of cake and laid it on Martin's plate. This too was quickly eaten and so was a third, followed by a number of biscuits, all washed down with lemonade. A fourth piece of cake was firmly refused.

"I reckon I've had enough," he said.

"I should just think you have," Ginny muttered. "Great greedy, gobbling thing."

Katharine, however, observing him, did not think it was pure greed. She suspected that he was undernourished in body just as he was in mind and this precisely at an age when both were growing and developing fast. "No wonder he's so fine-drawn," she thought. "The boy is in danger of outgrowing his strength. Something will have to be done about it."

When he left at half past twelve, at the end of his first morning's lessons, she lent him two books from the schoolroom shelves: *Gulliver's Travels* and *Crabtree's English Dictionary*. She also gave him a commonplace book in which she had set him a few tests for him to do in his spare time. This would help to nourish his mind, but what of physical nourishment? "I must have a word with Cook," she thought.

Katharine's concern for Martin Cox was aggravated by feelings of guilt, and these feelings were renewed during the course of a conversation that took place at lunch-time that day, when her father enquired how she had got on with her new pupil.

"He is very teachable," she said. "He also has a mind of his own. But—"

Before she could say any more, her sister Ginny interrupted.

"He certainly needs to be taught his manners. And I think you ought to know, papa, that before Kate came into the schoolroom, Martin Cox was making remarks about your owing his father money."

"Indeed?" Tarrant said, with a lift of his brows. "And how did that subject arise?"

"It was all Ginny's fault," Hugh said. "She was jeering and sneering at him for not being a gentleman and just out of interest I asked him what he thought a gentleman was. And he said, 'It's a man who can afford not to pay his bills.'"

"Then, as you so rightly say, Ginny was obviously to blame. And the boy is quite correct, of course, for people of our sort can almost always get credit and can let it run on pretty much as they please." Tarrant turned to his younger daughter. "But I am grieved to hear that you have behaved like this, my child, especially when I asked you to help the boy as much as you could."

"I did try to be nice to him, papa, but he is such a *lump* of a boy, and looks at one with such a scowl, that it's really rather difficult."

"Then you must try harder," Tarrant said.

After lunch, when he went to his study, Katharine rose and followed him there, wanting to speak to him alone.

"It is about this wretched matter of the money you owe Rufus Cox."

"It isn't just Rufus I owe money to. It's various other people as well. But yes, what about it, my dear?"

"I wondered, as the Coxes are so very poor, whether you need keep them waiting like this?"

Tarrant smiled.

"You don't need to worry yourself. Rufus is not so poor as he seems. In fact, according to local gossip, he's a very warm man indeed."

"But is the gossip true, do you think?"

"I have reason to believe it is, for I heard by way of an old friend, whose name I had better not divulge, that Rufus puts his savings to work by loaning sums to needy men at an interest of six or seven per cent. So your solicitude on his behalf is somewhat misplaced, as you see."

"My solicitude," Katharine said warmly "is not for Rufus Cox himself but on behalf of that boy of his."

"Yes," Tarrant said, soberly. "His son and daughter, I'm afraid, derive no benefit whatsoever from their father's usury. And I doubt very much if they suspect he is anything but the poor man he seems."

"I think it is monstrous!" Katharine exclaimed, and her voice, normally so quiet and equable, became for a moment almost harsh. "That he should deny himself the common decencies of life is one thing but denying his children in the same way—" She broke off and took a deep breath. "If what I gather is true, they don't even live in a proper house, and from what I have seen of Martin this morning, I feel sure he's not getting enough to eat."

"That may well be true. But whether I pay Rufus now or in three months' time, it will not make the slightest difference to the way he and his children live. As for this business of the boy's education, I don't know what's behind that. It may be that Rufus has got ideas … or it may just simply be that he likes to feel he is getting something for nothing. But if Martin really wants to learn … "

"Yes, he wants it most passionately."

"Then we are already helping him to the best of our ability. Except, perhaps, in the matter of food?"

"I thought, if you agree, papa, we might do something about that too."

"Excellent," Tarrant said, and patted her arm. "I leave it to you, my dear Kate, to do whatever you think best."

Just after one o'clock Martin arrived at Dipsikes Farm, where Rufus had that morning begun building a new cowshed. The boy took his working-clothes from the cart and changed in the barn. He joined his father in the yard, where they ate their lunch of bread and cheese.

"Well, and how did you get on?"

"I dunno. All right, I suppose."

"What've they been learning you?"

"English grammar, first of all. Afterwards, geology."

"Geology? What's that?"

"About the stone and other things that make up the earth's crust."

"I'd have thought you knowed enough about stone."

"Not how it got there," Martin said. "Not what made it in the very beginning, hundreds and thousands of years ago, or how the fossils got into it, that we come across oftentimes."

"What're you talking about?" Rufus said. "I told you that my own self – about the earth being under the sea. I told you when you was tuppence high and kept asking questions about them old shells."

"Yes, but that was *all* you told me, and there's a whole lot more than that."

"Geology!" Rufus exclaimed. "All you need to know about stone is what I've learnt you all these years. And what does Miss Katharine know about that? She's not a mason that I ever heard. Nor she don't work a quarr, neither. Strikes me she's been wasting your time."

"It was your idea, sending me there."

"Yes, well, I must've been touched."

"Am I to stop going, then?"

"No, we'll persevere for a bit. Give it a fair crack of the whip." Rufus, munching his last crust, cocked an eyebrow at his son. "You don't seem to've minded it much, for all the tarnal fuss you made about going there. You look a lot less hipped, anyway, than when you went off this morning, first thing. Now don't take all day eating your bait, cos I've got some *geology* here for you to do, and you've got a bit of time to make up, having taken a half holiday."

CHAPTER
2

It was a fine summer that year and often during June and July lessons were held out of doors, sometimes on the stone-paved terrace, sometimes in the summer-house, and sometimes in the Tudor garden, depending on the time of day and whether Katharine and her pupils went in search of sunshine or shade.

The Tudor garden, enclosed by stone walls, against which vines and fig-trees grew, was a favourite place with the young Tarrants, and was also known as the knot garden. It was laid out in criss-crossing paths between which were beds, geometrically shaped, planted with York-and-Lancaster roses; with old-fashioned herbs such as bergamot and balm; southernwood, hyssop, and sage; lavender, rosemary, rue, and germander. At the centre of this garden grew a mulberry tree, around which was a wooden seat; and there were many other seats placed at intervals here and there close against the surrounding walls, between the vines and the fig-trees.

For Martin, to whom everything at Railes was a new experience, these various parts of the grounds became inextricably linked with the things he learnt in those early weeks. His introduction to algebra meant the loud buzzing of bees in the lime-trees behind the summer-house. Charting the travels of Marco Polo meant the scent of new-mown grass as Jobe the gardener, with his scythe, mowed the lawn below the terrace. And the names of the kings and queens of England, recited aloud from memory, were always to be mixed up in his mind with the cooing of doves in the mulberry tree.

Sometimes, at Katharine's suggestion, Hugh took over the teacher's rôle, especially in mathematics, and as this was a subject for which Martin had a natural aptitude, he was, within a few weeks, not only solving the problems Hugh set him, but propounding problems of his own. Once the two boys were absorbed in this way for more than an hour, and Ginny, at the far end of the terrace, engaged in sketching a portrait of Katharine, who, in turn, was sketching her, kept glancing towards them impatiently.

"The rule for lessons has always been half an hour for each subject, but ever since Martin Cox has been coming, the rules are all at sixes and sevens. And they are only playing games. They're not really learning anything."

"Martin is."

"Well, Hugh is not."

"Never mind," Katharine said. "It's good for him to have a boy to pit his wits against for a change."

"Why is it," Ginny asked, "that you always side with Martin Cox?"

"Why is it," Katharine countered, "that you always do the opposite?"

"I haven't forgotten what he said about papa not paying his bills."

Ginny herself took no direct part in Martin's education, but liked to point out the mistakes he made, whether in speech or in general behaviour. Often she stored these corrections up until some moment occurred when she and he were alone together.

"It isn't misch*eev*ious – it's *mis*chievous. And it's different *from*, not different *to*. And when my sister leaves the room, you should rise and open the door for her."

"Anything else?" Martin said.

"Oh, yes, dozens of things, but judging by the look on your face, you would rather not hear them."

"I daresay you'll tell me, anyway."

"Only if you wish to learn."

"I reckon I'm learning plenty from you."

"And what do you mean by that?"

Martin shrugged and looked away. He could never keep up these exchanges for long – not when he was alone with her – and sooner or later he was obliged to take refuge in stubborn silence. At first he felt this to be a weakness, and in one sense it was, for her darting remarks fretted him; caused a scattering of his wits; but in another sense it was his strength because Ginny, like all spoilt young people, could not bear to be ignored. Hobbledehoy he might be: she craved his attention all the same; and sometimes he would smile to himself, despising her for her vanity and enjoying a moment of sweet revenge.

Such moments did not last long; he was awkward in her company and knowing that she watched him so critically served to make matters worse. He found himself saying things back to front, such as "kissamore" for sycamore, and often a dialect word would slip out, such as "quarr" for quarry and "stwoon" for stone. He was awkward physically, too, and once, stepping out of her way on the stairs, he trod on the spaniel puppy, Sam, who gave a terrible high-pitched yelp. Ginny picked the puppy up and made a tremendous fuss of him. She rounded on Martin in a rage.

"Great clumsy, lumbering thing! Why don't you mind what you're doing?" she said, and when Martin put out a hand to fondle the puppy, she stepped back a pace or two, hugging it to her protectively.

"I didn't do it on purpose," he said.

"Didn't you? I'm not so sure!"

Sam was now wagging his tail, squirming ecstatically in her grasp, and reaching up to lick her face.

"He doesn't seem too badly hurt, anyway."

"*You* wouldn't care if you'd killed him," she said, "seeing that you don't care for dogs."

"Who says I don't care for them?"

"It's obvious from the way you behave."

"I reckon I like them well enough, though I wouldn't make such fools of them as you are doing with that pup."

"No, you'd sooner tread on them! And what are you doing here, anyway, tramping all over the house in those great heavy boots of yours?"

"I'm going up to the schoolroom to fetch a book Miss Katharine wants."

"Yes, and that's another thing! I wish you wouldn't call my sister 'Miss Katharine' as you always do."

"Why, what should I call her, then?"

"As she is my father's eldest daughter, she should be called 'Miss Tarrant' by rights."

"But nobody ever calls her that. Not Cook, nor the maids, nor anyone else. They call her Miss Katharine, all of them."

"I know perfectly well what they do, but I thought your father sent you here to learn a few of the social graces, and if you wish to be correct, you should call her Miss Tarrant as I say. If, on the other hand, you choose to copy the servants instead, that of course is up to you."

"Yes. It is. And as Miss Katharine herself never seems to mind none, I think I'll stick to calling her that."

His attendance at Railes was irregular and depended on his father's decisions which, more often than not, were sudden and unpredictable.

"I shall need you at Buckley's in the morning, my son, to help me raise those chimney-tops. You can go to Railes in the afternoon." Or they would have an order for stone and delivering it, one load at a time, would take three or four days in a row. "Never mind. It can't be helped. You can have extra lessons next week instead."

Martin hated these sudden changes. He felt the rudeness of such behaviour, as it must appear to the Tarrants, and it made him hot with embarrassment. Miss Ginny, of course, disapproved strongly and told him so without mincing her words; but Miss Katharine, as always, was kindness itself.

"You must come when your father can spare you," she said. "It won't inconvenience us in the least."

She always made things easy for him; quietly, without any

fuss. If he was there at lunch-time, a place was always laid for him, and if he came too late for lunch, she would always ring for the maid and have some cold pork pie brought for him, or some slices of cold roast beef, often with potatoes and salad. Martin at first was extremely reluctant to accept this extra hospitality, but Katharine overrode his objections and, in addition to the meals he was given, there was always a package to take home for Nan: the last of a boiled bacon joint, or a cold mutton pasty with vegetables. He had never eaten so well in his life as he did on these days at Newton Railes, and some of the food was new to him.

"What, never eaten lettuce before?" Ginny said in astonishment.

"No, never."

"Do you like it?" Katharine asked.

"Yes," he said. "It tastes like rain."

Lunch in the dining-room at Railes, although it made him nervous at first, proved such a simple, informal affair that he soon lost the worst of his fears and was able, by watching and listening, to pick up all he needed to know of correct behaviour at the table, at least so far as it prevailed in this gracious but easy-going household.

John Tarrant was a large-minded man of liberal outlook and encouraged his children to air their views on whatever subjects interested them, especially on current events, as reported in the newspapers. Martin at first took little part, because such discussions were new to him, and he was less ready of speech than the twins, but sometimes Tarrant would turn to him and ask directly for his opinion, as when they were discussing the Chartists, much in the news at that time.

"What do you think of the matter, Martin? Would you say their demands are reasonable?"

"Yes, sir, I would."

"So you think all men should have the vote?"

"Yes, every one of them. – Thread and thrum."

"And why do you think so?" Tarrant asked.

"Because I hold it's only right that all men should have

some say in running their lives."

"I agree with you," Hugh said.

"Well, I do *not*," Ginny said, "because most common working-men wouldn't know how to use the vote even if they were given it."

"They would know well enough," Hugh said, "if only they were educated."

"And who is to educate them, pray?"

"Those of us who are lucky enough to have some education already."

"The stupid ones would still be stupid, whether educated or not."

"Oh, my dear girl!" Hugh exclaimed. "There are plenty of very stupid people even among the upper classes."

"Yes, that's true," Martin said, "and some of them sit in Parliament."

Hugh and his father laughed at this; so did Katharine, at Martin's side; and the way they all looked at him brought a warm flush to his face, of pleasure mixed with embarrassment. Only Ginny remained aloof, looking at him appraisingly, as though the reddening of his face were a good deal more amusing to her than his quiet rejoinder had been.

"I suppose, as you are a Chartist," she said, "you would like to see revolution here?"

"No, indeed I would not," he said.

"What, don't you want to see the heads roll?" she asked in exaggerated surprise.

"Well, just one or two, perhaps."

Later that day, when lessons were over, Ginny met him in the great hall.

"What is that book," she asked, "that you are taking out of the house?" And when he showed it to her she said: "*Paradise Lost*. Good gracious me! And what do you expect to make of that?"

"First of all I shall have to see what the author makes of it."

"You consider yourself a fit person to pronounce

judgement, then, it seems."

"I can have an opinion, I suppose."

"Did my sister say you could borrow that book?"

"Yes."

"Well, I hope you will take care of it. It is a particularly fine edition and if any harm should come to it—"

"No harm will come to it. I'll make sure of that."

Katharine had been lending him books right from the very beginning and he valued her trust too highly ever to risk losing it. Always, on getting home, therefore, he would hide these borrowed books away, under the pallet of his bed, where they were perfectly safe. He would scrub his hands punctiliously before attempting to read them and was careful never to leave them about where his father might perhaps toss them aside or spill his tea over them.

Nan knew where the books were hidden and sometimes, when alone in the cottage, she would, with Martin's permission, steal half an hour from her day's work and spend it in reading, always guiltily alert for the sound of her father's return. For although Rufus had decided that his son needed some education, he did not for one moment consider that his daughter had any similar need. Men had their way to make in the world; women merely stayed at home; and Rufus frowned on Martin's attempts to share his new learning with Nan.

"It won't do that girl a morsel of good, filling her head with all this stuff about history and whatnot. It'll make her discontented, that's all. If you and her have got time on your hands, there's plenty of work for you both outside."

When Nan's chores in the cottage were finished, she was expected to work in the quarry: dressing the stone and stacking the blocks; tending the lime-kilns; splitting tiles; even sharpening and setting the saw, a job requiring great patience and skill. She had worked like this since the age of nine and took it as a matter of course, but Martin was often indignant for her, especially in the wintertime, for then her hands, badly chapped by cold winds, became unbearably painful to her as the limestone dust, caustic and rough, got into the cracks in her skin, forcing them open until they bled. Even in summer it was bad enough; her hands were always tender and sore; and Martin felt bitterly angry that his father should make her do such work. These days, especially, when he compared Nan's life with that of the girls at Newton Railes, he was even more indignant for her, but whenever he spoke of it to his father, he received the same rough reply.

"And what would she do with herself all day, if she didn't give a hand with the stone?"

"There are plenty of things she might do if only she had the chance," Martin said. "Handling stone is a man's work. She ought not to do it. It's heavy and hard and – unsuitable."

"Has she been grumbling about it to you?"

"No, but—"

"Then it seems to me," Rufus said, "that you may as well get on with your own work, my son, and leave your sister to do hers."

But if Rufus would not hear the complaint that Martin lodged on Nan's behalf, neither would Martin hear his father's complaint that teaching her was a waste of time.

"If I'm not allowed to teach Nan, I won't go for lessons myself," he said. "Besides, talking to Nan about what I've learnt helps me to remember it better. It drives it further into my brain."

"H'mm," Rufus said, sceptically. "I will say this for you – you're good at thinking up reasons for doing what you want to do."

But although he continued to grumble about it, he did not forbid it outright.

It was perfectly true that talking to Nan helped to fix information in Martin's mind. It also served to clarify things which, until then, were only half grasped. But above all else was the sheer pleasure of sharing his new experience with her, and this applied not only to lessons but to everything connected with Railes.

"Is the house as lovely inside as you always imagined it to be?"

"Yes, and it's full of lovely things. A whole library full of books. Beautiful paintings everywhere. Carpets and rugs on all the floors. Silver spoons and forks to eat with, and knives with ivory handles on them. Oh, I can't tell you what it's like! And yet the Tarrants think themselves poor!"

"Do you still feel angry, then, about their owing father money?"

"Well, I still think it's wrong, but – how can I be angry when they are all so good to me? All except Miss Madam, that is, and I don't take too much account of her."

"Why does she treat you as she does?"

"To keep me in my place, I suppose."

"Perhaps she's a little in love with you, and that's why she behaves like that."

"Now you're talking plumb foolishness."

"Just think – if you and Miss Ginny Tarrant should one day be married!" Nan exclaimed, stopping her work to look at him.

"Ah, just think of it!" Martin said. He gave her a dark, sardonic glance.

"You're quite a good-looking boy, you know."

"No, I don't know."

"Of course you do."

"Well, I'd have to be something more than that before Ginny Tarrant would marry me. Yes, and *she'd* have to be something more than she is before I'd consider marrying *her*."

"You're not in love with her, then, pretty though she is?" Nan said.

"No, nor I don't intend to be, and that's all-about-it," Martin said. "She's a spoilt, vain, spiteful mommet and goes out of her way to make me feel small. Well, so she may, and be damned to her! She's not going to make a gowk out of *me*."

*

But then, only a few days later, a small incident occurred at Railes and lo, amazingly, out of the blue, Ginny Tarrant's attitude to him was changed utterly and forever.

It was a morning in late July, sunny and warm, and lessons were being held on the terrace. Katharine and Martin sat at a table, discussing an essay he had written, while the twins sat some distance away, testing each other on passages learnt from *Cymbeline*. Suddenly there was a loud barking down in the garden below: a barking so urgent, so full of distress, that it brought the young people to their feet; and when they looked over the balustrade they saw the spaniel bitch, Tessa, some fifty yards away, down on the lawn, attacking something close to the hedge. As they watched, she darted forward with a quick, angry snap-and-snarl, causing a flurry under the yews. Then she recoiled with a yelp of pain and they saw her rubbing her face with her paw.

"Tessa, what is it?" Katharine called. She turned to go down the terrace steps.

"Watch out, it's an adder!" Martin said. He had seen something writhing on the grass. "Don't go too close, Miss Katharine, please!"

He leapt clean over the balustrade, into the flower-bed below, and ran across the lawn towards the dog, who was now crying piteously, trying to rub her face on the ground. Before Martin could reach her, however, Tessa's puppy, Sam, appeared, and, seeing the adder on the grass, went scampering boldly up to it, yapping and snapping and clicking his teeth, and making threatening feints at it. The adder, already injured by Tessa, lay writhing and squirming on the ground, its forked tongue flickering, glistening silver-green in the sun. But the puppy, now doubtful, had drawn back in time, and before he could scamper forward again, Martin had descended on him and was scooping him up out of harm's way.

By now Katharine and the twins had arrived, and Martin, turning quickly towards them, bundled the wriggling puppy-dog into Ginny's outstretched arms. Hugh went and picked up Tessa. Katharine stood staring at the snake. Then, as Martin went quickly towards it, she called out to him in alarm.

"Martin, don't! It's dangerous! Leave it and Jobe will deal with it!"

But Martin was already on the snake, treading it down with one booted foot while he stamped on its upreared head with the other, a great crushing blow that killed it outright, though its body arched itself into a coil and its tail flipped the grass two or three times before it finally lay still.

At that moment Jobe and one of his boys arrived, drawn by the commotion, and Katharine gave orders that the whole of the garden should be searched in case there were adders elsewhere. The little group then withdrew, their first concern being for Tessa, whining and squirming in Hugh's arms and pressing her face against his chest. She was taken straight to the stables where the groom, Jack Sherard, tended her, cutting open the swollen area surrounding the snake-bite on her cheek, squeezing out the poisoned blood, and soaking the wound thoroughly with a strong solution of lunar caustic.

"Will she be all right?" Ginny asked. "She's not going to die, is she, Jack?"

"I reckon she'll be all right, Miss Ginny, so long as we look after that wound and keep her quiet for a day or two. But it's lucky it wasn't the pup that got stung cos I doubt if he'd have stood a chance. Older dogs, they're tough as a rule when it comes to adder-bites, but young ones, well, that's another matter, and they're generally dead in a two-three hours."

So Martin, unexpectedly, became something of a hero, and the story of how he had saved the puppy, without thought of the risk to himself, was soon being told to Cook and the maids, and, in a while, to John Tarrant, coming home from business in Sharveston while the little drama was still fresh and warm.

"It appears from what my children say that you acted with great presence of mind, and I am grateful to you, my boy. I hope, if there are any more adders in the grounds, Jobe will deal with them as efficiently."

Martin, though gratified, was also rather self-conscious at finding himself the centre of attention. He did his best to make light of it.

"There was no danger to me," he said. "No adder could've stung me through these great thick boots of mine."

"There *was* a danger," Katharine said, "because when you snatched Sam away, the adder might have stung your hands."

"Of course there was danger!" Ginny exclaimed. "You might have been stung most dreadfully, and Jack says that an adder's sting can cause the most terrible agony."

She had scarcely spoken till then, for the incident had frightened her, and Martin's prompt action in killing the snake had impressed her in such a way as to render her thoughtful and subdued. Now she had found her voice again and there was a note of respect in it. She was looking at him in a new way; even with a hint of admiration; but, knowing that this abrupt change of face was bound to draw teasing remarks from Hugh, she added with a touch of asperity:

"It's silly to try and be modest about it. You were very quick and clever and brave, and you may as well own up to it." She picked up the puppy, Sam, who was being kept on a collar and leash until the grounds were declared safe, and, turning his small muzzle towards Martin, she said: "You're a very lucky puppy-dog. Say thank you to Martin for saving your life."

Thus, after this incident, Ginny treated him differently. She was devoted to the dogs, just as all the family were, and Sam was her special favourite. So she was in Martin's debt and henceforth she would be his friend. She still scoffed at him, of course; still criticized his manners and speech; but now, instead of trying to make him feel foolish, she wanted only to see him do well. She would help him with his lessons now and say encouraging things to him, though she always rounded them off with a touch of the old mockery.

"You're getting to be quite clever," she said, when he gave a good account of himself, answering her questions on the

Wars of the Roses. "We shall make a scholar of you yet."

As a further sign of her favour, she would ask him to do certain things for her.

"Martin, will you sharpen my pencil? You do it much better than I do. And would you mind fetching my sketchbook? I've left it in the summer-house."

Hugh, looking up as Martin passed, offered a dry observation.

"Winning my sister's goodwill is proving a mixed blessing, I fear. She will have you running errands for her until your legs are worn to stumps."

"Oh, Martin doesn't mind," Ginny said. "He likes to do these things for me."

"I don't know about that," Martin said.

"Well, whether you like it or not, if you want to learn a gentleman's manners, you must just put up with it!"

One morning when Martin arrived late for his lessons, he found that the Tarrants had visitors. He had entered the garden by a side gate and was stepping onto the terrace before he perceived the little group strolling on the parterre below. He would have withdrawn immediately, but Ginny had already seen him and in a moment she was there, taking him firmly by the hand and leading him down the terrace steps to meet the four visitors. These were Mr and Mrs East with their grandchildren, George and Leonie Winter, who had driven over from Chacelands, the estate adjoining Newton Railes; and if they were somewhat surprised at having this youth in his ill-fitting clothes presented to them in this way, they were too polite to show it.

"This is Martin Cox," Ginny said. "He comes and has lessons with us and he's very good at killing snakes."

The story of the adder was then told and Tessa, now quite herself again, was called so that the visitors could see where the snake-bite, although healed, had left a bald scarred patch on her cheek.

"I do hope," Mrs East said, with a nervous glance around

the garden, "that there aren't any more adders here."

"Rest assured," Tarrant said. "The servants searched the grounds that day and have kept a vigilant eye ever since. There is no danger, I promise you."

The family and their visitors strolled along the green walk and down as far as the round pool, and Martin found himself strolling with them, included in the company as though it were the most natural thing in the world. Natural, that is, as far as the Tarrants were concerned; not so for Martin himself; and he was still looking for a means of escape when Ginny drew close to him and slipped her arm into his.

"Even if there *were* more adders," she said, "nobody need be the least bit alarmed, since Martin is here to deal with them." And she gave his arm a little squeeze.

As the party strolled on, it somehow divided into groups, Tarrant and Katharine leading the way with Mr and Mrs East; Hugh a few paces behind with George and Leonie; while Ginny and Martin brought up the rear. Leonie Winter was roughly the same age as the twins, her brother a few years older, and this young man, all the time as he walked, kept glancing back at Ginny and Martin.

"George and Leonie are our oldest friends, and our nearest neighbours," Ginny said. "Their parents both died some years ago and Mr East is their guardian. The Easts live at Chacelands with them but George is sole heir to his father's estate and next year, when he comes of age, he will take full possession of it. The Easts will return to London then and Leonie talks of going with them. George is my oldest beau. He is also the richest – so far, that is."

"Shall you marry him, then?" Martin asked.

"Oh, I don't think so," Ginny said. "It *would* be very nice, of course, to be mistress of Chacelands and live right next door to Railes. But I've known George all my life and ... there are so many men in the world ... I feel sure someone more dashing and rare is waiting for me somewhere, if only I had the chance of meeting him." She gave a sigh, followed soon by a little laugh. "Poor George! He's thoroughly hipped.

D'you see how he keeps looking at us? He's jealous because I'm walking with you."

"Isn't that why you're doing it? _And_ why you're hanging on to my arm?"

"Of course!" she said, unabashed, and looked up at him, wrinkling her nose. "You don't mind, do you?"

"No, I don't care twopence," he said. "But if I was the other chap—"

"Yes, what?" Ginny asked.

"It'd be a different matter, that's all."

A few minutes later the party re-grouped and Martin, talking to Mr East, heard Ginny urging George to go with her to the Tudor garden, to see what a good crop of mulberries they had on the old tree that year.

His sister Nan was delighted to know of the change in Miss Ginny's behaviour, particularly on hearing that she had made a great point of presenting him to the visitors. Rufus, too, was impressed by this, and had a few questions to ask.

"Mr East, did you say? Him that runs the Chacelands 'state on behalf of the young squire-to-be? How did you get on with him?"

"He was very friendly to me."

"Ah, that's right. That's good, that is. You want to get in with all that sort." Rufus sucked at a loose tooth. "Did you tell him about the quarry?"

"Yes, because Mr Tarrant had mentioned it to him and he said he thought he'd heard of us."

"Did you ask if they ever had need of stone for building and such at Chacelands?"

"No, I did not."

"Then you was a fool," Rufus said. "You missed a good opportunity."

"Mr East told me that Chacelands repairs are always done by the Fowlers of Pibblecombe who get their stone from Hawker's Hill."

"He could always change to us."

"If I had spoken to Mr East, cadging for custom like that, he would have thought it a breach of good manners."

"A breach of good manners!" Rufus exclaimed. "And what sort of mouthful of words is that? One you learnt from the Tarrants, I suppose?"

"I thought that's why you sent me there – so that I should learn from them."

"I sent you there to learn something useful, not a lot of precious cant. Mr East's got a 'state to run. That means he is a man of business and business is something you've got to discuss. It don't just happen by itself."

"He is also a gentleman and when gentlemen discuss business matters there are certain rules they observe."

"Oh, is that so?" Rufus said.

"Furthermore," Martin said, "when Mr East told me that Chacelands work is done by the Fowlers, it was his way of warning me not to expect business from him."

"How do you know that?"

"Because I could see what was in his mind. Because he *meant* me to see it, that's how."

"H'mm," Rufus said, still sceptical, and his gaze remained fixed on Martin's face. But he was impressed in spite of himself and after a while he gave a nod. "Yes, well, so be it, my son. I daresay you're in the right of it. I put my trust in your judgement and hope, in the fullness of time, some sort of goodwill come of it."

Rufus had a genuine respect for this young son of his: it was why he expected great things of him. The boy had a certain quickness of mind and a certain sensibility that enabled him to understand other people's feelings and thoughts in a way that Rufus himself could not. He was also adaptable and already, in a matter of months, Rufus detected a change in him, brought about by his lessons at Railes. For one thing his speech was much improved; he had shed some of his Gloucestershire burr and could even talk quite fine when he chose; but, more important than that, was his ever-growing fluency. Under Katharine Tarrant's tuition, he was learning how to express himself; to get his tongue round difficult words and to frame his thoughts in sentences that no one could fail to understand. All of which gave him confidence, so that nowadays, when he talked, it was with a certain authority.

All this Rufus observed, though his satisfaction was tinged sometimes with a kind of resentment; a feeling that the boy was *too* independent; that he had too much to say for himself and needed to be kept in check. Perhaps it was because of this that Rufus tended to heap scorn on those aspects of Martin's studies that were outside the range of his own experience.

"Poetry! What use is that? Where will it get you?" he would say. "It won't put bread into your mouth, nor clothes on your back, so why waste time on such flummery?"

This was a frequent complaint of his since overhearing Martin and Nan reciting their favourite passages from *Romeo and Juliet* while working together in the quarry.

"Filling your sister's head with such stuff! And some of it not even decent!" he said. " '*Well, Juliet! I will lie with thee tonight*'! Now what kind of talk is that?"

"It isn't indecent, it's sad," Martin said, "because Romeo thinks Juliet is dead and he intends killing himself so that they may lie together in the grave."

"And is the girl dead or not?"

"No, just asleep. But when she wakes up and finds he has taken a cup of poison, she stabs herself with his dagger."

"Is she dead this time?"

"Yes, they both are."

"Just as well for them if they are. They'd find themselves in trouble, else. It's against the law to take your own life. Didn't they think of that?"

"It's only a story," Martin said. "None of it happened in real life."

"Then where's the point of it?" Rufus asked.

"Well ... a story takes you out of yourself and sets you thinking," Martin said. "You see it all happening in your mind and you *feel* it as though it's happening to you. It gives you something to think about when you're doing dull, monotonous work. But it isn't just the story alone … it's the poetry too … the way the words are put together so that they sound exactly right. It's like a language all its own, that gets down deep, to the heart of things … the things you've often thought and felt but never been able to talk about."

There followed a long pause in which father and son eyed each other, one with a hard, satirical stare, the other self-conscious but defensive. Finally Rufus gave a grunt.

"That monotonous work you spoke of earns us our living, don't forget."

"Our living, yes. Such as it is."

"If you would improve it, my son, you should get Miss Katharine to learn you something worthwhile, that'll be some proper use to you, instead of giving you poetry and other such trash to read."

But Miss Katharine *was* teaching him useful things, among them the art of writing letters, and Rufus, seeing the few samples that Martin had written so far, gave his approval unstintingly.

"That's good, that is. There's sense in that. You're doing well and I'm proud of you."

The first of Martin's sample letters were written to Miss Katharine's dictation and were meant to test his spelling and punctuation while conveying the rudiments of a letter's construction. Some were written as though to tradesmen: one to a nurseryman, for instance, ordering twenty apple trees; another to a firm of clock-makers, requesting a copy of their catalogue. But others were written as though to friends: one accepting an invitation to dine; another refusing, with regret, and giving the reasons therefor. Later, Katharine set him to study a page of readers' letters published in *The Chardwell Gazette* and, as an exercise, to write his own answers to them. It happened one week that there was a letter from a Mr Hunt, deploring the use of red brick in the building of three new cottages on the outskirts of Wembleford, a village which until now had been built exclusively of stone.

"I have heard it said that good quality Cotswold stone cannot now be obtained from anywhere nearer than Bowden Hill and that consequently the expense of transporting it such a distance obviates against its use. But surely all right-minded men engaged in the building trade in this district should be prepared to meet the extra expense involved so as to ensure that their work is in harmony with what already exists?"

This was a subject close to Martin's heart and he wrote supporting Mr Hunt's complaint with strong, simple eloquence. Miss Katharine, as always, corrected the letter and improved on the sentences here and there, but the substance of it was his own, and when a fair copy was made it ended with these words:

"Obviously it is too late to prevent the use of red brick in the cottages Mr Hunt mentions, but whoever has said that good quality Cotswold stone cannot be obtained nearer than Bowden Hill has either been misinformed or been guilty of falsehood, and I beg to put the matter right. Stone of first-rate quality can be obtained from Scurr Quarry, on Rutland Hill, near Chardwell, leased and worked by my father, Mr Rufus Cox, a banker-mason of skill, experience, and good repute. As this quarry is less than a mile from Wembleford, the cost of transporting stone thereto would be less than that of transporting bricks from the Kinnington brick kilns.

> I am, dear sirs, yours respectfully, Martin Cox."

Miss Katharine was much impressed by this letter; so were the twins; and although Martin had written it purely as an exercise, Katharine now suggested that he should send it to *The Chardwell Gazette*.

"Yes, why don't you?" Ginny said.

"Is it really good enough?"

"Of course it is," Hugh said. "I'll get you a stamp."

A week later, the letter was published. The Tarrants saw it first, of course, for they had the paper delivered to them, and when Martin arrived for his lessons, Katharine put it in front of him, open at the relevant page.

"There!" Ginny said, watching his face. "I knew they were sure to print it! What a clever boy you are, to be sure! You're really quite a credit to us."

Martin, flushed with pleasure and amazement, gave credit where it was due.

"It was Miss Katharine's doing by rights." And he turned towards the older girl. "It was all your idea that I should learn how to write letters."

"It would not have led to this," she said, "if you hadn't been such an apt pupil."

When he took the newspaper home, his father and sister read the letter over and over, again and again. They could not believe their eyes, and Rufus in particular was fascinated by the sight of his name, and Martin's, in print on the page, together with the name of the quarry.

"That's a good letter. You've wrote it well. What's more, it tells the truth."

During the following weeks there was further correspondence in *The Gazette* on the subject of brick versus stone, all of it endorsing the stand taken by "Messrs Hunt and Cox" and urging that stern measures be taken to "halt the incursion of alien brick at present threatening our Cotswold towns." During these weeks, too, as a result of Martin's letter, a number of people from various parts of the county found their way to Chardwell and walked or rode up Rutland Hill on purpose to see Scurr Quarry. Most came simply out of curiosity. – "Nosy parkers!" Rufus said. "Asking fool questions and wasting our time!" – But one was a builder from Sharveston, Robert Clayton by name, and he had recently been asked by the Cullen Valley Turnpike Trust to submit a tender for repairs to the old bridge over the Ail, between Chidcot and Newton Ashkey.

"I thought it would mean getting the stone from Bowden Hill, but you are so much nearer to Newton Ashkey, I decided to come and investigate the claim your son makes in his letter, that you can supply good quality stone."

Also, Clayton had doubted whether a quarry worked by

two men would be able to meet his requirements, but when he saw the reserves of stone, already cut and dressed, his doubts were removed. There remained only the problem of transport.

"One cart and one horse? Is that all you've got?" he said in some amazement.

"Don't you worry about that," Rufus said. "I can always hire horses and carts to get the stone down to you. That's what I've always done in the past, when I've had a big order like this."

"In that case perhaps we can discuss quantities and reckon out a bill-of-costs? I can then send my tender in, and if so be I am given the work, we are well on the way to doing business together, Mr Cox."

In due course, Clayton secured the contract, and placed his order for the stone; Rufus hired extra horses and carts, with reliable men to drive them; and over the next three weeks or so, more than fifteen hundred tons of stone were delivered to Newton Ashkey for use in repairing the old bridge.

On meeting Martin for the first time, Clayton had been surprised and amused to find that the author of the letter published in *The Chardwell Gazette* was only a boy of fifteen.

"You've got a good businessman in the making there, Mr Cox."

"Yes, and I know it," Rufus said.

A few weeks later, when repairs to the bridge were finished, Clayton promised that if ever he had more work in that area, he would again come to Scurr for his stone; and time was to prove him a man of his word. Through Clayton, also, Rufus received a few orders from other builders in the Cullen Valley and was altogether well pleased with himself, because these benefits were the result of the "schooling" Martin was getting at Railes.

"I did the right thing, sending you there. I knew some good would come of it."

The Tarrants, too, were delighted that Martin's letter had brought such results.

"Does it mean you'll be rich?" Ginny asked.

"Seemingly not," Martin said.

He could not understand why it was that in spite of these extra sales of stone they were living as frugally as before. No better food came to the table; nor was there money to buy better clothes: Nan had to make-do-and-mend just as she had always done. And still they continued to live in the quarry, in the cottage, scarcely more than a hovel, built against the rock-face. Martin brooded long over this until one day, in a burst of anger, he spoke to his father about it.

"When are we going to be able to live in a proper, decent dwelling-house, down in the town, with other folk, instead of up here by ourselves, like primitive people in a cave? Surely we're doing well enough to rent a proper cottage by now?"

"You think so, do you?" Rufus said. "Just cos we've got a bit of extra coming in just now, you think we may as well throw it away? Seems to me you are forgetting all the extra expense I've had, hiring extra horses and carts and men to drive them to and fro."

"Don't we make any profit, then?" Martin asked sarcastically. "Do our expenses swallow it up and leave us just as poor as before? Strikes me there must be something wrong if we can sell off all that stone and be left with nothing to show for it."

"Oh, so you think there's something wrong? And what do you know about it, boy, when it comes to the way of running things and attending to the business side?"

"I know nothing at all," Martin said, "because you never tell me anything!"

"And what is it you want to know?"

"Well, what you just said yourself, about the business side of it all ... Profits and losses and things of that sort, and how they balance out in the end."

"So, at fifteen years old, my son, you expect to know as

much as me. And no doubt in another few months you'll be wanting to take over the reins and run the whole perjandum yourself!"

"No, I don't expect any such thing—"

"Just as well if you don't, my son, – you'd be in for a disappointment, else. Now listen to me and mark what I say. This here quarry is leased to *me*. The lawyer's papers are in *my* name. *I'm* the one that pays the rent. When I'm dead, the lease'll be yours, and you'll be running the quarr yourself, but until that day comes, I'm Master here and you're just Jack, and you had better remember it."

"Have we got to wait till you die, then, before we ever stand a chance of getting a decent place to live?"

"No, no, not as long as that. But a while yet. Be patient, that's all. I'd like to feel a bit more secure and get a bit more savings put by before thinking of taking a house."

"It doesn't cost all that much to rent a cottage in Chardwell."

"Doesn't it?" Rufus said. "Been looking into it, then, have you?"

"Yes. There's a nice cottage in Shady Lane to let for eighteen pence a week."

"And can you afford eighteen pence?"

"I could if you paid me for my work."

"What work?" Rufus asked. "Half your time is spent at Railes, sitting at a table, studying, or lounging about in the gardens there, learning snippets of this and that. Only the other half is spent doing a proper job of work and what you earn from that, boy, just about covers the cost of your keep! You're not a grown man yet. Not by a long chalk you're not! And when you are – well, we shall see!"

Martin, although shamed and defeated, had one last defiant speech to make.

"It was you who sent me to Railes in the first place and now you talk as though you think I am just wasting my time there. But I *did* write that letter to the paper, remember, and you said yourself it did us some good, bringing Mr Clayton to buy our stone."

"I yunt forgotten the letter, my son. You did well and I'm proud of you. And because I know you're a good boy at heart I shall do my best to overlook the saucy things you've been saying to me. But I am your father, don't forget, and it is your duty to honour me. I'm a lot older and wiser than you and I know better what I'm about. Take this matter of quarrying, now. – How many times have you asked me, 'Why must we always be cutting stone when we don't hardly sell none of it?' And how many times have I answered you, 'One of these days our luck will change. The stone will be needed. You mark my words'? Well, now you know that I was right, and you can be sure it'll happen again, which is why we must always make sure that when it's needed in a hurry, we've always got it ready to sell. So you just get on with your proper work and give your tongue a holiday."

The fine summer came to an end and the evenings began drawing in. Autumn at Railes meant rust-red leaves fluttering past the schoolroom window, from the vines and creepers that clothed the walls. It meant white mist spreading out over gardens and parkland, with the trees towering up out of it, many of them aflame with colour: the beeches all burnt sienna; the American maples crimson and vermilion; the tulip trees pale lemon and gold. Autumn meant a nip in the air, log fires lit in the house, and the smell of woodsmoke everywhere.

"I love the autumn," Ginny said, coming in late from her morning ride. "Which season do you like best, Martin?"

"I don't know … All the seasons are beautiful here."

Even November, cold, wet and dark, seemed less gloomy at Newton Railes, because of its welcoming comfort and warmth. However early he arrived, the lamp would be lit on the schoolroom table, casting a cheerful circle of light over the red velvet table-cloth, and a fire would be burning in the grate. And soon after he arrived, the maid, Annie, was sure to come in with a cup of hot chocolate for him to drink. Often, arriving early like this, he had the schoolroom to himself, and would settle down to half an hour of private study before Katharine and the twins arrived. They had granted him this privilege and he valued it very highly indeed.

Often he felt guilty, enjoying such comfort and luxury while his sister Nan remained at home, a prisoner in the quarry cottage, where rain trickled down the inner wall, soaking the stone-chip floor underfoot, and where smoke billowed out from the fire-face, filling the kitchen with its smuts.

"I don't know why I am singled out to receive such good fortune," he said to her. "But one thing I do know – that as soon as it is in my power, I shall make it up to you in every way I possibly can."

"You needn't feel guilty about it, Martin, when you're sharing your good fortune with me. – Teaching me everything you learn. Telling me all about Newton Railes. I feel I know it as well as you do. And I feel I know the family."

Nan could never hear enough about what the Tarrants said and did: what dresses the two girls wore and what their favourite colours were; what music they played and what songs they sang. Every detail was manna to her, and Martin, well aware of this, would do his best to remember those things that gave her the greatest pleasure. Sometimes, he would tease her, too.

"Master Hugh takes sugar in his tea but the girls do not. They all take milk, of course, and it has to be poured in *after* the tea. You must be sure and remember that if you are ever lucky enough to get milk to put in your tea."

"I hope you won't tell them that I'm always asking questions about them."

"Of course I won't."

One day at the end of November Rufus gave Martin a grubby sealed envelope for him to give to Mr Tarrant.

"That's my account for the work we done back in the early summer," he said. "He asked us to give him time to pay and it's now six months. Seems to me that's long enough."

Martin took the envelope and looked at it with a sombre frown.

"I suppose that means no more lessons, then?"

"Eh? Why should it?" Rufus asked.

"Because, from what I understood, that was what you arranged with him. – Lessons for me in exchange for allowing him time to pay this bill."

"Miss Katharine still teaches her brother and sister, don't she? Then she can still teach you just the same. I can't see it's any bother to her. Nor to her father, neither. That don't *cost* them nothing, does it?"

John Tarrant, receiving the bill that afternoon when he joined the young people for schoolroom tea, looked at Martin in surprise.

"Your bill-of-work? God bless my soul! Is it due for payment so soon? How quickly the time passes these days." He laid the envelope aside. "Tell your father he shall have my draft just as soon as it can be arranged."

When he left the room, however, the envelope remained on the table. Katharine saw it and picked it up and, a little while later, took it to him in his study.

"You won't forget to pay it, will you, papa?"

"Of course not, my dear. But Rufus won't hurt for waiting a while. I'm rather hard-pressed just now, what with Ginny outgrowing her frocks so fast and Christmas only a few weeks away—"

"It will be Christmas for the Coxes, too. And it is all wrong, papa, that you should spoil us with luxuries while that bill remains unpaid."

"I doubt if it will make any difference to the way the Coxes spend Christmas, whether I pay this bill or not."

"I fear what you say is probably true and it grieves me very much indeed. But I feel the bill should be paid all the same. That work was finished six months ago and it is not honest of us, papa, to delay payment any longer."

"Us?" Tarrant said, with a quizzical look, and shook his head at her, ruefully. "When were you ever dishonest, Kate, in all your nineteen upright years?" He opened the bill and looked at it and gave a little weary sigh. "Very well. It shall be paid. I give you my word most faithfully."

Accordingly, when Martin next came, an envelope lay on the schoolroom table.

"My father asked me to give you this, with his thanks and compliments," Katharine said.

Ginny, sitting with Hugh at the table, was watching Martin with prim satisfaction.

"Now you know, Master Cox, that gentlemen *do* pay their bills."

"Yes," Martin said, absently. He put the envelope into his pocket.

"Is anything wrong?" Katharine asked.

"Well, it's about my lessons," he said, and because he was troubled in his mind, he spoke roughly and clumsily. "Now that the damned bill is paid, I don't rightly know where I am, or whether I'm to come any more."

"Do you want to?"

"Yes. I do."

"Then I'm happy to go on teaching you."

"Of course you must still come!" Ginny said. "You've got a great deal to learn yet before we shall have done with you!"

But soon much of the schoolroom talk was of preparations for the festive season. There would be a party on Christmas Eve, with carol singers from Newton Childe, and a second party on Boxing Day, with dancing and a hired quadrille band. There would also be a round of visits to the homes of friends in the neighbourhood, all of which meant that formal lessons would be suspended for two weeks at least. Martin received an invitation to the party on Christmas Eve but this he declined with an awkward excuse.

"Too busy?" Ginny exclaimed. "Why? Shall you be entertaining at Scurr?" Then, seeing the look on his face, she was all contrition at once. "Oh, Martin! *Don't* look like that! It was only a joke. I meant no harm."

"I know you didn't," he said with a shrug. "There's no

bones broken. It's you that's upset."

"But why can't you come on Christmas Eve?"

"For one thing, I've got no decent clothes. Besides, I'm not fit for fine company."

Ginny tried to persuade him but here Katharine intervened.

"Martin knows his own mind. We shall only make him uncomfortable if we persist."

"Well, at least you can stay to supper today, seeing it's just the family, who are *not* such very fine folk," Ginny said. "And now let us go down and begin decorating the house."

Taking Martin by the hand, she led him down to the great hall, where, on one of the Tournai carpets, lay an enormous heap of holly, and where, at that moment, a side door opened to admit two of the garden boys, both grinning from ear to ear as they squeezed their way through with shuffling steps, carrying a wooden tub containing a tall green Christmas tree.

"Have you ever seen one before?"

"No, never," Martin said.

"You can help us to dress it," Ginny said.

Christmas at Newton Railes, Martin thought, as he walked home that evening, would certainly be a different affair from Christmas at Scurr Quarry. There, little was made of it, beyond what he and Nan might do to brighten the cottage with greenery. They had no money for buying presents. Nan always knitted mittens or scarves for her father and brother, using wool she had spun herself from wisps collected in the hill pastures, and Martin would give her a picture he had sketched or something carved from a piece of stone. But all Rufus ever did was to bring in a paper cornet of nuts and raisins, or a few sleepy apples, bought for a penny in the market last thing on Christmas Eve.

Still, at least their Christmas dinner this year would be much better than usual, for the Tarrants had given Martin a goose, with fresh vegetables and herbs to go with it, and a plum pudding in a white cloth. Nan almost wept on receiving these gifts. "Oh, what a feast we shall have!" she said. And sure enough, on Christmas Day, when she served up the big handsome bird, roasted on the open hearth, the sight and smell of it on the dish, surrounded by sage and onion stuffing, with roasted potatoes and mashed swede, brought a murmur of appreciation even from Rufus himself.

"I yunt had goose for I don't know how many years," he said. "But whoa, whoa, go carefully, girl! That bird won't last us no time at all if you carve slices so thick as that."

In addition to the welcome gifts of food, Martin had received a personal gift from the young Tarrants: *The Last Essays of Elia*, in soft brown calf, printed on delicate rice-paper, its pages gilt-edged. On the fly-leaf, in Miss Katharine's hand, there was an inscription: "To our friend Martin, Christmas 1844, from the family at Newton Railes." He in return had given them an ammonite: one of the fossils he so often found when cutting stone; the largest and best from his collection, being almost a perfect coil, which he had polished assiduously until it had the delicate glow of an ornament in palest amber.

"Were they pleased with it?" Nan asked.

"I don't know. They seemed to be. They know I've got no money, of course, so they understand how I'm placed."

Brother and sister were out on the hill. Their father, unused to eating so well, had fallen asleep in his chair by the fire, and they had quietly left him there. They walked together up the track, pushing against a strong north wind that had a few flakes of snow in it.

"Have you ever thought," Martin said, "that father may not be so poor as he has always made out to us?"

"Well, he has some money put by," Nan said. "He has always told us that."

"Yes, but how much? And what is it for? Where's the use of putting it by if we never get any good from it?"

"Father says we shall some day. But we've got to guard against the hard times."

"Hard times!" Martin exclaimed. "When have we known anything else?"

"Father must surely know best," Nan said.

"Do you think so? I'm damned if I do! Promises! That's all we get! And that's all mother ever got. He promised *her* a decent house and all she got was a box in the ground!" He walked in silence for a while and then: "Sometimes I think he's got so used to scrimping and scraping all these years that now he just doesn't know how to stop."

"Let's not talk about father," Nan said. "Let's talk about something else."

"The Tarrants?" he said, with a teasing glance.

"Yes, and the house and everything, and what it looks like at this time of year."

So he told her about the great hall and how it was decked for Christmastide.

"It's the largest room in all the house, and although it's so grand, it's homely too. There's almost always a fire in the hearth – even in summer, if the day is damp – and there are settles and chairs and stools round the fire, and all manner of other furniture round about, some of it as old as the house itself. The whole of one wall is all mullioned windows, including a great square bay, which rises to the very roof, all glazed with small leaded panes of glass. They stood the Christmas tree in the bay and when we had got it all decked out … Oh, I wish you had seen it, Nan! … The green branches all hung with delicate gold and silver baubles … with tinsel ribbons strung on it in loops … yes, and small wax candles in different colours, though they won't be lit, Miss Ginny said, because Mr Tarrant is nervous of fire. The whole of the hall is decked out with holly and ivy and mistletoe and there's a musical box playing carols …"

"Do you wish you'd gone to the party last night?"

"In some ways I do. If I could have been invisible, now … "

"Oh, but surely you'd want to take part? To talk to people and dance with the girls?"

"Yes, if I had the right clothes to wear, and wasn't worried all the time about doing and saying everything wrong."

"I wish you had gone. Then you could have told me about it." Nan looked at him and laughed. Her hair and eyebrows were flecked with snow. "Whatever did we find to talk about before you began going to Railes? And whatever shall we do with ourselves when the time comes for you to stop?"

"I don't know," Martin said. "I don't like to think about that."

They turned back towards Scurr, and the wind hurried them down the hill.

In fact he thought about the future only too often, and because the ending of his lessons at Railes would be like the ending of life itself, he was all the more determined to make the most of them while he could.

At this time he lived two lives, each the antithesis of the other. On the one hand, his life at Scurr: a mean habitation, comfortless, drab. On the other, Newton Railes: richness and colour wherever he looked; a quiet, unhurried feel to the days; and yet a kind of excitement too, because, through his lessons and the books he read, the world was opening out for him, in his imagination at least. Every hour that he spent with the Tarrants brought some new discovery; something to start a train of thought; to stimulate his own ideas and create a sense of wonder in him. In part it was the companionship; the endless argument and debate, sometimes serious, sometimes not; but always of a quality that made him feel he was really alive.

It was a strange relationship that he enjoyed with the family. Seeing so much of them as he did, in the intimacy of their home, he had come to know them very well, and felt he was sharing a part of their lives. It was just an illusion, of course, because his life and theirs were poles apart, and when the lessons came to an end, his friendship with them would end, too. It would soon be forgotten, on their side at least, – that, he knew, was inevitable – and he warned himself against the danger of becoming too strongly attached to them. He knew he would have to see to it that he made an independent life of his own, though what that independent life would be, he had as yet no idea. All he had was a firm resolve to arm himself against the loss of those things which, at present, made his life worthwhile.

Meantime, whenever at Railes, he stored its riches away in his mind: impressions; incidents; scents and sounds: every detail was precious to him and became engrained in his memory. Sometimes it was the lessons themselves: Miss Katharine's quiet voice explaining the structure of a sonnet, or Miss Ginny's excitable one quizzing him on the emperors of Rome. Sometimes it was a little scene, creating a picture in his mind: the two girls in the music-room, observed through the half-open door, Miss Katharine at the piano, Miss Ginny singing; and with the picture, inevitably, went the songs they played and sang together: "Greensleeves", "The Oak and the Ash"; "Afton Water" and "Robin Adair".

The music Martin heard at Railes had been a revelation to him, for as well as the old familiar songs, there was music of a kind that he had never heard elsewhere: the delicate sonatas of Haydn; the measured preludes and fugues of Bach; and, touching him even more closely, a Chopin study which Miss Katharine played occasionally. Surely such music as this must have come from another world? He could scarcely believe it had been composed by men who had lived mortal lives on earth.

Ginny enjoyed his astonishment and liked to try out "new" pieces on him.

"Which did you like best – the Beethoven or the Villeuse?" she asked once.

"I liked them both in different ways but – I think the Beethoven has more soul."

"All music has soul, silly. It wouldn't be music otherwise."

"Yes, you are right," Martin said. "I stand before you in a white sheet."

"Oh, goodness!" Ginny said. "You are beginning to talk like Hugh."

CHAPTER

3

In April he had his sixteenth birthday and a few weeks later the twins had theirs. It was then Whitsuntide and the Tarrants were away on holiday, staying with friends in Pembrokeshire, but soon after they returned, there was talk of a party at Railes; a belated birthday celebration, to be held on May the twenty-first, and, "This time you must come," Ginny said. She brushed aside all his objections. "If you haven't any suitable clothes, well, you must get them, that's all. As for not being able to dance, the party is not for a week yet. That's plenty of time for you to learn."

His sister Nan was also invited – that of course was Miss Katharine's idea – and Martin, in a state of excitement tinged still with nervous dread, carried the news home to Scurr.

"A party at Railes, eh?" Rufus said. "With company and dancing and that? Yes, well, I think you should go."

"We shall both need new clothes," Martin said. "Evening clothes. And special shoes. We can't go in the clothes we've got."

"Your sister will not be going, my son. You will go alone. It will cost me money enough, fitting you out with all you need, but at least there is some point in that, cos you're a young man and got your way to make in the world."

"And what about Nan?" Martin cried. "Surely she deserves the chance of getting some pleasure for a change?"

"Martin, hush," Nan said. She laid her hand hard on his arm.

"No, I won't hush! I will have my say!" He turned back to

his father and said: "If Nan is not allowed to go, I will not go myself."

"As to that, you may please yourself. It's just about all-as-one to me." Rufus drank the last of his tea and set down his mug. He rose from the table and reached for his cap. "You are not dictating to *me*, my boy, over this or anything else, and the sooner you swallow that fact, the better we shall get on, you and me."

Grimly, he stalked out of the house. Martin and Nan looked at each other.

"You shouldn't have spoken to father like that. It was bad of you."

"I meant what I said all the same."

"Martin, you're being silly, for I would not have gone, anyway. It is kind of the Tarrants to ask me but I wouldn't be happy going there. It's different for you – you're used to them. But I shouldn't know what to do or say. I'd be all at sea, like a pea in the pond."

"Come to that, so shall I, seeing there'll be such fine folk there, all of them strangers to me, excepting just the Tarrants themselves."

"Well, go for *my* sake, if not your own. How else shall I ever know what an evening party at Railes is like?"

Persuaded by Nan, he decided to go, and Rufus, on hearing of his decision, took him that very evening to be measured by Dunne, the Bridge Street tailor, for a suit of clothes appropriate to the coming occasion. And if the cloth for tail-coat and trousers was perhaps on the coarse side, being the cheapest on Mr Dunne's shelves, he did not, even by a flicker, betray surprise at his customer's choice. And if, as Rufus insisted, coat, waistcoat, and trousers, were all cut on the generous side, to allow for a young man's growth, nevertheless, when made and fitted, they were without argument the most impressive suit of clothes Martin had ever worn in his life. Guided by Mr Dunne, he was outfitted with further essentials: a white shirt, with butterfly collar; cuff-links, studs, a fine white tie; a pair of black dancing-pumps and a pair of white wash-leather gloves.

"I think you look very handsome," Nan said, when she saw him in his finery.

"I don't *feel* very handsome. I feel as though I'm nothing but *clothes*."

"You won't be nervous on Tuesday evening? I'm sure you have no need to be."

"It's easy for you to say that. Now if you had been going with me—"

"I shall be with you in spirit," she said.

"Then I hope your spirit will watch over me and keep me from making a fool of myself."

The evening of the party was fine and warm; so unusually warm for May that all the casements were open at Railes, letting in the strong sweet scents of lilac blossom and new-mown grass. Even in the great hall, high and spacious though it was, doors and casements were open wide, for here most of the guests were assembled and here, in due course, they would dance. The carpets had been taken up from the floor, revealing the smooth yellow flagstones, and most of the furniture had been removed. Up in the minstrels' gallery, five musicians, seated on small upright chairs, were playing softly and quietly a medley of old traditional tunes. The dining-room and drawing-room doors were open and through them Martin caught a glimpse of tables spread with eatables. In the background, the maids went to and fro, and once he saw Miss Katharine talking to Jobe, who, in dark green livery, was acting as butler for the evening.

Just inside the main door, the twins stood receiving their guests, but Martin, disliking the thought of arriving with the carriage-folk, had entered the house from the stable-court and gone first to the servants' quarters, there to brush away the dust which, in the course of his three-mile walk, had whitened his trousers to the knees, and there to change into his dancing-pumps. Now, from choice, he stood alone in a quiet corner of the great hall, a glass of wine-cup in his hand, trying hard to master his nerves as he watched the gathering of the guests. Most of these were in their teens: the sons and daughters of local gentry or of notable Chardwell families. Some were known to him by sight because his work had taken him to their homes, but although one or two of these nodded to him in passing, there was no recognition in their eyes, for who, in this well-bred gathering, expected to find a stone-mason set down in their midst?

As more and more guests filled the hall, so more and more glances came his way, until Martin was left in no doubt that he was the object, not only of speculation, but of puzzled amusement too. At home, when he had looked in the glass that Nan had held up for him, the tailed coat and breasted waistcoat, the pleated shirt and white neck-tie, had seemed to him absurdly fine; he had felt the pretension of wearing such clothes; but here in the hall at Newton Railes, watching the girls in their gossamer gowns, the young men supremely elegant, he realized how clumsy and countrified his own evening dress appeared. And with this dawning realization, he felt his face begin to burn.

One small group nearby – a youth and two girls – were passing remarks quite openly. The youth, aged nineteen or twenty, his curls sleek with bandoline, his shirt-front resplendent with pearl buttons, stared at Martin for some seconds, raking him over in an insolent way, with a faint smile and a lift of the brows. He then turned back to his two companions, making a drawling remark that brought a splutter of laughter from them.

"No, I've no idea who he is. The fellow's a total stranger to me. And so is his tailor, I'm glad to say."

The three young people moved away, to join a group at the foot of the stairs. Martin looked into his glass, at the candied violet floating in it, and swirled it round and round in the wine. When, in a while, he looked up again, Ginny stood smiling in front of him.

"So this is where you've been hiding yourself! You didn't come in through the entrance hall. I suppose you sneaked in at the back. What's the matter? – You're as red as turkeycock."

"It's a warm evening."

"Fiddle-de-dee!"

"Yes. Well. If you must know, I overheard somebody enjoying a joke at my expense, with particular reference to my clothes."

"Male or female?"

"I'm not sure."

Ginny laughed in huge delight.

"Come, now, tell me who it was."

"The dandified sprout over there, with black curls, sweetly scented, and the kind of face you see in a spoon."

"Better and better!" She laughed again. "I don't need to look to know who that is." But she turned and looked all the same. "Yes, I though so. It's Sidney Hurne."

"One of the Hurnes of Brink End Mill?"

"Yes, he's Oliver Hurne's eldest son. But you mustn't heed what Sidney says. They are terrible snobs, you know, some of these clothiers' families, and Sidney is an odious youth, altogether too full of himself."

"If you think him odious, why did you invite him here?"

"Oh, because if we did not, we should never be invited to Aimbury House. Besides, Sidney can be quite amusing sometimes, in his spiteful way. But he had no right to be rude to you and I've half a mind to tell him so."

"I'd rather you didn't," Martin said. "I prefer to fight my own battles."

"Well, finish your drink and come with me and I'll introduce you to some other guests."

At that moment they were approached by a tall, burly young man whose fresh, open countenance Martin recognized instantly.

"Ah, here's someone you already know," Ginny said. "You remember George Winter of Chacelands? You met him here one day last summer when he called with his sister and grandparents."

"Yes, I remember, of course," Martin said.

"And so do I." George Winter's gaze was steady and frank. "Have you killed any more adders since then?"

"Not here at Railes. Only up at the quarry, that's all. We're often troubled with them on the hill."

"My sister Leonie is here somewhere. She will enjoy meeting you again." George, turning, looked all round the room, but Leonie was nowhere to be seen. "She's probably out on the terrace with Hugh." He turned and addressed himself to Ginny. "I hope I may have the pleasure of dancing the first dance with you – if you are not already engaged."

"For the first dance? I'm afraid I am. I've promised it to Martin here." Ginny opened the tiny card dangling by a ribbon from her wrist. "I'll write you in for the second instead."

George bowed and went away. Martin looked at the smiling girl.

"This dance you say you've promised me—"

"Don't worry. It's just a quadrille. Well within your abilities."

"And favouring me is part of your scheme for keeping George Winter on a string?"

"I suppose it hadn't occurred to you that I might *prefer* dancing with you?"

"No. It had not."

Up in the gallery above, the musicians were playing a series of chords, their signal that dancing was about to begin, and a moment later the leading musician, coming close to the balustrade, called down to the guests below, asking them to form their sets. Laughing and talking, the guests complied, and the band struck up with the opening bars of "Belle and Beau". Five sets took the floor and this meant that the great hall, spacious though it was, only barely accommodated them. For the couples in one set, indeed, the figure was made difficult by the lower part of the staircase, the curtail-step of which jutted out in a wide curve. Martin and Ginny were in this set and there was much merriment as two of the couples, in swinging round, were obliged to mount the lower stair.

"You look very fierce," Ginny said, as they stepped down

together, hand in hand.

"I have to concentrate, that's why, otherwise I'll go all wrong."

"Oh, that doesn't matter! It's part of the fun."

"Only for those who are looking on."

He got through the dance without any serious mishap and Ginny was very pleased with him.

"There! You see! It wasn't so bad!" She looked at him with a glowing face, fanning herself with a small silk fan. Then, laughing, she fanned him too. "Now, if you're not too lost for breath, you can get us both some wine-cup."

When he returned with the two glasses, he found her talking to Sidney Hurne. She looked at him with mischievous eyes and made a formal introduction.

"Cox?" Hurne said. "Do I know that name?"

"Probably, yes," Martin said. "My father is well known in the district. He is a mason. So am I. And we did some work on your father's mill about eighteen months ago. An extension to your engine-house."

"Indeed? Well, I wouldn't know about that. My father has little to do with the mill these days. He leaves it to his manager. As for myself, I never set foot in the place."

"No?" Martin said. "Then perhaps you should."

"What?" Hurne said, with a haughty stare.

"I mean if you *were* to set foot in it – you or your father, that is, – you would find the law being broken there."

"What the devil are you talking about?"

"I'm talking about the Child Labour Bill, which made it illegal to employ children under the age of nine in any mill or factory. But such young children *are* employed at Brink End. At least, they were when I was there eighteen months ago."

"And what business is it of yours?"

"The breaking of the law is anyone's business."

"Brink End is not the only mill where young children are employed. Most of the mills in the Cullen Valley do the same."

"Then you *do* know something about it, after all?"

"I know this much at least – that the weavers themselves take no account of the law. They *want* to put their children to work just as soon as they possibly can because they need the extra money."

"They would not need it, though, if they were paid a proper wage that enabled them to raise their children without turning them into slaves."

"I suppose you are one of those people who think the children of the poor should go to school till the age of nine?"

"Yes."

"And who is to pay for that schooling, pray?"

"Those who have money to pay for it."

"Would that include you?"

"No. It would not."

"It's a very remarkable thing that the penniless nobodies of this world are always so quick to tell the others how their money should be spent."

"It's not just the penniless nobodies. An example has been set by the work of men like Lord Ashley and Lord Brougham."

"Indeed? And are their lordships friends of yours?"

"No. But they are both good friends of the poor."

"You are poor. You said so yourself."

"Not so poor," Martin said, "that I am obliged to sell myself into slavery at Brink End Mill."

"Now look here, Mason, or whatever your name is—"

"Cox, not Mason," Martin said.

The two young men, silent now, glared at each other, eye to eye. And here Miss Ginny, although enjoying the argument that had flared up so fiercely, now saw fit to intervene.

"I would remind you two gentlemen that you are both guests in my father's house and that as such you have no business arguing in this unmannerly way." Smiling at each of them in turn she added: "You ought to be thoroughly ashamed of yourselves and I think you should apologize for behaving thus in my presence."

There was a pause. Sidney Hurne was the first to speak.

"Miss Virginia, you are quite right. I beg pardon most abjectly for allowing myself to be provoked, and I hope you will demonstrate your forgiveness by granting me two dances at least."

Ginny, with a gracious nod, gave him her card and pencil and watched him write his name in it. When he had finished, she smiled at him, and he, after a bow for her and a cold, flickering glance for Martin, went off to join a group nearby. Ginny sipped her wine-cup and looked at Martin over the glass.

"Do you feel better," she asked, "now that you have had your revenge on poor Sidney?"

"Perhaps."

"I have not had your apology yet."

"No. Well. I apologize."

"That is hardly to be compared with Sidney's, but I suppose it will have to do." She turned and set down her empty glass. "Now finish your drink and come with me and I'll introduce you to some of the guests before dancing begins again."

"Just at present," Martin said, "I would prefer to stand and watch."

"But you should be asking some pretty girl to dance and you can't if you haven't been introduced." She studied his face, so stubbornly set, and: "I don't know why you came," she said, "if you're not going to enjoy yourself."

"I am enjoying myself, in my own way, but—" he cast a glance round the crowded room "I am not brave enough to dance with a girl I've only just met. Besides which, most probably, all your young ladies would turn me down, thinking it beneath them to dance with such a hobbledehoy."

"Well, at least you can ask Kate," Ginny said. "You don't have to be brave for that. And as she is one of your hostesses, it is in fact your duty to ask her."

"Yes. So I shall. In a little while."

"Very well. I'll leave you, then."

*

Later, with a third glass of wine-cup in his hand, he stood in the square-bayed window recess, close to where one of the open casements let in the soft warm summer air. At half past seven it was still light and the evening sun, shining almost horizontally through the huge expanse of glass, cast a pattern of the small leaded panes over the greater part of the hall, so that the people gathered there stood or strolled about in reticulations of light and shade.

It was a relief to him to stand alone again for a while, and although by doing so he attracted attention, as before, somehow it no longer worried him. Ginny had been quite right: he did indeed feel better for talking to Sidney Hurne as he had, for anger in some strange way had cleared his brain and removed his self-consciousness; and as he brooded on it now, he saw how easy it was to feel contempt for another human being. Just as Hurne despised him for being a mason and ill-clad, so he despised Hurne's pretensions and hypocrisy. Somehow this discovery – that every man had it in him to look down on another – gave him a fresh view of his life, and the knowledge that he, in a worldly sense, was inferior to the people about him no longer caused him anxiety. He was here by invitation, and if the Tarrants treated him as a friend, what was Hurne's contempt to him?

Suddenly he felt sure of himself, as though all things were possible, and nothing in the world could assail him; and with this feeling he was aware of a pleasant glow spreading throughout his whole being. In a while it occurred to him that the wine-cup might have something to do with this. He had never drunk wine until this evening. Perhaps he was intoxicated. He drained his glass and smiled to himself. That, he thought, must be his last. Another might undo the good and create mischief in its place.

Up in the minstrels' gallery, the leading musician, with his fiddle, struck up "Sir Roger de Coverley", and the young people down below greeted the tune with applause. Martin watched as they moved about, taking their positions for the dance, behind the two leading couples: Ginny partnered by

George Winter, Hugh with George's sister Leonie.

After "Sir Roger" there was a waltz. Ginny's partner was now Sidney Hurne, and Martin observed, with scornful detachment, that the youth danced with verve and panache, keeping up a flow of talk which Ginny obviously found amusing. Deliberately, Martin looked elsewhere, and saw that Miss Katharine had joined the dance, her partner a tall, dark-haired young man, rather older than most of the guests, being in his mid-twenties, and with a look of assurance that made him appear older still. He and Katharine, dancing together, made such a strikingly handsome couple that many eyes were turned their way; but of this they seemed unaware, and the man certainly, Martin thought, was utterly absorbed in his partner.

A touch on his shoulder and Hugh stood beside him.

"You are not dancing."

"Neither are you."

"After 'Sir Roger' I needed a rest. I have to respect my poor lungs, you know."

"Who is that man dancing with Miss Katharine?"

"Oh," said Hugh, turning to look, "that's Charles Yuart of Hainault Mill."

"I don't think I've ever seen him before."

"Charles has been away quite a lot, travelling abroad on his father's business. But two months ago his father suffered a stroke and Charles came home to take over the mill. My father met him at a meeting of the Turnpike Trust and invited him back afterwards. Since then he's been a regular visitor."

Hugh paused, watching as Katharine and her partner whirled past, just a few yards away.

"Charles is very much taken with Kate, as you will observe for yourself, and she seems strongly attracted to him. Ginny, who thinks she knows the signs, is sure it will come to a match one day. But that is confidential, mind."

"Yes, of course," Martin said, and then, after a little pause: "Is he good enough for her, do you think?"

"With regard to birth and breeding, do you mean, or regarding his wealth?"

"No, I mean as a man," Martin said.

"Well," Hugh said, weighing the question. "I don't know that any man could ever be good enough for Kate...but he seems a decent enough sort of fellow and my father thinks very highly of him."

"He has the look," Martin said, "of a man who is seldom troubled by doubts."

"He's certainly an ambitious one. He thinks the woollen trade needs pulling up and is all in favour of modern ideas. He wants to extend Hainault Mill and bring in the new power-looms, but his father won't hear of it. The cloth trade is still in a bad way and old Mr Yuart has had a struggle to keep going these past twenty years. But Charles thinks that is all going to change and so do some of the other clothiers. There's already been a lot of expansion in the north of England but down here we're lagging behind. Charles would like to be the one who sets things moving in the Cullen Valley and restores Gloucestershire to its former glory."

"Let's hope he succeeds, then, because that will be good for everyone. But I thought these new power-looms had already been tried a few years ago and were not what they were cracked up to be."

"Yes, but they've been improved since then."

While Martin was talking to Hugh, John Tarrant came up to them.

"Well, Martin. I'm glad you could come. I hope you are enjoying yourself?"

"Thank you, sir. Very much indeed."

"Why aren't you dancing, you two boys? Aren't there enough pretty girls for you?"

"Oh, there are pretty girls in droves," said Hugh, "but they will keep for a while, papa, and the summer night is young as yet."

The lively waltz came to an end; the couples stood, some clapping their hands as they looked up at the gallery; and after a moment the five musicians stood up and bowed their acknowledgement. They then sat down again; the couples drifted about the hall; and John Tarrant moved on, going the round of his children's guests, making sure, in his affable way, that he spoke to every one of them.

The sun had gone from the windows now and the hall was growing shadowy, but during the present lull in the dancing, Jobe, in his rôle of butler, appeared, with three of the maids, bringing lamps and candelabra, already lit, which they set down on tables and shelves, here and there about the hall. As they went to and fro, bringing more lamps and candelabra, sometimes carrying two at a time, Martin noticed that John Tarrant was watching them very carefully. It seemed from his frown that he was displeased and in a moment something happened that drew an exclamation from him and brought him striding across the hall, for one of the maids, Prissie by name, as she set down the first of two candelabra, allowed the other to tilt so badly that a number of candles fell to the floor.

Martin instinctively darted forward; so did Hugh; but other young people, closer to the scene, were already gathering round the maid, taking the two candelabra from her, setting them safely down on the table, and retrieving the candles from the floor. Tarrant now came and reproved the maid. His face showed that he was angry, though he spoke, as always, with restraint.

"Prissie, we have a rule in this house, and I'm sure you are well aware of it, that no one should ever attempt to carry more than one light at a time. Candles and lamps are dangerous things and I hope I never have occasion to remind you of this rule again." Turning, he looked at the other maids, standing sheepishly nearby. "Yes, you may well hang your heads. Prissie is not the only culprit. Now go on your way, all of you, and be thankful the accident was no worse."

The three maids curtseyed and fled away. The young guests exchanged smiles and those who had hastened to Prissie's rescue now spoke on her behalf. Of these Ginny was one, and now, as she replaced the douted candles, she said:

"Don't be too hard on her, for there really is no danger, papa. Not when the stone floor is bare. They wanted to bring all the lights in before we began dancing again."

"They did wrong nevertheless. And I insist that my rule should be observed at all times. Are these candles damaged, my child? If so, they must be replaced."

"No, they are all in good order, papa."

Ginny took one of the lighted candles and with it re-lit the others, carefully and delicately, so that no drop of wax was spilt. Tarrant, with a nod, turned away. He crossed the hall to join Katharine who, standing with Charles Yuart, had been watching the little incident. Hugh now turned to Martin again.

"My father, as you see, is frightened of fire. Rather excessively so, perhaps. That is because of an accident that occurred in the night-nursery when Ginny and I were two years old. A lighted candle was left on a shelf and somehow it fell into my cot. The bedding caught fire and I was burnt. I don't remember it, of course, but I know it happened because of this." And Hugh, tilting his fair, handsome face, displayed the ugly pink-mottled scar that puckered the skin on his throat and jaw. "Hence my father's stringent rule."

"You could have been burnt to death," Martin said.

"There's no doubt that I should have been, too, but for Ginny waking up. She saw the fire and began to scream. The nursemaid came in and I was saved." Hugh gave a gentle, lop-sided smile, and ended with a touch of self-mockery. "Thus the son and heir was spared and perhaps – who knows what lies ahead? – a Member of Parliament to boot."

"Perhaps even," Martin said, "a future Prime Minister."

"Ah!" Hugh said, with a bright glance. "All things are possible, I suppose."

The maids were coming in with more lamps – one to each maid this time – and Katharine, leaving Charles Yuart in conversation with her father, went to intercept Annie, reminding her that lamps were needed up in the gallery, for the musicians. She then stood, surveying the company, and Martin, excusing himself to Hugh, took this chance of approaching her. Nervous but resolute, he made his bow.

"Miss Katharine," he said, and cleared his throat. "I hope you will do me the honour of dancing with me, if you have a dance to spare."

Her grey eyes smiled at him. She understood perfectly that this formal speech, on this formal occasion, had required courage on his part; and he knew that she was pleased with him. But she offered no word of commendation: she paid him the greater compliment of taking his good manners for granted.

"In truth I have plenty of dances to spare and I shall be delighted," she said.

"I hope one of them is a quadrille, for I can do no other, I'm afraid."

"Come, now, I cannot believe that, for I saw you practising the waltz with Ginny only a few days ago, with Hugh playing the violin."

"Yes, but practice did not make perfect," he said, "and I'm bound to make janders of it."

"Very well. A quadrille it shall be." Katharine consulted her card. "That means the very next dance, so you may as well stay and talk to me until it begins."

"Yes," he said, and was instantly dumb.

"Poor Martin. I'm afraid the evening is proving rather an ordeal for you. But you're bearing up very well."

"All part of my education."

"Well, I hoped you would find that you were able to *enjoy* at least some part of it. But it *will* become easier in time, you know, and all experience, whatever its nature, is bound to be useful in some way or other."

"You mean," he said, thinking of Ginny, "it will help me when entertaining at Scurr?"

Katharine looked at him steadily.

"You will not always be at Scurr. Somehow or other, in God's good time, you will make something different of your life and arrange it more to your own liking. I am utterly sure of that."

"Well, if I do," Martin said, "it will all be thanks to you."

"No, not all of it," she said. "You *must* take some of the credit yourself. When you first came to us my father said you were worth helping, and he was right. You have a gift for learning things. And, what is more, for *enjoying* them."

For a moment Martin was dumb again, and because he valued Katharine's esteem above anything else in the world, her words brought a warm flush to his face.

"It seems," he said, when he found his voice, "that I shall *have* to make something of myself if only to justify your faith in me."

"Yes. I'll be disappointed, otherwise."

The musicians struck up the Hampton Quadrille, and couples moved across the great hall, converging and forming into their sets. Martin turned to Katharine and bowed. She curtseyed to him and gave him her hand. Proudly he led her into the dance.

It was well after midnight when he returned home to Scurr, and the cottage was in darkness. Nan was still awake, however, and as he crept past her bed, she sat up and whispered to him.

"Did you enjoy the party?"

"Some bits I did. Others not."

"Oh, dear," she whispered, dismayed.

"It's all right. I'm glad I went. The good bits made up for all the rest."

"Tell me tomorrow?"

"Yes. Good night."

During the next few days, whenever brother and sister were together, the subject of the party was discussed exhaustively between them, until even Nan became satisfied that every detail was known to her. Rufus, on the other hand, demanded only a few solid facts.

"Were there many people there?"

"Between forty and fifty, all told."

"Gentry, of course?"

"Mostly, yes. Including some of the clothiers' sons. If you class them as gentry, that is."

"How else would you class them, might I ask?"

"I don't rightly know."

"Speak to any of them, did you?"

"Just one, that's all."

"And did you get on all right with him?"

"No, I did not."

Rufus, on hearing Martin's account of his meeting with Sidney Hurne, was gravely displeased.

"I didn't let you go to that party just for you to make enemies there. It isn't no concern of yours what children the Hurnes employ in their mill, and telling them they're breaking the law is just about the most foolish thing I've heard in all my born days. We've done work for them in the past, but I doubt if we'll get the chance again, due to your foolishness. It's your job, with people like that, to make yourself agreeable, not go falling out with them."

"Even when they make it plain that they're looking down their noses at me?"

"You don't need to fret about that. You just stay mum and bide your time." Rufus paused, his gaze still severe. "I hope you didn't have words amiss with nobody else you met there."

"No," Martin said, sullenly; and, seeking to distract his father's attention, he repeated what Hugh Tarrant had told him concerning Charles Yuart's ambitions and plans. "It seems he's got some idea for extending Hainault Mill and installing the new power-looms there. He thinks the woollen trade will pick up if modern methods are introduced."

"Extending, eh?" Rufus was all ears at once. "He will need stone for that. – Unless he intends using brick!"

"I don't know what he intends. It's only so much talk as yet. And it seems old Mr Yuart himself is against any such scheme to expand."

"Ah, but he's sick," Rufus said, with a pounce. "I heard that myself just recently. He's had a seizure, poor old man, and chances are he won't last long. Young Mr Yuart's the only son. – Only child, too, I believe. – And he'll have a free hand when his father's gone. That means work for builders, my boy, and that in turn means more work for us." He patted Martin on the back. "I've always said our time would come and now it may not be all that far off."

Often during the days that followed Martin wished he had never repeated what he had heard about Charles Yuart and his plans for extending Hainault Mill, for his father fastened on it in such a way that it became an obsession with him. He talked of it as a settled thing that "the new looms" were coming to the Cullen Valley, and that this meant prosperity for the whole district and for Scurr Quarry especially.

"Have you seen young Mr Yuart again, to find out what he's got in mind?" he would ask, whenever Martin had been to Railes.

"No, I only saw him that once, on the evening of the party. And I never spoke to him even then, so there's no question anyway of asking him about his plans."

"What about the Tarrants, then? Don't they never talk of him?"

"No. They do not."

In saying this Martin lied, for the twins in fact had mentioned the young man recently, though not in connection with the new looms. What they had told him was that Charles Yuart had sought, and been given, their father's permission to pay his addresses to Katharine and that already there was an "understanding" between them.

"They are as good as engaged," Ginny had said. "But it can't be made public at present because of old Mr Yuart being so ill."

This having been told him in confidence, he would not betray it for worlds. He had not even told his sister Nan but she, by chance and perhaps intuition, had somehow divined it for herself simply because, recently, she had seen Miss

Katharine in Chardwell one day, driving with her sister in the governess-cart, around the crowded market square.

"Did you tell me, after the party, that Miss Katharine had a suitor?" she asked.

"Yes, I did. But I was speaking out of turn and we must keep it to ourselves. Miss Katharine is more or less engaged but no announcement has been made because old Mr Yuart has taken a turn for the worse."

"Oh, dear. How sad for them all."

"What made you ask about it now?"

"There was something about her … some look in her face … Oh, I can't explain it exactly, but it made me remember what you'd said about her dancing with Mr Yuart and what Master Hugh had told you about there being an attachment between them. Somehow, as soon as I saw her, I thought to myself, 'She is engaged.'"

"And how come you know about such things?"

"I don't know. I just do, that's all. She and Miss Ginny passed us quite close. There was a terrible crush in the square – you know what it's like on market day – and they had to drive very slowly, which meant I had a good view of them. How very attractive they both are, and yet so different from each other. The one so dark, the other so fair, you would never think they were sisters at all."

"They're not only different in looks," Martin said. "They're different in every possible way."

"Oh, yes, I know that, because you've told me so much about them. But even those *deeper* differences can be seen in their faces, don't you think? I mean, you can see what they're like underneath … what manner of people they really are … just by the way they hold themselves and the way they look at other folk." Nan paused, still seeking to define what she meant about the two Tarrant sisters, neither of whom she had ever met. "The difference is this – Miss Ginny is pretty and knows it," she said, "but Miss Katharine is beautiful and doesn't know it."

*

Increasingly, during that summer, Ginny was growing restless. The schoolroom had become irksome to her. She felt it was time to spread her wings. In September she would be going to London to spend three months, perhaps even longer, with some old friends of the family, who had a house in Belman Square. This it was that made her impatient with ordinary lessons. – The only things worth learning now were those that would be useful to her while enjoying the London season.

She practised her music assiduously, and was always sending to Metzler's for the latest piano pieces and songs. She studied ladies' fashion journals and worried whether her new gowns, being made for her in Sharveston, would prove smart enough for London wear. At sixteen she felt herself to be fully a woman. At the same time she recognized that she was still too excitable and, longing for her sister's poise, she read books of advice on deportment and walked everywhere, indoors and out, with a carefully studied grace, much to her family's amusement.

The visit to London filled her mind. She could talk of little else but the parties the Wilsons had promised her and the conquests she expected to make.

"Who knows?" she said once. "I may even come back engaged!"

"I sincerely hope not," her father said, "for I should want to see the young man and to know a great deal about him before you committed yourself to him."

"Oh, papa! I should not engage myself to a man unless he was suitable in every way, especially with regard to his income."

"Are you as mercenary as you sound, my child?"

"Now that is a very confusing thing to say, bearing in mind that you've always told us that we must be sure to marry well."

"Marry well, most certainly, but there are other considerations, my dear, besides the pecuniary one. And I do most sincerely hope you will marry a man you can really love."

"Oh, I shall love him, be sure of that! – So long as he is rich enough!"

While Ginny wished the time away, Martin wanted to slow it down. For him the summer was going too fast. "Only ten more weeks," Ginny would say. "Only nine." "Only eight." And for him, a sinking of the heart, because not only would his lessons end, but all further contact with Newton Railes. The future lay in wait for him: bleak, empty, colourless; though he said nothing of this to the Tarrants, even when, as happened sometimes, they spoke as though his friendship with them would continue indefinitely.

"You'll come and see us, of course," Ginny said. "When I've come back from London and Hugh is back from the Continent—"

"I hope you'll come before that," Miss Katharine put in. "My father and I shall be at home and we should so like to see you and hear how you are getting on."

"Thank you, Miss Katharine. You're very kind."

But he knew he would not visit them. He had already made up his mind about that. They had been very good to him and he would be grateful all his life. But he would not be a hanger-on – the thought of it was hateful to him. Probably, in a year or two, he and his father would be called in to carry out repairs on the house, but that was a different matter entirely. It lay in the unseen future and by then time and chance would have re-opened the natural gap that divided him from the family at Railes.

Meanwhile, with an ache in his heart, he made the most of the time that was left. He was at Railes only one day a week now – his father considered that quite enough – and every moment of that one day had to be savoured to the full. Lessons on the paved terrace, followed by a stroll through the gardens with Hugh; the jokes, the discussions, the fellowship: would he ever know anything like it again?

Afternoon sunlight on the garden; the old house, half in the shade, cool and quiet among its trees; the two girls on the rose parterre, Katharine in white, Ginny in pink, bending over the rose bushes, snipping the blooms, – which, also, were white and pink, – and placing them in the shallow basket that Katharine carried on her arm.

"Why are you looking at us like that?" Ginny asked.

"May not a cat look at a queen?"

"And which of us is the queen, pray?"

"Which of me is the cat?" he quipped.

She was flirting with him quite openly these days, and her family often teased her about it. She was full of high spirits, especially during these last few weeks, and, eschewing elegant deportment and poise, she lived like a swallow on the wing. One day she took it into her head that they should all enact certain scenes, which she had selected, from *Much Ado About Nothing.*

"I shall play Beatrice and Martin will play Benedick."

"Naturally," murmured Hugh.

"Kate will be Hero, of course, and you will be Claudio. Also Don Pedro and Leonato."

"And shall I be pleached arbour, too?"

"No. We shall enact the scenes in the Tudor garden. It will serve most beautifully for the arbour scene, and Benedick will be hidden behind the mulberry tree."

But Ginny's venture into dramatics was spoilt by a sudden thunderstorm, which brought down such a torrant of rain that the players were obliged to flee, out of the walled Tudor garden, along the green walk, and into the shelter of the summer-house. They burst in, the four of them, breathless, laughing, and very wet, and stood looking at one another, trying to shake the worst of the rain from their hair and their clothes. Ginny had suffered much the worst for she, as befitted an actress, had reddened her cheeks and lips with rouge, and now, with the streaming rain, the colour had run down her face and throat and onto her pale yellow frock. The frock itself, being of light organdie, had become utterly soaked with the rain and clung to her body in limp, sodden folds. Her fair hair had escaped from its ribbon and hung, a mass of corkscrew curls, dangling about her red-streaked face.

"What, my lady Disdain, is it you?" Martin said, and made a great show, Benedick-fashion, of peering, astonished, into her face. "Are you living yet?"

For a moment Ginny glared at him, her mortification made worse by the way her brother and sister applauded the scene; and during that moment she was, like a child, suspended between temper and tears. But then good humour intervened; her lips twitched; and she flew at him in a laughing fury, pounding his chest with her clenched fists.

"Oh, you! *You! You!*" she exclaimed, gritting her small white teeth at him. "You are a brute! I could kill you sometimes!"

Laughing, she pounded and pummelled him: short, sharp blows with the edge of each fist; while he, partly in self-defence, partly in response to her closeness, flung his arms around her and held her tight, thus impeding the force of her blows. Briefly, she was his prisoner, enclosed in the circle of his arms, and he felt the slim young shape of her, warm through the folds of her wet clinging frock. He felt the curve of her waist and hips and, as she turned within his grasp, the soft but firm shape of her breasts lightly touching his wet-shirted chest.

He loosened his hold and she escaped, to go dancing all round the summer-house, holding up her wet skirts so that they flared and made a "cheese". She appeared self-absorbed, and hummed a tune, but the deep bright glance she threw at him was full of mischievous awareness; of delight in her own feminine powers; and conveyed, too, without shyness or shame her own sweetly sensual response.

Katharine and Hugh were looking on. They had grown accustomed, recently, to their sister's displays of coquetry, and they merely watched, indulgent, amused. But later that day, when they were all indoors, having dried themselves and changed their clothes, there came a moment when Hugh and Martin were alone together in the schoolroom, the two girls being next door, practising piano duets. And Hugh spoke, casually yet pointedly, of his twin sister's behaviour.

"Ginny's a thorough baggage these days. She's flirting madly with everyone. It's all this excitement at going to London. It's scattered her wits to the four winds. She takes no account of the harm she might do and my father says she will break a good many fellows' hearts before she finally sobers down."

The two youths regarded each other. There was a good understanding between them.

"You don't need to worry," Martin said. "She shall not break mine, I promise you."

In August there were more thunderstorms, bringing the summer to an end. September came in dull and cold but on Martin's last day at Railes a fitful sun brought some warmth. The Tarrants saw him off at the door and he shook hands with each of them, thanking them for all they had done, and Miss Katharine especially.

"You *will* come and see us, won't you, Martin?"

"Of course he will," Tarrant said. "There's work for him and his father here, as soon as I can see some chance of finding the money to pay for it."

" 'A gentleman'," Hugh quoted, " 'is a man who can afford not to pay his bills.' " He looked at Martin with a slow, gentle smile. "Do you remember? The first day you came? That is what you said to us."

"Yes, I remember only too well, but I wish you did not," Martin said.

Ginny would not shake hands with him. Instead she slipped her arm into his.

"I'll come with you part of the way and say my adieu in private," she said.

They walked together through the gardens, with the two dogs, Tessa and Sam, lolloping ahead of them.

"Will you miss me?" Ginny asked.

"Yes," he said, "I shall miss you all."

"You'll think of me, then, while I'm away?"

"I daresay I shall – now and then."

"Is that all? Only now and then?"

"Why?" he said. "Will you think of me?"

"Of course I shall!" She squeezed his arm. "But I'll be most terribly busy, you know, what with all the parties and concerts and things, and going to see the sights of the town."

"Whilst I shall have nothing to do," he said drily, "except earn my living, that's all."

"Yes," she said with a sudden frown. "Such hard, heavy work it is, too, handling stone all day long. I wish you did not have to do such work. You are worth something better than that. And that horrid mean old father of yours doesn't even pay you a wage. You ought to speak to him about that. You ought to stand up for yourself."

"I have tried once or twice but it hasn't done much good so far."

"Then you must try again and again until you get him to see some sense. You are not just a boy now. You're a grown man, more or less, and it's time he began to treat you like one. You may tell him I said so if you like."

Still arm-in-arm, talking together, they strolled along the green walk, down the steps past the summer-house, and along the path by the round pool, until they came to the wicket gate leading out into the park.

"This is where we must say goodbye."

"Yes," he said, and held out his hand.

"Oh, don't be so silly!" she said. "I didn't walk with you all this way just to shake hands with you. I could have done that back at the house."

"Yes. Well. Why didn't you?"

"Because I want you to kiss me, of course."

"Ah. I thought it might be that."

"Of course you did. You knew all the time."

They looked at each other steadily, she frankly provocative, he half responding, half holding back; enjoying a certain masculine scorn; quite deliberately teasing her, to show that *he* would not be teased.

When she came close to him, however, his arms went

round her immediately, and when his lips touched hers there was no question of holding back, nor any question of masculine scorn. Ginny's mouth was gentle but firm and she kissed him, not in a teasing way, but with honest enjoyment, letting him know by her delicate sigh and the movement of her lips against his that the kiss was as sweet to her as to him.

She drew back at last, breathless and flushed, and touched his lips with her finger-tips, as though putting her seal on them.

"You're the first man I've ever kissed. In that particular way, I mean."

"I doubt if I shall be the last. In fact, by the time you come back from London, I shall probably be just one of many."

"So that is what you think of me?" She tilted her face, laughing at him. "Anyway, it won't alter the fact that you were the first, – the very first. Doesn't that mean anything to you?"

Martin took time to consider this.

"Decide what it means to *you*," he said, "and by that you'll know what it means to *me*."

"Such deviousness does not become you, Signor Benedick," she said. "But now it really is goodbye."

Again she reached up to him, to kiss him lightly on the cheek. Then, with a last vivid blue glance, she turned and hurried blithely away, half walking, half running, along the path, pausing just once and waving to him before the shrubbery hid her from view.

When she had gone, he remained for a while looking up at the old house, seen from here at a slight angle, its windows reflecting the sun in a glow that leapt like living tongues of flame. In silent farewell he passed through the gate and began walking across the park, taking one of the short cuts that would lead him downhill, then up again, until he reached the quarry at Scurr.

As he went, he became aware of a tantalizing taste on his lips, and after a moment of puzzlement remembered that Ginny, a few hours before, had been eating half-ripe mulberries picked from the tree in the Tudor garden. Their red juice had been on her lips. Now, sweet-yet-sharp, it was on his, too.

CHAPTER
4

In the autumn of that year the steam railway came to Chardwell, thus linking the Cullen Valley with the Great Western line, and on a fine day in October Martin and Nan walked to the top of Rutland Hill to watch the three o'clock train go puffing along the valley side, just above the river Cullen. For Nan the outing was a major event, and her excitement knew no bounds. Even when the train had vanished round a distant curve of the track, she continued to stare after it, and she talked about it all the way home.

"Just to think of all those people travelling through our valley like that, some of them very important, no doubt, with serious business on their minds. Oh, I would love to ride on that train, wouldn't you, and see all the different towns on the way?"

"You'd better ask father for the fare."

"Do you think he would give it to us?"

"No, but there's no harm in asking," Martin said.

But their father's response, when he was asked, was precisely what they had thought it would be.

"Ride on the train? Just for fun? You've been staring too long at the moon!" he said.

"Lots of other people are going. There's a special excursion ticket offered at eighteen pence, to celebrate the opening of the line."

"Well, all I can say about that is, some folk have got more money than sense. But I am not one of them, so you can put it out of your mind."

But although Rufus dismissed the idea of riding on the train for novelty's sake, he welcomed the coming of the railway with immense satisfaction, and expected great benefits from it. For one thing, coal could now come into the district more easily and economically, thus reducing the cost of steam-power for the woollen mills in the Cullen Valley. For another thing, the railway link would mean an improvement in trade because of the speed with which manufactured goods could be carried to towns all over England and to seaports for shipment abroad.

"Prosperity! That's what it means! And we shall have a share in it."

"Shall we?" Martin said once, with a touch of sombre cynicism. "And how shall we know when we're prosperous? Shall we live in a proper house and have decent food to eat? Shall I be paid a weekly wage and be treated like a grown man?"

"Oh, there'll be changes, right enough! I have always promised you that and you must just have faith in me. You've got your life ahead of you and it's going to be a whole lot different from what my own life has been. You'll be *somebody* one of these days and hold your head up with the best. I'll swear you that. Bible oath. And it won't be too long, neither, the way things are looking these days. The new looms are coming – there's no doubt of that – and when they do our stone will be needed to build new mills to hold them all. Oh, yes! You mark my words."

"And how shall we supply so much stone, just the two of us, working alone, with only one poor old horse just about on his last legs?"

"Ah, well, when the time comes, we shall employ extra men. Everything will be different then. We shall need extra equipment for a start. Extra horses, extra carts. It'll mean laying out money, of course, but that's something that can't be helped. Oh, yes, you may stare, my son! But I've got it all worked out in my head and I know exactly what we shall do – when the right moment comes."

Meantime, when they worked in the quarry, they used the same tackle and gear they had always used, most of it improvised, all of it old; like the primitive hoisting gin, also known as the "tripod", though in fact it had four legs: tall stout wooden poles tied together near the top with rope, from which hung the pulley-block with its big iron hook.

"Seems to me it would make more sense if we spent some money *now*," Martin said, "and set ourselves up with proper equipment, beginning with a proper hoist instead of this jam-dangle here."

"Why, what's the matter with it?"

"Everything," Martin said. "For one thing the ratch doesn't always hold. It slipped a few teeth yesterday, and not for the first time, as you know. Now, this morning, the pulley-hook's opened out again. That's the third time at least."

"I thought you said you'd mended it."

"So I did, after a fashion, which means I hammered it back into shape so that it looks like a hook again. But it's weak now. It ought to go to the smith by rights so that he can re-temper it. That hoist isn't really safe as it is. It's like everything else here and should have been thrown out years ago. It's like that old cart of ours, falling to pieces under us. Yes, and poor old Biffin, too. *He's* been past his prime for years."

"All in good time, boy. All in good time. I will make changes here, sure enough. When the right moment comes."

"Ah, *when*!" Martin said. "I hope I live to see it, that's all."

That winter they were working at Rowell, a lonely crossroads out beyond Meer, building a small Methodist chapel intended to serve the dozen or so hamlets that were scattered among the hills there. Being high up, the site was exposed, and often they worked in a raw north-east wind that brought down showers of cold, stinging rain. In the new year the weather was worse, and Rufus, often soaked to the skin, took a severe cold on the chest. Martin and Nan tried to persuade him to stay at home, but he would not hear of it.

"Our working day is all too short at this time of year and

I've promised Mr Wilkinson that we'll have his Ebenezer ready in time for Easter."

Soon, however, he was seriously ill. Martin, who shared a bed with him, was awakened in the night by his fearful cough, and found him hot but shivering. He was scarcely able to breathe and complained of a terrible pain in his side. "I think I've taken pneumonia," he said, and when Martin, in the small hours, fetched the doctor out to him, this diagnosis proved correct.

Dr Whiteside, a young and energetic man, new in the district, was appalled at conditions inside the cottage and, after examining the patient, made no bones about saying so. Grimly he eyed the trickling moisture that formed black slime on the inner wall and grimly, with a face of disgust, he looked at the matting on the floor, which squelched wetly under his feet.

"I have been in some poor habitations in my time but I've never seen anything like this." He was addressing Martin and Nan. "Why do you live in such a place? Your father's a skilled banker-mason and sole lessee of this quarry. Surely he is not so poor that you *need* live in such dreadful conditions?"

Brother and sister exchanged a glance. They led the doctor outside and there Martin answered his question.

"My father doesn't like spending money."

"Then to some extent he has brought this illness on himself."

"Will he be all right?" Nan asked.

"Oh, he will pull through it, I think. But whether he'll ever be well again depends on a number of things. First, he needs to be kept warm, and how you will manage that in this dripping wet hole of a place I cannot imagine. He will also need careful nursing and when he begins to pick up, he will have to avoid all exertion, otherwise he will damage his heart." The doctor took a notepad from his pocket and made a few notes on it. "Come down to the surgery at half past eight and I'll have a prescription ready for him. Some linctus to ease his cough and some digitalin for his heart. I will come and see him again tomorrow. Meantime, give him plenty of liquids to drink, and something very light to eat. Arrowroot, if you have it. If not, barley gruel and milk."

There was a pause while he looked at them: a look that expressed deep concern.

"Now, regarding your own health. – Living in this place, in such close contact with your father, you are both in danger of infection. That, unfortunately, cannot be helped. But I urge you to take the greatest care in all matters of hygiene and to keep this room as fresh as you can. Also – and this is vital – to ensure that you are adequately fed. At present, I'd say from the look of you, *that* is far from being the case." The doctor's gaze, keen and shrewd, came to rest on Martin's face. "Your father must be persuaded that you need the right kind of food. Hot nourishing stews with plenty of meat and vegetables in them. Plenty of cheese and butter and eggs. Fresh fruit, if you can get it, and porter to drink. And for God's sake, both of you, avoid getting wet and cold."

A moment later, when Nan had gone indoors, he spoke a few words to Martin alone.

"The onus of nursing your father will fall most heavily on your sister. But you are the head of the family, while your father is ill, and the onus of looking after *her* will be yours."

"Yes. I know it. And so I shall."

Rufus lay in the stump bed, propped up against extra pillows, and with extra blankets over him. His face and neck were darkly flushed and his breathing was painfully difficult. He looked at Martin with fever-bright eyes.

"Seems I'm in a bad way and got to lie up for a while." He spoke hoarsely, without any voice. "That young doctor said so straight."

"Yes, we've got to take care of you. And of ourselves as well. The doctor is worried about Nan and me, in case we should take the pneumonia, too. He says we must eat more nourishing food, so I'll need money to buy it."

"How much money?"

"Well, I'm not sure."

"Under the mattress ... up by here ..."

Martin felt under the mattress and pulled out a small canvas bag. His father reached for it at once but Martin, stepping back from the bed, put the bag into his pocket.

"I will take charge of this for now."

"You! Boy!" Rufus gasped. "Taking advantage—"

"There's no need for you to be worried, father. I'll spend it wisely, I promise you. Now lie still or you'll make yourself cough."

Martin went out to the scullery, where Nan was washing clothes in a pail. He took the canvas bag from his pocket and emptied its contents onto the bench, and at sight of the money his heart gave a leap. The gold, silver, and copper coins amounted to nearly twenty pounds. Nan stared in astonishment as he counted it out and placed it in piles.

"Did father give you all that money?"

"Not exactly. I took it from him. And now I'm going down to the town to buy all the things we need, including father's medicine. I'll have my breakfast when I get back."

This time, instead of going on foot, he took the horse and cart, and when he returned Nan saw why, for in it he had a heap of coal, collected from Harker's wharf. He also had a large sack filled with all manner of provisions, mostly of a kind and quality never seen in that household before. There were three pounds of boiling beef, a hunk of suet, and a bag of flour. There were carrots, parsnips, onions and swedes, and a half-hundred weight of potatoes. There were also some oranges, apples, and pears; eggs, butter, bacon, and cheese; cocoa and arrowroot, coffee and tea; white sugar in the lump and a blue paper bag full of Abernethy biscuits. There was also a bottle of Napolean brandy. At sight of all these luxuries Nan was almost overcome.

"Oh, Martin! However much did you spend? And whatever will father say when he knows?"

"Don't worry about father. *I'm* in charge while he's ill."

"You are very bold all of a sudden."

"And not before time."

"Did you bring the medicines?"

"Yes, they're in that package there. The doctor has written the dosage down."

Martin went outside and unloaded the coal from the cart. He brought as much as he could indoors, and left the rest in a heap on the ground, covered over with a tarpaulin. He then swept out the cart so that it would be clean enough to take the usual load of stone out to the chapel at Rowell Cross. So far the morning had been dry but as he went indoors again a sleety rain began to fall.

Before sitting down to breakfast he went and spoke to his father, who, having taken some arrowroot, was still sitting up against his pillows. His colour had improved slightly but his breathing was as painful as ever, and the noise of his congested lungs struggling to do their work made Martin wince for him.

"Well, father. I am sorry to see you like this."

"Are you?" Rufus said hoarsely. His sideways glance was sceptical. "Thought ... maybe ... you was ... pleased." A terrible rattling in his throat and: "Where's ... my ... money?" he asked.

"I'm keeping that for the time being, in case I need to buy more things. After all, as the doctor said, I am the head of the family, while you are laid up like this."

"Suits you, does it?"

"Only until you are better again."

"Chapel," Rufus said in a whisper. "You ... will ...have ... to ... work ... alone. Manage, can you?"

"Yes, I can manage all right. Try not to worry yourself. Just think about getting well."

"You're a good boy. I rely on you."

Rufus closed his eyes and slept.

Although the illness was severe and pulled him down grievously, he came through the worst of it without further complications, partly because of his native toughness, partly because of the tender care with which Nan looked after him. Luckily, she and Martin escaped the infection altogether, and although they were often very tired, after nights of broken sleep, they bore it without ill-effects. All this, Martin felt sure, they owed to the doctor's good advice, which they followed to the letter.

With a fire burning day and night, they kept the cottage constantly warm, though the extra heat, inevitably, drew moisture out of the walls until it hung on the air like fog. The curtain dividing the room was removed so that the air could circulate and the one small window was kept ajar to let the fresh air in. Dr Whiteside approved of this. He attached great importance to it. And he further advised that a kettle of water be kept boiling at all hours, for the steam would help the sick man to breathe. The doctor came every day and on his fourth and fifth visits found Rufus much improved, with a temperature almost back to normal.

"I think, in another day or two, you could get up and sit by the fire. You will be better for getting up. But you mustn't go out of doors, nor must you exert yourself. Your heart is not right yet and you'll have to take things quietly for another three or four weeks at least."

"What's the matter with my heart?"

"Your illness has put a strain on it."

"But it will get better?"

"That depends on you, Mr Cox, and whether you heed my advice. But one thing is certain – another winter in this cottage will probably give you pneumonia again and *that* will most probably finish you off."

"You don't mince your words, do you, young man?"

"Why, is that what you would prefer?"

"No. I'd sooner have it straight. That way, I know how I stand. And if you say I'm to coddle myself, well, so be it, that's what I'll do."

"You're a sensible man, Mr Cox, and you're lucky in having a son and daughter who are looking after you so well."

"Yes, they're good children, both of them. I'm a lucky man, just as you say."

To his children's surprise, in the weeks that followed, Rufus proved a docile convalescent, accepting help when it was needed, yet doing his best to save them trouble. During the day, alone with Nan, he sat quietly by the fire, reading some old almanacks that Martin had found on a rubbish-dump. Later, when he felt up to it, he would do a few light chores: chopping sticks for the fire, perhaps, or mending the big leather gloves he sometimes wore at work in the quarry. Sometimes he would talk to Nan while she was doing her own chores, but he never had much to say to her, and the great moment of his day was when Martin came home from work.

"How've you been getting on? Did you remember to take that lime? What about the water for mixing it? Seems to me it must be time you took another barrel out."

"I've been getting on pretty well. Mr Wilkinson came out this morning. He seemed very pleased with the place. He said you were not to worry about getting finished for Easter. He said you must think about getting well. But I think it *will* be ready in time. I'm taking the door-lintel out tomorrow and once I've got that up it won't be all that long before the joiners can start on the roof."

"Ah, you've done well," Rufus said. "That's been a great relief to me, knowing you was getting on with the work while I was laid up like this. But it comes hard on you, my son, having to do it all by yourself, out there in that lonely place."

"I don't mind," Martin said. "It doesn't worry me in the least."

In fact he enjoyed working alone on the little chapel at Rowell Cross. He liked the independence of it; the sense of responsibility; and he was working very hard, determined to have the place ready for its first service on Easter Day. His father, he knew, would be well pleased. So would the minister. But most of all, being human and young, *he* would be well pleased with himself.

*

At first light the following morning he was out in the quarry, getting ready to load the chapel door-lintel onto the cart. The lintel-stone was large and heavy: ten feet in length; one foot in depth; and two and a half feet wide. It weighed roughly a ton and a quarter, which meant using the hoisting-gin, with the horse, Biffin, harnessed to the chain that would work the pulley and lift the stone.

Martin began by laying the sling-chains out on the ground and levering the stone on to them, carefully, so that it shouldn't be chipped. He then jiggled the legs of the gin into place over the stone, drew the hook down from the pulley, and, gathering the ends of the sling-chain together, slipped the hook into the rings. At the far end of the tackle-chain, the twin ends were already hooked to the hames on Biffin's collar and the horse stood patiently, facing away from the gin, awaiting Martin's word of command.

"All right, Biffin. Haul away! Easy, now...That's the style."

The old horse moved off, the slack of the chain jingling behind him; a slight jolt as it grew taut; and he leant to the collar, beginning to haul.

"Gently, now!" Martin called. "Ge-ently! That's the style." Anxious to avoid too sudden a jerk on the pulley-hook, old and worn, he watched, alert, as it took the strain. "Gently, now. Tha-at's right! Haul away! That's the style."

The horse, long accustomed to the work, pulled slowly and steadily, and the lintel-stone rose in the air. Martin steadied it with his hand; judged the height with a practised eye; and called again to the horse.

"Stand now, Biffin! Stand, boy!"

The horse stood, perfectly still; the stone hung in its sling from the pulley; and Martin, still holding it steady, curbing its tendency to swing, looked again keenly at the great iron hook. It was holding well, he thought, and he turned away to fetch the cart. He took hold of the ends of the shafts and, facing towards the rear of the cart, wheeled it carefully into place between the four straddling legs of the gin, until it stood correctly positioned under the dangling lintel-stone.

The stone was eighteen inches longer than the bed of the cart and would have to be lowered into it so that these eighteen inches jutted out of the rear end, from which the tail-board had been removed. Satisfied with the cart's position, Martin now went round to its rear, ready to guide the stone into place. As he did so his heart gave a leap, for he saw that the old worn pulley-hook was very slowly opening out. In that same instant, too, he heard the tiny rasping sound of the sling-rings sliding down its curve.

Steadying the stone with both hands, he called to the horse; quietly, in his ordinary voice, so as not to startle him.

"Back now, Biffin. Ge-ently back. Easy, now. That's the style."

Obediently, Biffin backed; the pulley cheep-cheeped in its block; and the stone slowly began to descend.

"Gently, Biffin. Ge-ently, boy."

Looking up as he guided the stone, he saw that the hook was opening further; uncurling itself, slowly but surely, as though it had a will of its own. Then, quite suddenly, the stone lurched towards him, still suspended, but only just. Instinctively, he thrust against it, pushing it away from his chest. The pulley-hook opened out altogether, the sling-rings slid off and separated, and the lintel-stone crashed into the cart, smashing through its worm-eaten boards and shattering the axle-tree. As the rear of the cart tilted towards him, Martin, too late in stepping clear, was thrown onto his back on the ground. His left foot was caught under the cart and as the smashed timbers bedded down, so his leg was trapped underneath them, somewhere between ankle and shin. He felt the terrible pain of it go shrieking throughout his whole body. His senses clouded; he felt he was falling away into darkness; but then voices spoke his name and dimly he saw that his father and sister were bending over him.

"Can't move leg," he said, speaking through lips that felt like indiarubber. "It's caught fast."

"I know, I've just looked," his father said. "The axle-tree is lying across it – at an angle, where it's broke – and all the rest is lying on *that*."

"Oh, Martin!" Nan was in tears. "What shall we do?"

"You'll have to fetch help from the farm."

"It'll take so long!"

"The boy's right," Rufus said. "You run to the farm and tell them what's happened. Say we need two strong men and get them to send for the doctor too. You can go faster than me. I'll stay with Martin here."

"Yes. Yes. All right, I'll go."

Nan ran off as fast as she could. Rufus fetched an old sack, folded it into a pad, and placed it under Martin's head.

"The tackle-hook gave?"

"Yes," Martin said.

"And I'm to blame. I know that. You said it should have gone to the smith." Rufus spoke in a husky voice. His face was pinched and grey with distress. "Is the pain very bad, my son?"

"Bad enough."

"I'll get you some of that brandy you brought up with the goods that time. It'll maybe help a bit."

Rufus had gone but a few steps when there was a creaking noise from the cart that brought him hurrying back again. Under the weight of the lintel-stone, the broken timbers were still yielding. The pressure on Martin's leg increased and he cried out in agony. Face contorted, eyes closed, he lay stiffly on his back, arching his body against the pain and pressing with his hands against the ground. When, in a while, he opened his eyes, his father was standing close to the cart, and he cried out yet again, this time not in a pain but in fear.

"No! It's too heavy! You'll kill yourself!"

"Don't be so foolish," his father said. "The damned cart is still bedding down and if I don't get you out of it you'll very likely lose your foot."

He positioned himself carefully, his feet to the left of Martin's trapped leg, and took hold of the lintel-stone where it jutted out at the end of the cart.

"Now! Ready, are you? Right! Here goes!"

With knees bent and shoulders bowed, Rufus, straining with all his might, lifted the stone a fraction or two up off the broken end of the cart. But the stone, thus lifted, began to move, and Rufus, with a little grunt, was forced to let it down again, bending low and bracing himself to stop it sliding towards him, down the cart's steeply sloping floor.

"Father, don't do it!" Martin cried. "For God's sake leave it alone!"

Rufus made no answer. He was breathing heavily and his face was darkly suffused with blood. On forehead and neck his veins stood out, and his eyes had the blind, baffled look of a man lost in the sense of his own weakness. But he was determined to lift the stone and determination gave him strength. Doggedly, he changed his position: took hold of the lintel-stone; and again, straining with all his might, raised it from the bed of the cart, this time shifting it gently sideways so that, instead of sliding towards him, it was wedged against the cart's side. For three seconds he held it there while Martin, with a squirming movement, rolled himself over onto his side and, using his right foot as a fulcrum, dragged his damaged left foot from under the wreckage of the cart.

"All right, father! I'm out! I'm out!"

Lying back, propped on his elbows, he saw his father let go of the stone; saw and heard it drop into place; then saw and heard how the cart gave, yielding and splintering yet again under the force of this second impact and smashing the other end of the axle, so that stone and shattered timbers sank together in a cloud of dust, settling down close to the ground.

For a time Rufus remained quite still, arrested in the very position he had assumed while lifting the stone, his legs bent, his spine in a curve, his head sunk between his shoulders. He had no strength now to straighten himself; his legs were yielding at the knees; and as Martin wriggled towards him he sank very slowly, slowly, down until he was sitting on the ground. It happened that he came to rest beside one of the poles of the hoisting-gin and he leant against it, instinctively, wedging the lower part of his spine against it while the rest of his body crumpled and shrank. And all the time he was struggling for breath, his tortured lungs labouring, squeezed as they were by his overtaxed heart.

Martin, who had humped himself round until he sat close to his father, looked at him in horror and fear, appalled by the darkening of blood in his face; by the way the swollen veins stood out, pulsing, on his temples and neck; above all by the terrible pain rending him as he struggled for breath.

"Oh, father!" the boy cried. "Why did you do this to yourself? I told you, *told* you, to leave it alone." He reached out and touched his father's hand. "Bear up, father, if you can. The doctor is coming. He'll be here soon."

Rufus heard. He turned his head. And he was making an effort to speak when the killing pain transfixed his heart. His right hand flew from Martin's grasp and became a claw, clutching his chest, while his left arm moved in a powerful spasm, arching itself in mid-air. His face now was dark blue; his eyes bulged; and his mouth became a mis-shapen hole, gasping to let out a long, silent scream.

Martin watched, helplessly, his own face contorted with pity and pain. Sobbing, he felt he could no longer bear to watch what his father was forced to bear, but turning away would be treachery. His father's eyes were fixed on him, pleading with him in some way, and he felt he had to answer that plea, if only by sharing the agony. At last a faint sound like a drawn-out sigh and the suffering was over. The grizzled head fell forward, the hands fell limply away, and the body, which suddenly seemed very small, sank slowly to one side, away from the pole of the hoisting-gin, into Martin's outstretched arms.

So when, in a while, Nan came, bringing help from the farm, this was how she found them: her father dead – she saw that at once – and her brother holding him close in his arms, rocking him gently to and fro and weeping, weeping bitterly.

*

The farm-hands laid the body out on the quarry workbench
and covered it with a canvas sheet. They carried Martin into
the cottage and laid him on the bed. They then went to see
to the horse, still harnessed to the hoisting-tackle, and to deal
with the lintel-stone, which they levered out of the cart to the
ground, for the sake of safety. By this time the doctor had
come and the two men departed with a brief word to Nan.

"If you need us again, you have only to ask. But we'll stop
by later to see that you're all right."

The doctor, on hearing that Rufus was dead, did not ask
to see the body – that could wait, he said brusquely – but went
straight into the cottage to examine Martin's injured ankle
and to hear his account of the accident.

While Martin talked, the doctor was busy with a pair of
scissors, opening up the trouser-leg and cutting away the
leather boot. This, Nan had been nervous of doing, and now,
as she stood watching, she let out a cry, appalled at the way
the ankle and leg began immediately to swell, stretching the
thick woollen sock so that it became taut on the flesh. The
sock, too, had to be cut, and the flesh when revealed was a
terrible sight, being darkly contused, purple and black, all
the way from the knee to the toes. But although the bruising
was severe and there was damage to the tendons, the doctor's
given opinion was that matters could have been much worse.

"At least there are no bones broken. That's something to
be thankful for. And in fact, from what you've told me, you
are a very lucky young man. If that cart had fallen right
down, with a ton-weight of stone on top of it – well, I hardly
need tell you that your father undoubtedly saved your foot."

"Yes, and killed himself doing it."

"He knew what danger there was to his heart. I had
warned him clearly enough. It seems, therefore, that he
made his choice."

The doctor, very matter-of-fact, now advised them on the
treatment Martin's injured leg would need: cold compresses
applied at frequent intervals, and the leg to rest on a number
of pillows in a way that would elevate the foot.

"It will probably be two or three weeks before you can put that foot to the ground, but when I get back to the surgery I'll send someone out to you with a pair of crutches for you to use. I will also send some medicine which I hope will help to reduce the swelling. You two young people, I'm afraid, will have much to do in the next few days, dealing with funeral arrangements and so on, and you'll need to hire some form of transport."

The doctor then went outside to examine their father's body. In a few minutes he returned, sat down at the table, and wrote a certificate of death.

"It is hardly suitable that the body should remain outside. Nor can you possibly have it in here. But with your permission I will call on Jessop the undertaker and get him to deal with the matter at once. He will arrange for your father's body to be removed to a suitable place to await burial."

"But won't we have to see Mr Jessop to discuss the funeral arrangements with him?"

"Yes. But first you must see your parish priest. There's also the business of registering the death. I'll write these things down for you. I hope you will find that people are helpful but if you have any problems you can always come to me."

"Thank you, doctor. That's kind of you."

Having seen the doctor off, Nan fetched a bowl of water and some pieces of white flannel cloth, and returned to where Martin lay on the bed. She soaked the pieces of cloth in the bowl, wrung some of the water from them, and placed them one by one on his leg. Martin lay quietly watching her but when she reached his ankle, the touch of the cloth made him cry out, for this was where the pain was worst and the flesh most tender.

"Oh, Martin, I'm so sorry!" She looked at him with anguished eyes.

"Not your fault. Can't be helped. And it's better now. It's soothing it."

"Is it truly?"

"Yes. I swear."

He put out a hand to comfort her, and with loving care she completed her task, covering his foot with the last two cloths. Her own face was as white as his because she, scarcely less than he, was in a severe state of shock. For a little while they were silent together, two young people alone in the world, drawn together more closely than ever because of what had happened that day, but still numbed by the magnitude of it. At last Nan spoke, composed now, though her voice was still tremulous; still unsure.

"Poor father, lying out there. I can't really believe he's dead. Poor boy Martin, too, that you should have seen him die like that. It seemed such an ordinary morning at first ... and a good one, too, what with father feeling so much better ... He was standing at the window there, watching you dealing with that stone, and he said he was praying every night that he would soon be himself again so that he could get back to work ... And now, – oh, Martin! – now he's dead. Whatever are we going to do?"

"The first thing for you to do is to make some tea," Martin said. "I need it. So do you. We'll feel better after that and then we'll be able to think it out."

They had never had to make decisions before. Now, in a day, they had to learn. But they came to it, in their own way, by talking matters over between them, and with Nan writing out a list of all those problems and questions which, at the end, remained unresolved.

"We needn't worry about money yet," Martin said. "I've still got more than eighteen pounds left in father's money-bag. We can pay for the funeral out of that ... And hire a trap, like the doctor said ... We'll still have plenty left to keep ourselves for some time to come ... And there must be more money put by, I'm sure, though where it is and how much it might be, I've no more idea than the man in the moon."

This soon led them both to the thought that they must look into their father's box: a small wooden chest, iron-bound, always locked and jealously guarded, and kept under the bed where Martin lay. So Nan drew out the box and placed it on the chair where she had been sitting. She went to her father's jacket, which hung on a hook on the back of the door, and found the key in an inside pocket. With trembling fingers, – and a strong sense of wrongdoing, even now, at prying into her father's affairs – she unlocked the box and raised the lid.

But there was no money inside; only a collection of their father's work-books, each tied round and round with string, and an envelope on which was written: "This here is a summery of my Will and Tesstament. The Will Proper is in the keeping of Mister Sampson Godwin, Solissiter, of Sage Street, Chardwell." The summary of the Will, when opened, yielded no detailed information but gave, in simple direct terms, a statement of their father's wishes. "I, Rufus Frederick Cox, leave Every Thing I pozess to my dear Son, Martin, safe in the knollige that he will always provide for the Cumfort and Needs of his Sister."

Martin, when Nan read this aloud, gave a little sardonic smile.

"So! We'll have to wait a while longer yet before we know how rich we are. But I am to provide for your 'comfort and needs' – which is more than father himself ever did."

"Martin, you ought not to say things like that."

"I am only speaking the truth. And the truth doesn't suddenly change just because someone is dead."

"It's a question of showing respect."

It was a new experience for him, to see inside his father's work-books, and while Nan went about her chores, he lay all morning deeply absorbed, reading the neatly written notes of "Work Undertaken" and "Stone Supplied", interspersed with remarks in which he could hear his father's growl: "Stubbs demanded discount on stone. Gave him ½ per cent. Added this to his labour bill." And, scanning the details of "Account Rendered" and "Payment Received", he learnt for the first time in his life something of his father's costs and charges, though his father's method of accounting was such that Martin had to study the figures hard before he could make sense of them. There were regular entries, too, of a kind he did not understand at all: "Received from Mr King £2.6.8"; "Received from Mr Bennett £1.15.0"; names of men who, he was sure, had never ordered stone from the quarry or had any building work done.

He was puzzling over these entries when the doctor's messenger arrived, bringing the promised wooden crutches. He rose from the bed, cautiously, and began to practise using them, first in the narrow space of the cottage, then out in the open quarry, with Nan standing anxiously by. While he was doing this, the undertaker's men arrived, bringing, in their covered cart, a coffin of plain unvarnished elm. It made Nan cry again, to see her father put into the coffin, and to see the coffin taken away, jolted about inside the cart as it bumped its way down the quarry track.

"Poor father," she said again, and stood for a moment, overcome, letting the tears stream down her face.

Martin, on his crutches, also watched until the cart had gone from sight. The pain in his leg was bad again now. His ankle, most especially, felt as though it was still being crushed; and in his foot, which he kept off the ground, there was a hot, liquid sensation, as though flesh and bone and muscle together were melting painfully away. A little groan escaped him, and immediately Nan was at his side. She helped him to hobble back indoors and there he stretched himself thankfully on his bed again; and after a while, as the pain receded, he fell into a deep sleep that seemed deliciously sweet and cool.

Early the next morning Nan walked down into Chardwell, to Lotto Smith's livery yard, and returned with a pony and gadabout. In this small vehicle, chosen because it was low to the ground and easy for Martin to step into, they went together into the town to deal with those matters of business that fall to the recently bereaved. They went first to Mr Hickson, the vicar of St Luke's at Old Church End; next to Mr Jessop, the undertaker; and then, with the funeral arrangements settled, which was something of a relief to them both, they drove to Arch House, in Sage Street, where, after a brief wait, they were shown into the presence of Mr Sampson Godwin, solicitor, who rose from his seat behind his desk and came round to shake hands with them. A grey-haired man in his early fifties, fatherly and courteous, he saw them both into chairs and returned to his own, regarding them both with close interest as Martin explained the reason for their visit.

"Your father was an old and valued client," he said. "I knew him for nearly thirty years. His death comes as a great surprise. He was always such a vigorous man." He offered his condolences and then spoke in a general way, referring to their father's early life, when, as a young man of twenty, he had first settled in the district and rented the quarry on Rutland Hill. "I arranged that transaction for him and have the deed in my possession, together with other documents relating to other aspects of his business, and, of course, his last will and testament."

Mr Godwin rose and turned to a tall cupboard behind him. He took out a black metal box, one of many that filled the shelves, and brought it to the desk. It bore the name, R. Cox, painted on it in white letters, and Martin and Nan, seeing this, looked at each other in surprise. They watched as Mr Godwin unlocked it and took out a handful of documents.

"The essence of the will you already know. You, Martin, are your father's heir. But as to the nature of the estate, I long ago formed the impression that your father kept his business affairs very strictly to himself."

"Yes, we know nothing," Martin said.

"Well, now, let me see." Mr Godwin consulted one of the papers taken from the box. "Your father has funds on deposit at Coulson's bank amounting to five hundred pounds." He passed the paper across to Martin. "It earns interest of roughly two per cent."

Martin frowned at the sheet of paper. Mention of the sum, five hundred pounds, had made his heart beat fast. He could scarcely believe it. But there it was, in black and white.

"Yes, well," he said huskily. "We thought there might be a tidy sum put by somewhere."

Mr Godwin smiled gently. He took up two more documents.

"There is also a matter of seven hundred pounds at present out on loan to two gentlemen of this town, namely Mr King of Unity Mill and Mr Bennett of The Bridge Street Brewery. Mr King has borrowed four hundred pounds, repayable two years from now, and Mr Bennett has borrowed three hundred pounds, repayable next December. At present they pay only the interest, which is seven per cent. These are the mortgage deeds."

He passed the documents across. Each was folded narrowly and tied with green ribbon, and each had a summary of its contents written on the outer fold. Martin now understood the entries for Bennett and King in his father's work-books and the explanation came as a shock.

"My father was a money-lender, then, and much better off than we ever thought." He passed the documents to Nan, who looked at them with incredulous eyes. "He has left twelve hundred pounds in all."

"No, Mr Cox, there is more than that." Another two documents were passed across the desk. "One thousand pounds invested in The Sharveston and Craye Railway Company and five hundred pounds invested in The Ricknell and Fordover Turnpike Trust. The capital value of your father's estate is therefore some two thousand, seven hundred pounds, but in fact the railway shares, if sold, would be worth a good deal more now than when he bought them eight years ago."

"How much more?"

"Possibly as much as forty per cent."

"So, altogether, you could say that my father has left more than three thousand pounds."

"Yes. Less certain charges levied against the estate. The first is probate duty, charged at two and a half per cent of the whole. There are also my own charges, for professional services, set at one and a half per cent. Which still leaves a substantial sum, as I'm sure you'll agree." Mr Godwin smiled. "Thanks to your father's thrift and hard work, you are a very lucky young man."

Martin sat perfectly still, looking at the documents in his hands. Yes, he was a lucky young man, but at that moment he felt no joy. His initial excitement, when the sum of five hundred pounds had been mentioned, had given way to disbelief; disbelief to a kind of disgust; until now, on learning the full value of his father's estate, he felt only a sick, bitter rage. He was breathing heavily, his nostrils dilated, his lips compressed. Nan watched him. She understood. And Mr Godwin, a kindly man, who knew something of the life these young people had lived at Scurr, wished he had phrased his congratulations differently. After a while he spoke again.

"The extent of your inheritance has come as a shock to you, I'm afraid. Following on your bereavement, and the injury to your leg, that is understandable. Perhaps you would prefer to postpone all further discussion until some future date."

Martin looked up. He was very pale. His ankle was throbbing painfully and he was trying to hide the fact.

"No, I'd sooner discuss it now. There are some questions I'd like to ask and the first one is this – how long will it be before I can start spending the money?"

"Well, strictly speaking, not until probate has been granted, which will take a few weeks. But in practice the law allows for necessary expenses to be met and paid immediately. Before I go any further, however, in answering your question, I must explain the situation that arises from the circumstance of your being a minor. It means that you cannot have control of your inheritance or hold property in your own name until your twenty-first birthday."

"Do you mean to tell me that although the money is now mine I can't touch it for another four years or more? Because if so—"

"Please," Mr Godwin said gently, "bear with me a while

longer and I will explain more fully.

"When your father made his will, we discussed the possibility that he might die before you came of age, and on my advice he provided against that sad event by appointing me executor of his will and trustee of his estate. In other words, I am now your guardian, which means that I have control of your affairs until you come of age. But you need not be cast down by that. It's merely a question of my looking after your interests until such time as the law considers you to be capable of looking after them yourself. My duty as trustee is to help you in every way I can, and so long as your spending is not, in my view, ill-judged, there shouldn't be any problems between us. But any real property you wish to acquire – which is to say, any buildings or land – will have to be held in my name. Don't blame me for that, Mr Cox. Blame the law. Though I must say, for the most part, I think it a very sensible law."

"I want to buy somewhere decent to live. Can I do that?"

"Certainly. But the deeds, as I say, must be in my name."

"What about the quarry?" Martin asked. "Can I take over my father's lease?"

"So long as your landlord agrees, yes. But that, too, must be in my name."

"And what if I want to make changes there? Buy new equipment? Employ a few men?"

"So long as you can satisfy me that the changes will be all to the good, I shall not stand in your way. We'll have to see the agent, of course, and tell him what you have in mind, but I doubt if there will be any difficulty. The more stone you cut and sell, the more you will pay in royalties, and the Nashwood estate won't object to *that*."

There was a pause. Mr Godwin smiled.

"Are there any more questions you wish to ask?"

"Yes. It's a long time till I come of age. Presumably your duties as my guardian will not be carried out free of charge."

"My usual fee for this service is five guineas a year, though there may be additional charges if complications arise."

"Five guineas," Martin said. "That seems reasonable."

"I think I can promise you, Mr Cox, that you will find me a reasonable man in most of our dealings together. Your father put his trust in me. I hope you feel you can do the same. Now, there are still a few things to be discussed, and I think we had better begin with the matter of buying a place for you to live …"

On leaving Mr Godwin's office, brother and sister scarcely spoke. For one thing, the street was thronged with people. For another, they were both intent on getting Martin, with his two crutches, into the little gadabout. It was not until they were out of the town, on the quiet road leading to Fordover, that Martin at last gave vent to his feelings.

"All that money! – A fortune!" he said, clenching his fists in his lap. "Three thousand pounds! Just think of it! And father talking all these years of 'trying to put a little by'."

"Yes, I know," Nan said. "I can scarcely believe it even now."

"All that meanness over the years! The penny-pinching! The going without! Forcing you to work in the quarry till your hands were so sore that you cried with them. Forcing us – and mother too – to live scarcely better than rats in a hole. Mother was ill for six months and all father ever did was make the same old promises. 'One of these days, Annie. – One of these days!' Mother *died* of his promises. And all the time there was all that money, lying there, year after year, doing nothing but fatten itself!" Martin's bitterness went deep. His young voice was choked with it. "Oh, Nan, I *hate* him for that! I shall never forgive him. *Never!*" he said.

"Hush, you mustn't say such things. You don't really mean it, I know."

"Oh, but I do! I mean every word!"

"Father thought the world of you. Everything he did was for your sake. Even yesterday, when he died, it was because of lifting that stone to save your foot from being crushed."

"I know that! But I didn't ask him to kill himself! And if he hadn't been so miserly, refusing to spend a few pence sending our tackle to be repaired, it would never have happened at all. He would not have died as he did and I should not have had to bear this *damnable* pain in my leg and foot!"

Nan said no more but took him straight home. She made him lie down on his bed and saw that his leg was comfortably propped on its pillows. She then drove out to Meer, to call on the Methodist Minister and explain why work had stopped on the new chapel at Rowell Cross. When she returned, Martin was asleep, and it was some hours before he awoke. By then the worst of his rage had passed, but a core of bitter resentment remained, and everything he said now had an unrepentant hardness in it.

"Do you realize that with three thousand pounds invested like that, we could live on the interest it earns, without ever having to work?"

"And is that what you intend to do?" Nan asked in astonishment.

"No. It is not. I was just trying to show you how we've been cheated all these years, because you don't seem to understand what a great lot of money father's left."

"I do understand. I'm not a fool."

"Then why aren't you angry?" Martin asked.

"Because," she said, in her gentle way, "*you* are angry enough for both of us." Then, after a pause, she asked, "Will you still work as a mason, then, when your leg is sound again?"

"Oh, I shall work, most certainly. And if I'm allowed to take over the lease, I shall still work here at Scurr. But it's all going to be a whole lot different from how it's always been in the past. Oh, yes, I promise you that! Father always had faith in our stone because it's some of the very best in all this part of the Cotswolds. He always said the day would come when it would be in demand again and he talked about being prepared for it. But *I* intend to prepare for that day in a way that father never imagined even in his wildest dreams. *I'm* going to put some of that money back where it'll do the most good, – back into the quarry itself – because I have faith in our stone, too. – Ten times the faith father had. – And I'm going to put that faith to the test just as soon as I possibly can."

Nan was silent. He looked at her.

"But it's not just the quarry that's going to be changed. It's the whole of our lives. And the first most important thing is to find a decent place to live. A cottage somewhere down in the town, where you'll have neighbours to talk to, just as you've always longed for. Not a rented cottage, mind, but a place of our own, which we'll buy outright. We'll have proper furniture to go in it – oak or mahogany – you shall choose. And you shall have a stove to cook on – one of these iron kitcheners, with an oven at the side, and bits of shiny brass on it. And of course you'll have new clothes to wear, made for you by a dressmaker, and the very latest thing in bonnets."

Nan smiled. She was both touched and amused by what he intended to do for her, but at the same time there was a hint of wistfulness in her smile, and Martin perceived it.

"What is the matter? Are you not pleased to think that soon you will have all those things you've wanted and longed for all these years?"

"Yes. Oh, yes, I am pleased, of course. It's just that I wish you would remember, when you are talking of these things, that we have father to thank for them all."

"Oh, I remember it well enough! But I also remember what it's been like, all through our lives, up until now. How we've always gone without the common decencies of life when all the time there was money enough to buy them over and over again. And you mean to tell me that you see nothing wrong in that?"

"All I am trying to say is, that father did what he thought was best."

"Well, my ideas are different from his, and from now on I am the one who will decide what's best. And tomorrow, when we go into town again, we'll call in at the auction rooms, to see what there is in the way of cottages for sale."

"I think we should wait a while. It hardly seems decent to do that when Father's been dead scarcely thirty-six hours."

"When *will* it be decent?" Martin asked.

"I think we should at least wait until after the funeral," Nan said.

Two days later they stood in the churchyard of St Luke's and watched their father's coffin being lowered into the grave where their mother's coffin already lay. They were the only mourners and when the undertaker's men had gone, the vicar, Mr Hickson, walked with them out to the green, there to shake hands with them and to help Martin, still on his crutches, into the back of the gadabout.

It was a fine, sunny day with a hint of spring in the air, and rooks were noisily at work repairing their nests in the churchyard elms. On the two acres of green a tethered nanny-goat and her kid were grazing, together with a few geese, while three ducks were having a bath in the stone trough under the pump. On the far side of the green stood a row of six cottages, each with its own strip of garden in front, enclosed by a low stone wall. These were the cottages that Nan had so much admired whenever she had come to the churchyard to tend her mother's grave. And now, as she drove in a circle round the green, rather than turn on the narrow track, she saw that the gate of one of these cottages had a white board attached to it, on which, in bold block letters, were the words "For Sale By Auction", with the auctioneer's name underneath. It was the cottage at the other end of the row – beyond it were the fields and meadows sloping down to the Chickle Brook – and Nan, scarcely believing her eyes, drew up outside the gate.

"Martin, look."

"Well, I'm blessed!"

"Do you think—?"

"It's up to you."

The cottage was empty; they could see that; the windows were curtainless, upstairs and down. The sale would be held on March the tenth and viewing permission could be obtained from Messrs Thompson and Hargreaves of Crocker's Yard. After a brief discussion, therefore, Martin got down from the gadabout and Nan drove off by herself to see about obtaining the key.

Awkwardly, because of his crutches, he opened the gate and walked in. On his left, quite close to the path, a low stone wall divided the garden from the one next door. On his right, but further away, a similar wall divided it from the open field. Under both walls, in the well-kept borders, most of the shrubs were still bare, the roses and quinces neatly pruned, the currant bushes and cherry tree showing as yet no more than their buds. But among them were a few evergreens: laurustine and Jerusalem sage; holly, box, and sweet bay; and below, in their shelter, daffodil spikes stood erect among clumps of primrose and violets.

Because it was the endmost cottage, its garden was wider than the rest, and from the main path, running straight to the door, another path went off to the right, leading round past the gable end, into the garden at the back. Here there were fruit trees, apple and plum; a small area of grass sloping down to a hedge of lilacs, and, on the other side of the hedge, a kitchen garden, winter-dug, with a row of raspberry canes in it, and a few wizened broccoli stumps. When Martin went close to the boundary wall, he could see down over the fields and meadows to the brook, which ran shallowly at this stretch, rippling over its bed of stones. Two or three hundred yards further down, the brook ran into the Leame, and another hundred yards further still, beyond the two weirs, stood one of the valley's many mills, known as Jervers. Martin could not see the mill because of the trees along the bank but he could hear the clatter and swish of its two big water-wheels, and the heavy thump-thump-thump of its fulling-stocks pounding the wet cloth in the troughs.

He turned and hobbled back to the cottage and was peering in through a rear window when Nan returned with the keys.

"Mr Thompson offered to come with me but I thought it would be better just to look round by ourselves."

Yes, it was better indeed, for it meant they could marvel at everything without any self-consciousness. And Nan, who had rarely entered a "proper house" in the whole of her life, found plenty to marvel at because these cottages at Old Church End were of a very superior size and quality, and number six in particular, having been occupied until now by a well-to-do ironmonger, boasted certain refinements that made it quite exceptional. In the front parlour, for instance, not only was there an iron grate with Delftware tiles surrounding it, but also an oakwood chimney-piece carved with a pattern of vine leaves and grapes. And in the kitchen-cum-living-room, behold, an iron cooking-range such as Martin had spoken of, its surfaces black-leaded to perfection, its ovendoor vainglorious with polished brass handle and hinges, and the maker's name on a brass lozenge: J. G. Stoot, Bushbury, Staffs.. Beyond the kitchen was a scullery with a copper-lined boiler in it and a stoneware sink.

Nan could not get over it. She went from one room to another; up to the bedrooms and down again; out to the scullery, the coal-house, the privy. But it was the two living-rooms that drew her back again and again; the kitchen because she imagined it with a good coal fire in the stove, and furniture such as she had seen in the kitchen at Hey-Ho Farm; the parlour because, with its white plaster ceiling and blue-sprigged paper on the walls, its polished oak window-seats with little cupboards underneath, and its panelled oak door with Delftware knob and finger-plates, was simply the most beautiful room anybody could have devised. And everywhere was so clean and dry! The roof, the walls, the stone-flagged floors: all were just as dry as could be; and this, after Scurr, was a miracle. Admittedly, Martin had found a patch of damp on the kitchen wall, underneath one of the windows, but what was one small patch of damp, scarcely the size of a human hand, when everywhere else was dry as a bone?

"Oh, it's nothing," Martin agreed. "It's a very well-built cottage indeed, there's no doubt about that."

"It's more than a cottage – it's a palace," Nan said.

"You like it, then?"

"Oh, Martin, don't *you*?"

"Yes," he said, smiling at her. "I think it will suit us very well."

"I can't believe it even now. Just to think of you and me living in such a place as this!" And then the brightness in her face was overcast by a shadow of guilt. She looked at him with tear-filled eyes. "Oh, dear! It seems all wrong for us to be here, laughing and talking like this, when father's only just been laid to rest in the churchyard over the way."

"I don't see why it should be wrong. Father's dead and we're alive. The living have got things to do and may as well get on with it." He turned and hobbled towards the door. "Come and see the garden," he said.

There were other cottages for sale in Chardwell, and a few fine houses, too, and during the next three weeks, taking Mr Godwin's advice, Martin and Nan went to see them all. But nothing they saw pleased them so well as number six, Church Row, and they looked forward with some impatience to the day of the sale.

Slowly, Martin's leg was improving. The worst of the swelling had gone down and he suffered less pain. At the end of a fortnight, he was putting the injured foot to the ground and walking on it a little each day, without the aid of his crutches. And after another week or so he was able to discard them altogether. Soon he was back at work again, on the chapel at Rowell Cross, with two hired men to help him, recruited by means of an advertisement placed in *The Chardwell Gazette*. He had bought a new cart, stoutly built, with extra-strong axles and wheels; also new tackle for hoisting stone; and with this he and his helpers raised the lintel into place over the chapel doorway.

These two men whom he had engaged were not only

skilled banker-masons but quarrymen too. Formerly they
had been employed at Stennets, a famous quarry on Beeches
Hill, some sixteen miles away; but this quarry was now
worked out and as a result they had lost their jobs. The older
of the two, Tommy Nick, had been foreman-in-charge at
Stennets. He was a man in his early forties, rather small in
stature but tough, wiry, and surprisingly strong. The other,
Bob Sellman, was in his twenties; a great lumbering ox of a
man, devoted to his older mate. Martin got on well with them
both; they were clever, hard-working, reliable; and work on
the chapel was going ahead at a very satisfactory pace. If they
were interested, Martin said, he could offer them permanent
work, and he told them about his plans for Scurr. Yes, they
said, they were interested, and they gave him the names of
three other men, all old work-mates of theirs, who might well
be interested, too.

"What happened to all your gear when Stennets closed
down?" Martin asked. "Was it sold?"

"Yes, it was bought by Radley Brown, over at Appleton.
But if you're wanting to set up smart, you should go to Wattle
and Son, who've got a foundry down Badston way. That's the
place to go if you want the latest in all sorts of gear, and *that's*
the place where you'll get the best."

"Very well, Wattle's it is. And you two can go with me, to
give me the benefit of your advice."

But first things first and on the evening of March the tenth
Martin and Nan attended the sale of the Church Row
cottage. Mr Godwin joined them there and it was he, in his
rôle as guardian, who bid for the cottage on Martin's behalf,
and, when it was knocked down to him for a hundred and
ninety five pounds, it was he who signed the auctioneer's chit
and paid the deposit of ten per cent. Martin and Nan were
jubilant, and Mr Godwin, kind man that he was, invited them
to celebrate by dining with him at The Post House Inn, an
experience so novel to them that it made a fitting culmination
to an already momentous day. He toasted them in a glass of
wine, wishing them years of comfort in their new home, and

every success to Martin's plans for expansion at Scurr.

The promise Mr Godwin had made, that Martin should find him a reasonable man, was fulfilled in every possible way, for his guardianship, though conscientious, was never intrusive. Finding that his ward had a level head on his young shoulders, he treated him in a straightforward way, completely without condescension. He watched over him diligently and offered good, sound advice, but, duty being done in that respect, he gave the young man a free hand, letting him do things for himself. He was courteous and considerate and in a short space of time Martin and Nan both knew that in him they had a good friend. Once, when Martin expressed surprise at being allowed so much freedom, Mr Godwin smiled and said:

"I know more about you than you think. Not only from your father but from my good friends at Newton Railes. Katharine Tarrant thought highly of you – of your intelligence and your integrity – and that is a high commendation indeed. There! Now I've embarrassed you! But that tribute, coming as it does from such a source, will not be unwelcome to you, I'm sure."

Nan could scarcely contain herself during the three weeks that elapsed before the purchase of the cottage was completed. But at least she could go there whenever she pleased, to keep it clean and tidy; to pull up the weeds in the garden; and – a great joy for her – to get acquainted with the neighbours. And at least she and Martin could go in to town and bespeak the furniture they wanted; not to mention the carpet, the curtains, and the household linen; the chinaware, the cutlery, and all the new pots and pans.

"Gracious, what a lot of things we need, now we're going to live in a fine cottage! And oh, what a lot of money you're spending! Whatever will Mr Godwin say when he receives all these bills?"

"We've spent hardly more than three hundred pounds so far, including the cost of the cottage itself. That is only a trifle out of the total sum. And what we've bought only *seems* a lot because we've had so little till now."

"But what about all your plans for developing the quarry?" she said. "How much will you be spending on that?"

"I don't know precisely as yet. I am still looking into it. But it certainly won't cost so much that there will be any risk involved. We won't ever be poor again, if that is what you are frightened of. In fact, if my plans work out as they should, we shall be very comfortably off. And in time to come – who knows? – it's possible we may even be rich."

Nan looked at him for a while; a smiling look, happy and fond; but with something else in it, as though she were trying to search him out.

"Have you some particular reason for wanting to make yourself rich?" she asked. "Something to do with a certain person?"

"It's nothing to do with Ginny Tarrant if that is what you are hinting at."

"Are you sure?"

"I am positive."

"I thought perhaps you had it in mind to – to put yourself on a level with her."

"I am not in love with Ginny Tarrant. I told you that once before."

"You said you wouldn't let yourself be."

"Did I? Well. It's the same thing."

"If it's got nothing to do with the Tarrants … why *do* you want to be rich?"

"Because," Martin said, with a touch of impatience, "it will make a nice change from being poor."

"Martin," Nan said.

"Yes. What?"

"It's a good six weeks since father was buried. Don't you think it's about time you took your tools down to the churchyard and put his name on the headstone, along with mother's?"

"I've been very busy. You know that. And I doubt if he

himself would worry. Mother had been dead almost a year before he put that stone on her grave."

"That was because he was waiting for the ground to settle."

"Then I'd better leave it a year too – so that the ground can settle again."

One day when Martin got home from Rowell, Nan handed him a letter. A servant had brought it from Newton Railes. It was from Katharine Tarrant, offering her condolences on the death of his father.

"I am sorry not to have written to you before but my father and I have been away, visiting friends in Shropshire and Wales, and only heard of the accident at the quarry when we returned yesterday. My father joins with me in sending thoughts of sympathy to you and your sister in your loss and in hoping that your injured leg is by now thoroughly mended.

"Ginny remained behind in Llangollen and Hugh is travelling in Scotland with a friend, but they should be home in two or three weeks, and I hope soon you will keep your promise of coming back to see us all here.

"Sincerely, your friend, Katharine Tarrant."

Martin gave the letter to Nan and she read it aloud.

"How very kind of her to write. Will you go and visit them?"

"I don't know. I'll have to see."

"You'll answer the letter?"

"Yes, of course."

His work on the chapel at Rowell Cross was finished shortly before Easter. By then the purchase of the cottage had been completed and he and Nan were installed there. On an evening in early April, they ate their first meal at the new mahogany dining table; sat on the new mahogany chairs, upholstered in green and gold brocade; and used the green and white chinaware; and while they ate they kept looking round at all the many luxuries, grand beyond words, with which they had furnished their living-room. The weather was sunny and warm; one of the casements was open wide; and the air coming in from the back garden was sweet with the scent of plum blossom.

"Can you really believe this is us?"

"No. It must be somebody else."

"How very different the tea tastes when you drink it out of a china cup …"

"It's even better," Martin said, "when you stir it with a silver spoon."

"It's funny to think of there being neighbours living right next door to us."

"They seem to be friendly folk."

"Yes, they are. Mrs Beech has been so helpful … So has Mrs Colne, next door but one … And they said they hoped we'd be happy here."

"Do you think we shall?"

"What a thing to ask!"

"You certainly won't lack for company. You may even find there's too much of it."

"Oh, no!" Nan exclaimed. "You'll never hear me complaining of *that*!"

They had brought nothing with them from Scurr except their recently purchased clothes and Martin's few precious books. Nothing else was worth bringing, he said, and one day, alone in the quarry, he dragged the few bits of rickety makeshift furniture out of the lean-to cottage, piled them against the old broken cart, and lit a fire under the pile. He then took his heaviest sledge-hammer and knocked down the cottage itself. It only needed a few good blows, delivered against the front wall, for walls and roof to collapse together, raising a cloud of dust and grit. He stood back and watched them crumple; waited until the sagging roof had finished caving inwards, bringing down the two end walls; and then went round, methodically, till the work of destruction was complete.

In twenty minutes it was done; all that remained was a

ruckle of stones with a few bits of timber among them: the plank door and the window-shutters; the rafters and laths, sticking up like smashed ribs. These he pulled out and threw on the fire before setting about the task of clearing away the heap of stones. It was ugly and pitiful and he was resolved to be rid of it, so he went to and fro with a wheelbarrow, taking the stones to that place where the flat quarry floor gave way to the downward slope of the hillside. Here all the quarry rubbish was thrown and among it the stones and tiles of the cottage would soon lose their identity, lying scattered about the slope among the rubble, the chippings, the brash, and the loose, shifting soil dislodged by rabbits.

Soon, where the cottage had stood, there was only a patch on the rock-face, a different colour from the rest, and that would not last long, he thought. There was great satisfaction in this, – even a kind of angry elation – and he turned his attention back to the fire, now burning very low. Using a long-handled shovel, he pushed all the unburnt bits of timber deep into the central heat, so that they too should be consumed. These were mostly the remains of the cart: the side-timbers, the shafts, the wheels; and as he pushed them all together, the fire burnt up fiercely again, sending flames and sparks high into the air.

He laid his shovel on the ground and walked about the silent quarry. It was no longer his home, and he thanked God for it; but it was still his place of work; the centre of his ambitions and plans; and as he looked up at the rock-face, towering above him like a cliff, a certain excitement moved in him. This quarry had been his father's kingdom. Now it was his. But he meant to rule it differently and he felt impatient to begin.

Briskly, he turned and went back to the fire, collected shovel and sledge-hammer, and went to put them into the tool-shed. On his way he caught sight of the hoisting-gin standing some twenty yards off and suddenly, in his mind's eye, he saw his father on the day of his death, sitting with his back against one of the poles, his whole body bent with pain as his crippled heart beat its last. Then, in a moment, he saw himself, holding his father dead in his arms, and, with a little shock of surprise, saw his own face wet with tears.

Had he really wept that day? Perhaps he had. Because *then* he had not known the full extent of his father's savings. Once that had been revealed, anger had taken possession of him, hardening the blood throughout his veins. Anger had kept other feelings at bay. But now, in a wave, those feelings came, ushered in by a sense of guilt. Guilt because of the sacrifice his father had made for his sake. Guilt because his father's death meant freedom and independence for him and he was rejoicing in these things. Guilt because, while that anger remained, he had felt no sense of loss. Now, suddenly, it was there: an unexpected ache in his heart; and he looked all round the quarry again, almost like a small boy, puzzled at finding himself alone. For the first time since his father's death, he understood the finality of it, and just for a while he almost regretted pulling the old cottage down.

Such regret was foolish, of course. He shrugged it away impatiently. But a few minutes later, when he left the quarry, driving the little gadabout, he took with him his bag of masoning-tools. What Nan had said was right: it was time he went to the churchyard, to his parents' grave, and added his father's name to the headstone.

CHAPTER
5

Even before probate was granted on his father's will, Martin's plans for developing the quarry were already under way because Mr Godwin, fully approving of his ideas, felt that they should be put into action with the maximum expediency.

"The changes your father foresaw are certainly on their way. The Cullen Valley is waking up. Our clothiers are beginning to realize that they must keep abreast of the times if they are to compete successfully with their confrères in the north. It's just a question of who will be the first to bring the new power-looms in, and some of the sporting fraternity are laying bets among themselves. Hurne of Brink End is first favourite, of course, with Yuart of Hainault close behind. They are two of our biggest men and they are expected to lead the way."

"I heard that the elder Mr Yuart is against the new looms," Martin said, "though his son is all in favour of them."

"Old Mr Yuart is a sick man. He has suffered a severe stroke and is now confined to a wheelchair, with a manservant to push him about. He's still against the power-looms, but he can no longer run the mill, and his son has got power of attorney to run it for him."

"So the son may well decide to adopt the new looms?"

"Yes. And will do, almost certainly. For my part, if I were a betting man, I would put my money on him, because Charles Yuart is an ambitious young man who likes to be first with everything. But Hurne or Yuart or anyone else, they can't build without stone, so let me know what plant you need and I'll write a letter to cover your orders."

Within a few weeks, therefore, the quarry at Scurr had been transformed, and although the stone was still dug by hand, in the old traditional way, there was now a mechanical crane, moving on a series of tramways, to carry the lumps of raw stone from the quarry face to the work sheds. The work sheds, which were open-fronted, stood at the eastern side of the quarry, well away from the main workings, but not far from the quarry entrance. In this same area, other buildings had sprung up, forming a miniature township. There was stabling for twenty horses; a harness-room, with hayloft above; sheds for tools, trolleys and carts; and a blacksmith's shop, with a good-sized forge, so that all essential repairs, including the shoeing of horses, could be done on the spot, without delay. There was also an office for Martin and, at Mr Godwin's suggestion, a notice-board, ten feet by five, set up on two posts at the quarry entrance, painted with the following words in bold white letters on a black ground: Scurr Quarry; Rutland Hill; Good quality building stone; Lessee: M. Cox, 6, Church Row, Chardwell.

Martin employed twenty men and the place, so quiet in his father's time, seemed now to be filled with noise. It was very strange at first, to hear so many tools at work, and the voices of so many men; the masons chatting in the work sheds; the stone-cutters shouting to one another, directing proceedings at the quarry face. There was also the noise of the heavy crane as it travelled to and fro on its rails or revolved, with a slow grind-and-squeak, on the central turntable, which enabled it to change direction.

Sometimes, standing alone, gazing up at the stone cliff that rose in jagged terraces eighty feet to the blue spring sky, he allowed his mind to dwell on the past, seeking and finding the quietness that always came, a sweet relief, conjured from old memories. Then he would shrug and deride himself, aware that these acts of remembrance carried a hint of regret with them, a weakness he viewed with youthful contempt.

The old ways were gone and a good thing too. And although the noise often irked him, the activity itself was source only of satisfaction. For this was how the quarry *should* be, yielding great quantities of stone, just as it had done in earlier times, fifty and sixty years before, when the new woollen mills had been built all along the Cullen Valley, and the clothiers, growing steadily richer, had built great houses for themselves out in the countryside around. There had been half a dozen quarries at work in the district then, and Scurr had been the most famous of them, because of the quality of the stone. Now it was coming to life again and soon its fame would be renewed. His father's prophecy would be fulfilled. "Our day will come. Mark my words. And when it does – we'll be ready for it." But Martin was ready for it in a way that had not been part of the prophecy, and already, by the end of April, the stocks of dressed stone were such that his father would have been struck dumb at sight of them.

He did no building work now. His days as a jobbing mason were over for good. All his time and energy were concentrated on the quarry. Often he worked as hard and as long as ever he had done in the past, but now, at the end of a working day, a comfortable home awaited him, with all its many luxuries. A hot tub in the scullery, and a huge white huckaback towel, clean every day, for him to rub himself dry with. A clean shirt and underclothes laid out ready for him, and a tidy, well-made suit of good quality Cotswold cloth. Then to sit down to a well-cooked meal. Not the thin stew, tasting of soot, that had been their daily fare at Scurr, but butcher's meat, the best to be had, simmered to perfection on the hob of the range or roasted in the capacious oven.

Afterwards, if the evening were fine, an hour or two in the garden with Nan, or a leisurely stroll around Old Church End, stopping to talk to the folk they met. And – the day's last luxury – to sit for a while in the pleasant parlour, he with some new book he had bought, reading passages to Nan while she did her needlework: not coarse flannel shirts or make-do-and-mend, as in days gone by, but fine embroidery, which she loved, and delicate drawn-thread work, learnt from their neighbour, Mrs Beech. Her hands were becoming quite smooth and soft, now that she no longer worked in the quarry, and she took a certain pride in them, rubbing them every night with a salve of dock-leaves pounded in honey and cream, and trimming her nails most carefully, until in time they lost their thick horny hardness and became quite clean and delicate. She had nice clothes to wear now; not greys and browns, in the coarsest stuff, but pretty dresses of cotton or silk, in summer colours, pale blue or pale green, made by Miss Gray of Bennett Street.

"Do you like this frock, Martin?"

"Yes, it suits you very well."

"You don't think it's a little showy, perhaps?"

"No, not at all. If it seems so to you, that is because until now you have been so poorly clad. And I'm sure you can depend on Miss Gray in all matters of good taste."

Nan had no trouble in making friends. Neighbours in Church Row and Church Lane were soon inviting her to tea with them, and she was only too delighted to return their hospitality. They drew her into the life of the town: the sewing circle and the concert club; the Ragged School Fund-raising Group and the Hospital Helping Hands Committee; all of which meant for her an ever-widening circle of acquaintance. And although in one sense Nan was shy, in another sense she was quite the reverse, because this new life, in the swim of things, was so miraculous to her that she took each experience as it came and, having no preconceptions, was never disappointed and rarely hurt. Even when she met with snobbery, it made little impression on her. Endowed with the gift of happiness, she was almost impervious to slights, and nobody could put her down. She had too many other things on her mind to spare more than a passing thought for the petty behaviour of the petty genteel. There was too much to do, every day, every hour.

For one thing, Martin had bought her a cottage piano, and

engaged Mr Lloyd, the best teacher in Chardwell, to come and give her three lessons a week. She was learning dancing with Mrs Sweet and singing with Miss Underhill and the fees for all these lessons together cost Martin six guineas a term. Nan worried about this. The singing lessons, especially, seemed an absurd extravagance. But Martin brushed her objections aside.

"Do you enjoy these things?"

"Yes, but—"

"Then you shall have them. I insist."

"Oh, Martin!" Nan exclaimed, looking at him with tear-bright eyes. "You are so *very* good to me!"

"Nonsense," he said, in a gruff voice. "Who's good to *me*, I'd like to know?"

They had always been very close. Drawn together in early days by their isolation at Scurr, they were just as congenial now in sharing this new life together, revelling in their freedom and the future that now lay open to them.

"I saw Miss Ginny Tarrant today, in the Railes carriage, driving along the High Street. She looked just as pretty as ever and she carried a lovely blue parasol ..."

"I saw her, too, as it happens. But that was in Marton Street, when I had just come from seeing Mr Godwin."

"Did you speak to her?"

"No. She was too far off. And she didn't see me."

"You've never been back to Newton Railes. And Miss Katharine wrote such a kind letter when father died. She invited you most particularly. Why is it you never go, when they were so very kind to you?"

"Because I will not presume on that kindness and because I will not be a hanger-on."

"Oh, but Martin, surely—"

"Please, Nan, allow me to decide such things for myself," he said.

During the following weeks three items of interest appeared in *The Chardwell Gazette*, the first being a paragraph

announcing the engagement of Miss Katharine Elizabeth
Tarrant and Mr Charles Henry Yuart. The second was a
notice announcing that tenders were invited from builders of
standing and good repute for the erection of a new cloth mill
of substantial size, the same being an extension of the
premises known as Hainault Mill, at Catchpool, near
Chardwell, Gloucestershire, proprietors Henry Yuart and
Son, of Saye House, Chardwell. Applications were to be
made to G. M. Chadwick, architect, of 21, North Street,
Sharveston.

The third item was a notice informing the public that
operations at Scurr Quarry, Rutland Hill, Gloucestershire,
had been expanded and modernized and that output of its
excellent stone, already well known in Chardwell and its
environs, was now greatly increased. Visitors would be
welcome, the notice said, whether their interest lay in the
stone itself or in the up-to-date plant. And sure enough
visitors come, among them the builder Robert Clayton who,
two years before, had repaired the bridge at Newton Askhkey
with stone from Scurr.

"I said then I'd be back again and here I am. But I'm sorry
to hear of your father's death. Please accept my condolences."

"Thank you, sir."

Clayton had brought his son with him, a fair-haired young
man of twenty-three, with a freckled face and candid
expression, and a handshake that was strong and warm.

"Edward is my right-hand man. I rely on him a good deal
these days, now that I am feeling my age."

Clayton was deeply impressed by the changes Martin had
made in the quarry and he looked at the stocks of new-cut
stone with an appreciative gleam in his eyes.

"Seems you're expecting an increased demand."

"Yes. I think there's building in the air."

"Mills, not castles, eh?" Clayton said. "Which brings me to
the purpose of my visit. But perhaps you've already guessed
what that is?"

"You're submitting a tender for the new Hainault Mill."

"Exactly so. And from what I see here, Mr Cox, the contract is as good as mine."

Strolling about, inspecting the piles of ashlar blocks, Clayton began talking business at once.

"Hainault belongs to a man named Yuart but he, it seems, is an invalid and the mill is now managed by his son. Young Mr Charles is in a hurry. He wants to be the first man to bring the new looms into this district, so the builder who promises the earliest start – and the earliest finishing date – will almost certainly win the day. I've told Chadwick, the architect, that, depending on my supply of stone, I can begin in three weeks' time. So unless these stocks are already bespoke—"

"They are not bespoke," Martin said, "except those three small lots over there, which are marked; but it scarcely matters, Mr Clayton, because I can produce as much again during the next six weeks, and if there should be the slightest doubt over future supplies, I would take on extra men."

"Capital! Capital!" Clayton said, and took a notebook from his pocket. "Let us get down to business, eh?"

Four days later, the Claytons were at the quarry again. The contract was theirs, signed and sealed, and they had come immediately with a written order for the stone. It was four o'clock in the afternoon and, their main business being soon concluded, Martin invited them home to Church Row.

"We can discuss further details there," he said.

Nan was out in the back garden, on her knees under a fruit bush, trying to pull up a wild briar, when Martin came in search of her, bringing the Claytons with him. Breathless and red in the face, not to say somewhat dishevelled, she was more than a little put out at finding herself facing visitors, especially when the younger man stepped forward and helped her up. But her dismay did not last long – she had too much sense of humour for that – and as soon as introductions were over she was making the Claytons welcome and inviting them indoors.

"Is it all settled about the mill and have you got the contract to build?"

"Yes, Miss Cox," Robert Clayton said, "and your brother is going to supply the stone."

"That's good news. I'm so glad."

They were in the living-room now, crowding into the small space between the table and the Welsh dresser, where, on a large cooling-rack, stood a newly baked fruit-cake, an apple tart, and a heap of scones. Nan, having shed her pinafore, led them out along the passage and into the parlour, with Martin following behind.

"Will you excuse me for a moment while I make myself tidy?" she said. "And then can I bring you some refreshment? A glass of Madeira wine, perhaps? Or Marsala if you would prefer it?"

"Thank you, Miss Cox, that's very kind, but what I would like more than anything else is a nice cup of tea," Robert Clayton said. "I don't know about Edward, of course. He will have to speak for himself."

"Oh, tea for me as well, Miss Cox, if it is not too much trouble for you." Edward Clayton stood gazing at her, his expression an artless combination of earnestness and impudence. "And perhaps a slice of that sugar-topped cake which I couldn't help observing on the kitchen dresser as we came through."

Early one morning in the following week, Martin drove out to Hainault Mill, to meet Charles Yuart on the site of the new extension and discuss arrangements for delivering the stone. The mill stood on the bank of the Cullen, at a place where the river swung round in such a wide loop that the land jutting into it formed a large, peninsular bluff of some fifty acres. The oldest of the mill buildings was the original fulling-mill, scarcely bigger than a modest farmhouse, its exact age not known; but towards the end of the eighteenth century, when the woollen trade had been flourishing, a large handsome new mill had been built, of four storeys and ten bays, with a loom-shop capable of housing fifty looms. In time this too had been extended until, with all its adjunctive buildings,

Hainault Mill formed three sides of a large enclosure, which functioned as its workyard.

Now there was to be a further addition, larger and more handsome still: five storeys and twelve bays, with a porticoed central section, and a clock tower at the end, surmounted by a cupola. As soon as this new mill was completed – which should be within a twelvemonth – the old mill would be used for spinning and, with extra machinery, would supply the greater quantities of yarn needed to feed the new power-looms. In turn, the old spinning-sheds would be used as a dye-works, so that, in the course of time, all the many processes comprised in the manufacture of cloth would be carried out on this one site.

Martin had seen the architect's plans, both for the new building itself and for the alterations to the old, and he knew that no expense was to be spared in making Hainault the most thoroughly up-to-date woollen mill in the whole of the Cullen Valley. And, with fifty acres of good flat land at the owner's disposal, there was room for further expansion still, should it be needed in the future. Yuart had no doubt that it would, for the West of England, he declared, had lagged too long behind the north: now was the time for it to catch up and, perhaps, even take the lead.

"I'm going to put Chardwell and the Cullen Valley back on the map, beginning here at Hainault," he said. "That's why I hired the best architect in the district, so I hope the builder made it clear that I want the very best quality stone you can provide."

"Yes. He made it perfectly clear."

"I already know Scurr stone, of course. Also the good reputation your father had as a mason. Mr Tarrant of Newton Railes certainly thought well of him and I've seen the work you and he did on the manor stables two years ago." There was a slight pause and then: "In fact, I gather from Miss Tarrant that you were once acquainted with the family on a somewhat more personal level as well."

"Yes, I did have that honour," Martin said. "It is kind of

Miss Tarrant to remember me." In the same strictly formal manner he added: "I would like, if I may, to offer my congratulations on your engagement and to wish you both every happiness."

"Thank you. I will convey your good wishes to her."

Once again there was a pause. Charles Yuart's gaze was keen.

"You are very young to have been left the responsibility of running your late father's business alone."

"I am not entirely alone. I have the benefit of Mr Godwin's guardianship and may look to him for help and advice at all times."

"Perhaps I should really be dealing with him?"

"No. The quarry itself, and all its transactions, are in my hands. I should only need to consult him if any problems were to arise."

"I sincerely hope there will *not* be any problems. I want this work to go ahead with the utmost dispatch, and the builder has promised faithfully that it will be finished within a year."

"Then you may rest assured that it *will* be, for Mr Clayton is a man of his word."

"I am glad to hear it."

Yuart now led the way across the site, already marked out with pegs, to an area of open ground beyond, where the stone would be stacked on delivery. There followed some further discussion and Martin, talking thus to the man whom Katharine Tarrant was to marry, studied him with close interest, noting his dark good looks and the strong, almost hawk-like cast of his features. He was conscious of the man's drive and energy; of his passionate belief in progress and the great renascence that lay ahead for the woollen trade in the Cullen Valley. Above all, Martin was struck by the unimpeachable confidence with which this young man of twenty-seven had assumed the rôle of leader, forging the way that others would follow.

The Yuarts were an old family, Flemish in origin, who had come to England in the early part of the eighteenth century and settled in Chardwell as clothiers, a trade they had followed successfully throughout its many ups and downs and from which, in the course of time, they had amassed a respectable fortune, together with the status of gentlemen. This status would be enhanced when Charles Yuart married into the Tarrant family, and as he was sole heir to the Yuart fortune, the alliance was a matter of satisfaction on both sides. But the young couple were not marrying to please their families; nor out of worldly considerations; it was a genuine love match, as Martin knew, for he had watched them dancing together at Newton Railes on the evening of the twins' birthday party, and even to his inexperienced eye it had been plain that they were in love.

The business discussion came to an end; arrangements for delivering and stacking the stone were settled; and Charles Yuart, being a man with much to do, excused himself and hurried away.

Building began at Hainault early in May and although Robert Clayton, the builder, came regularly to inspect its progress, it was his son Edward who organized and controlled the work and took responsibility for it day by day. Martin and the young builder, therefore, soon became well acquainted, and a warm friendship sprang up between them. Edward, for the sake of convenience, had taken lodgings in Chardwell, but as these were comfortless, and the food poor, Martin often invited him home to supper. In return Edward would entertain Martin and Nan at The Post House and afterwards the three of them would stroll together through the quiet streets or up the hill to the castle ruins.

"I like this little town of yours. It's got so much variety. There's the grand new part around Trinity Square, built in the last century. There's the older part, round the market place, with its narrow streets and alleyways. And then there's the *really* old part, out on the Burr, which has a country village feel about it, especially on the green where you live. In fact I like the town so much that I'm thinking of buying a house here – when something suitable turns up, that is."

"Whatever will your father say to that?" Nan asked.

"Oh, my father knows and approves of my plan. He thinks there'll be a lot more work for us, all around Chardwell in the next few years. So it's only common sense for me to make my home here."

"Permanently?" Martin asked.

"Well, that depends."

"Surely, being a builder," Nan said, "you could build yourself a house?"

"Builders can never find the time. They're too busy building for other folk. So I hope I can rely on you two, as my friends, to help me find a suitable place. A woman's opinion, especially, will be of great value to me." Edward looked earnestly at Nan. "But only so long as you have the time and will not find it too tedious," he said.

"Oh, no! On the contrary. I love seeing inside people's houses and this will be a good excuse."

"You will tell me honestly what you think of any house I take you to?"

"It's what *you* think that will matter, surely, seeing it's you that will live in it?"

"Yes. Oh, yes, you're right, of course. But I may not *know* what I think of it until I hear somebody else's opinion."

Work on the new Hainault Mill was going ahead rapidly. Day after day, week after week, loads of stone were delivered there, the carts going endlessly to and fro, up and down Rutland Hill and along the winding valley road, the empty ones passing the full ones, often thirty times in a day. Course by course, the mill walls grew; wooden scaffolding was erected; and on it the building-masons toiled, often from first light of day to last. Below, at their stone workbenches, the banker-masons were hard at work, cutting the dressings for windows and doors: the sills, the mullions; the lintels, the quoins; the fluted sections of the pilasters which would support the pediment. Soon the first iron pillars were raised and on them the iron brackets and beams that would carry the storey above, for everything in this new mill was to be as safe from the risk of fire as modern building methods could make it.

Over the weeks, as the building rose, it attracted a number of visitors. Most of these were clothiers, of course, who came as a rule without prior appointment, and although Charles Yuart was always willing to show them round, he rarely allowed any one of them to take more than half an hour of his time. But one day when Martin was there, talking to his foreman, Tommy Nick, the Newton Railes carriage, with two ladies in it, came slowly along the valley road, turned into the busy mill yard and drew up at the counting-house door. Charles Yuart emerged at once, helped the two ladies down from the carriage, and spoke briefly to the coachman, Sherard, directing him to the mill stables.

For a while the little group stood talking together, gazing at the surrounding buildings. Yuart, pointing, was obviously explaining the function of each, bending his head while he spoke because of the volume of noise all around: the clack and rattle of the looms; the high-pitched hum of the spinning-machines; and the thump-thud, thump-thud, of the great wooden mallets pounding wet cloth in the fulling-stocks – a sound that travelled through all the buildings and reverberated across the yard. Miss Ginny was clearly complaining about it. She had raised her hands to her straw hat and was pulling the brim down at the sides to cover her ears. Yuart conducted the sisters away, bringing them out of the mill yard, into the open, where the worst of the din was diffused.

They turned towards the new building, as yet only two storeys high, and encaged in its framework of scaffolding poles, but presenting already a striking appearance, partly because of its clean new stone, pale as biscuit in the sunlight, partly because of its mullioned windows, five on each side of the portico, and twelve in a row on the first floor, giving some idea of how the new mill would look when all five storeys were built.

"Goodness! What a lot of windows!" Miss Ginny exclaimed. "However many will there be altogether when the whole mill is up?" But Yuart's answer went unheard because she had now caught sight of Martin and broke in to say excitedly: "Oh, look, there's Martin Cox! We wondered if he'd be here today. You will excuse us, won't you, Charles? We simply must have a word with him."

Martin was in his shirtsleeves but now, as the visitors came towards him, he took his jacket from the branch of a tree and went to meet them, putting it on. The two young women seemed genuinely pleased to see him and smiled at him in such a way that he felt himself colouring boyishly.

"Martin, how nice," Miss Katharine said, and gave him her hand. "This is a happy meeting indeed, though you hardly deserve to be greeted thus, for you promised to come and visit us and you have not kept your word."

"Miss Tarrant," he said, with a little bow, and then, as Ginny gave him her hand: "Miss Virginia. How do you do."

"Oh, how formal you are to be sure!" Ginny said, with a bright, mocking stare. "That's what comes of neglecting old friends. You hardly know what to say to us."

"Would it be too formal to say that I'm glad to see you both looking so well?"

"Yes, too formal by half. He'll have to do better, won't he, Kate?"

"Formality has its uses," Miss Katharine said, "and doesn't necessarily mean that the feelings expressed are not sincere."

"We've come to see the new mill," Ginny said. "Would you like to show us round?"

Martin, smiling, shook his head. He was all too well aware that Yuart, standing some way off, was glancing towards them impatiently.

"That is Mr Yuart's privilege and I should feel myself in the way."

"Very well. Be strait if you must. But you *will* still be here when we come out? Or are you so busy these days that you have no time to talk to old friends?"

"I am not too busy. And I *shall* be here."

Scarcely twenty minutes later, Ginny emerged from the new mill alone.

"It is, I suppose, Katharine's duty to admire every single block of stone and every girder Charles points out to her, but it's not mine and I've seen enough. Let us go for a walk somewhere, away from all this, where we can hear ourselves talk. We have a lot of news to exchange."

So they left the mill site behind them and strolled across the rack-ground where, on the rows of tenter-frames, some "pieces" of olive-green cloth, forty yards long, newly removed from the fulling-troughs, hung drying in the warm summer air. From the rack-ground they followed the curve of the river bank and continued along the meadow reach, where comfrey and purple loosestrife grew; where clumps of meadowsweet scented the air; and where ducks came and went among the reeds.

"Did you enjoy your three months in London last year?"

"Surely you don't need to ask that? How could anyone fail to enjoy a city which is known as the greatest in the world? – Where there is always so much to do. – Where you can see the Queen herself and all manner of eminent people."

"You saw the Queen?"

"Yes. Twice. Once driving along the Mall and then, which was more exciting still, at the theatre with the Prince."

"What play did you see?"

"Oh, I saw nothing of the play! I was too busy watching *them*. But I did hear the speech Macready made at the end—"

"You actually saw the great Macready?"

"Oh, yes, and dozens more. Not to mention the operas and concerts. I've heard the great Cotoni sing and I've heard Frederick Kosski play the viola …"

"What about the city's great buildings? St Paul's, for instance, and Westminster Abbey?"

"Oh, yes, of course I've seen *them*. The Tower, too, and the Traitors' Gate. The Houses of Parliament. London Bridge.

I've been to all the great galleries. To Hampton Court and the gardens at Kew... Oh, yes, I went *everywhere*."

"Gloucestershire, then, must seem very quiet, and country life very dull after that."

"Yes. And yet no. I cried when I left the Wilsons' house and felt so jealous of Anne and Marie who live there almost all the year round. But there's something nice about coming home ... And there's no place quite like Railes after all ... Now, if I could marry the right sort of man, I'd spend two or three months in town in the winter, travel abroad in the springtime, and spend the rest of the year in my own dear hills, in a large country house with every comfort money can buy, somewhere not too far from Railes."

"Have you not found him, then?" Martin asked. "This rich husband you're looking for, who will give you everything you want? Were there no suitable candidates even in London in all those months?"

"No, there were not," Ginny said. "Most of the eligibles were either old or ugly or disagreeable. Those who were charming were mostly poor. And those few who were charming *and* rich were already married or engaged. But never mind. There's plenty of time. And if all else fails, there is always George Winter of Chacelands, you know, to fall back on as it were."

"Is he still waiting for you, then?"

"Oh, yes. He called on me twice in London and proposed each time, and then, no sooner was I home at Railes than he called on me there and proposed again."

"And still you refused."

"I said I felt I was too young to commit myself to him as yet." Ginny, meeting Martin's glance and perceiving the scepticism there, gave an impish smile and said: "Well, I *am* only seventeen, after all, and it wouldn't be very kind of me to enter into an engagement now, only to break it later on. But that is quite enough about me! Let us talk about you instead and the things that have happened to you this past year."

They came to a halt, facing each other, and she treated him to a long, cool look, assessing the changes that his new life had wrought in him.

"Yes, you're different from how you were ... And yet somehow you are still the same ... Your father left you a lot of money. I've heard all about it, you may be sure. And you've bought yourself a cottage somewhere out at Old Church End. You're also doing great things at the quarry, with dozens of men under you, tearing the heart out of Rutland Hill, and everyone says you're in a fair way to make a fortune out of it."

"Do they say that? Let's hope they're right."

"Charles seems to think so, anyway. He says every clothier in the district will follow his example in the next ten years and that means that *you* can be sure of a constant demand for stone. So! You will very likely be rich! How will you like that, I wonder?"

"I think I could probably bear it, once I'd got used to it," Martin said.

Ginny laughed; the kind of laugh that lit up her face and had no affectation in it; a laugh that made her blue eyes appear more deeply blue than ever, under the delicate flaxen brows.

"You won't hide all your money away and horde it the way your father did?"

"No. I will not."

"Well, then, who knows?" Ginny said. "If you should become *really* rich, – and provided you don't take too long about it – I might end up by marrying *you*."

"Always supposing I were to ask you."

"That is not very gallant, Mr Cox."

"I imagine you get more than enough gallantry from all the fine young gentlemen of the district who wait on you every whip-stitch."

"Don't be silly. Girls can never have enough of such things. Surely even you must know that."

"When you do marry," Martin said, "will you expect your

husband to treat you with gallantry all the time?"

"Of course. I shall expect him to adore me and make a fuss of me and give me plenty of money to spend."

"Then I wish you luck in your search."

For a moment they stood in silence together, Ginny still regarding him with a look that was at once critical, detached, amused, and yet had a hint of warm pleasure in it.

"I am just trying to picture how you will be in a few years from now, and to guess what sort of girl you will marry, when the time comes for you to choose."

"And have you succeeded?"

"No. I have not. The future is too well hidden from us. It keeps its secrets most stubbornly."

They turned and walked back along the path, talking about Newton Railes; her sister's forthcoming marriage; and her brother's recent travels abroad.

"Hugh was not well in the spring and papa sent him to Switzerland. That is the fifth time he's been to Europe whilst I have never been at all. Now why couldn't I have been asthmatic and travelled abroad now and then? It really is very unfair..."

With Ginny prattling on in this way, they returned to the site of the new mill, there to stand for a little while, watching as a great iron girder was winched up to the scaffolding platform level with the mill's second floor.

"How long will it be before the mill is finished?"

"It should be ready by next May or June."

"Charles says it will be the biggest, most modern and efficient mill in the whole valley. It's certainly a very fine-looking place. But I do rather wonder at you, Martin, helping to build a woollen mill, for I thought you saw them all as places in which the poor spinners and weavers are kept in a state of slavery."

"Not all of them are so bad as that and Hainault has always had a good name for treating its work-people pretty well."

"Your conscience is clear, then?"

"Certainly."

"And what about all the extra noise the power-looms will make in the valley? Doesn't that prospect trouble you?"

"We shall get used to that, I daresay, just as we're used to the noise there is now."

"You may be used to it but I am not, and I pity poor Kate when she gets married and has to live in Saye House, with the din she will have in her ears all day long from the town mills."

"It isn't heard all that badly up in that part of the town."

"Badly enough, to my mind, and I'm thankful to goodness I live out at Railes, where we cannot hear it at all. Also, where we don't get the smell, except now and then when the wind is contrary."

They walked on together, past the new mill, making their way carefully between the endless stacks of stone; of iron girders and pillars and brackets; of wooden scaffolding poles and planks; and so into the old mill yard, where Katharine and her betrothed stood talking together, and the carriage waited, with Sherard on the box.

"Oh, dear! Have I kept you waiting? I *am* so sorry!" Ginny said. "Martin and I went for a walk and I rather lost count of the time. We had a great deal to talk about and I have just been chaffing him for supplying stone to build a *mill*." With a smile of pure mischief, she explained herself to Charles Yuart. "Martin is something of a Chartist, you see, and thinks the poor weavers are harshly treated. However, he tells me that Hainault has a good reputation in this respect, and that *your* weavers are treated quite well."

"Indeed?" Yuart said, a slight edge to his voice. "I'm glad to know that we have his approval." He turned and addressed Martin directly. "Purely as a matter of interest, Mr Cox, – if you were asked to supply stone to a clothier of whom you did *not* approve, would you refuse?"

"I'm not sure. But probably not. Because my refusal would make no difference to the way the clothier ran his mill. He would merely go elsewhere for his stone and I should be out of pocket by it."

"Quite so, Mr Cox. I'm glad you take a realistic view of the matter and I commend your honesty in expressing it. It seems to me we are in agreement, that whatever we may feel about the poor, business considerations must come first. We who are engaged in commerce have a duty to uphold its principles, for if we fail in our endeavours, it is not only we who suffer, but all our employees as well."

"But surely," Ginny said archly, "it is the poor who would suffer most?"

"My dear child!" Yuart exclaimed. "Since when have you interested yourself in the poor?"

"Oh, I'm not interested in them at all! My brother Hugh is the one for that. And when he goes into Parliament, he will probably introduce reforms that will make it quite impossible for you or Martin ever to become rich at all. What do you think, Kate?"

Katharine, though she laughed, refused to be drawn.

"I think you and I between us have taken up quite enough of these gentlemen's time for today and we really ought to be going home."

"Yes, I suppose we must." Ginny relinquished Martin's arm but turned towards him appealingly. "Now *do* come and see us, won't you?" she said, and then, before he had time to reply: "Kate! He takes more notice of you. Tell him he has *got* to come."

"Martin knows he is welcome at Railes. He will come in his own good time, I am sure."

Katharine turned towards the carriage and Charles Yuart handed her in. Ginny followed, glancing into Yuart's face and bestowing a dazzling smile on him.

"Thank you for showing us the mill, Charles. It was really quite fascinating."

"I am glad you found it so, Ginny."

Yuart's tone was gently sardonic and Martin saw an amused glance pass between him and Miss Katharine.

The carriage steps were folded in and the door was closed; and while the two sisters settled themselves, arranging their wide-spreading skirts, Yuart stood with one hand on the ledge, exchanging a few last words with them, concerning a garden party they were to attend at Kingsnorth House. Martin, feeling himself out of place, stepped back a little, but stayed to watch as the carriage drove away. He raised his hand in salute; graciously, they acknowledged him; and Ginny, turning in her seat, gave a last, small, intimate wave, intended specially for him. When the carriage had gone out onto the road Yuart turned towards Martin.

"Miss Ginny was in humorous mood today. I'm not sure whether I was its chief object or you. Certainly her tour of the mill was something of a disappointment to her, and it was a very fortunate thing that you were on hand so conveniently, to keep her more happily entertained. Now, if you will excuse me, I must get back to my desk."

Some six or seven weeks later, on a sunny day in September, Katharine Tarrant and Charles Yuart were married in the church at Newton Childe. Nan wanted Martin to go with her, to watch the bride and groom leave the church, but Martin had business in Sharveston, so Nan went alone.

"Oh, it was such a lovely wedding! They made the most perfect couple together, the groom so tall and distinguished-looking, the bride so serene and beautiful. She wore a white satin gown, very simple and plain, and carried a white prayer-book with a spray of white rosebuds. Miss Ginny and the other bridesmaids wore dresses of the palest green and carried posies of mixed flowers. I saw Mr Tarrant and Master Hugh … And old Mr Yuart in his wheelchair … Poor man, to be so reduced! His face is twisted, you know, from his stroke. But he looked quietly pleased all the same, sitting there, wrapped in his rugs, and Miss Katharine, before she got into the carriage, – Mrs Yuart, I *should* say – leant over him and kissed his cheek and was plainly very much concerned that he should not feel left out of things. Then his manservant lifted him up and put him into one of the carriages, to go to Railes for the wedding breakfast. It was sad to see him like that, having to be lifted up, but it was all done so naturally that it didn't spoil the day at all. It was a very happy wedding and I wish you'd been there to see it for yourself."

"I see it better from your description than I would have done with my own eyes, for I should never have noticed one half of the things you did."

"I wonder how long it will be before Miss Ginny follows suit."

"Yes, I wonder," Martin said.

"She has a great many beaux, I hear, but seems in no hurry to choose one of them."

"She is hoping to do better, that's why. And as she is only the same age as I am, she has plenty of time before her yet."

"Yes," Nan said, reflectively, and looked at him for a little while. "I'm apt to forget you're only seventeen. You've always been older than your years and nowadays, what with running the quarry and becoming such a man of business, you're really very mature already."

"I also have the responsibility of being the head of this family."

"Surely that's no great worry to you?"

"Indeed, I hope it may not prove so," Martin said, in a grave tone, "but just lately, whenever Edward Clayton's been here, I have found myself thinking—"

"Oh!" Nan exclaimed, pink to the ears. "And what have you been thinking, pray?"

"That I may soon be called upon to assert my position in a rather particular way—"

"Is it so obvious, then?"

"It was perfectly obvious from the moment Edward set foot in this house," Martin said, enjoying himself. "It was your sugar-topped cake that did it. He saw that on the dresser there and immediately he was a lost man."

"Was he indeed?"

"Without a doubt."

"So, if Edward should propose to me, I'll know it's only because of my cakes?"

"If Edward intends proposing to you, he will, of course,

have to ask my permission."

"Oh, how absurd! The very idea! He's older than you by a good six years."

"Nevertheless, the fact is that I am the head of this family, and as such I have certain rights—"

"Rights! Poof!" she said scornfully. "I've half a mind to box your ears!" Then, her face still flushed with happiness, her voice still bubbling with laughter, she said: "And what if Edward does ask your permission? How shall you answer him?"

"I'm afraid I shall have to tell him the truth."

"The truth? What truth, for goodness' sake?"

"That I cannot think of anyone I'd sooner have as a brother-in-law."

"Oh, Martin! You are a dear!" She came to him and hugged him tight. "You're always so *very* good to me!"

Charles Yuart and his bride, after a honeymoon in Wales, returned to live at Saye House, the large square mansion in William Street, which had been the Yuart family home for ninety years. Old Mr Yuart still lived there and every day, weather permitting, his manservant would take him out for an hour or so and wheel him about the streets of the town. Martin had seen them oftentimes, the old man slumped in his chair, his hat pulled down over his eyes, being pushed along at a rattling pace by the tall young man dressed in dark green who carried himself with a military air and never spoke to passers-by. One day soon after Christmas, however, on leaving the bookshop in Powder Street, Martin saw the old man in his wheel chair coming along on the opposite side, but this time, instead of the manservant, it was Katharine Yuart who pushed the chair. Martin, crossing the narrow street, raised his hat and spoke to her.

"Martin! What a pleasant surprise!" And, as always with this young woman, the pleasure she expressed seemed genuine. "Do you know my father-in-law?"

"Only by sight," Martin said.

"Then let me introduce you. Father, this is Martin Cox. He's a friend and former pupil of mine."

"Cox?" the old man repeated, and looked up at Martin squintingly. "Any relation to Rufus Cox?"

"Yes. I'm his son."

"Knew your father. Long ago. Before you were born, that would be. He supplied the stone for my second dam."

The old man's mouth was badly twisted and his speech slurred, but Martin, meeting him thus for the first time, was surprised by his lucidity. Surprised, too, by the touch of humour with which he went on to speak of his son.

"How's Hainault Palace coming along?"

"Very well. It's up to its fourth storey now."

"How many storeys will there be altogether? Eighteen?"

"Not quite so many as that. Five in fact."

"Five? Is that all? I thought my son had it in mind to rebuild the Tower of Babylon." The old man gave a hollow laugh. "But *you* won't object to that, eh? Not in your trade? And no doubt, being young yourself, you approve of all these new ideas?"

"Well, I think there has to be progress, sir."

"With what end in view?"

"Greater efficiency, increased production, and, it is hoped, greater prosperity for the community at large."

"All due to the new looms?" The old man grimaced. "Personally, I have my doubts. Increased production is all very well but ... how do you sell the extra goods? My son talks of progress, the same as you. He's very keen to lead the way. Myself, I prefer a middle course, the same as my father before me, and *he* always used to say this:

"'... Be not the first by whom the new are tried,
      Nor yet the last to lay the old aside.'

"That's good advice, Mr Cox. But the young men these days ... They want to be racing ahead all the time ... And my son Charles the fastest of all." Awkwardly, the old man turned, looking up into Katharine's face. "Isn't that so, my dear? But there! You're his wife. And much too loyal to say a word against him."

He raised his one good hand to her and she clasped it firmly between her own.

"These are fast-moving times, father, and you know what Charles says – if we don't move with the times, we may get left behind altogether."

"Yes. Well. Perhaps he's right. I'm an old man. Set in my ways. No good trying to stop the clock. The new age belongs to chaps like Charles. And your young friend, Mr Cox, here."

The old man's voice was growing tired; he spoke as though with a thickened tongue; but still he persisted, stubbornly, reluctant to let Martin go.

"Never get a chance to chat as a rule cos Wiskens … Wickens … whass the man's name? … pushes me at such a rate … everyone gets out of the way. But we've given him the slip today … and oh, what a difference it makes … to be pushed along … slowly … by my lovely Katharine here." Again the old man looked up at her. "But I'm worried about you all the same … pushing me back up that hill … If Charles knew, he would not approve."

Katharine laughed, and a faint tinge of colour came into her face. But her look was perfectly tranquil, and there was no prudishness in her.

"I am expecting a child, Martin, and although it will not be born till July, my husband and my father-in-law are already fussing over me."

"Mrs Yuart, that is happy news. Please accept my congratulations. But may I say, without offence, that I'm inclined to share their concern. With Mr Yuart's permission, therefore, I will push him the rest of the way, and promise to do it slowly. No, it's no trouble at all. It will give me great pleasure, I assure you."

So Martin now wheeled the chair and together they proceeded, in a leisurely way, up through the quieter part of the town, into the residential area, and so to the door of Saye House, a great square block of a place, standing a little way back from the road, behind tall railings and wrought-iron gates.

Katharine had always been so very much a part of the old manor house at Railes that Martin had found it difficult to picture her living anywhere else. And there could have been no greater change, he thought, than to come to this sombre-looking house in the town, so closely surrounded by fir-trees and laurels that its tall sash-windows, viewed from outside, had always a sea-green tint to them. Inside, however, the house was all comfort and luxury, and Katharine's influence was as strong here as it had been at Railes, creating a circle of homeliness where everyone, on crossing the threshold, was made welcome as a matter of course. And Martin, sitting with her and her father-in-law in the richly furnished drawing-room, drinking tea from pale blue Rockingham china, eating hot toasted muffins thickly spread with butter and jam, saw with what tact and consideration she waited on the afflicted man, and with what pleasure and affection his gaze so often dwelt on her.

"My son is a lucky young man, Mr Cox, to have married such a wife as this, and I am very lucky, too, having gained such a daughter-in-law. I could scarcely speak two words … after my stroke… but Katharine came and… she took me in hand, teaching me and encouraging me. My voice gets tired. You'll have noticed that. But I rest it a while and… it comes back. That's all due to her. Oh, yes! She gave me back my speech again. This house is a much better place because of Katharine being here. And my disabilities are easier to bear … now I have her to cheer my days."

"Yes, I'm sure that is so," Martin said, "and I'm glad of it, sir, for your sake." Then, turning to Katharine, he said: "Sadly, however, what this house has gained, another has lost, and I wonder what Newton Railes is like now, since losing its mistress."

Katharine smiled. "Ginny is mistress of Railes now and rather enjoying it, I think. But why don't you go and see for yourself how matters are there? It's a good fifteen months since you left the Railes schoolroom and still you have not yet been back. Of course, I realize you are a busy man these days—"

"That's not my reason for keeping away."

"Keeping away? It's deliberate, then? And you do have a reason for it?" she said.

"Yes. You were all very kind and generous to me and I will not presume on that kindness."

"Neither my father nor the twins would regard it as presumption. Not for one moment."

"Other people would call it that."

"And do you put other people's opinion before ours?"

"No, but I can't be indifferent to it. And I do have another reason of sorts, though it's rather difficult to explain."

"Try."

"Well, Railes being the place it is, anyone who knew it would find it hard to keep away. . . And I wanted to prove to myself that I could."

"An act of self-denial, then?"

"Yes. In a way."

"And how long must you persevere in it before you are satisfied with your strength of mind?"

"I doubt if the question will arise. People's lives change all the time. They take different paths."

"Not such different paths, surely, since we live in the same small town, you and I, and Railes is only two miles away. However, I will not tease you any more, nor subject you to further reproaches. It is enough that you are here and in a while you must tell me your news. But I am neglecting my duties as hostess and have let the tea get cold. Martin, will you ring that bell? I'll have a fresh pot brought in."

Early in the new year, Nan was married to Edward Clayton, and they set up house together in Morgan Street. The prediction Edward's father had made, that there would be a good deal of work for them in the Chardwell area, was

coming true, and Edward was a busy man. Other clothiers
were following Yuart's example and, the Hainault extension
being much admired, the firm of Clayton and Son was in
demand. Other builders were busy, too, and soon the orders
for stone were such that operations at Scurr Quarry were
being expanded further still.

The building fever was not confined to the Chardwell
area: it was spreading along the Cullen Valley; and in
February 1847 Martin took the lease of a disused quarry at
Clinton Hill, near Wimpleton, intending to re-open it. The
freestone there, though not so good as Scurr stone, shared
two of its great advantages: it was impervious to frost and did
not require long seasoning. Martin had begun taking on the
men he would need and had ordered plant from Wattle and
Son, resolved that when the far end of the valley began to
follow Chardwell's example, New Start Quarry would be
ready to supply it with the stone it required.

Because of his activities, not to mention his growing
prosperity, Martin was the subject of much interest in
Chardwell, and although there were a few who sneered,
remembering the shabby boy driving his father's ramshackle
cart about the district, with a half-starved nag between the
shafts, the majority of Chardwell's citizens were pleased to
receive him into their midst. There was excitement in the air
at this time; a spirit of progress and enterprise; and Martin,
because of his trade, had a place at the very heart of it. He was
a young man with a future, likely to do well for himself; he
was also Sampson Godwin's ward, made welcome in the
Godwin household; and his sister was married to Edward
Clayton, son of the well-to-do building contractor. Altogether,
then, Martin's credentials were favourable, to say the least of
it. Even the more prominent townsmen would speak to him
in the street these days, and the mothers of marriageable
daughters made a point of getting to know him.

"You are becoming quite important, although you are
only eighteen," Nan said, and Edward told him he'd better
watch out or some young miss would snap him up. "Be

warned, my dear chap, by what's happened to me."

"The warning is dire," Martin said, "for marriage has already made you fat."

"You are just piqued, that's all, because I've taken your housekeeper from you. But if what I hear is true, you could replace her soon enough if you chose, and take your pick from a clutch of nice girls, including little Amy Godwin."

"Oh, don't tell him that," Nan said, "or he will be so puffed up with himself that there will be no bearing him."

But Nan, though she teased, was proud of her brother; proud of his looks, and the way he talked; proud of his growing business ability; and, perhaps most of all, proud of the way he got on with all manner of people. He had always been a good-looking boy, with his fine-drawn features, and sensitive mouth, which yet had a look of strength about it; and now, freed from the heavier work of the quarry and from the squalor of the quarry cottage, he was able to make the best of himself. He wore clothes of the finest quality, with a change of linen every day, and his straight dark hair was neatly trimmed. He carried himself with his shoulders well back and, walking through the streets of the town, looked like a young man of consequence.

"People may say what they like, but money *does* play a part in shaping people's lives," Nan said, "and it's made you into a gentleman."

Martin, smiling, shook his head.

"It takes more than one generation to produce a gentleman. And money alone cannot accomplish it."

"Well, it's done *something* for you, there's no doubt of that."

"Yes, it's enabled me to be myself."

This conversation, inevitably, had made him think of Newton Railes; of his first day in the schoolroom there, now almost three years ago; and of how, in a fit of righteous anger, he had defined a gentleman as "a man who can afford not to pay his bills." The thought of Railes caused him a pang and perhaps because it was springtime, a season when the human heart is most susceptible to the pain of nostalgia, he had a great longing to go there: to walk in the garden, the shrubberies, the park; to see the family, the servants, the dogs; to experience again, however briefly, the delicate atmosphere of the place, with all its many felicities.

It was a lure he was determined to resist. "An act of self-denial", Katharine Yuart had called it, and she, being the person she was, knew that pride lay at the root of it. "How long must you keep it up before you are satisfied with your own strength of mind?" she had asked. It was three months since that meeting with her. Longer still since his meeting with Ginny. And whatever Katharine might say, it was only a question of time, he thought, before the family at Railes had forgotten him altogether.

In this he was mistaken because one day later that spring Ginny and her brother Hugh called on him in Church Row. It was a warm evening in May, and Martin, in waistcoat and shirtsleeves, was working in the front garden, hoeing the border beside the path, when he heard the sound of hooves and wheels and turned to see the governess-cart drawing up at the edge of the green. Leaving his hoe against the wall, he went to meet them, and was in the act of opening the gate when Ginny, helped by her twin, sprang lightly to the ground in a little billow of pale pink organdie skirts.

"Yes, you may well look surprised," she said, giving Martin her hand, "but if the mountain will not come to Mahomet … what is poor Mahomet to do?"

"I seem to remember," Martin replied, "that Mahomet gave thanks to the mountain because it did not overwhelm him."

"Well," Hugh said, in his quiet way, "we have come to overwhelm *you* instead."

"You have succeeded. My surprise is complete. Do please come indoors."

In the hall, as he led the way, he took his jacket from the hallstand and put it on. The twins followed him into the parlour, sat together on the settee, and accepted a glass of

Madeira wine. Ginny, with frank curiosity, looked all round the room.

"So this is where you live now? And alone, I hear, now your sister is married? What a very pleasant room, and what a lot of books you have in it. Do you ever have time to read them, being so busy as I'm sure you are?" Her glance came to rest on a watercolour that hung on the wall above the fire-place. "Oh, look, it's a picture of Railes! The west front from the top of the Knoll. Did you paint it, Martin? I'm sure you did. From memory, too. How clever you are!" And, fixing him with her bright gaze, she said: "It seems you *do* think of us, then, sometimes?"

"Yes," Martin said, "sometimes I do."

"We heard you had been to Saye House and had tea with Kate, and we were hurt – weren't we, Hugh? – because you never come to us."

"I met Mrs Yuart quite by chance—"

"Yes, and wheeled old Mr Yuart home in his chair. We heard all about it, you may be sure. And now we have come on a special mission, with an invitation to dine with us on Friday week. Kate and Charles will be there, with the old gentleman, of course, but no other guests besides you because Kate is expecting a child, you know, and it's only two months to her lying-in. So it's just an informal family dinner and you can't possibly refuse or you will give the gravest offence—"

"I am not refusing," Martin said. "I'm honoured to be asked to a family party and I shall be delighted to come."

"Very well. It's settled, then. And now perhaps you will realize that we Tarrants are a stubborn breed, who are not to be cast aside easily, as though we were an old glove. Isn't that so, Hugh?"

"Absolutely," her twin agreed. "Polonius speaks for us when he says, 'Those friends thou hast, and their adoption tried, grapple them to you with hoops of steel'." Hugh took a sip from his glass of wine. "Ergo, my dear fellow, consider yourself well and truly grappled."

"We dine at six," Ginny said, "but come earlier than that

– between four and five if you can – and then we can walk in the garden before dinner and it will be like old times…"

They stayed only a short while because they were on their way to visit other friends at Craye and were expected there at eight o'clock. But they lingered with him in the front garden, on their way to the gate, and Ginny, looking back at the cottage, complimented him on its neatness.

"You keep it all most beautifully, inside and out, and it is such a pretty spot to be in, even if you *can* hear those awful stocks pounding away in the valley down there. But no doubt in time, when you become rich, you will buy yourself a larger house."

"Shall I?" Martin said, amused.

"Well, *won't* you?" she said, with a little frown. "Why, with all that stone at your command, you could build yourself the finest, most beautiful house in the whole of the county. That's what *I'd* do if I were a man."

Here her twin put in a word.

"You wouldn't like it, Ginny, I'm sure. A brand new house would have no soul."

"It's all very well for you to talk! *You* can live at Railes all your life. It will be yours in the course of time. But I'm only a wretched girl and papa has always made it clear that he won't have much to settle on *me*."

"Well, you will marry, of course. You're bound to do that. I can't imagine you remaining single all your life. Now come along. We've stayed long enough. We'll be late at the Stewarts' if we don't watch out."

Hugh helped her into the governess-cart and climbed in himself. Martin stood alongside and they were exchanging a few last courtesies together when Hugh suddenly looked up at the sky. A lark was singing somewhere above and he tilted his head until he found it: a tiny dark speck of a bird, soaring on small fluttering wings, throbbing with its transcendental song, which came, a fast-trilling tumble of sound, down to those watching and listening below.

"I envy that lark," Hugh said, "expressing its joy so easily, and with such perfection ... taking itself up into the sky and singing straight from the heart like that."

"Perhaps you will write your own ode," Martin said.

Hugh, smiling, shook his head.

"No, I will spare you that," he said. "I should probably fall into the same error that Shelley does. 'Bird thou never wert', he says, and compares it instead to glow-worms and rain-drops and clouds of fire and – let me see, now, what else? – maidens singing from a lofty tower! When all the time the whole *point* of the lark lies in the fact that it *is* a bird. That is the miracle of it. – The thing itself. Don't you agree, my dear fellow?"

"Yes. Perhaps."

"It's gone out of sight now," Ginny said.

"Has it?" Hugh looked up again, raising one hand to shield his eyes. "No. Not quite. It's there – look – veering over to the left."

"Oh, yes, I can see it now. But only just."

Sitting together in the governess-cart, brother and sister looked up at the lark, and Martin in turn looked at them: at the two faces, so absurdly alike, the young man's as delicate as the girl's, his complexion as pure; except where, under his chin, the mottled burn-scar spread up from his neck, relic of the accident in early childhood, when a candle had set fire to his cot. Now, because his face was upturned, and the evening sun was full upon him, the scar could be seen very clearly: an angry red blemish, puckered at the edges; all the more startling, Martin thought, because of the beauty of the face. Then Hugh looked down at Martin again and the scar was almost completely hidden in the shadow cast by his jaw.

"The lark is gone and we must follow its example." He took up the reins and began turning the governess-cart. "But on Friday week we meet again. Five o'clock. We'll be looking for you."

"Earlier, Martin, if you like," Ginny said, glancing round at him.

The governess-cart moved slowly, making a crescent-

shaped turn on the green that brought it round again onto
the track. Martin watched it drive away, and in the garden
next-door-but-one, his elderly neighbour, Mrs Colne, stood
at her gate and watched it, too. Hugh, as he passed, raised his
wideawake hat to her, and Ginny gave her a nod and a smile;
and Mrs Colne, quite overcome, bobbed a deep curtsey to
them. She knew who they were, of course, and her round
pink face was alight with pleasure; and the moment they had
passed from sight, she turned to call across to Martin who, by
now, was back in his garden.

"Such a nice young lady and gentleman, to acknowledge
me in that gracious way. And to think of their coming to call
on you – driving themselves up to your gate just as any friend
might do! I heard when you first came here that you were
acquainted with the family and now I know it is really so. And
you are to see them again, it seems, for I couldn't help
hearing what the young man said just as he was driving
away—"

"Yes, I'm invited to dine with them."

"Goodness me! How very nice. Invited to dine at Newton
Railes! Such an agreeable young lady and gentleman, and so
very attractive, both of them."

The old lady was full of it, but she went indoors eventually,
and Martin took up his hoe again. His own surprise, not to
mention his pleasure, was scarcely less than his elderly
neighbour's, and he was obliged to laugh at himself. So much
for his stern resolve in keeping away from Newton Railes!
Where was it now? Well, the circumstances were changed, of
course; the case was altered, as the old phrase had it; and all
because they had sought him out. Hitherto he had pictured
himself calling at Railes and feeling himself a stranger there.
Now, at a stroke, that fear was dispelled. And oh, how simple
it was, after all! For *them*, how perfectly natural! And he found
himself making a new resolve: that in future he would do his
best to behave without fear of rebuff.

In ten days' time he would dine at Railes. Later, after a few
weeks, perhaps, he would ask the Tarrants to dine with him.

If they did, well and good. If not, there would be no offence. Friendship was like a precious cloak, but he must learn to wear it more lightly, he thought. It was easy enough with Edward Clayton; with Mr Godwin and his daughters; and with his neighbours here in Church Row. Why should it be any different with people such as the Tarrants?

For the moment, there was no difference at all. His mind was at ease; his heart serene; and as he hoed his way along the border, the prospect of an evening at Railes, with all the family gathered there, filled him with pleasure so complete that he could think of nothing else. The spring sunshine was warm on his back; the scent of lilacs filled the air; and, high in the blue sky overhead, Hugh's skylark was singing again.

CHAPTER
6

M artin, in the time to come, could never think of the skylark, or hear its song, without thinking of Hugh Tarrant. He was always to remember the young man's face, upturned to watch the bird's flight, and to hear his light-toned voice saying: "I envy that lark, expressing its joy so easily, and with such perfection..." Martin would also remember Hugh, the soul of natural courtesy, raising his hat to Mrs Colne as he drove away in the governess-cart. All these things Martin remembered because four days later Hugh was dead, killed in a fire that had broken out during the night at Newton Railes.

He heard the news on Monday morning when he walked down to Lotto Smith's to collect the pony and trap. It was shortly before eight o'clock, but news of the terrible tragedy had already reached the town, and here and there along the streets small groups of people were gathered, exchanging whatever details were known to them so far. Accounts varied from group to group. The only single definite fact was that young Mr Hugh was dead. Even when Martin drove out to Hainault Mill, he learnt nothing further, except that Mr and Mrs Charles Yuart were with the family at Railes. It was not until almost midday, when he spoke to Dr Brewster, that the whole story became known to him.

The fire had begun in the servants' quarters, somewhere in one of the first-floor bedrooms, occupied by Cook and the two older maids. It had spread to the small attic bedroom, occupied by the two younger maids, Alice and Bronwen. The alarm had been raised by Jack Sherard, who had seen the flames from his room above the coach-house. He had woken the other men and together they had roused the whole household. Cook and the two older maids had been brought down to safety by the grooms while John Tarrant and his children, together with Jobe and the other gardeners, had run to and fro with buckets of water, trying in vain to put out the fire, which had already spread to the upper staircase. Hugh, with a wet rug wrapped around him, had fought his way up to the attic where Alice and Bronwen lay unconscious, overcome by smoke and fumes. He had carried Bronwen down to the first-floor landing, where Sherard received her, and had then gone back for Alice; but while he was bringing her down, the burning staircase had collapsed under them, and they had been killed. John Tarrant had been badly burnt, dragging their bodies from the wreckage, and the doctor feared that his lungs were damaged.

It was the same with all those concerned: each had been hurt in some degree, either by the fire or the smoke, and Katharine Yuart, the doctor said, would be staying at Railes indefinitely, with two servants from Saye House, to help in caring for the stricken household. Ginny's burns had not been severe but the death of her twin had affected her deeply and she was in a profound state of shock.

"Will she be all right?" Martin asked.

"Yes, I think so, given time. For one thing, she is very young. For another, she's being well cared for. Yes, she'll recover, I'm sure of that."

"What about Mr Tarrant?"

"That is a different matter entirely. He is in his mid fifties. His body, his hands, his head, were burnt, and he took hot smoke into his lungs. Worst of all, he has lost his only son. He may recover. I just don't know. But when I left him an hour ago, he confessed he had little wish to do so."

The cause of the fire was not known then, but later investigation showed that a beam supporting the first-floor joists had been built into the kitchen chimney. It had caught fire from the inside, where the masonry had crumbled away, and had smouldered secretly for months, possibly years, all through the thickness of the chimney wall and under the floor of Cook's bedroom, until, on that night of strong winds, draught had fanned the smouldering beam so that joists and floorboards had burst into flame.

For this was the "new" part of the wing, built some forty years before, when, for the sake of economy, home-grown materials had been used: inferior stone dug on the estate; poor quality timber cut from its woods. The fire, taking hold, had spread quickly; the pinewood staircase up to the attic had been destroyed in a matter of minutes; and long before the firemen arrived, to put out the last of the fire, the two upper storeys had collapsed, bringing down the whole of the roof and much of the outer gable wall.

Martin wrote to the family, and it was the most difficult task of his life. On the day of the funeral he sent two wreaths of flowers to the house: one for Hugh, and one for the maid, Alice Hercombe, because the two burials were to take place together, and there was to be one service for both, in the little church at Newton Childe. The service would be a private one, with only the bereaved families present, a fact made known in a brief announcement published in *The Chardwell Gazette*.

But John Tarrant was much respected in the district around, known as a fair-minded magistrate who had served many years on the bench; also as a good landlord to his tenants in the cottages he owned in the town and elsewhere. Added to this, the whole family had always been well liked for their friendliness and their lack of show. Now young Mr Hugh had died trying to save the life of a servant, a local girl from Yateley Bridge, daughter of the farrier there; and this so affected the local people that on the day of the funeral, some two or three hundred of them lined the narrow winding lane outside the east gate of Newton Railes park to watch the sad cortége go by.

Everything about it was perfectly simple, the coffins borne on an open farm-cart, covered only by wreaths of flowers, with the mourners in three closed carriages following behind. There were no black streamers on the hats of the coachmen. No black plumes on the horses' heads. Only the carriage windows were heavily draped with black net, shutting out the bright sunshine and completely hiding the mourners from view. Not that the watchers in the lane peered into the carriages. Nor did they follow the cortége to the church. They respected the wish of the two families, to bury their dead in a private manner, with no outsiders to observe their grief. And when the procession had gone past, out of sight round a bend in the lane, the watchers quietly went away, breaking up into small groups, some going homeward across the fields, most going back along the lane to the town. Martin and Nan were among these last, and although she had never met Hugh Tarrant, Nan wept for him most bitterly, because of what she knew of him and because of the way in which he had died.

"How old was he, Martin?"

"He was just eighteen. He had his birthday a few weeks ago. I remember that because it's soon after mine."

"The only son, and his father's heir...What that poor man must be feeling now..."

A few days later, Martin received a letter from Katharine Yuart, who was still at Railes, thanking him for his letter of condolence and for his flowers. Her tone was restrained, almost matter-of-fact, but it was only too easy for him to imagine that house of mourning. The sense of numb disbelief was conveyed in her plain simple statements; so was her anxiety; for her father, who had borne up well throughout the ordeal of the funeral, had collapsed soon afterwards and was now keeping to his own room, while Ginny, grieving for her twin, was like a lost child, Katharine said. Still, she was being very good, caring tenderly for her father, and helping to nurse the injured servants.

"Ginny hopes, and I do, too, that when things are better here, you will come and visit us. Meantime, we thank you yet again for your friendship and your sympathy."

One day towards the end of June, Martin walked out to Newton Childe to look for Hugh's grave in the churchyard. He found it beside a cobbled path that ran round behind the church: a simple mound, newly made, covered with neat squares of turf which had not yet knitted together, though the grass on them was neatly trimmed; and at the head of the mound a small wooden cross carved with the initial H.J.T.. Beside the cross was an earthenware jug filled with flowers from the fields and meadows: buttercups, cowslips, and ragged robin, forget-me-nots and cuckoo-flowers; together with sprigs of rosemary, rue, and southernwood, which had come, no doubt, from the Tudor garden at Newton Railes.

The position of the grave, out in the open churchyard, came as no surprise to Martin, because Hugh had strongly disapproved of the family vault, under the floor of the church itself, and had often said – cheerfully, though in all earnestness, – that he would prefer a grave of his own, "decently filled in with earth, and the green grass allowed to grow over it." Aged eighteen, he had his wish: the pale Cotswold soil lay over him; green grass covered the mound; and over all was the open sky, where, in the years to come, the soaring skylark would often sing.

Not far away, between two birch trees, Martin found the second new grave; that of the maid, Alice Hercombe. This too had its small wooden cross, with the dead girl's initials on it, and beside it a pot filled with wild flowers. The crosses would serve until such time as the earth in the new graves had settled. They would then be replaced by permanent headstones.

When he returned to Hugh's grave, he found Ginny standing beside it, and although she was in his thoughts just then, her sudden appearance startled him. Dressed all in black, she looked very small, and her face, under the black bonnet, was deathly pale. Her eyes, too, were devoid of their colour, as if pain and weeping had washed it away, so that when she turned towards him, her look was that of an elderly child.

"Oh, Martin," she said in a whisper, and made a little gesture with her black-gloved hands, looking at him in helpless appeal.

For a moment he was unable to speak and when he did his words got caught up in the back of his throat.

"I knew you'd been here … recently … because of the flowers being so fresh."

"Yes, I come here every day. Somehow I can't keep away from this spot… It's very stupid of me, I know, because Hugh isn't here in the ground, is he? Only his poor burnt body is here … and that's not the dear good boy I knew, who was always such a kind brother to me."

She began very quietly to weep, and Martin, in the most natural way, went close and drew her into his arms. He held her with great tenderness and she leant against him, thankfully, her head, in its small close-fitting bonnet, resting sideways against his chest. She wept with tired hopelessness, and when she spoke between her sobs, her voice was only just audible, so close was it to exhaustion.

"Martin, how can God be good when he does such terrible things to us? It seems Hugh was *meant* to be killed by fire… First the accident years ago, when we were still in the nursery… Now this … and this time he's dead. But why should God do that to Hugh? That's the question my father asks, and so do I."

"Yes," Martin said, "I've asked it too."

"And can you understand it?" she asked, drawing away to look up at him. "Can you forgive it? Because I cannot! That God should be so dreadfully cruel… I cannot forgive it. I shan't even try."

She took a hankerchief from her sleeve and dried her eyes. She was trying hard to compose herself.

"I still can't believe Hugh is gone…That I shall never see him again…" She stood very still, looking down at the grave.

"I don't care about another life. It's too long to wait. I want Hugh as he always was." She drew a deep, tremulous breath, and turned to look across the churchyard. "Alice is buried over there."

"Yes. I saw."

"I can't feel anything for her. I keep thinking to myself that if Hugh had not tried to save her, he would still be here with us."

"You have put flowers on her grave all the same."

"Yes, because *he* would have wanted me to."

On leaving the churchyard, they walked together along the lane till they came to the first bridle-gate opening into Railes land.

"Don't leave me yet," Ginny said. "Come with me part of the way."

So they walked together through the belt of trees and out onto the open parkland, and Ginny, in answer to his enquiry, talked about her father.

"He's sick, Martin, and very weak. He was badly burnt, you know, and he is still in terrible pain. His breathing is better than it was but … the slightest exertion makes him cough and … it's a terrible thing to see and hear… But all that would be as nothing, I'm sure, if it were not for losing Hugh. That is what has struck him down. And oh, Martin, if you saw him now, you'd find him so changed from what he was! He's very brave. Or he tries to be. *Too* brave, for it costs him dear. Kate and Charles are still with us, thank God, and will stay until after the lying-in. It is papa's wish, you see, that Katharine's child should be born at Railes… Because now that Hugh is no longer here, the estate will go to Katharine and Charles. Papa has spoken of it quite often. Death is much on his mind just now so naturally he is hoping—"

Her voice broke; she was in tears; and Martin said what she could not say.

"He is hoping, before he dies, to see his grandson and future heir."

"Yes."

"I hope and pray that his wish may be granted. But I hope too that he is mistaken in thinking himself so close to death. And I think perhaps, with the birth of the child, he may find the will to live."

"Oh, Martin, I pray you are right! Because I don't know how I should ever bear it if papa were taken from us as well."

She came close and took Martin's arm and he, looking down at her pale, pinched face, usually so full of mischief, thought how very cruel it was that the first real sorrow of her life should be one of such magnitude. They walked on slowly together, over the green slopes of the parkland, where grazed the Manor Farm cattle and sheep, then down into the golden valley, and along the bank of the trout stream, where the water ran pure and clear over its bed of broken stone and where, in the warm air above, bright blue dragonflies darted swiftly to and fro. And now, as they walked along together, Ginny talked about the fire.

It had not spread to the kitchen or to the rooms above it because the wall dividing the old part of the wing from the new was, of course, the original gable-end, built of good stone, four feet thick. Only one door, at ground level, connected the two parts of the wing, and this door, though badly burnt, had not been breached. Still, neither the kitchen nor the main part of the house had escaped completely, for a number of windows had been broken and smoke had got in, causing much damage.

The burnt-out section of the wing had now been demolished and the debris removed. The hole in the outer wall of the chimney, where the culprit beam had burnt away, was now filled up, and the roof-end had been repaired. Charles had arranged for these things to be done and he had also brought in a number of men to deal with the damage to the house. The broken windows had been replaced; the blackened rooms cleaned and redecorated; the carpets and furniture were being restored. Scarcely a visible trace remained, Ginny said, though the smell of the smoke still hung everywhere and would, it was said, for a long time to come.

"Charles has offered to rebuild the end of that wing. Indeed, he has insisted upon it, for papa has not money enough to do it, and we need those rooms most desperately. Papa wants your advice on the matter but he's not really well enough to see anyone just at present." Ginny squeezed Martin's arm. "When he is, you will come, won't you?"

"Yes, of course."

"I'm so glad I met you today. You and Hugh were such good friends in the days when we had lessons together. I've been thinking a lot about those days. I can't get Hugh out of my mind. He was always such a dear, kind brother to me, and I was often horrid to him. I said some spiteful things to him sometimes – *and* to papa – because there was always money enough for Hugh to go travelling abroad but *never* enough for me to go too. And oh, if I only had him back! I'd never be jealous of him again!"

She came to a standstill, overcome by tears, and stood, small and childlike, with her head deep-bowed. Martin turned towards her and blindly she put out her hands to him. And as they stood thus together, silent in grief and sympathy, a man came briskly along the path on the opposite side of the stream and across the wooden footbridge some twenty yards from where they stood. It was Ginny's brother-in-law. He had come from the house in search of her.

"Katharine was beginning to worry," he said, as she and Martin turned towards him, "and so was your father, needless to say."

"They need not have worried," Ginny said. She dabbed her eyes with her handkerchief, then blew her nose. "Kate knew where I had gone. And I am perfectly safe, as you see, for I met Martin in the churchyard and he has kindly walked back with me."

"Yes, quite so," Yuart said. He acknowledged Martin with a nod. "But we were not to know that, Ginny, and as you've been gone longer than usual, it is natural that we should be concerned. I feel bound to say, too, that I think it inconsiderate of you to worry your family in this way, when your father is still far from well, and your sister is so close to her time."

"Please don't scold me, Charles," Ginny said, speaking with frail dignity. "I'm quite sure neither Kate nor papa would want you to scold me on their behalf."

For a little while Yuart was speechless. He looked at her in blank dismay, undone by the simple truth of her plea.

"My dear child!" he said then, but this time his exasperation was softened by a note of remorse. Gently, he went to her and drew her arm into his. "Come along. I'll take you home. And not one further word of reproach shall I utter, now or at any future time." He turned and addressed himself to Martin. "I'm much obliged to you, Mr Cox, for your kindness to my sister-in-law, and I know both my wife and my father-in-law will be pleased to know she was safe in the company of someone they know."

Martin gave a little bow.

"It was my pleasure to meet Miss Ginny as I did and it was my privilege to escort her part of the way home."

He was about to speak to Ginny when she forestalled him.

"I hope you are not going to be so stiff and formal with me, Martin dear. It really would be too absurd when only a short while ago I wept on your shoulder in the churchyard. Indeed, I might well have done so again, if Charles had not come along when he did." She smiled at him: a brave, wistful smile; and reached out with her free hand to touch his arm. "It's been such a comfort, talking to you. You're so much a part of the old days, you see. And I hope it won't be too long before papa is well enough for you to come and talk to him about – well, you know what about."

"I hope so, too," Martin said.

A fortnight later, he read in *The Chardwell Gazette* that Katharine Yuart had given birth to a son, and that mother and infant were in good health. The child would be named Richard Hugh. Soon after this announcement, Martin received a letter from Ginny, asking him to come to Railes to

discuss the rebuilding of the wing-end, and to take luncheon
with the family.

"My father's hands still give him pain, so I write for him. He
is in better spirits at present, thanks to the birth of his grandson,
but is still far from strong. Be prepared to find him changed."

Accordingly, on the day appointed, he drove out to Railes
in the pony and trap. From the gravelled carriage-road, as it
traversed the upper slopes of the park, the old house looked
as serene as ever, and just as beautiful, Martin thought. Even
as he drove round to the stables and glanced across at the
kitchen wing, he could see little sign of the damage done,
though when he stood in the stable-court, talking to the
groom, Jack Sherard, there were signs enough, and all too
plain, for the man's face was badly scarred, and so were his
hands.

"We're all of us marked one way or another, Mr Cox, but
the hurts we got that night, well, – we'd go through it all
again, and worse, if only it would bring the young master
back to us, and the poor girl he was trying to save."

While Martin was talking to Sherard, John Tarrant came
from the back of the house, with the two spaniels at his heels,
and Martin went to meet him. Prepared though he was to
find the bereaved man changed, he was nevertheless shocked
by the full extent of that change, because John Tarrant, at
fifty-four, was already an old man. His once handsome face,
scarred worse than Sherard's, was only barely recognizable,
and his hair, having been burnt away, was only just beginning
to grow, patchily, in a grey stubble. He still wore loose cotton
gloves, to hide and protect his damaged hands, and he still
walked with the aid of a stick, in pain from an injury to his
knee. When he spoke, it was with an effort, drawing each
breath stressfully, up from the depths of his scorched lungs.
But the worst wound of all, as Martin knew, was the loss of his
son; and the suffering he endured from this showed in the
haunted look of his eyes; in the moments of absent-
mindedness that came over him while he talked, when he

would break off in the middle of a sentence and stare into space, having lost his way.

Yet still, in spite of his afflictions, he was as courteous as ever, talking to Martin as a friend, apologizing for his lapses of memory, and, on reaching the kitchen courtyard, ushering him to a wooden seat placed against the wall of the kitchen garden. From this position they looked across the yard to the back of the house and could see the whole of the kitchen wing, reduced now to its original length. Because the burnt-out section had been demolished, and a certain amount of repair-work done, there was little visible evidence of the fire, and a stranger, in all probability, would have been surprised to learn of its occurrence. But the signs were there, nevertheless, and to Martin, who not only knew the house but knew so well the nature of stone, those signs were all too eloquent.

The gable wall, which was also, in part, the wall of the chimney, had been blackened by a thick coating of soot, but this had since been scraped away, leaving the surface startlingly clean. But the stonework, subjected to so great a heat, had undergone a change of colour and was now flushed a deep dusky pink. No amount of scraping would remove that colour, as Martin knew, for he had once handled stone taken from a burnt-out mill and, sawing it up for use elsewhere, had seen how that same pink flush had gone right through each ashlar block, staining it to the last granule.

Along the side wall of the kitchen wing, both upstairs and down, all the windows had been replaced, and some, too, in the main back wall of the house, where it joined the wing at a right angle. The ivy that had covered the kitchen wall had been burnt away completely, of course, but juice oozing from its thickest stems had stained the stonework, leaving a ramified pattern behind, limned like the ghost of the ivy itself.

These things, and many more, Martin observed as he sat talking to John Tarrant. The workmen brought in by Charles Yuart had done a very thorough job. Yuart himself had made sure of that, anxious to see the ruin demolished and

the debris cleared without delay, for safety's sake. He had
also done his best to ensure that every grim reminder of the
tragedy should be removed, eradicated, or disguised.

"He wanted to spare our feelings in every way possible,
and I have much to thank him for. Without him I do not
know how this household would have got through these
terrible weeks. But in spite of all Charles has done ... there
can be no forgetting for me. I keep going back over the past,
to the time when Hugh was burnt as a child. It's as though
that was meant as a warning to me, and I did take heed of it,
God knows. I made such stringent rules in the house ... and
all of them to no avail ... because the cause of the fire this time
lay elsewhere ... My grandfather had that extension built,
and did it all on the cheap, as you know. And now, years later,
it has cost Hugh his life. But I am just as much to blame. If
I had done as your father advised and pulled that damned
extension down—"

"Sir, you could not have foreseen *this*. Nobody could."

"No, no. You are quite right. And I have not brought you
here to inflict my self-reproaches on you but to ... to ask your
advice about rebuilding. These past weeks I have lacked the
will to take any firm decisions whatever. I could not bear the
thought of further disturbance, further mess. But matters
are somewhat different now. Katharine has a son, as you
know, and it's high time I looked to the future, even though
my share in it is likely to be of short duration. So ... did you
know that my son-in-law has offered to pay the cost of the
work?"

"Yes, Miss Ginny told me."

"Well, then, the point is this. You and your father did all
my repairs and what building I could afford, and excellent
work it was, too. But you are a busy man these days and
Charles seems to think you wouldn't have time ... He says
you no longer do such work and he talks of calling contractors
in."

"It is not that I am too busy, sir. I would always have time
to do whatever you asked of me, so long as it was within my

capabilities." Martin paused. He detected awkwardness in John Tarrant's manner and, confident that he knew its cause, he gauged his answer accordingly. "The plain truth of the matter is that I am not an accredited builder, and when it comes to work such as this, I must confess to having my doubts."

John Tarrant looked relieved.

"Well, that's as honest an answer as anyone could wish for, and I'm grateful for it. But you will of course supply the stone?"

"Yes. Most certainly."

At half past eleven Charles Yuart arrived, riding into the stable-court on a handsome dun mare. At the same moment Ginny emerged from the back of the house, still dressed in black but with a grey stole over her shoulders. Martin rose and she gave him her hand. Then she stooped and kissed her father's cheek.

"I got tired of waiting for you to come in so I came to see what you were about. Kate is talking to the nursemaid. Baby Dick has got the gripes."

Yuart now joined the group at the bench and, after an exchange of civilities, addressed himself to his father-in-law.

"I shall not be staying to lunch, I'm afraid. I have urgent business in Sharveston. It really is most unfortunate but I hope Mr Cox will understand if I come to the point immediately and ask what decision you have reached together as a result of your discussion."

"Well, you'll be glad to know, Charles, that Martin feels as you do, that this is work for a firm of contractors."

"Ah!" Yuart said, gratified, and looked at Martin directly this time. "I'm glad we are in agreement, Mr Cox. It simplifies matters considerably. As a matter of fact my own idea is to engage a reputable architect – probably Lunnett of Cheltenham, the leading man, I understand, when it comes to restoring older houses – and be guided by him in choosing a builder."

"You must do as you think best, of course, but I hardly think you need give yourself any such extra expense. The work will be simple and straightforward, well within the scope of a first-rate builder, and you really couldn't do any better than call on Robert Clayton and Son, whom you already know."

"It is not a question of this rebuilding work alone," Yuart said. "Mr Tarrant may not have mentioned it but I intend, in a year or so, to enlarge the west wing quite substantially, and to do that work, Mr Cox I shall *not* be employing Clayton and Son."

"I'm sorry," Martin said in surprise. "I meant no presumption, I assure you. I merely thought, as the Claytons had built your new mill at Hainault and you knew the quality of their work—"

"I believe Edward Clayton is your brother-in-law, so it is quite understandable that you should wish to put work in his way. However, I have my own reasons for not employing him again, and I hope you will not be offended if I choose to reject your recommendation."

Martin was angry. He felt the blood rising hot in his face. But he did his best to answer with a coolness equal to Yuart's own.

"You quite mistake the matter, Mr Yuart. Clayton and Son have contracts for work that will keep them busy for some time to come. They certainly do not need *me* to drum up custom on their behalf."

"Mr Cox, I apologize. I mistook the matter, as you say." Yuart glanced at the stable clock and begged the company to excuse him. "I just have time for a word with my wife and then I really must be gone."

He hurried away into the house and John Tarrant looked up at Martin.

"I'm afraid my son-in-law is somewhat over-brusque at times, but he has a lot on his mind just now, and I hope you will make allowances for him."

"Charles is not only brusque," Ginny said, "he is also very

high-handed, papa." She moved close to Martin and took his arm. "I'm afraid he rubbed you up the wrong way, but never mind. – I will soon smooth you down again. Papa, dear, you won't object, I'm sure, if I take Martin away from you? I want to show him the bean-tree in flower."

"No, my child, I don't mind one bit. Martin and I can resume our discussion over lunch."

They walked arm-in-arm through the gardens; along the green walk into the *allée*; around by the small summer-house, where pigeons called from the sweet-scented limes, and back by way of the Tudor garden, where the York-and-Lancaster roses bloomed, their delicate scent mingling strangely with the burnt-coffee smell of the clipped box trees.

"You are not offended with Charles, I hope?"

"I think I would rather not answer that."

"Then you *are* offended. Oh, dear! Oh, dear!"

"I took exception, I must admit, to the way he spoke of my brother-in-law."

"He did apologize for that."

"Yes. I will put it out of my mind."

"Charles has been very good to me. He is also very generous. He gave me twenty-five pounds last week, to spend exactly as I pleased, and I had a simply wonderful time choosing materials for next winter's gowns."

Bleakly she looked down at herself; at her black silk dress, with its black net sleeves, relieved only by a touch of grey in the lace on the collar, which matched the grey of her silk stole.

"I long to be dressed in colours again. I feel so *old* when I'm wearing black. But papa, you know, is quite strict in some ways, and I must wear it for ages yet."

They had left the Tudor garden now and were standing under the Indian bean-tree, looking up at the sprays of blossom, white flecked with purple-brown, amongst the large pale luminous leaves.

"Isn't it beautiful?"

"Yes, it is."

"It seems so terribly cruel, somehow, that everything is extra lovely this summer, and Hugh not here to see it all. I can't get used to not having a brother. I still find myself thinking of things to tell him ... and then I remember that he is not there."

The stable clock began to strike. Ginny took Martin's arm again.

"That's twelve o'clock striking. Lunch will be ready at half past. Katharine should be free by now, so let's go back to the house, shall we, and you can meet baby Dick." She looked up at him with a sweet sad smile. "The new heir to Railes," she said.

On leaving Railes that afternoon, Martin, instead of going straight home, called on Edward at his office in Prince Street.

"What has Charles Yuart got against you?" he asked, and related what had passed that morning.

"Well, we had a few tussles, he and I, during the last weeks at Hainault. He complained that we had overrun our promised date, though that, as you know, was due to the fact that he wanted certain changes made earlier on. He delayed settling his final account on the grounds that we had failed to fulfil the terms of the contract. All arrant nonsense, of course, and it has been cleared up now. His accountant has just written to say that we shall receive our cheque shortly."

"So what's behind it?" Martin asked.

"I suppose he wanted time to pay and chose this way of getting it rather than ask us openly."

"Do you mean the man is not *sound*?"

"Oh, I should think he's sound enough. But he's spent a fortune enlarging his mill, and another fortune on the new looms, and just at present it's money tied up. Trade has been stale recently but it's picking up again now, and once he gets his new looms under way, Yuart will be nicely placed to bag a large share of it. Hainault will be first in the field, and although the other cloth-men are following his example, he should be able to keep that advantage for a good many years to come."

"I'm relieved to hear it," Martin said. He was thinking of Charles Yuart's wife, but after a little while he said: "You never breathed a word to me about having these arguments with him."

"No. I did not. Because such matters are, as a rule, kept private between the parties concerned. But now that Yuart has seen fit to make his insinuations to you, I am exercising the right to explain the Clayton side of it. As for his not employing us for the work he wants done at the manor house, that, my dear Martin, is a piece of bare-faced impertinence. After our experience at Hainault, we should be very reluctant ever to work for him again, as he well knows, and what he said to you was just an example of the old trick of refusing before he could be refused."

"But he must know also that I was bound to ask you about it and that we two at least would see the ploy for what it was."

"I don't think Yuart cares twopence what we think of him so long as he can feel satisfied that he has got the better of us. We are beneath his notice, my boy, and as far as I myself am concerned, long may it continue so. Of course, I realize it's different for you, being a friend of the family at Railes, and *that* was yet another reason why I didn't speak up before."

"I care no more than you do that I am beneath Yuart's notice, but yes, where the Tarrants are concerned, it is a different matter entirely. It grieves me very much indeed that the one member of the family deserving the very highest respect should be married to a man of such doubtful honour."

"Oh, come, now, that's rather strong! I deplore the man's lack of principle, of course, but he's done nothing really heinous, you know. Indeed, some of our fellow businessmen would say that Yuart's methods are merely an everyday part of business practice."

"Yes. No doubt. But Mrs Yuart is a woman of integrity, and I know that she would not share that view."

"It is unlikely that Mrs Yuart will ever know about such

things so you need not have any fears that she will be caused distress on that score."

"I hope you are right," Martin said.

By late August, stone for rebuilding the domestic wing-end had been delivered at Railes, and Martin's banker-masons, working in conjunction with the builder's men, were cutting the dressings. Martin himself was there two or three times a week, partly to oversee his men's work, partly for consultations with the builder, but chiefly because John Tarrant was anxious that he should be there.

"I've nothing against this builder. I'm sure he is a first-rate man. And Charles is sparing no expense to see that all the materials used are the very best that can be got. Come and look at this pile of timber. Stout seasoned oak, all of it. Beams and joists every bit as thick as those in the old part of the house. Floorboards the same. Rafters, too. They won't burn very easily. But I'm glad you're keeping an eye on things because no builder, however good, knows this house so well as you do, and having you here makes me feel safe."

Martin, on these visits to Railes, saw little of Katharine Yuart: the duties of motherhood kept her indoors. Nor did he often meet her husband: *he* was busy with his new looms. But Ginny would always come running out of the house the moment she knew Martin was there and, whenever possible, would insist that he walk in the garden with her. She was always pathetically pleased to see him, for visitors were few and far between during this period of mourning, and the family rarely left home to pay visits elsewhere.

"It's all so silly!" she complained once. "We see hardly anyone. Just a few close friends, that's all. And we shan't be asked to parties and balls for another two or three months at least, though at times like this we *need* cheering up. Never mind – at least I've got you! Come and see the little oak tree Kate and Charles have planted in celebration of baby Dick's birth."

*

John Tarrant's health was failing and Martin, perceiving it, was grieved. On each visit he noted some change and could see that Tarrant still suffered great pain, though he always hid it as best he could, especially when his daughters were present. Alone with Martin he spoke in a way that showed the tenor of his thoughts at this time; how he dwelt on the past with wistful regret but looked to the future with resignation.

"It saddens me that when I am gone the Tarrant name will pass from this place. We've been here since 1565. Still, there it is, and cannot be helped. Change is ordained from above and we must bow our heads to it. And at least Newton Railes will be in good hands... Charles takes almost as much pride in the house as I do myself... Furthermore, he has the money to take care of it as it deserves. That's more than I ever could, scrimping and scraping all these years..."

There was a pause. Tarrant, as was his custom now, sat on the bench in the kitchen courtyard, whence he could watch the men at work, rebuilding the end of the kitchen wing. Martin sat beside him.

"Charles is full of plans, as you know, for making improvements here and there. He always discusses them with me and asks my opinion ... but I shan't be here to see them fulfilled. *This* work, perhaps, but not the rest... The sands are running out for me, Martin, and soon there will be no turning of the glass. I know it. So does Charles. And I think my daughters know it, too, in their hearts. Please don't be distressed, my boy. The end, for me, will be a sweet release. I admit I worry sometimes about Ginny... I should have liked to have seen her settled, with a good husband to look after her... Still, there again, I am thankful for Charles. He and Kate will take care of her and in due course see to it that she makes a suitable marriage. Meantime, she is desolate. The restrictions of mourning weigh hard on her, and when I am gone, poor child, she will be in mourning again."

By the end of September, the banker-masons' work was finished, and Martin was no longer needed at Railes.

"But you *will* still come and visit us?" Ginny said, imperatively. "Of course you will! – You'll come as a friend."

"Well..."

"You must come. I insist on it. Papa enjoys talking to you and so do I. Indeed, I don't know what I should do without your visits to look forward to. Apart from George Winter and you, I see no friends of my own age, so do please come, Martin dear, otherwise—" Her lip trembled; her voice broke. "Otherwise I think I shall die."

"Yes. I will come."

"You said you would bring me *Barry Lyndon* when you had finished reading it."

"Yes, and so I shall," he said.

But when, a few days later, he called at Railes with the book as promised, he learnt that Ginny had gone away.

"She was in such low spirits that we feared for her health," John Tarrant said. "We sent her to stay with our friends in Llangollen and she will be there for two or three weeks. We have had a letter from Mrs Lloyd, who says the child is already improved."

"I'm sure you have done the right thing," Martin said.

"Will you stay and have lunch with me? I am all alone today because Katharine is at Saye House, visiting her father-in-law. So it would be a kindness indeed."

"I should be delighted," Martin said.

Ginny came home at the end of the week, because by then her father was gravely ill. Three days later he died, and on a cold wet morning in October, he was laid to rest in the churchyard at Newton Childe, in a grave close beside that of his son. Martin wrote to Katharine Yuart; sent flowers; and attended the funeral. Both sisters were heavily veiled; nothing could be seen of their faces; but Ginny, towards the end of the service, broke down and wept into her hands.

At the end of October, Martin, for the first time in his life, went away for a holiday. He had always wanted to visit London; now he had the money to do it; and, with the quarry safe under Tommy Nick's management, he could absent himself for two weeks without any anxiety.

He stayed in a small hotel called Coote's, just off Ludgate Hill, and spent his days exploring those places and buildings associated with the famous names and events of history. St Paul's Cathedral, Westminster Abbey, and the new Houses of Parliament, part of which was still under construction. Windsor Castle, Hampton Court, and the Royal Botanical Gardens at Kew. He attended a concert where he heard Jenny Lind sing and Anton Harnische play the piano. He also attended a Chartist meeting but thought the speakers too violent to do anything but harm to their cause.

He had been home little more than a week when, on a mild Sunday afternoon, Ginny Tarrant called on him. The governess-cart stood at the gate. She had driven herself and was quite alone.

"Are you terribly shocked?" she said, as he ushered her into the parlour; and, when she was seated – "Yes, you are, I can see by your face."

"It will certainly cause some comment among my neighbours."

"And whose good name do you mind about most? Mine or yours?"

"Chiefly, I am wondering about your sister, and whether she knows you are out alone."

"Yes, yes, of course she knows, though she doesn't approve, I must admit. Neither does Charles, needless to stay. But never mind about Kate and Charles. I wanted to see you and here I am."

She removed her black hat, with its heavy black veil, and set it beside her on the couch. Her face had the tired, expressionless look that comes after prolonged weeping, and although she had coloured her lips with rouge, this only emphasized her general pallor and the cold limp texture of her skin.

"I would like you to give me a glass of wine, if it is not too much trouble to you. Whatever is in that decanter there. It doesn't much matter what it is."

Martin poured two glasses of malmsey and put one of them into her hand. He stood looking down at her.

"Ginny, what is it? Why have you come?"

"I needed to talk to somebody. I needed to get out of the house. So I bravely told Katharine and Charles that I was coming to see you. I wish I could be brave enough to rebel against wearing this horrible black. Just look at it, how loathsome it is! – It makes me feel a hundred years old. I hate the whole business of mourning – I would abolish it if I could. What good does it do? It doesn't bring the dead back to life. It only makes everything harder to bear."

Her voice trembled and she came close to tears, but an angry defiance possessed her and she was borne up by it.

"Can you imagine what it's like? We see scarcely any company and those few friends who do call talk only on solemn subjects. Mrs Bourne was very shocked when I asked for an account of the concert at West's. And that is how we must live our lives for another five months at least! It's all very well for Katharine – she has Charles and baby Dick – but I have nobody of my own, and the only person who seems to have any understanding is George Winter." She took a few sips of her wine. "You remember George, don't you?"

"Yes, of course."

"He has proposed to me again."

"While you are still in mourning?"

"Yes."

"And do you intend accepting him?"

"I don't know. I'm not quite sure. But I think most probably I shall. I don't like living at Railes now... The memories are more than I can bear. Oh, Kate and Charles are kindness itself. Kate says it is still my home, just the same as it ever was, and Charles says so, too. But nothing *is* the same as it was, now that Hugh and papa are gone, and I have a longing to escape."

There was a pause. She drank her wine. For a while she looked into her glass, but presently she rose from her seat and moved to the small hearthside table, where she set her glass down on the tray. She was now standing quite close to him, her wide black skirts almost touching his knee. "Anyway," she said lightly, "I have to marry somebody, sooner or later, don't I? – If only to have a home of my own."

"That doesn't, by itself, seem a very good reason."

"What *is* a good reason, would you say?"

"Well, of all those set out in the marriage service, surely the most important is love."

"It's all very well to talk of love, but how are we supposed to know whether we love someone *enough*? Do *you* know what it is to love?"

"We are not discussing my affairs. We're discussing yours."

"Yes. Well. Kate says when you love someone, you know it at once, without any doubts. Certainly she and Charles were like that. And George is very positive about the feelings he has for *me*. He's been so sweet and kind to me all through these terrible, terrible months, and in spite of my being in mourning, he says he will marry me straight away and take me on a tour of the Continent. It will cause no end of talk, of course, but he says he doesn't care about that. And oh, to think of going abroad! Seeing new sights every single day, with a chance of forgetting the horrible past. George says we can stay away for just so long as I choose to. We may even go to Istanbul."

"It seems as though it is settled, then." Martin raised his glass to her. "I wish you both every happiness."

"Is that all you have to say?"

"Why, what more can I say than that?"

"Oh, I don't know! Some word! Some sign!"

Martin, setting down his glass, answered with a touch of impatience.

"Ginny, what are you talking about? If you're not sure about this marriage, then for God's sake don't commit yourself to it."

"Oh, yes, I'm sure enough. I *want* to be married and I feel safe with George. It's just that everything has turned out so *differently* from how I used to imagine it. Such a wedding I meant to have! I had it all planned to the last degree. I never dreamt that when I married, neither Hugh nor papa would be here to see it ... and now, somehow, the wedding itself no longer matters one iota. I still can't quite believe they are gone... And oh, Martin, I do miss them so!"

Gently he took her into his arms, holding her and comforting her while she wept against him with little choked sobs. Soon, however, the weeping ceased, and her arms crept up behind his neck. She raised her face, wet with tears, and, reaching up to him, urgently, kissed his mouth with unrestrained passion, her lips moving against his in a way that was sweetly, tenderly sensual.

"There, you see, you knew all the time." And she kissed him again, with a little sigh, seeking and finding forgetfulness in the way that came most naturally to her. Then, hiding her face against his, she spoke in a whisper close to his ear. "Do you remember, two years ago, on the day our lessons came to an end ... and you kissed me goodbye at the wicket gate? And *Much Ado*, when the storm came on, and we sheltered in the summer-house? You didn't kiss me then, of course, but I'm quite sure you would have done if Kate and Hugh had not been there. I remember the feel of your hands on my body, warm through the cold wet stuff of my dress, and I thought then—"

"What did you think?"

"That you would make a very good lover."

Still with great gentleness, but firmly, too, Martin disengaged himself. He removed her hands from behind his neck and held them clasped between his own.

"You mean, if you could arrange it so, you would take Winter as your husband and keep me as your paramour? Is that what you are proposing?"

"No, of course not."

"What, then? And why did you come?"

"Because I've been thinking about George... Trying to imagine what it will be like to be married to him... At the same time I was thinking of you ... of what I felt when we kissed that time … and I wanted to find out if I should still feel the same now."

"And do you?"

"Yes, of course. You know I do. And I don't feel like that with George."

"And yet you will marry him just the same."

"You need not speak to me in that tone or look at me in that critical way. I'm really quite fond of George and I mean to be a good wife to him."

"I'm glad to hear it," Martin said.

"Are you? Why?"

"Because Winter, from what I know of him, is a thoroughly decent sort of man. He's head over heels in love with you and he's only getting half a loaf."

"Oh, what a vulgar thing to say!"

"I'm a vulgar fellow."

"Yes. You are."

But she was neither offended nor hurt. She had come to him in search of solace; some respite from the incumbent grief she felt for the loss of her father and brother; and, her nature being what it was, she had, for this interlude, found what she sought. Her face now was warmly flushed; there was a little smile on her lips; and her pale, tear-washed eyes, searching his face, had even a hint of mischief in them.

"Martin, do you care for me?"

"I think you know the answer to that."

"No, I'm not sure that I do. How *much* do you care? Tell me that."

"As much, or as little, as you deserve."

"That is no answer."

"It's the best I can give."

"You will not commit yourself."

"No. I will not."

"I suppose you think I'm a hussy," she said.

"I'm more concerned with what the neighbours will think."

"Meaning, it's time I took my leave. Very well. You are right, of course. But aren't you going to wish me well?"

"I've already done that."

"Well, then, will you kiss me goodbye?"

Martin stooped to kiss her cheek but she turned and kissed him full on the mouth.

"Surely there's no harm in that? I'm not married to George yet."

She collected her hat and put it on, letting the veil down over her face.

"If you knew what the world looks like from behind this horrible stuff," she said, "you would pity me indeed."

He accompanied her out to the green and helped her into the governess-cart. He stood watching her as she turned. Then he waved to her from the gate.

Three weeks later a notice appeared in *The Chardwell Gazette* announcing her marriage to George Winter. The wedding had taken place in London, quietly, from the home of some family friends, and the couple had left immediately, to spend their honeymoon on the Continent.

"Poor Martin," Nan said, calling on him soon afterwards.

"Poor Winter is more to the point, for she will lead him no end of a dance."

CHAPTER
7

During the next few years there were people in the Cullen Valley who deplored the coming of the power-looms and the consequent growth of the woollen industry because of the increased noise from the mills and the greater volume of effluent pouring into the rivers and streams. These complainants, needless to say, were not connected with the woollen trade; but even they recognized that with its growth and prosperity, other trades prospered too. Chardwell in particular, after fifty-odd years of taking second place to Sharveston, was now showing signs of moving ahead, due to the impetus and example provided by one of its native sons, Charles Yuart of Hainault Mill.

Chardwell's superfine broadcloth, out of favour for some time past, had now come into its own again, and at the Great Exhibition of 1851, cloth from three mills in the Chardwell area had been highly commended by the judges, and Hainault Pastello had received a medal. As a result, these four clothiers could rest assured that their best quality broadcloth would be snapped up eagerly by wholesale buyers in London, Manchester, and even Scotland. There was also a very good trade abroad, especially in America.

"You certainly started something, Charles, when you brought the new looms into our midst," Lewis Bakerman said to him. "You stirred us all up and no mistake, and you've put Chardwell on the map."

"Yes, and we must keep it there. Not sit back with folded hands as though there's nothing more to do."

Yuart's attitude to Chardwell was a mixture of scorn and loyal attachment. He often spoke in a scathing way of its narrowness and complacency but took pride nevertheless in his family's long connection with it. This dated from 1705, when his great great grandfather, Pieter Youweerts, coming from Flanders to England, had settled in a cottage in Tub Street and installed two handlooms there. Yuart was proud of the town's traditions and its reputation for fine cloth, and he felt it did not make enough of itself. He was ambitious on its behalf; he wanted to see it grow and develop; and many of his fellow clothiers, respecting him as a man of vision, looked to him as their natural leader, a rôle he accepted without demur. Already, in his early thirties, he was an active member of the Chardwell Chamber of Commerce and of the Cullen Valley Clothiers' Association, and for two years running had occupied a seat on the Borough Council. He was energetic and go-ahead, and, following the recent cholera epidemic, had been tireless in promoting the Board of Health's scheme for giving Chardwell a completely new drainage system and a much improved water supply.

Being the kind of man he was, he had already introduced modern ideas into his own household. There was a bath-room at Railes now; water-closets on both floors; and water, both hot and cold, was piped to all the bedrooms. The new wing had been built by this time, providing billiard-room, gun-room, and smoking-room, with three extra bedrooms above. The staff had been increased, of course, and now included a butler and footman, while his two children, a boy and a girl, had a trio of nursemaids to care for them. There were more horses in the stables and more grooms to look after them. And in the grounds Jobe the gardener had all the help he could require.

Yuart enjoyed spending money. In particular he enjoyed providing those comforts and luxuries which, he felt, were his wife's due, and which, for so many years, she had gone without. That Miss Tarrant of Newton Railes should have acted as governess to her brother and sister and managed the whole household with nothing more than a cook and four maids had, in the days of their courtship, filled him with fierce indignation. It could not be helped, of course: the family fortunes had declined; but he had made up his mind that once Katharine became his wife, all that would be drastically changed, and this promise he had fulfilled. At Saye House, in the first few months of their marriage, she had had everything she could desire. Now she had Newton Railes as well, and although this had come to pass because of a terrible tragedy, Charles could not help feeling that everything had worked out for the best. By marriage Newton Railes was his and he, unlike her late father, was in a position to bring the house, together with its gardens and park, into a state as near perfection as money, time, and care could achieve. This was his greatest gift to her; the one in which he took the most pride.

But there were other gifts as well: expensive jewellery and furs; holidays touring the Continent; a rented house in the West End of London, overlooking the Green Park, where, throughout a fortnight's stay, fresh flowers from Covent Garden were delivered every morning at the door. It needed no special occasion for him to lavish gifts on her. He liked to surprise her at any time. But special occasions were specially marked, and on the fifth anniversary of their marriage, he gave her a carriage of her own: a handsome landau in midnight blue, its panels picked out in silver leaf; and a beautiful pair of thoroughbred bays.

Her sister, calling at Railes that day, viewed the carriage with admiration and was quite openly envious.

"Charles is much more generous with you than George is with me. George is really quite mean sometimes. He questions me about bills and things and is really quite disagreeable."

"I suppose it is not possible that you are sometimes extravagant?"

"Oh, you may tease if you wish, but I didn't marry George just to go short of everything. And you, my dear Kate, are a fine one to talk, for what is this new carriage of yours if not a piece of extravagance?"

"What indeed?" Katharine said.

"The stupid part of it all is that most of these wonderful gifts are only wasted on you," Ginny said.

There was a good deal of truth in this because Katharine's personal tastes, on the whole, were simple, and extravagance for its own sake induced a feeling of guilt in her. She had spoken of this to Charles but he had brushed her objections aside.

"Would you deny me the pleasure of giving you what I think you should have? I am only making up to you for the poverty of your early days."

"We were never so poor as all that. Certainly we never lacked the things that mattered most to us. Our childhood days were happy ones. My father made sure of that."

"Yes. I know. And I intend to make sure that you are even happier now."

Chardwell found him generous, too, and early in 1852, when his father died, he presented Saye House to the township, to be used as a library and reading-room, open to the public, with an art gallery and museum and a number of lecture rooms. At a meeting of the Borough Council, the Mayor, formally accepting the deed of gift and expressing the town's gratitude, proposed that Saye House should be known as the Charles Yuart Institute, and this was agreed unanimously. The Mayor further proposed that the Council should commission a portrait of this, the town's foremost benefactor, which portrait should then be hung in the outer hall of the Institute. This motion, although carried, did not receive a unanimous vote, for there were a few councillors whose admiration for Charles Yuart stopped short of idolatry; who felt indeed that their elderly Mayor was under Charles Yuart's thumb and that as a result the younger man's influence was altogether too strong.

Certainly there was a group, composed chiefly of clothiers, who tended to dominate Council proceedings, and on one notable occasion, Councillor Edward Clayton proposed that "a small sum of money be subvented for purchasing a pack of playing-cards so that those of us at the lower end of the Council table may have some means of passing the time while all the most important decisions are being made at the upper end." Councillor Yuart's response was brief and dry. "It seems we already have the Joker," he said, and *The Chardwell Gazette* later reported that this good-humoured exchange had caused much amusement around the Board.

"Good-humoured be damned!" said Edward, talking to Nan and Martin later. "There's nothing good-humoured in what I feel for Charles Yuart, nor the other way around, and the sooner we have some new blood on the Borough Council the better pleased I shall be."

In the Council elections the following year, Edward Clayton kept his seat; so did Dr David Whiteside; and so too did Charles Yuart, along with three of those clothiers who formed his staunchest following. Martin, twenty-four that year, was one of the new candidates, and to his surprise he was elected: the youngest Councillor, it was said, ever to take his place on the Corporation of that ancient Borough.

"And a good thing, too!" Edward said. "You can help stop the clothmen from running the whole duck shoot!"

One of the subjects under discussion at this time was a scheme proposed by Charles Yuart, for the purchase of a piece of land to be made into a public park, for the recreation of the townspeople. The scheme included a suggestion that the park should be named after the Queen; that a letter should be sent to Her Majesty, requesting her gracious permission; and that with this letter the Council should send a gift of that superfine broadcloth for which Chardwell was noted all over the world. Yuart said that he would be honoured to donate the said bolt of cloth, which would be woven specially on one of the newest Hainault looms.

During the preliminary debate, he had won a fair degree of support for his scheme, but some councillors averred that its chief object was merely to gain the attention of Her

Majesty – known to favour the creation of public parks – and thus promote the clothiers' own private interests. Alderman Lewis Bakerman, of Daisy Bank Mill, retorted that anything promoting the interests of the cloth trade was bound to be for the general good, and that with this particular scheme the townspeople would reap a double benefit, since the park would provide them with much needed amenities, including a band-stand and tennis-courts. Here Councillor Dr Whiteside joined the discussion.

"The amenities you mention are not needed nearly so badly as those which would be provided by the building of a new hospital. This is a subject that has been raised here more than once—"

"Indeed, don't we know it!" somebody said. "And each time you have been reminded that Chardwell already has a hospital."

"Yes, we have a hospital. – A cold, dirty, unhealthy place, formerly a dyeworks. There are just three nurses there, all of them elderly, all untrained, and one almost totally blind. There are bugs in the walls of that hospital and rats in its drains. The place is meant for the poor, of course, but they go there only in dread, knowing they will probably die there. That is what hospital means to them – a place of death."

"Can it not be improved?"

"No amount of improvement would make it adequate to its purpose. What is needed is a hospital built to appropriate specifications, equipped and staffed to meet the needs of our growing population, *not* merely to provide a place where sick people are sent to die, but where, with proper medical treatment and care, they stand some chance of recovering. The recent outbreaks of cholera have shown how ill-equipped we are to deal with any epidemics of a serious nature. They were, I feel, a warning to us, and as Chairman of the Board of Health, I would say this – we ignore that warning at our peril."

Following the doctor's speech there was further discussion, as a result of which it was found that support for each of the two schemes was now roughly equal: seven in favour of the hospital, eight in favour of the public park, with three as yet undecided. Among those supporting the hospital scheme were Edward Clayton and Martin Cox.

"Well, of course, they would, wouldn't they?" said Sidney Hurne, of Brink End Mill. "The one a builder and the other a quarryman? – Obviously it is in their interest to foster a scheme that involves the erection of an expensive building, and I would ask Messrs Clayton and Cox whether they have already calculated their bill-of-costs for the material and work involved?"

Edward, though angry, remained quite calm.

"Anticipating that the matter of cost was bound to be raised at this meeting, yes, I have with me a sheet of figures drawn up by Mr Cox and myself, in consultation with Dr Whiteside, and will pass it round for the Board's perusal."

While the paper went from hand to hand, Edward spoke a few more words.

"At this stage the figures quoted can form only a rough guide but I would like to make two points: that Mr Cox has in fact offered to supply all the building-stone required at cost price and that I have offered my own services as a contractor at a discount of twenty-five per cent. These points are noted at the foot of the page."

A number of councillors murmured their appreciation of this and the Mayor, presiding over the meeting, offered Councillors Clayton and Cox its formal thanks. A moment later the paper was in his hands and he was pursing his lips over it.

"Nevertheless, with all due respect, six thousand pounds is a great deal of money and, bearing in mind that most of it will have to be raised by public subscription, it compares badly with the two thousand five hundred pounds which the public park is expected to cost."

Dr Whiteside answered him.

"Two thousand five hundred pounds spent on something the town does not really need is a greater extravagance, surely, than six thousand pounds spent on something essential to its general health."

The debate continued for some time and was then adjourned so that those few councillors as yet reluctant to commit themselves should have further opportunity to make up their minds. Dr Whiteside suggested that this might well be achieved if the three gentlemen in question were to visit the present Infirmary and see for themselves the shameful conditions prevailing there.

"But I doubt very much if they will," he said, alone with Edward and Martin later. "What will most likely happen is that between now and the next meeting, Yuart will get to work on Fenyon, Hedges, and Samms, and try to win them over to his side. That's what he usually does and more often than not he succeeds."

"In that case," Martin said, "I think we should press for a meeting of the ratepayers and thrash the matter out with them."

"Yes, but think of the time it will take!"

Charles Yuart was much put out that his scheme for creating a public park had not won the Council's full support, but there was little doubt in his mind that he would be able to remedy matters. He spoke of it to Katharine that evening.

"I thought I would ask Joe Samms and his wife to dine with us one evening next week. Then, later, Frank Fenyon. Perhaps you'd select suitable dates."

"I have always had the impression that you disliked Joe Samms and avoided him as much as you could."

"Oh, the man is a lout, certainly. He will make a noise drinking his soup and bore you with the tale of his life. – How he was born the son of a blacksmith and now has the largest ironmongery business in the whole of the Cullen Valley. But just at present I need his support and ... well, it's surprising what an invitation to Railes can do, with men of his sort ... not to mention their good wives."

"Is he opposing the park scheme?"

"No, he hasn't made up his mind. But others are opposing it, among them Edward Clayton, needless to say, and your old friend Martin Cox, who has recently got himself onto the Council."

"Why are they opposing it?"

"Well, Clayton always opposes me as a matter of course, and Cox being his brother-in-law, I suppose he feels bound to do the same."

"That doesn't sound like the Martin I knew. Even as a boy of fifteen he always had a mind of his own. Perhaps he and his brother-in-law support some alternative scheme?"

"Well, naturally, there are other schemes on the agenda just now. Probably half a dozen at least—"

"Including Dr Whiteside's proposal for building a new hospital?"

"Yes. That has come up again."

"Charles, I have something to tell you. Dr Whiteside is quite right. The new hospital is much needed. Ginny and I have been looking into the matter. We went together this afternoon to visit the Infirmary and it is true that conditions there—"

"Katharine! I am very much grieved! You had no business exposing yourself to the risk of infection in that place! As for your sister Ginny – since when has that giddy girl taken an interest in such things? It seems to me she wants something to do!"

"That could be said of both of us."

"You have two children. She has none."

"Both Ginny and I, placed so fortunately as we are, have a great deal of leisure time on our hands, and naturally we both feel we should like to do something useful with it."

"I cannot see that you have achieved anything useful by visiting a place which has obviously caused you great distress."

"Charles, have you ever been there yourself?"

"No, never. Unlike you I do not have a great deal of time on my hands."

"Then let me tell you what it is like—"

"There is no need. I have heard about it often enough from Dr Whiteside."

"Then why do you still oppose him?"

"Because, from what I have heard elsewhere, I've always been given to understand that the doctor is prone to exaggeration."

"In that case, Charles, you have been misled, because if you were to visit the place, you would find that it is not *possible* to exaggerate the conditions in it."

There was a long silence, during which Katharine watched the conflicting emotions at work in him, seen clearly in his face: the angry stare giving way to a frown as his mind reluctantly received the substance of her argument, until in a while his gaze fell and he turned from her with a sharp sigh and a sideways movement of the head, conveying plainly that his anger was now directed towards himself.

"Yes, well," he said at last. "It seems I have been most gravely at fault. I should have done what you have done – informed myself more fully on the matter before taking such a positive stand." He turned again and faced her directly. A wry smile touched his lips. "I'm going to look a rare fool over this, but I have only myself to blame. And I might have been made to look a lot worse – had it not been for your good sense."

Within a few days every member of the Council had been informed by letter that Charles Yuart's views concerning the issue of hospital versus public park had undergone a radical change. He explained himself with great frankness: "I discussed the matter with my wife and as a result of what she said I visited the Infirmary. That, gentlemen, changed my views."

He also let it be known that if the hospital scheme was adopted, he would head the subscription list with a donation of one thousand pounds; and such was the effect of his conversion that when, at the next Council meeting, the motion was put formally to the vote, it was carried nem. con..

Councillor Sidney Hurne then proposed a further motion, which was also carried: that the new hospital should be called The Chardwell and District Victoria Hospital; that a letter should still be sent to the Queen, requesting Her Gracious Majesty's blessing upon the undertaking; and that the letter should, as originally suggested by Councillor Yuart in another connection, be accompanied by a gift of cloth woven in the Cullen Valley. He too signed the subscription list, promising a handsome donation. Councillor Yuart then called for a vote of thanks to Dr Whiteside, Mr Clayton, and those others who, from the very first, had advocated the hospital scheme with such conscientious fervour and zeal.

"It is now up to the rest of us – especially us late recalcitrants – to make such amends as we can by promoting the project with all possible expedition."

"And that," as Dr Whiteside later observed, on leaving the meeting with Martin and Edward: "*that*, my friends, is turning defeat into victory with a vengeance."

"Yes, it's a favourite trick of his," Edward said. "He will soon take over the Project Committee lock, stock, and barrel, you mark my words, and we, along with everyone else, will be left gaping in admiration."

"Well, we shall see," the doctor said. "Definitely I think it better that he should be with us instead of against us. But the one person I would most like to thank is Charles Yuart's wife. I have never met the lady. It's an honour I hope to be granted one day. Perhaps you, Martin, could arrange it for me, since you have I believe some acquaintance with the family."

"Not now," Martin said. "It has fallen into desuetude. I see Mrs Yuart occasionally, driving through the town, and sometimes her sister, Mrs Winter, and they always acknowledge me most pleasantly. But that is all, I'm sorry to say."

"What a pity. I shall have to find some other means of getting to know the lady."

The doctor, being a straightforward man, solved his problem in the simplest way by riding out to the manor house and introducing himself to its mistress. As a result of this meeting, Katharine became a member of the Hospital Building Fund Committee, and was soon actively engaged in organizing fêtes and bazaars, concerts, dances, and lotteries. Thus Martin renewed his acquaintance with her, not only at committee meetings, but often at the functions themselves. Later, at the Grand Midsummer Ball, held during "Hospital Week", he met her sister, Ginny, too, for the first time in almost six years. They were partners in a Scotch Reel and afterwards stood talking together, drinking cool rum-shrub.

"Why is it so long since we met?"

"We move in different circles," he said.

"Well, the circles have impinged at last, and here we are, two old friends, who have left their youth behind them."

"Not the whole of it, I hope."

"You have grown quite mature, anyway. And you have a certain something about you that marks you out from the general run of men. I think, speaking by and large, that you do us credit, Kate and me."

"I'm glad to hear you say so."

"Do you think me changed?"

"Not in the least."

"Which means I must still be pretty, then."

"You don't need to ask me that. Almost all the men here are looking across the room at you. Including your husband."

"Oh!" Ginny said, wrinkling her nose. "Don't spoil things by speaking of George. Husbands are no fit subject for amusing conversation. And I insist on being amused."

"Then I leave it to you to introduce a subject more to your liking."

"There, now! You couldn't have said anything better devised to drive all ideas clean out of my mind."

"That I refuse to believe. I never knew you at a loss before."

"That is what marriage does for one. It stultifies one's brain in the most depressing way and stifles all spontaneity."

"So marriage as a subject of conversation is not taboo, though husbands are?"

"Marriage as a subject for *speculation* offers possibilities and is therefore allowed. You have avoided it so far, though I understand from the gossip I hear that it is not for want of candidates. So tell me, as an old friend, is there not one young lady in this town, or anywhere in the county, capable of engaging your interest?"

"You have set your snare very well. I cannot answer without appearing either a coxcomb or a liar. And neither part appeals to me."

"Well, as tonight is a special occasion, and we are renewing an old friendship, I will dance another dance with you." Ginny set down her empty glass and consulted her card. "The next is free and it is a polka. You are not engaged? Then all is well. We have time for another glass of shrub."

From the far side of the ballroom, Nan and Edward stood watching.

"Oh, what a nuisance it is that *she* should be here tonight, as pretty as ever, and as fascinating! And just this evening of all times when the Chapmans are coming and bringing their niece. Martin and May got on so well when she stayed with them earlier this year and I thought if they were to meet again – There! Look at that! They are dancing together a second time."

"Well, there can't be much danger in it, seeing she is a married woman."

"There is *every* danger that she will revive his feeling for her. Why do you think he's remained unmarried all this time if it is not because of her?"

"Oh, what nonsense!" Edward said. "You speak as if he's a middle-aged man instead of a mere twenty-four. He will marry no doubt, when the spirit moves him, but meanwhile he's a busy man."

"Yes, but why must he always be so busy, making more and more money all the time? What is the point of it? What is it *for*?"

"Martin has a gift for it. It's only right he should exercise it."

*

Martin was certainly busy. He controlled three quarries now, all in a high state of production, and that year had obtained a lease to dig for gravel at Culverstone. There was also his work on the Borough Council, and, stemming from this, other work of a public nature. He took a keen interest in education, especially that of the poorer children, and was active in promoting improvements in the district's free schools. He also took an interest in Pettifor's, Chardwell's ancient grammar school, and was on its board of governers. He had paid for the school house to be enlarged; had donated a plot of land to be used as a playing-field; and, by means of an annual endowment, had provided ten free places for boys from poorer families.

That year, too, he had bought for himself a house called Fieldings, standing in ten acres of garden, a mile or so south of Fordover, just off the turnpike road. It was a Jacobean house, stone-built and in good repair, and needed only refurbishing to satisfy his own taste. The garden, however, was another matter, being full of old neglected trees, many of which had to be felled. So now he had yet another interest, re-planning his ten acres: laying down new lawns, planting new trees and shrubs, and renovating the stone-paved terrace, which work he did himself.

He had an elderly cook-housekeeper, a manservant, and two maids to look after him now, but Nan, a regular visitor, still maintained a watchful eye, just as she had done at Church End. She helped him to choose new furnishings; offered sensible advice on managing his domestic staff; and, whenever he entertained friends, acted as surrogate hostess. She was pleased enough to do this but told him she would be more pleased still when he had found himself a wife who could look after his household and preside at his table in the proper way.

Nan was so happy in her own married life, with her growing number of sons, that she longed to see her only brother settled as happily as herself. Her efforts at matchmaking, however, all ended in disappointment. Time and again she did her best, putting suitable girls in his way, and each time her hopes were high; for Martin was agreeable to them all; took delight in their company and even flirted with this one and that; but—

"Nothing ever comes of it!" she said to Edward despairingly. "And new girls are becoming scarce."

"Well, if there's no one to suit him here, who knows what he may find, travelling in Europe later this year? Perhaps he will bring back a foreign wife."

But this was 1853 and Martin, returning home from Europe, brought only fresh news of the conflict growing between France and Russia; a conflict in which, the following March, Great Britain was also embroiled, allied with France in supporting Turkey against the greed of the mighty Czar.

Soon Chardwell, like the rest of England, was in the grip of patriotic fervour. The fund-raisers were busy again, collecting money to buy comforts for the soldiers suffering in the Crimea, and to help their families at home. At a bazaar held in the Town Hall Martin was talking to Katharine Yuart when her sister Ginny came and joined them. She was wearing a small fur busby and a dark green jacket frogged in gold, *à l'hussar*, and was selling lottery tickets, collecting the money in a round box painted to look like a military drum.

"I hear you have bought Fieldings and are turning it into something very fine. It seems you must be very well off."

"If it seems so, then so it must seem."

"Come, now! You're a rich man. Why not own up to it?" Ginny said.

Martin, with a smile, put a coin in her hand.

"Very well, I'm a rich man, though poorer now by a sovereign," he said.

"That is very generous. I hope you may win the prize."

"What is it?"

"A basket of mulberries from the old tree at Railes. In the Tudor garden – do you remember? I was there early this morning, helping Katharine to pick them."

"Ah, well, if I win *that*, I shall think myself rich indeed."

"Why, Martin!" Ginny exclaimed. "I do believe you have just been gallant."

"I believe I have," he said equably. "My education must be complete."

He did not win the lottery but next day a basket of mulberries was delivered at Fieldings with a note.

"Consolation prize," it said, and was signed Katharine Yuart.

Two years of war brought extra profits to the woollen mills in the Cullen Valley and one clothier at least was said to have made a fortune by producing flannel for soldiers' shirts and coarse serge for their overcoats. Whether this was true or not, the trade in general continued to prosper, and with the welcome return to peace, various projects were revived. Chardwell, rejoicing in its prosperity, spent freely, and towards the end of that decade had much to be proud of. Its hospital was one of the best equipped in the west of England; the town's streets had been greatly improved and were now lit by gas; and expensive restoration work had been carried out on St Benet's Church.

In 1859 there was a scheme afoot to build a fine new Town Hall on a site endowed by a former mayor, but by now voices were heard expressing some anxiety. There were hints that the present prosperous period might be coming to an end. Wool at this time was very expensive and Gloucestershire clothiers, raising the price of their cloth, lost sales to their Yorkshire brethren who produced the lighter, cheaper worsteds. Some of the Cullen Valley clothiers, still paying off the loans by which they had purchased their power-looms, ten or twelve years before, were seriously worried.

Their worries were soon made worse by news of events in America, where, it was feared, the growing unrest would affect trade between the two countries. This fear was substantiated when America imposed a heavy tariff on cloth imported from England. A number of clothiers ceased production and sold up, lock, stock, and barrel, to avoid the threat of bankruptcy. Mills and plant were sold at a loss and in most cases the mill buildings were adapted to different industries. One became a paper mill; two ground corn; and another manufactured flock. A fifth mill, at Belfray, was bought by Martin, who let it to a friend named George Ainley, formerly a shearman at Daisy Bank. Ainley, eschewing traditional broadcloth, set about making the lightweight worsteds and knaps so popular now with tailors and cutters.

"That is where the future lies," he said to Martin. "Broadcloth is a thing of the past. It costs too much to make and customers won't pay the price. They want a bit of variety, too, such as Yorkshire is offering. And I am taking a leaf out of the Yorkshireman's pattern-book!"

Ainley's views were well known and his warnings discussed throughout the Cullen Valley. Even some of the bigger clothiers were made nervous by the state of the trade and some, remembering the slump of '40s, decided to retrench. Others talked of following Ainley's example and giving in to the demand for cheaper cloth. But braver spirits rejected these expediencies and Charles Yuart was one of them.

"These trends come and go. We've seen it happen time and again. We've also seen depressions in trade. But always the best quality cloth has risen above these difficulties and come out on top. Gentlemen, *it will happen again*."

To demonstrate his faith in the future, Yuart bought three looms from Lewis Bakerman, who was cutting down, and a steam engine from Joseph Dunne. He was buying top quality wool and making more cloth than ever before, and while other clothiers were reducing their work-force, Yuart's remained at full strength.

"There will be no men laid off at Hainault Mill," he said, and this popular speech was reported in *The Chardwell Gazette*, along with an announcement that Mr Yuart had been invited to stand as Conservative candidate for Chardwell and the Cullen Valley in the forthcoming bye election and that he had formally agreed to do so. He would stand against

Mr Wyatt Jones, representing the Liberal interest.

Edward Clayton, discussing this item of news with Martin, weighed Yuart's prospects of success in carving out a career for himself in public affairs.

"If his optimistic predictions for trade are correct, he will be riding on the crest of a wave. But if they should turn out to be wrong—"

A few weeks later, in the same paper, it was announced that Mr Yuart of Hainault Mill had with regret been obliged, for reasons of a private nature, to withdraw himself from the candidature.

Martin, when he read this report, could guess what the private reasons were because by now there were cogent rumours that all was not well with Charles Yuart. The present depression in trade, together with the heavy duty imposed by America on English cloth, had affected the whole of the Cullen Valley, but Yuart, running his mill to capacity, was now suffering worse than most. Not only was he losing his American sales but, in the disturbances in Virginia, a huge consignment of his cloth, waiting to be shipped back to him, had been burnt in a warehouse at Perry Springs. At Hainault, now, only three of his looms were at work, and even this, rumour stated, was merely an act of stubborn defiance. When his stock of wool ran out, Hainault Mill would fall silent. How long for, no one could tell.

Martin heard all these things and feared they were true. And, thinking of Katharine Yuart, he was filled with anxiety for her.

Some five months later, on a wet morning in April, Charles Yuart stood at the window of his solicitor's office, looking out at the traffic in Bold Street. He was smoking a cigarette, and the hand that held it trembled palpably. Behind him, Alec Stevenson sat at his desk, studying a number of papers and making notes from them. Eventually, he laid three of the papers out before him, and tidied the rest into a pile. Yuart turned and looked at him; came and sat in the visitor's chair;

and stubbed his cigarette out in the ash-tray.

"Well?" he said, in a harsh voice.

"This is a bad business, Charles."

"How bad, precisely?"

"It could not be worse. I've been through the figures supplied by your own accountant, Mr Verney, and those supplied by your creditors, and altogether they make sorry reading."

"You mean I'm ruined."

"It's not a word I care to use, especially to an old friend, but—"

"It's true all the same."

"I'm afraid it is." Stevenson studied Yuart's face, watching the colour drain from it. But, distressed though he was on his friend's behalf, he did not mince his words. "If only you had come to me when you first began to run into trouble, something might have been done about it, and you might still have been in business. Trade has been slack for two years or more but you have ignored all the signals – buying wool you couldn't pay for and making cloth you couldn't sell. You've even bought extra looms and made costly changes in your spinning-shop. But in addition to all this I am bound to say that there has been a great deal of extravagance of a private and personal nature."

"Not lately, there hasn't. I've been economizing in every way possible. I've sold most of the horses at Railes. I've reduced the staff—"

"Those economies came too late. I am talking about the past. I'm sorry, Charles, but the truth is you've been living beyond your means for years. You have also been over-generous in making donations to good causes. Now, in the last year or two, you have had a run of back luck. But this cloth at Perry Springs – even if it had come safely home, with trade here as it is at present, I doubt if you could have sold it even at a knock-down price."

"I know that. I have reason to know. I'd be glad if you would stick to the point."

"Very well." Stevenson consulted his notes. "To put it bluntly, your debts are enormous, especially for wool. Thirteen thousand and three hundred pounds to Burrows and Oates. Nineteen thousand to Pirrie and Son. Your coal account stands at twelve hundred pounds and you still owe five hundred on the steam engine you bought from Dunne. Repairs to the dam ... and the dyehouse furnace ... and certain sums you have borrowed here and there... Five thousand pounds from your brother-in-law, Mr George Winter, and a further three thousand from Henry Preece. Then there are the domestic bills... Rent on the house in Coniston Square... Wine merchant's and grocer's bills..."

"How much do I owe altogether?"

"Upwards of forty-three thousand pounds."

"Shall I have to go through the bankruptcy court? You said you hoped it could be avoided."

"Yes. I think we may be able to negotiate a private agreement with your creditors. I've already sounded one or two and I think there's a good chance they'll agree. Now we come to the subject of your assets, most of which, inevitably, are somewhat problematical. Your warehouse is stacked to the roof with cloth. Its value two years ago would have covered your debts and left you solvent but today it is practically worthless. It will have to go to the auctioneers and in present conditions I doubt very much if it will fetch five thousand pounds. Then, of course, there is the mill."

Again Stevenson consulted his notes; not because he needed to, but so as to avoid Yuart's gaze.

"According to Verney's estimate, and that of Mr Meed, acting as adviser to your creditors, the mill and its machinery may with luck realize something between three and four thousand pounds."

"With *luck*, did you say?" Yuart spoke savagely, and Stevenson, obliged to look up, saw that his face was darkly suffused. "D'you know what I spent on that new extension? The cost of building alone was close upon seventy thousand pounds, without the plant, and now, together with the old buildings and all the improvements I've made on them, Hainault Mill as a whole must be worth twice that at the very least."

"Not today, Charles, as you well know. A mill is only worth whatever it will fetch at auction and no man at a time like this will lumber himself with a place like Hainault. Its very size goes against it. You must surely see that."

Yuart made no answer. Stevenson returned to his notes.

"Last of the items listed here are a few sums owing to you, which, if we can get them paid, amount to nearly three thousand pounds. So, the estimated value of your assets so far is some twelve thousand pounds. If realized in full – and that is doubtful – it means that your creditors can expect to receive seven shillings in the pound."

Stevenson laid down his notes and sat back in his chair. After a while he spoke again.

"There is of course one more realizeable asset we have not yet mentioned."

"Yes," Yuart said, "Newton Railes." He drew a deep, quivering breath. "Can they make me sell that? The estate came to me through my wife."

"Nevertheless, by law it is yours. You know that as well as I do. And certainly they can make you sell it. Being offered only seven shillings in the pound, they are within their rights to press for more. And in the bankruptcy court there would be no question whatsoever but that the estate should be sold. If, however, your creditors agree to a private arrangement, and I'm sure they will, there is just a possibility that they may be lenient. They are almost all Chardwell men and when I lay the full facts before them I shall, with your permission, of course, remind them that you have done a great deal for this town and been very generous over the years. For one thing, when your father died, you gave Saye House to the Borough, and all its amenities are enjoyed by a great number of people. Whenever money has been needed for worthwhile projects, you have always been one of the first to put his hand into his pocket. You have also been an able and energetic Councillor and a leading light in the Clothiers' Association. I shall also remind these gentlemen of the benefit we have all derived from your energy and example in promoting our most important trade, which, in recent times, has brought Chardwell to the fore and given it a name known all over the world."

"Do you expect to influence them?"

"Well, here again I have already sounded one or two, and from their response I would say there's a chance. They know Newton Railes is your wife's old family home, and as the Tarrants have always been highly esteemed in the district, that is another point which may count in your favour."

"Am I to attend the meeting on Friday?"

"I think, if I'm to plead on your behalf, it would be better if you were not there."

"Very well. Let's hope you are right."

The two men rose and Stevenson accompanied Charles to the door. They shook hands and Charles said:

"If only we can save Railes – well, you'll do what you can, I'm sure of that."

"How much have you told your wife? Does she know the seriousness of your position?"

"Yes. Oh, yes. She knows full well."

When he got home, Katharine was waiting for him in the morning-room. A tray, with tantalus and glasses, lay on the table, and, the day being wet and cheerless, a good fire burnt in the grate. Charles poured himself a brandy, drank half, and came to stand in front of the fire. Katharine looked up at him.

"Is it as bad as you feared?"

"Yes. Worse, if anything, because until now I have been hoping—" He broke off and gave a shrug. "Hoping for a miracle, I suppose." He drank the rest of his brandy and put the glass on the mantelpiece. "I'm ruined, Kate. The mill and everything I've worked to achieve – it's all to be thrown away for nothing. I'm to be beggared. Stripped to the bone.

Everything will have to go."

"Oh, my dear!" She rose and went close to him, to take his hands into her own and to hold them an instant against her face. "How cold you are. You're trembling. Let me get you another drink."

She took down the glass and went to refill it at the tray. She brought it to him and watched him drink. A small sharp shiver went through him, but the brandy was already taking effect, and some slight suggestion of colour could be seen returning to his face. For a while they stood in silence together, close to each other, in front of the fire. Then he leant forward and kissed her cheek; put aside his glass once more; and told her of Stevenson's hope that his creditors would probably agree to a private settlement of his affairs.

"And will you be able to pay your debts?"

"Well, not the whole, of course. That's what is so damnable. I am forced to sell my very soul and all my creditors are likely to get is seven shillings in the pound! Whereas if they would only give me time – time for trade to pick up again – I could perhaps pay them in full."

"Seven shillings? Is that all?" Katharine looked at him, appalled. "Even with the sale of the house?"

"I'm hoping the house will not have to be sold. Stevenson thinks there's a good chance that my creditors will not press for it. He intends appealing to them, reminding them that I've done a great deal for my home town, one way or another, and that it has good reason to be grateful for my generosity in the past. He feels that it is only right that they should be generous in return."

"Do you agree with him?" Katharine asked. "Have you sanctioned this appeal?"

"Well, I don't much care for the thought of humbling myself to these men but certainly, as Stevenson says, I *have* done a great deal for the town and *given* a great deal, too. And if the only way of keeping Railes is to throw myself on their mercy, then obviously that's what I must do, and swallow my pride as best I can. Stevenson intends to reinforce his appeal by reminding them that Railes is your old family home. And I should be very surprised, not to say disgusted, if Pirrie and the rest of them were to force the sale of this estate, which has been in your family for so many years."

There was a silence in the room. Katharine returned to her seat on the sofa. She sat looking up at him.

"You have spoken of swallowing your pride. But it's not only *your* pride that's at stake. It's mine as well."

"I'm not sure that I take your meaning."

"Charles," Katharine said, vehemently, "surely you can't possibly consider keeping Railes when it means asking your creditors to be satisfied with so small a proportion of their dues?"

For a long moment he stared at her, an angry flush darkening his face.

"Small proportion it may be but at least *they* will still be in business whereas I shall not!" Then, seeking to gain command of himself, he went on: "This is our home. Under the terms of your father's will, your brother Hugh being dead, it came to you, and thereby to me, and in due course it will go to our son. It is only right that it should. You of all people must feel that! And what is my son going to say to me if I tell him I'm selling Newton Railes which is *his* by every expectation and right?"

"Dick is almost thirteen. He is an intelligent boy. He also has a sense of honour. What will he say if you tell him that you intend keeping Railes while leaving your debts unpaid?"

"Are you trying to suggest that by keeping Railes I should be guilty of a dishonourable act?"

"I think, because of what has happened, and the shock of it all, you are not seeing things quite as you should."

"Indeed?"

"For instance, what are your plans for the future, now that you know you must leave Hainault?"

"I shall have to find work, of course. Probably running another man's mill!"

"And how much will you earn by that?"

"Precious little, I assure you!"

"Then how can we possibly afford to stay here in this house?" she asked, and, when he failed to answer her: "Charles, there is another thing. Supposing, when your creditors meet, they should *reject* Mr Stevenson's appeal? How will you feel then? – You will wish it had never been made. You will feel ashamed. Humiliated, even. And, if it matters to you at all, so should I."

"From all you have just said to me, it seems that *you* would feel ashamed even if the appeal were to be successful."

"Yes. I should. I could never live happily here again, under such circumstances."

Watching her husband's face, and the painful struggle visible in it, Katharine could read his every thought; could feel, in her own heart, all the anguish he felt in his; and she thought how hard it was for a man, at times like this, that he should be denied the relief of tears. Presently he spoke again and his voice, though strained, was under control.

"You have no wifely qualms, it seems, at forcing my hand in this way. But no doubt you will say that it is the circumstances that force my hand, not you, and that they are of my own making. Well, you are right, of course. But that knowledge, I would point out, doesn't make it any easier to bear."

"I wish there were something I could do, or say, that *would* make it easier to bear."

"I wish it too. But there is nothing. I'm going back to Stevenson now. I will tell him I've talked matters over with you and that as a result we have decided that Railes must be offered for sale. Then, later, when I return, I shall have the painful duty of breaking the news to Dick and Susannah."

"Would it help," Katharine asked, "if I were to speak to them first?"

"Yes," he said, "I think it would."

CHAPTER 8

Martin had been abroad for a month, travelling on the Continent. When he stepped from the train at Chardwell station, almost the first thing he saw was a board with two posters on it. One announced the forthcoming sale of Hainault Mill, the other the sale of Newton Railes. Each property was to be sold by auction, without reserve, unless previously sold by private treaty.

Outside, in the station yard, he hired a fly. But he did not go straight home to Fieldings. Instead he went down into the town to call on Sampson Godwin, formerly his guardian, still his solicitor and close friend.

The following morning, at eleven o'clock, Alec Stevenson was shown into the study at Railes, where Charles Yuart sat writing letters. At Stevenson's request, the servant was sent with a message to Katharine, asking her to join them there. When she and the two men were seated together, Stevenson explained the reason for his visit.

"I have asked you to be present, Mrs Yuart, because what I have to say concerns you both, though it may not at first be obvious." He then addressed himself to Charles. "I have been approached by a certain gentleman who has offered to buy Hainault Mill, together with all its machinery, etc., by private treaty, at a price to be agreed, and to let it to you on a three-year lease, at a rent also to be agreed, so that you may resume operations there and begin normal trading again."

Yuart stared. He answered curtly.

"Kind of him, whoever he is, but if he is acquainted with my circumstances, as he surely must be, he will know that I have no money to resume operations, nor any hope of obtaining it at the present time."

"The gentleman is aware of that and is willing to advance you the sum of two thousand pounds for the purpose, which sum you will repay when the state of your business enables you to do so."

"Who is this gentleman?" Yuart asked sharply.

"Before answering that question I must, further, inform you that the same gentleman wishes to buy Newton Railes, together with its contents, and has made a specific offer for it."

"Very well. You have informed us. Pray go on."

"He offers twenty thousand pounds for the estate, which sum comprises fifteen thousand pounds for the land and five thousand pounds for the house. He will also buy such of the contents as you are obliged to sell, at a figure to be agreed, subject to independent evaluation."

Charles and Katharine sat silent and still. Stevenson spoke again.

"It is a very generous offer."

"I don't know that it is," Charles said. "It is certainly higher than the figure you thought Railes would fetch, which makes me wonder whether your other estimates might also be wrong. If this one anonymous buyer is prepared to pay more than you expected, perhaps there are others who would pay more still. My own feeling is, therefore, that this gentleman should take his chance at auction, along with everyone else. Perhaps after all, Hainault, with its plant, together with the cloth in my warehouse, may fetch something approaching their true value, in which case I should not only be able to pay off my debts in full but have something left over at the end of it."

"That possibility is so remote, it is not even worth considering. With trade so badly depressed as it is, men are only buying property where it can be had dirt-cheap. You know as well as I do, Charles, that if Newton Railes goes under the hammer, it could be knocked down to this same buyer for as little as eight or nine thousand pounds."

"Is he aware of that?"

"Certainly. He is no fool. But he has offered a higher figure, knowing that your creditors are sure to accept it, which means that you and your family will be spared the distress of the auction."

"Do I have any say in the matter at all?"

"Regarding the mill, yes, you do, because he will purchase that *only* if you wish to take up the option of renting it from him. Otherwise he has no interest in it. Regarding the estate, well, your views and those of Mrs Yuart will be put to the creditors, of course, and will, I am sure, receive the fullest consideration. But, as I have already said, they are certain to favour acceptance of this generous offer because failure to do so would almost certainly be to their disadvantage."

"In other words, this discussion is only a mere formality."

"The formalities *do* have to be observed."

"And the name of this well-meaning gentleman?"

"Mr Martin Cox."

Yuart's face remained impassive, but it was some time before he could speak.

"Cox has offered to buy Hainault and lend me two thousand pounds to remain in it as his tenant. Why, I wonder?"

"Out of the concern and goodwill he feels for Mrs Yuart."

"Ah, yes. Quite so. Also perhaps because old habits die hard. Rufus Cox was something of a money-lender, I believe, and it seems the son is following in his father's footsteps. Well, regarding his offer to buy Hainault, the answer is no. I have no intention of selling myself in bondage to Martin Cox or anyone else. Regarding Newton Railes, however, I would like to discuss the matter with my wife, even though, once again, it is merely a formality. I will let you have our decision by the end of the day."

He rang for the maid to show Stevenson out.

*

"Martin Cox!" Yuart said when he and Katharine were alone together. "Strange how that quarryman's son keeps cropping up in our lives."

"Yes," Katharine said, absently, looking at him across the desk. But then, collecting her thoughts, she said: "And yet not so very strange after all, for whatever your feelings may be towards him, I and my own family have always regarded him as a friend."

"I confess I have never understood why you should hold him in such regard. As I myself see the matter, he was a cunning jackanapes who wormed his way into this house years ago and ingratiated himself with you all, especially with your sister, Ginny."

"No, Charles, it was not like that. Papa owed Rufus money and Rufus allowed him time to pay. In return, Martin came to have lessons with us, and that is how we became friends."

"However it was, you were kind to him, and in return for that kindness he would now turn you out of your home."

"That, I feel, is unreasonable. We have offered the house for sale. Martin wishes to buy it. And Mr Stevenson considers that the sum he offers is generous."

"Generous it may be, but only my creditors will benefit from it!"

Katharine was silent and he, seeing the look in her eyes, was stricken with shame.

"I know! I know! I ought not to have said that! But the present condition of my mind is not conducive to feelings of gratitude or reasonableness. I don't much like being pitied. Nor do I like being patronized with offers of help from Martin Cox. I suppose I'll get used to these things in time but until I do I must ask you to – to bear with me as best you can. As for this offer Cox has made, I take it you wish me to accept it."

"Yes. I do. Martin is quite right – I'd be glad to be spared the auction sale."

"You wouldn't have had to witness it. We should have gone from the place by then. But I understand your feelings, of

course. Even the thought of an auction here... People
tramping over the house ... poking into every cupboard, and
handling every ornament ... At least if we sell to Martin Cox
we shall be spared all that. I suppose I ought to be grateful
to him but all I can feel at the moment is – Oh, God, I don't
know! That *I* should have brought you to such a pass! It is
really more than I can bear!"

There was agony in his voice. His face was contorted, his
fists tight-clenched. He sprang from his chair and crossed the
room, to stand in front of the empty hearth, his back to her,
his shoulders hunched.

"When I think of the plans I had! All the things I meant to
do. I wanted to make myself worthy of you. To make myself
the sort of man that you and our children could be proud of.
I hoped to make a career for myself. Go into Parliament. Get
things done. What, I wonder, is wrong with ambition, that all
my hopes should come to naught? That I should have lost not
only the mill and everything I began with, but even this, your
beloved home, which has been in your family ever since it was
first built! I can't forgive myself for that. I shall *never* forgive
myself. To fall so low and to bring *you* so low! A failure. A
bankrupt. Destitute!"

Katharine rose and went to him. She put her hand on his
arm.

"Charles, we are not destitute. We have each other and we
have our two children. You are still a young man. You have
energy, knowledge, experience. There is still a place for you
somewhere in the cloth trade. It is a question of beginning
again."

"The bottom rung!"

"Well, why not? Other men have begun there, *and* got to
the top of the ladder, and a great number of those men did
not have your advantages."

Charles turned to look at her. His face, though drawn, was
calmer now. He placed his hand over hers, where it lay on his
arm.

"So long as you still have faith in me, I feel I can do almost anything. Though how I find a place in the trade after what has happened to me I cannot at present begin to conceive."

"Charles," Katharine said, in a tentative way. "Will you not even consider accepting Martin's offer of help? I mean his offer to buy the mill and lend you the money to run it again. It seems as though you suspect his motives but I know him better than you do and I wish I could persuade you—"

"No, Katharine! You may save your breath. You heard my answer to Stevenson. Nothing will ever budge me from that. Not even your persuasions. And that is my final word."

"I don't understand," Katharine said, "why you should dislike him so much."

"All the things I dislike about him have been made manifest by the fact that he wants to buy Newton Railes. He is an upstart. A parvenu. Furthermore, he's a hypocrite who supports the working-man's franchise yet sets himself up as a gentleman. And it is quite bad enough that he should take our home from us without my putting myself in a position that would give him power over me. Though as to this business of his buying Railes … there's many a slip twixt cup and lip and he could be disappointed yet."

"What do you mean?"

"Well, whatever Stevenson may say, there is always the possibility that someone else may come forward privately with an offer superior to his. It wouldn't do for my creditors to be over-hasty in accepting Martin Cox's figure, and when I write to Stevenson I shall make that point to him."

As events turned out, however, it was Yuart's own hopes that were disappointed, for his creditors, learning of Martin's offer, urged immediate acceptance lest by chance it should be withdrawn. The transaction was therefore put in hand. Shortly afterwards Hainault Mill, with all its stock and appointments-in-trade, was sold at auction without reserve. The purchaser was Oliver Hurne, who put his son Sidney in charge of it, which meant that the Hurnes, who still held Brink End, were now the biggest cloth manufacturers in the whole of the Cullen Valley.

In due course, the sale of his assets being completed, Yuart was able to pay his creditors fifteen shillings and threepence in the pound. The deed of composition was discharged; his business affairs were wound up; and, for the first time in his life, he became a man who had neither property nor occupation. All he had left in the world was a small sum of money realized from the sale of his wife's jewellery.

On a rainy morning in early July, he and his family moved into a cottage in Cryer's Row, at the bottom of Tack House Lane, in the lower part of Chardwell. They took with them such furniture as was suited to their new home: "the bare essentials," Dick said bleakly, speaking to his sister, Susannah; though there were in fact two items that were not purely utilitarian: the upright piano and the Welsh harp that had stood in their old music-room. Everything else had been left behind, sold to Martin Cox for the sum of two thousand, five hundred pounds.

"I wonder what he's like," Susannah said.

"Mother says we met him once, years ago, at Chacelands, when aunt Ginny held that fête in aid of the patriotic fund."

"I don't remember meeting him."

"Neither do I. It's too long ago."

Charles studied the local papers, but every week it was the same: there was nothing in the list of situations vacant that he could even consider taking. Millman wanted at Daisy Bank, twenty-one shillings a week. Clerk wanted at Longsides, nineteen shillings a week. Shearmen were wanted. And sorters, of course. But nobody wanted a manager.

Six weeks passed in this way and then he received a note from George Ainley of Kendall's Mill, who said he wanted an overseer and asked Charles to call on him to discuss the work and the salary. Kendall's was a small mill, three miles away, at Belfray, where Ainsley, formerly a shearman, had set himself up making lightweight worsteds and cheap coarse tweeds. His venture so far had been a success and recently, in a cautious way, he had extended his operations.

"I'm doing my own spinning now and as I can't be everywhere I need another pair of eyes. The job is yours if you want it and I'll pay you a hundred pounds a year."

"Very well. I accept. But it's not what I hoped for and I think it only right to say that as soon as something better offers I shall ask to be released."

"That's easy enough, Mr Yuart. A month's notice on either side. Now if you'll step along with me, I'll show you what we're doing here."

"What it amounts to," Charles said, savagely, to Katharine at home, "is that I shall be doing a manager's work for less than one sixth of what it's worth, yet to hear the way Ainley talked, you'd think he was doing me a favour."

His bitterness knew no bounds and when, at the end of his first day, Katharine asked how he had got on, his answer was curt.

"I do not wish to talk of it."

But one evening, on coming home, he flung some small samples of cloth upon the table in front of her.

"That, it may interest you to know, is the rubbish I help to make at Kendall's Mill, and which George Ainley calls cloth! 'Kendall's Suiting', he calls it, and it's no better than sackcloth!"

Still, at least he was in employment, which meant they could now afford a maid, and although Katharine protested that in this new home of theirs she and Susannah could manage perfectly well by themselves, Charles remained adamant. He would not have his wife and daughter doing the rough work of the house; nor would he listen to Katharine's suggestion that she might give piano lessons to supplement their income.

"I have brought you low enough – I certainly won't let you stoop to that."

"But I would enjoy doing it. And may I not be allowed to help? Surely, in our present position, we need to do everything

we can if you are ever to have the chance of renting a mill of
your own."

"Katharine, have you any idea how long it would take to
save enough money for that?"

"No. I only know it will take longer if we spend money on
things we don't need."

"The cost of a girl to help in the house is neither here nor
there," he said. "It is not even worth thinking about. As to this
question of your giving piano lessons, I wonder that you can
even suggest it. Perhaps the next thing I shall hear is that you
are thinking of taking in washing!"

For the two children, Dick and Susannah, the change that
had taken place in their lives was often difficult to bear. Dick,
removed from Scanfield College, now attended Pettifor's,
the old Chardwell Grammar School, and although he liked
it well enough, he was not making friends with the other
boys. This fact he confided to Katharine when she questioned
him in private once.

"The Head Master is a splendid man. No end of a scholar,
and a sportsman too. The trouble is the other fellows. They
keep making remarks all the time, about Petty's being a
come-down for me after being at Scanfield. Ryeland is always
doing it. 'We know it's not what you're used to,' he says, 'but
you'll just have to make the best of it.' And the stupid thing
is that it's simply not true. Petty's is every bit as good a
Scanfield. Even better in some ways."

"Then why not tell them so?" Katharine said.

"D'you think I should?"

"Certainly, if it is true."

Susannah had never gone to school; she had always had a
governess; now, of course, her mother taught her and this
arrangement pleased them both. But she, like Dick, found it
hard to adapt to their new life in Tack House Lane. The
cottage, though of "superior" size, was nevertheless very
small after Railes. The rooms were pokey, dark, and ill-
arranged, and their neighbours' voices could be heard

through the walls. There was no garden whatsoever; only a small paved yard at the back, shared with two other cottages; and always there was the noise of the town.

Tack House Lane was busy with traffic making its way to and from Fleet Mills; there was also the noise of the mills themselves: the heavy thud of the fulling-stocks echoing along the valley, and that conglomerate of sounds issuing from the steam-engines, the spinning-machines and the power-looms, the rushing of water over the weirs and the clatter of the waterwheels, along with the hubbub of people at work which together made up the "Cullen Hum".

This phrase had a double meaning, as Dick and Susannah soon discovered, for, even worse than the constant noise were the smells that all too often arose when effluent from the stocks and troughs was released into the rivers and streams. One was the smell of scalding-hot water in which the raw wool had been washed; the other was the smell of scalding hot "sig" in which the finished cloth had been scoured; and sig, the children learnt with horror, was urine collected from the town privies.

"Hainault never smelt like that," Susannah said indignantly; but, as her brother pointed out, no mill-man was ever allowed to empty his stocks while there were visitors at the mill. "Well, I don't know how the people bear it who have to *work* with such a smell."

The children found plenty to grumble about during these first weeks in the cottage, but they never grumbled when their father was present, for their mother had forbidden it.

"Papa has been under great stress and strain this twelvemonth past, and is still so now. You must not add to his burden by showing that you are unhappy here."

"Some of the fellows at school say it was papa's own fault that he failed as he did. Is that true, mama?"

"Your father made mistakes," Katharine said. "There's been a decline in trade, as you know, and he misjudged how long it would last."

"Pollard said that *his* father lost money when papa failed. Mr Pollard did some work repairing the dam at Hainault last year and never got paid in full."

"Are the boys still unfriendly towards you?"

"No. Not really. Not any more. I think in a way they feel sorry for me."

"Oh, how beastly," Susannah said.

The one bright gleam in their lives at this time was when their aunt Ginny came in the carriage and took them back to Chacelands with her. Ginny hated seeing her sister living in the cottage in Cryer's Row. It was more than she could bear.

"I wish you would let me speak to George about your coming to live with us. I'm quite sure he'd agree to it, for he feels as angry as I do at the thought of your living in this place."

"No, Ginny, it will not do. Even if George agreed, Charles most certainly would not. It isn't only a matter of pride. They have quarrelled badly, as you know."

"Oh, yes, I know all that! Just because George lent Charles some money and only got two thirds of it back. As though money mattered a fig! But George can be very mean sometimes. He has an unforgiving streak. I wanted him to buy Railes and let you go on living there but he wouldn't even consider it."

"Of course he wouldn't," Katharine said. "You should never have suggested such a thing."

"I don't know which I hate the most – Charles for losing Newton Railes or Martin Cox for buying it."

"Somebody had to buy it, Ginny."

"Yes. And I should hate them whoever they were. But Martin Cox of all people! That, I think, is the worst cut of all."

Martin had not taken possession of Railes immediately on receipt of the deeds because he had been ill with influenza, which had kept him in bed for some days and house-bound at Fieldings for another week. Thus, he had only barely recovered when, on a morning in mid July, he drove out to the old manor house and saw it for the first time as its owner.

The servants, who gathered in the kitchen at his request, were those he remembered from early days, for the butler and footman employed by Yuart during his early affluence had been dismissed, together with housekeeper, governess, and lady's maid, at the onset of his recent declension. So it was Cook and the older maids, with Jobe the gardener and Sherard the groom, who stood in a row, with expressionless faces, to hear what Martin had to say to them.

"I know how you must be feeling about the change of ownership here and it may be that you will find it too difficult to accept. If so, I shall quite understand. But my own personal wish is to make as few changes as possible. Therefore I hope you will stay."

They looked at him; then at each other; and it was Cook, downright as always, who took it upon herself to speak.

"It's true we don't like what's happened here. It's no good pretending otherwise. But Mrs Yuart asked us to stay on and look after you, and it seems that's what we'd better do, whether we like it or not. Besides, where should I go at my time of life? Who would want an old body like me? I've been in this house thirty-four years. I came the year Miss Katharine was born. And I had thought, in recent times, that I should serve her till I died." Here the old woman's lip trembled, but in a moment she recovered herself and went stubbornly on. "As it turns out, that's not to be, but at least I can still serve the house. And if that means serving you, Mr Cox, I give you my word I shall do it to the best of my ability. And so will these girls here."

Martin then looked at the two men.

"Ah," said Jobe. "Same as Cook."

"Me, too, ditto," said Jack Sherard. "At least for the time being, like."

Martin's illness had been severe, and as he walked about the house and gardens, he found it difficult to decide whether the queer, light-headed feeling that assailed him every now and then was due to the after-effects of flu or to the not-quite-believable fact that everything he saw was now his. There was the rarefied sense of elation; the feeling that he was not of this world, even though, at the same time, he felt he held the world in his hands. There was the sense of subtle refinement that so often comes with recuperation after illness, when all the perceptions are so delicately heightened that every detail of what is seen is felt to the very depths of the soul and is almost unbearably beautiful.

Pale sunshine, slanting into the great hall, through the leaded panes of the bay window. A Venetian vase set, empty, on a polished table, where it caught the light in its green-crackled glass. A shallow bowl made of beaten copper, filled with dried gourds of the palest colours: melon, yellow, and apple green. And, on the chest by the foot of the stairs, an earthenware jug full of sweet peas, pink, blue, and white, imparting their pure scent to the air.

It was thirteen years since he had last set foot in this house but, excepting only Yuart's new wing, built in 1849, little was changed. In the great hall, most certainly, the old heavy furniture stood ranged about much as it had always done: the oakboard table and joint stools; the high-backed settle, the wainscot chairs; the court cupboard under the staircase; the tall cased clock on the half-landing: he remembered them all from early days and now, amazingly, they were his. Not only the furniture but the carpets, the curtains, the tapestries; the pictures and portraits on the walls; the family silver, the china, the glass; even the books in the library. All were his.

But with the elation there was also a sadness that touched him through and through with pain, because everywhere, in every room, there were so many things that spoke to him of those who had recently departed. In the drawing-room, especially, the Broadwood piano spoke to him of Katharine Yuart, for the green-covered stool was drawn up to it, the lid was raised from the keyboard, and a piece of music stood on the stand. It was a Chopin étude and Martin well remembered how, hearing it for the first time, played on the piano in the music-room upstairs, he had declared it to be the most beautiful piece of music ever written. Had Miss Katharine remembered that? And was the music left here now as a sign to him of her forgiveness? He thought it was, and received it as such; but it did nothing to lessen the pain; for he was reminded of the ancient custom whereby a victim on the scaffold forgave his executioner.

From room to room he went, following the ghosts of the past, and so out to the rear courtyard, where he stood gazing at the end of the kitchen wing, rebuilt after the fire in which Hugh Tarrant had died trying to save the maid, Alice Hercombe. While Martin was standing there, Cook came out to speak to him. She wanted to ask him about luncheon but, struck by his stillness and his expression, she allowed her question to fade from her lips. She stood in silence behind him; but when he turned she found her voice.

"If it hadn't been for that terrible fire, Mr Hugh would still be here, and the house would never have had to be sold. He'd have been master here in time and everything would've been as it should. Instead of which—"

"Yes. I know. You have me instead. But let me say … that if I could undo the past, I would. And I mean that with all my heart."

"Do you?" she said sceptically. "Even though it'd mean that you wouldn't be standing here now, lord and master of all you survey?"

"Yes, even then," Martin said.

The old woman looked at him. Her fat round face was sombrely set; her eyes examined him, searching him out.

"Well, it's no good talking of that. Nobody can undo the past. We've got to put up with things as they are. But, as I've already said, Mr Cox, it'll be hard for us old ones, getting used to a new master, especially when—"

"Yes. I know."

"It's not as if you're a stranger, you see. It might be easier if you was. But we all remember you as a boy, coming here in your rough clothes, to work with your father, masoning. Then having lessons in the house, a scrawny bean-pole, all skin and bone ... I remember Miss Katharine telling me you weren't getting enough to eat and we'd got to feed you up a bit." The old woman paused, her gaze still keen. "Seems you haven't changed much, for all you're a gentleman these days. You're just about as scrawny now as you were as a boy-chap years ago."

"I have been ill with the flu, that's all."

"Yes. Well. Whatever the reason, Mr Cox, it's plain you still need building up, so I'll go and see about getting some luncheon ready for you. And it seems to me you can't do better than start with some good hot nourishing broth."

When she had gone indoors, Martin went over to the stables, to see his nag in her stall, and to have a word with Jack Sherard. Nearby, on a heap of straw, two spaniels lay dozing together, but got up and came to him, sniffing at him and wagging their tails. He stooped and made a fuss of them and Sherard said they were called Snug and Quince.

"Do you remember old Tessa, who was stung by the adder years ago? And her puppy, Sam, who *would* have been stung if you hadn't snatched him up so quick? These two are both Sam's sons. The blue one's Snug and the yellow one's Quince. The family had to leave them behind – no room for dogs where they're living now – and they sleep here in one of the stalls because Mrs Yuart thought perhaps you wouldn't want them in the house. But you'll have to be careful about that, otherwise they might nip in. They've always been used to it, you see, and of course they're missing the family."

"Yes," Martin said, huskily, and just for a moment could say no more. Stooping, he fondled the dogs' floppy ears, and they gazed at him with furrowed brows. "But there's no need to keep them out of the house. They are welcome to come and go as they please."

He stayed chatting to Sherard for a while, discussing arrangements for bringing his other horses over from

Fieldings that afternoon. Then he returned to the house for his lunch. As he went he clicked his tongue, and the two spaniels followed him in.

Charles Yuart, though he lived in Chardwell, no longer took any part in its affairs. He had resigned from the Borough Council and from all other public bodies and never attended public functions. He went nowhere, except to his work at Kendall's Mill, and to get there he walked across the fields, thus avoiding awkward encounters with former business associates. He refused invitations to dine with friends because, as he said to his wife, he could not return their hospitality now that he lived in a rabbit-hutch.

"But this is our home," Katharine said. "Surely friends will still visit us, wherever we live, so long as their friendship is genuine."

"I have no intention of putting it to the test."

"Is it your intention, then, to cut yourself off from the world completely?"

"The world is getting along perfectly well without me."

"But you have so much to give. Your circumstances may have changed but you are still the same man."

"To you, perhaps, but not to myself. And certainly not to my fellow townsmen. To them I'm a failure and a bankrupt, reduced to a level scarcely better than that of the mill-hands I supervise. I am not to be sought for in public counsel, nor sitting high in the congregation."

"You accept defeat, then?"

"What else would you have me do? I've lost Hainault to the Hurnes and I've lost Railes to Martin Cox. And oh, how pleased they must be with themselves! How loud they must crow, the pair of them!"

"Not Martin," Katharine said. "He would not think of it in that way."

"How do you know what he thinks and feels?"

"Because I know him better than you do. I knew him when he was a boy of fifteen, eager to learn and improve himself, sensitive to beautiful things."

"Yes, and in love with your sister Ginny, if I understood the signs. Well, at least the upstart quarryman's son has not got *everything* he wanted! There is some small comfort in knowing that."

"I am sorry to hear you say so."

"Katharine, I don't understand you! Do you not *mind* that Martin Cox is now living in your old home?"

"I mind very much that we were obliged to leave it, of course, but as far as Martin is concerned—"

"That's just the point. – We were *not* so obliged! If we had done as Stevenson suggested, we stood a good chance of keeping it. But *you* insisted it should be sold! – The house that should have been our son's!"

"Charles, you still had debts to discharge. Dick understands and accepts that. He knows it's a question of honesty. And always when we talk like this, you seem to lose sight of the fact that even if we had been able to stay at Railes, we could never have afforded its upkeep. Not on your present salary."

"If we had remained at Railes our circumstances might have been different. Men would still have respected me, whereas now that I live in this place, they see me brought as low as low and of course they treat me accordingly. I might, if I still lived at Railes, have been offered a partnership somewhere—"

"Wouldn't you need money for that?"

"Not necessarily. I could have worked for it instead. My experience all these years would be worth something, I can tell you, to any decent clothier willing to pay for it. Or I could perhaps have raised a loan, with Railes as my security, as I did once before, when I built the new wing. But now with things the way they are—"

Suddenly he turned away; stood for a moment, staring at nothing; then strode out of the house. His supper lay on the table: some slices of cold lean mutton, with cold potato-and-onion pie. Katharine rose and covered the plate and put it away in the meat-safe.

*

His only relief at times like this was to walk up and over the hills, and often he was gone for hours, returning exhausted, long after dark, and refusing the food she had kept for him.

He hated living in Cryer's Row, where there was no privacy. His children's chatter got on his nerves and he was often short-tempered with them. For weeks now he had raked the newspapers, still hoping against hope that he would find his salvation there. But the cloth trade was still slack, and most of the mills in the Cullen Valley were, it was said, merely marking time. Hainault Mill was one of them and although Charles felt a stab of satisfaction, knowing that his rivals, the Hurnes, had bitten off more than they could chew, the news in general only deepened his gloom. For how could he hope to make his way as a clothier again when everywhere in the west country the trade's very future was in doubt? When, on the markets of the world, good quality broadcloth was universally rejected in favour of cheap worsteds and tweeds such as were made at Kendall's Mill.

His work at Kendall's was hateful to him. Everything there was in a muddle, due to a system of "making do". The loom-shop was old and badly lit; the windows had not been cleaned for months; and everywhere the wooden floors were slippery with oil and filth. In addition to all this, he knew that the work-people jeered at him, enjoying the sight of a powerful man reduced to the status of paid employee, barely a cut above themselves.

One day a new man was taken on in the finishing-loft. George Ainley had engaged him. His face, Charles thought, was familiar.

"I know you, I think?"

"Yes, sir, you do. I worked for you at Hainault once. But we very soon parted company."

"Ah, yes, I remember now. Your name is Hopkins, I believe. I dismissed you for being insolent. Well, I hope you've mended your ways since then."

The man smiled and touched his cap.

"I hope we both have, Mr Yuart, sir."

Charles, complaining to George Ainley, received scant sympathy.

"You'd be wise to ignore that sort of thing. Better still – avoid provoking it in the first place."

He had worked at Kendall's almost two months when a bitter altercation arose over some pieces of "Belfray Tweave", which had been through the burling-room, where all knots and lumps should have been removed. Charles was dissatisfied and sent the cloth back to be done again. The burlers complained to George Ainley, who called Charles into his counting-house.

"My burlers know what they're doing. They've been told not to spend too much time on that cloth. It's part of a special order for Winterton's and I've promised delivery by next week."

"Not much use delivering on time if it only comes back as faulty."

"It won't come back," Ainley said. "I've quoted an extra-low price for it."

"Low price or not," Charles said, "I don't understand how you have the gall to make that rubbish and call it cloth."

"At least I sell what I make, Mr Yuart, which is more than you managed to do in your last two years at Hainault. Yes, and all my trade bills are met, too, along with all my running-costs."

"If you think I'm staying here to be spoken to in this way—"

"Please yourself. It's all one to me." Ainley looked at him with dislike. "I always knew it was a mistake, employing a man who'd been big in his day, especially when that man was you."

"You seem to forget," Charles said, "it was you who approached me in the first instance, saying you needed an overseer."

"Yes, but I did it against my better judgement, and only to please a friend of mine, who, as it happens, is also my landlord."

"What friend?"

"Martin Cox."

"Well," Charles said, in a voice like steel, "now you will have to find someone else!"

When he returned home to the cottage, he found the front door open and Katharine on her knees in the doorway, scrubbing the white stone step. The sight of his wife performing this task, where neighbours and passers-by could see her, was more than his present temper would stand, and Katharine, looking up at him, saw that his face was paper-white. In silence she leant to one side, and in silence he pushed past her, into the narrow passageway. There he stood waiting while she wiped up the last of the suds, rose to her feet, and closed the door. He then led the way into the kitchen, and his voice, when he turned and spoke to her, was only barely under control

"Why are you scrubbing the floors? Where is the maid?"

"Ellie's not well. I sent her home. Susannah has gone with her."

"And can't the damned doorstep wait till she's back?"

"That may not be for a while yet. I think she has the chicken-pox."

"Sometimes, Katharine, it seems to me that you take a delight in demeaning yourself. It's as though you deliberately set out to rub salt into your wounds. Or, more to the point, in mine!"

Katharine looked at him. She, too, was very pale. She had set down her bucket and was wiping her hands on a towel.

"Something has happened."

"Yes. It has. I have had words with George Ainley and have left Kendall's Mill."

"I was afraid of something like this."

"You are satisfied, then."

"Is there no hope of putting it right?"

"None whatsoever."

"You mean you do not intend to try?"

"I think I have already sunk low enough without humbling

myself further to an ignorant, jumped-up shearman who calls himself a clothier! And if it is what you expect me to do, then it seems you must despise me indeed."

"There is nothing despicable in making an honest apology."

"Katharine, I've had enough of this. Always you put me in the wrong!"

"Charles, you put *yourself* in the wrong by speaking of Ainley as you do. He has been very good to you—"

"You know nothing about the man."

"This much at least I know," Katharine said, "that he is in business and you are not."

"So, madam wife, there it is at last! – The truth about what you think of me!"

"The truth of what I am saying is that you are not seeing things clearly. You are not facing facts. And the most important fact is that without the goodwill of those men who are still in business, making cloth, you cannot even hope to begin working your way back into the trade."

"How can I ever work my way back when I have been left destitute? When everything has been taken from me and even *you* have turned against me!"

"That is not true," Katharine said.

"Oh, but it is! It is!" he exclaimed. "I can see it in your eyes!"

Katharine made a move towards him; a gesture of comfort and appeal; and just for an instant it seemed almost as though he would take her into his arms. But then, with a sudden exclamation, he flung himself away from her, snatched up his hat, and made for the door, stumbling against the pail on his way, so that water slopped over his trouser-legs. A moment later the front door opened and was slammed shut behind him.

Katharine sat down. She was trembling badly and was close to tears. But, knowing Susannah would be back shortly, she made an effort to compose herself. She rose from her chair and removed the pail; wrung out her muslinet cloth and wiped the spilt water from the floor.

*

Charles, on leaving the cottage, walked down to the river and stood on the bridge over the leats, close by Fleet Mills. Below him the water from the dam rushed in a swift white torrent, over the weir and into the mill-race, there to form a white-boiling foam before eddying out in swirls that gradually gave themselves back to the river and became part of its smooth dark flow.

Above the dam, beside one of the upper leats, two men were watching him, and over in the millyard, too, a few men at work, pressing bales, turned their heads to look at him. Could they see who he was, and did they think he might jump in? Well, they would be disappointed, for surely there must be some way out of his present problems, without that desperate, cowardly act? And with a queer grin that twisted his mouth, he walked on over the bridge and up the slope of the far bank.

To shade the dams and keep them cool, the slope was planted with alder trees, and he stood among them, hidden from sight, looking obliquely across the fleet to the opening of Tack House Lane. By choosing his position carefully, he was able to watch his own home, and after ten minutes or so he saw his daughter return and go in. There followed a longer wait until, as he expected, his wife and daughter came out together, each with a basket on her arm, and walked up the lane towards the town. He emerged from his hiding-place, re-crossed the fleet, and hurried home.

Upstairs in the bedroom he changed into his best suit and packed other clothes and essentials into a leather valise. He took a small chamois bag full of coin from its hiding-place under the wardrobe and put it into his inner pocket. Downstairs, in the living-room, he sat at the table and wrote to his wife.

"You are right – I do not seem able to see matters clearly here, therefore I am going away. I have lost all my self-respect and can see no prospect of regaining it. Not here in Chardwell, at any rate. I think I may go to America. It is a place that owes me something – I mean compensation for my cloth that was burnt –

and is said to be a land of opportunity. If it is – well, we shall see.

"I am sorry to take my leave in this furtive way but saying goodbye to you and the children would cause me more sorrow than I could bear. Please try to understand and get them to understand too. My own view of the matter is that you and they will be better off without me because then you will find it easy enough to accept your sister Ginny's offer and make your home at Chacelands."

Charles paused, read the letter through twice, and added a last few words.

"In spite of the course I am taking, I beg you will please believe me to be your loving husband always.

Charles."

He put the letter into an envelope, wrote Katharine's name upon it, and propped it against a vase on the table. He left the cottage and walked down to the fleet again. But this time, having crossed the bridge, he set off across the rack-field where Fleet Mills cloth, undyed, hung out, dirty white, on the reaming-frames. From the rack-ground he climbed the ridge and set off over Tull Hill, in the direction of Pibblecombe Halt, where he would take a train for Crewe. From Crewe he would travel to Liverpool and there board the first ship that would take him to North America.

The story of Charles Yuart's abscondence spread quickly through the town, but Martin only heard it when he met George Ainley outside Coulson's Bank.

"Yuart and I had a disagreement and he walked out. It was bound to happen sooner or later. The man is too stiff-necked by half. But I'm sorry about it all the same and if I had known it would come to this—"

"Come to what?" Martin asked.

"Yuart's gone. Hadn't you heard? Left his family and cleared off. According to rumour, he's gone abroad."

"When did this happen?"

"Three days ago."

Martin, making enquiries elsewhere, found the whole story to be correct. For two days he pondered the matter. Then he called at the cottage in Cryer's Row. Katharine, as it happened, was there alone.

"It's Dick's half-term holiday and Ginny has taken both children over to Chacelands for the day. I didn't go with them because ... well, I felt I wanted some time to myself."

"In that case I am intruding. Perhaps you'll allow me to call again, on a day better suited to you."

"No, of course not. Do sit down." She looked at him with unsmiling gaze. "You know that my husband has gone away?"

"Yes. And I am deeply sorry. It is in fact my reason for coming." Watching her, he did his best to gauge her response to these words, but her face remained closed to him. "I'm told that he has gone abroad. To America, I believe. That being so, then presumably he will be gone some time."

"Yes, it would appear so."

Her grey eyes were cold and bleak; her tone almost curt; and Martin, perceiving from this that she was still in a state of shock, was filled with anger against the man whose desertion was responsible for it.

"If it is not presumptuous, may I ask what you mean to do?"

"I am not sure. I haven't decided. Ginny wants us to go to her. She and George have been very kind. But I would prefer to be independent and I'm trying to decide how that might be achieved. I thought of trying for a post as governess but at my age, and with two children, I am not really hopeful of success."

"Well, that brings me to the point of my visit," Martin said, "for I wanted to ask if you would consider coming to Railes as my housekeeper."

Katharine sat very straight in her chair, her hands clasped together in her lap; but in spite of her rigid self-control, he could see how his words had affected her, and he spoke with all possible care.

"This is a strange and difficult situation. I know how painful it must be for you and the last thing I want is to add to your distress. It may well be that the thought of returning to Newton Railes, under such circumstances, is too painful for you even to contemplate. You may even feel that the mere suggestion is a gross insult to your pride but—"

"I am not insulted, Martin. Nor can I afford to be proud. But it is, as you say, a strange situation, and I must admit I am taken aback. Certainly a return to Railes would bring pain to my children and myself but ... our predicament is such that there can be no such thing as a really happy resolution."

"You mean you will consider my proposition?"

"Yes. I will consider it and discuss it with my children."

"You will, I hope, bear in mind that there will be certain advantages in the arrangement that might, in some measure at least, atone for its more distressing aspects. It would mean that you and your children would have security and comfort until such time as your husband returns, and a certain degree of independence. You would, if it is agreeable to you, occupy those rooms which are on the same landing as the schoolroom. That would include the small sitting-room, so that you and your children could always be private whenever you chose. Your work as housekeeper would not, I believe, be too onerous, and you would have ample time to instruct your daughter, as you do now, and help your son with his school studies. Your salary would be fifty-two pounds per annum, with all found for yourself and for them, and probably some further allowances."

"Yes. I see. Indeed, it seems very generous. But why are you offering me this post? Have you had no housekeeper at Railes all these weeks?"

"No. Mrs Nicholls, who kept house for me at Fieldings, chose to stay and serve the new owner. Cook has managed at Railes till now and I have been reluctant to bring someone new into the house. But Cook, as you know, is getting old and – well, she herself has repeatedly said that I ought to find someone suitable to run the place for me."

"Yes, I see," Katharine said again, but this time a little smile touched her lips. "Dear Cook. She is such a good soul. I have known her all my life, you know, and would dearly love to see her again."

"May I enquire how long you will need to think the matter over?" Martin asked, getting up. "Would it be in order for me to call again in three days' time?"

"Yes. I shall have decided by then."

She rose and saw him to the door.

At six o'clock Ginny returned. She was driving the carriage herself but left it standing in the narrow lane to come into the cottage with the two children.

"Well, Kate, have you made up your mind?"

"What?" Katharine said, staring at her.

"Whether you're coming to Chacelands and *when*. George was quite sharp with me when I said you wanted time to think – naturally, he assumes it's my fault – and he says there can be no question whatever but that you make your home with us."

"That is very kind of George and I'd like you to tell him how grateful we are for his kindness and generosity. But—"

"Well, if only you had come with us today, you could have told him that yourself and perhaps argued the whole thing out. You shouldn't have stayed here all alone. Not at a time like this. It's given you a fit of the blues."

"No, it hasn't. I'm quite all right. But I've had a visit from Martin Cox."

"Good heavens! What did *he* want?"

"He had heard about Charles going away and he came to offer me the post of housekeeper at Newton Railes."

"Oh, how *dare* he?" Ginny exclaimed, and so fierce was her indignation that it lit her fair face like a scarlet flame. "Oh, the effrontery of the man! I hope you sent him about his business."

"No. I said I would think it over."

"Surely you can't be serious?"

"Yes. I am serious enough. I've thought about it a good deal in the three hours since Martin left and I think there is much to be said for it."

"Children, did you hear that? Your mother has taken leave of herself! Kate, the idea is quite absurd. You have no need to do such a thing. Your place is with us and it's only right that George and I—"

"No, Ginny, it will not do. It would mean too great an imposition. And, as I've said before, I am anxious to keep my independence in whatever degree is possible to me."

"And going to Railes would give you that?"

"Yes, because there I should be earning my keep."

"A paid domestic."

"Yes, if you like."

"That's just it. I do *not* like."

"You seem to forget," Katharine said, "that I kept house for papa all those years, without any shame attaching to it."

"That was a different matter entirely, as you well know."

Ginny, in exasperation, looked across at her nephew and niece, who, throughout this interchange, had stood in silence, shocked but alert. Then she turned to her sister again and spoke with some acerbity.

"Will Martin expect you to *cook* for him?"

"I think not, since Cook is still there. But even if he did, what of that? I've cooked for my own family since coming to live here and it has not meant the end of the world. To tell you the truth, I rather enjoy cooking and baking, and even in the old days at Railes—"

"Well!" Ginny said, and threw up her hands. "It seems there's no reasoning with you at all because plainly you have made up your mind to accept this ridiculous proposition and are wilfully closing your eyes to the fact that by doing so you're demeaning yourself."

"I have *not* yet made up my mind. I have three days in which to do that. And first I need to discuss it all very thoroughly with the children."

"Yes, I am simply dying to hear what their views on the matter might be!"

"We shall find discussion easier when we are alone together."

"You want me to go?"

"Well, your carriage *is* blocking the lane, Ginny, and any moment now somebody will want to pass."

"Then I had better take myself off. I certainly don't wish to intrude on your private family councils. But I think I should warn you, Kate, that if you do as Martin Cox asks, instead of coming to Chacelands, I shall be seriously hurt and offended. And George will feel exactly the same."

The children, raised in the habit of obedience, had already accepted their mother's reasons for refusing to live at Chacelands, and Dick in particular, with his own strong independent streak, had endorsed her decision whole-heartedly. Furthermore, the children knew there was only one alternative, for Katharine had made that plain to them. She would have to seek employment; but what, and how, and of what kind, were questions that had not yet been resolved. Now, suddenly, employment was offered, and, sitting with them at the dining-table, she presented her own views of that offer, point by point, pro and contra, before inviting them to give theirs.

"The final decision, of course, must be mine, but I shall be helped, while weighing the matter in my mind, if I know what you both think about it."

Dick at this time was thirteen; Susannah eleven; and it was easy for Katharine to see the conflict of feeling in each young face: instinctive joy at the thought of returning to Newton Railes, darkened inevitably by doubts because of their changed circumstances. Railes had been their home from birth; they loved it as she herself loved it; and had suffered, with her, deep pain at its loss. Now it was another man's home and they would be retainers there. Would they be able to accept that or would it be too hard to bear?

"I certainly don't like the thought that you would be a servant, mama."

"Neither do I," Susannah said.

"But whatever work I secure, it will have to be service of some kind."

"Yes, but not *there*, and with *him*," Dick said.

"What kind of man is Mr Cox? Do you like him?" Susannah asked.

"Yes. I do."

"Even though he lives in our house? Aunt Ginny says she hates him for that. And sometimes I think I hate him, too."

"In that case we cannot possibly go."

"Oh, but I'd never show it, of course! I would take good care not to do that."

"Even to feel it would be wrong."

"Perhaps I might not feel it, however. Perhaps I might even like him, as you do, mama."

"Yes. I think perhaps you might. And you wouldn't see all that much of him because we should have our own quarters and mostly we should keep to them."

"*Servants'* quarters?" Dick said.

"No. You would have your own bedrooms, next to the schoolroom, and I'd have the bedroom opposite. We would also have the small sitting-room, just to ourselves, for our private use."

"Did Mr Cox say so, mama?"

"Yes indeed."

"Well," Dick said in some surprise, "that seems very decent of him, I must say." And, after further thought, he added: "I think, if you don't mind, mama, I'd like a few words with Susannah alone."

"Very well. By all means."

Upstairs, in Dick's bedroom, the children sat on the edge of the bed.

"What do you honestly think, Susannah?"

"I'm not sure. I keep thinking about papa. I'm sure *he*

wouldn't like the idea of our going back to live at Railes."

"Then he ought not to have left us." Dick's tone was uncompromising. "Sneaking off in that shabby way, leaving us to shift for ourselves, with nothing more than the few shillings mother had in her purse. Only think what it's like for *her*, suddenly being left like that, on top of all that's gone before."

"Yes, I know," Susannah said, "I'll never forget mama's face when we came back from shopping that day and she read the letter papa had left."

"My own view of the matter is that papa has forfeited every right to be considered in things of this sort. Mama is the only one we have to think about now. *She* wants to do what's best for us, so *we've* got to do what's best for her, and obviously, from the way she spoke, she is in favour of accepting the offer."

"Do you think so?"

"I'm certain of it."

"Then we must say we want it, too."

"Yes. I know it will be difficult, going back as outsiders… Being there on sufferance… But I daresay we shall get used to that. Anyway, whatever it's like, we must just make the best of it."

"I think I could bear it well enough, for mama's sake, if it's what she wants."

"Of course you can. So can I. If we could bear living *here* all these weeks—"

"Oh, Dick, just to think of it! To be gone from here and back to Railes, even though it isn't ours—"

"I know, I know," Dick said briskly. "But don't get upset, there's a good girl. It'll only bring you out in spots."

"I'm not upset. Truly, I'm not. Look at me. I'm perfectly calm."

"Well, just take care that you stay that way, otherwise you'll worry mama. Now let us go down and tell her what we think of the famous offer."

CHAPTER
9

A few days later, on a misty morning in mid October, Sherard came for them in the carriage and drove them out to Newton Railes. On the seat beside him was a trunk containing some of their clothes. The furniture and the rest of their things were to follow by van that afternoon.

Little was said during the journey, especially once they had passed through the main Newton Railes gateway and were driving through the parkland. Katharine, sitting between her children, exchanged an eloquent glance with each and knew that for them, as for herself, the moment was too full of feeling for words. But Susannah leant against her, clasping her arm with both hands, and in a while Dick did the same. Another hundred yards or so and they were rounding the long curve that gave them their first glimpse of the house, and Sherard, speaking over his shoulder, was saying in a quiet voice:

"There it is, the old place ... Doesn't change much, does it, ma'am?"

"No," Katharine said, "it doesn't change."

The stone-built walls, with their green creepers, just beginning to change colour; the steep-pitched roof and tall chimneys; the windows, not yet lit by the sun, gleaming darkly between their mullions; even the way the house stood, occupying, with its garden and park, a comfortable fold in the lower hillside, backed by the distant slopes of Ox Knap: all these things, imprinted on their minds and hearts from earliest childhood, touched them all in a certain way that no other place on earth could do.

"Is Mr Cox at home?" Katharine asked.

"No, ma'am. He had business in Culverstone. He won't be back till this afternoon."

Round the east end of the house they drove, under the stone-built archway and so into the stable-court; and there, as they got down from the carriage, Cook stood stolidly waiting for them, wearing her best marocain dress with a crisp white apron-and-bib.

"Welcome home, Mrs Yuart, ma'am," she said with strict formality. "Miss Susannah. Master Dick." But then, as the children went towards her, she suddenly opened her arms to them, and they, glad to be able to hide their faces, yielded themselves to her strong warm hug. "There, now! There!" the old woman said, and Katharine, meeting her gaze, saw that her eyes were full of tears.

It was only three months since they had left, but to Dick and Susannah that seemed an age, and it was with a sense of amazement that they found everything so little changed. Not only was all the old furniture there – naturally, they expected that, – but everything was in the same place: the oakboard table in the great hall, with the green glass vase on it, filled now with tall white and yellow daisies; the old settle beside the hearth; the way the carpets were spread on the floor ... And, the happiest thing of all, the two spaniels, Snug and Quince, who came lolloping in from the garden, were still allowed the run of the house just as they had been in days gone by. *Everything* was exactly the same.

But no, not quite, they soon discovered. There *were* some changes after all. New bookcases full of books in the alcoves in the drawing-room ... A glass-fronted cabinet containing fossils, beside the window in the library ... Some watercolours and pastels on the wall of the back staircase ... Indeed there were quite a number of things ... Still, in essence, the children felt, the house was as they remembered it; and Cook, in close attendance on them, agreed that it was so.

"Mr Cox said, right from the first, that he wanted everything to remain just as it was when the family was here. That's what he always calls you, you see, when talking in the general way. Always 'the family'. Nothing else."

A little silence fell on them all, and they looked at her reflectively, until Dick, with a touch of briskness, said:

"But we're *not* the family now, Cook, and we must take care not to behave as if this is still our home. You mustn't call us Master Dick and Miss Susannah any more. It wouldn't be right, would it, mama?"

"I think we shall find," Katharine said, "that Cook will very quickly get used to the new position we occupy here and will treat us all accordingly."

The old servant looked at her.

"Yes, Mrs Yuart. I'll do my best."

After lunching with the staff in the kitchen, the children went for a walk in the grounds, taking the dogs with them. Katharine went upstairs to her room and busied herself unpacking the trunk. When that was done, and the clothes had all been put away, she went out into the garden. The mist of the morning had thinned now, and a pale sun shone through it, bringing brightness but little warmth. The grass being wet, she kept to the stone-paved pathways, and went wherever they led her.

Shortly after four o'clock Martin returned and came looking for her. He found her in the lower garden, standing beside the oval pool, gazing downwards into the water. She was wearing a hat with a wide brim and it happened that the pale sun, glistening on the pool's surface, was reflected upwards into her face and down again, because of this brim, in slow spreading ripples of light. She stood motionless, absorbed in her thoughts, and Martin, when he perceived her expression, would have gone away again, feeling that he was a trespasser. But she glanced up and, seeing him there, came forward at once to meet him. Martin spoke first.

"I'm sorry I wasn't here to welcome you but I had business

in Culverstone and it took the greater part of the day."

Katharine smiled.

"I thought you had absented yourself because you knew how we should feel, coming back here like this, and you wanted to make it easy for us."

"Yes, I would always want to do that, if such a thing were possible."

"You have been very kind, Martin, and we are grateful, the children and I."

"I hope your rooms are to your liking. If there is anything you lack, you have only to say."

"We lack nothing. You have already made sure of that."

Together they turned away from the pool, following the formal path that led through an opening in the yew hedge and across the parterre to the lower terrace.

"The children have gone off through the park. Dick wanted to see the stream. But I have been on a tour of the gardens, quietly by myself."

"Everything is behind-hand this year, the summer having being so poor, and Jobe, as befits his name, predicts that autumn is bound to be worse."

"Let us hope he is wrong."

"You will have found that we've made a few changes, especially in the grounds lower down."

"Yes. You've built a second footbridge over the stream in the bog-garden. And you've planted a number of tree-ferns."

"The changes do not offend you, I hope."

"No, of course not." Katharine said. Then, in a while, as they walked on: "Martin, I think we should discuss the running of the house, and my duties as your housekeeper."

"That is simple. I want you to run the house much as you have done in the past."

"But we must discuss details all the same. I know nothing about your daily routine."

"Very well. I breakfast at seven; I lunch at twelve; and generally dine at half past six. But this is subject to change, of course, according to my day's work, and social engagements, if any. As for your own routine, I leave you to arrange that to suit yourself and your children, so as to be sure of having some time with them, in quietness and privacy."

"Yes, we shall be glad of that. But what is more important still is that we should not intrude on your privacy."

"I have no fear on that score."

"You may not fear it, but I do. Dick and Susannah are very young. I have spoken to them seriously and warned them both against the danger of treating Railes as though it were still their own home. But I find now I'm here – I was thinking of it as I stood by the pool – that I am in need of the warning myself. I am in danger, as much as they, of thinking I'm back in my own home."

Martin turned and looked at her.

"As far as I am concerned—" he began, but broke off abruptly, giving way to second thoughts.

He wanted to tell her that she and her children were free to treat the house as their home; that this was what he wanted for them; but he realized that to say such a thing would only emphasize the fact that it was *not* their home any more. Nothing he could say would alter that; nor remove the hurt of it. All he could do was give her time to adapt to her new situation here, hoping that its security would relieve her of immediate worries, especially those concerning money. Hoping too that Railes itself, even though it re-opened old wounds, would also in time effect its own cure.

"What were you going to say?" Katharine asked.

"Something clumsy, which is best left unsaid."

"In that case let us return to practical matters. The choice of meals, for instance. What about that?"

"I shall leave it to you and Cook, except when I have friends to dine, when some discussion may be needed. You will be responsible for ordering all household requisites and dealing with tradesmen generally. You will also keep the household accounts. I have done this myself till now – Cook did not feel equal to it – but I shall be glad to have the task taken out of my hands."

*

At the end of the lower terrace, the children appeared, returning from their ramble in the park. They were introduced to Martin, who shook hands with each of them.

"I have, as it happens, met you before, but you were very young then and I doubt if you remember me."

"No," Dick said, "I'm afraid we don't."

"How far did you go in your walk?"

"As far as the stream and along the bank a little way."

"See any trout?"

"Yes, just a few."

"We've been losing them to a pike," Martin said. "A huge brute that comes up from the river. We've put a grille in above the pool and I'm hoping one day to catch him there."

"How huge is he, exactly, sir?"

"Well, I haven't actually seen him myself, but according to Jobe's nephew Will he's twice the size of an alderman."

Dick smiled; Susannah laughed; and Martin was about to speak to her when a maid came from the house to say that Mr Nick from the quarry had called and was in the study. Martin excused himself, and the children were left alone with their mother.

"So that's the famous Martin Cox," Dick said. "I must say I was rather surprised to find him so gentlemanly."

"What did you expect?" Katharine asked.

"Well … the way papa always spoke of him … 'the quarryman's son' and things of that sort … I pictured somebody quite different."

"So did I," Susannah said. "And I wish he hadn't been called away because he was about to say something to me and now I'll never know what it was."

During the first three weeks, Martin's meetings with Katharine were few, and the conversations they had together were restricted to domestic matters. As for the two children, he saw them not at all. Dick, of course, was at school by day, and

Susannah was being taught by her mother in the schoolroom, as of old. But at all times their comings and goings were so quietly discreet that he scarcely knew they were in the house. Katharine was keeping her promise that neither she nor they should intrude upon his privacy. But Martin knew it was more than that. She had passed through difficult times: the failure of her husband's business; the sale of her home; and now, worst of all, her husband's desertion. All these had taken their toll, and now that she was back at Railes, centre of a lifetime of memories, with all the emotions they evoked, she had withdrawn into herself. Martin saw this and understood, but often he was troubled, too, and once he spoke to Cook about it.

"Tell me, did I do wrong, do you think, bringing Mrs Yuart back here?"

"I don't know, sir. It's hard for her – I do know that. She belongs here in this house and yet the house don't belong to her. But it isn't just that. It's everything. So many sad events have happened to the old family over the years … and now this latest thing, with Mr Yuart going off, leaving her and the young ones like that … It's something I can't understand, sir. But one thing I do know – such a thing should never have happened. Not to our Miss Katharine, it shouldn't. No, sir. It should not."

No, Martin thought, it should never have happened. Charles Yuart's desertion had inflicted the cruellest wound of all. He felt for Katharine and left her alone.

Although he saw so little of her during these early days, her presence in the house was manifest at every turn. For one thing, the household was better regulated: no longer were brooms and dusters left in corners here and there; nor did he come upon the maids gossiping together on the stairs. There were other improvements, too: he had always been given good meals, but now there was more variety in them, and they were served with greater care.

But in addition to these things, there were the hundred-

and-one little touches, so characteristic of her, and which he remembered from earlier times. Fresh flowers everywhere, chosen and arranged so that their colours were always exactly right for the room. Provence roses, cool yellow and white, in a bowl of nut-brown aventurine. Pink nerine lilies, standing tall in a vase, with the slender, sword-like leaves of the yucca, striped in pale green and white. Copper-coloured chrysanthemums in a well-polished pewter jug. And soon, in large stoneware pots, there were branches of leaves in their autumn colours: sugar-maple, crimson and scarlet; flat sprays of beech, turning now to burnt sienna; and homely horse-chestnut leaves, speckled yellow, with rusty brown edges.

Katharine had always possessed this gift, for bringing light and life and colour to every corner of the house, and in spite of the shadow of recent events, she possessed it still.

One Saturday afternoon, when Katharine and her children had been three weeks at Railes, her sister Ginny drove over from Chacelands. Martin, from an upper window, saw her arrive. He went down at once and met her on the rear staircase.

"Mrs Winter. What a pleasant surprise."

"*Is* it pleasant?"

"Yes, of course."

"You have no objection, then, if I visit my sister and her children here?"

"On the contrary. You are welcome to come whenever you please."

"I'm not sure Kate deserves to be visited all that often. I have not yet forgiven her for choosing to come here to you instead of to me at Chacelands. However, I have my nephew and niece to consider, and I don't intend to deny myself the pleasure of seeing them merely because of their mother's contrariness. I think I shall blame you instead, for bringing her here in the first place."

"By all means," Martin said. "It is always wisest to lay blame upon those who are best able to bear it."

"By which you mean me to understand that you don't care twopence if I blame you or not."

Martin smiled. He would not be drawn.

"I think you will find Mrs Yuart and her children in their own sitting-room. That is to say, on the west landing."

"Then I will go up and surprise them."

"I hope," Martin said, as he stepped aside for her to pass, "that you and they will do me the honour of taking afternoon tea with me."

"How very kind." Ginny paused, looking back at him. "Shall I instruct Kate to see to it? Presumably it is one of her duties."

"That will not be necessary. I will speak to Cook myself."

A little while later, Ginny was strolling with Kate and the children in the garden, in the last of the day's sunshine.

"And how does it feel to be back here at Railes, in service to Martin Cox?"

"It feels very strange, of course, and sometimes I can't quite believe that this is how things really are. But Martin has been very kind to us—"

"I should hope so indeed!"

"—and we are getting used to the situation, gradually, the children and I."

"Yes, I daresay. But at what cost to your finer feelings!"

"It isn't all pain, you know. There is comfort of a kind in being here at Railes again."

"And is there comfort, my dear Kate, in being a paid menial?"

"Yes. The comfort that comes with independence. But please, I entreat you, let us not argue again over that."

"Very well. But if you knew how I feel at seeing Martin Cox here, stalking about, so full of himself—"

"Whatever your feelings may be, you are a guest under his roof, and I beg you will remember it."

"I am hardly likely to forget it. He will no doubt see to that." Ginny turned to her niece and nephew. "And what do you think of your mama's employer?"

"We've only spoken to him once," Dick said. "That was the day we arrived. Since then we've kept out of his way. – Obeying Mama's instructions, you know."

"How very wise," Ginny said. "I hoped to keep out of his way myself but alas, it was not to be, and we came face to face on the back stairs. However, all was well, and your aunt Ginny carried the day."

Brother and sister exchanged a grin. They were used to their aunt's histrionics.

"Was it difficult?" Susannah asked. "Did you have to fight tooth and nail?"

"Oh, my dear, it was much worse than that, for I had to *smile* and be *pleasant* to him! As a result you'll be glad to know that he has graciously granted permission for me to visit you whenever I choose. We are also invited to take tea with him. Yes, my dears, all four of us! And there, unless my eyes deceive me, is Dorrie coming to say it is ready."

During the course of tea, the children, mindful of their mother's strictures, were careful not to put themselves forward; but their aunt Ginny, admitting no such need for restraint, chatted away without pause. Chiefly, she addressed herself to Martin and was in a mood for reminiscence, quite openly taking delight in reminding him of his early days.

"How many years is it since you first came here, helping your father with the masoning, doing repairs on the stone-work for us?"

"I was ten the first time I came, so it was twenty-one years ago."

"And how long is it since you came to join us in the schoolroom?"

"Sixteen years. I was fifteen."

"You were very different then. – A gangling youth, all legs and arms, in a suit of clothes you had long out-grown. Katharine used to feel sorry for you. She thought you were half-starved and often she asked you to stay to lunch. Poor boy, you were so uncouth, you could hardly handle a knife and fork. We couldn't help laughing sometimes. Once there was green salad to eat – something you'd never had before – and you said the lettuce tasted like rain. Do you remember those days, Martin, all so very long ago?"

"Yes. I remember everything."

"Everything? That's a large boast. Shall I test your memory?"

"On some other occasion, perhaps. At present it would be too boring for Dick and Susannah if they were forced to listen to their elders raking over the distant past."

"Oh, but you are too modest, Martin! How could they be bored by such a story as yours, which is worthy of Samuel Smiles himself? For who would have thought that the stone-cutter's son, once so glad to receive charity from us, should one day be lord and master here and that we should be nothing but guests and retainers, accepting his hospitality?"

"Ginny, *please!*" Katharine said.

"Why, what's the matter? Am I speaking out of turn?" Ginny turned to Martin again. "Am I causing you embarrassment, Martin, by speaking of the past in this way?"

Martin, unsmiling, met her look. He knew this excitable mood of hers. He remembered it from the days of their youth.

"I'm aware that such is your intention," he said, "but if you will only reflect a moment, you will see that whatever embarrassment you are causing me, it is nothing to the very real distress you are causing your sister."

For a moment Ginny stared at him, a bright flush invading her cheeks, a sharp rejoinder on her lips. But she knew she had earned this reproof and although she was angry she was also ashamed. The rejoinder remained unspoken. Instead, she turned and spoke to Katharine.

"*Mea culpa,*" she said, in a small voice, and made a gesture with her hands, of humility and submissiveness. "Impose whatever penance you choose. Come, now, Kate, don't shake your head! I insist on a penance, if you please, otherwise how shall my guilt be purged?"

"Very well. So be it." Katharine picked up a plate piled high with rock-cakes and offered them to her sister. "You must eat one of these," she said.

"Is that a penance?"

"Yes. Cook has forgotten to put in the sugar."

There was a good deal of laughter at this, and the rest of the tea-party passed off without untoward incident, much to the relief of the two children. And although in a while their aunt Ginny, recovering her sang-froid, engaged in further badinage, again at Mr Cox's expense, she was careful to keep within those bounds that his earlier rebuke had set for her.

"In fact, if you ask me," Dick said, alone with Susannah afterwards, "far from hating him, as she pretends, I think she likes him very well."

"And does Mr Cox like *her*, do you think?"

"Oh, well, as to that, everyone likes aunt Ginny, of course."

Ginny was often at Railes after that, and although she continued to make remarks about her sister's position there, she soon came to accept it. Even, in time, to approve of it.

"At least you don't dress like a housekeeper – that's something to be thankful for. And I must say you are looking heaps better now than you have done this long while past. Perhaps it was not such a bad thing, after all, your coming back here. You were always good at adapting to change, and the children seem to be, too."

Always, on these early visits, Ginny came alone, driving herself in the Denbigh carriage, with her prized team of silver greys.

"No, I have not brought your uncle George," she said, in answer to the children's enquiry. "He's a very tiresome man these days and when we're together we're bound to quarrel."

Katharine, in private, tried to dissuade Ginny from speaking of George in this way when the children were present, but Ginny only scoffed.

"Dick and Susannah must already be well aware that

marriages are not all made in heaven. It is all part of their education and may teach them to take care whom they choose when the time comes."

"What is it you and George quarrel about?"

"He's always complaining that I spend too much of his money."

"And do you?"

Ginny shrugged.

"As he refuses to tell me what his income is, how can I possibly know whether I spend too much of it? But it isn't only money, of course. He's bitterly disappointed in me because I haven't given him the son and heir he longs for so desperately. Naturally, he takes it for granted the fault is mine. But that is quite enough about George. Let us talk of other things. Sherard said Martin was out. Will he be back soon, do you know?"

Martin was glad of Ginny's visits because as a result of her goodwill a small but difficult problem was solved.

Katharine, since coming to Railes, had not attended church service due to the awkwardness of her position. That she, a paid housekeeper, should sit with her employer in the Newton Railes pew was plainly out of the question. But equally difficult was it for her – daughter of the old family – to sit at the back of the church with the servants. Not only would it have caused talk, but the servants themselves would have been distressed.

Now, the problem was gently removed: Ginny and George, in the Chacelands carriage, called for Katharine and her children; and in church they all sat in the Chacelands pew. And although, on the first Sunday, this caused a stir in the congregation, the feeling conveyed was, on the whole, one of understanding and approval.

There was another reason why Martin welcomed Ginny at Railes: she brought Katharine and the children out of their self-imposed seclusion. Her high spirits enlivened them; her nonsensical chatter made them laugh; and as the family quartet usually took tea with him, the children came to know him better; became more relaxed in his company. Dick had a passion for the Classics and Martin was able to draw him out on the subject of the *Iliad*.

"What do you think, sir?" the boy asked. "Is it just pure myth or is there some real truth in it?"

"I cannot say. Even the experts disagree. But there is a new work on the subject, by Professor Scudamore, which summarizes the theories so far and draws some interesting conclusions. I have the book in the library and you are welcome to borrow it."

"Thank you, sir, but mama said we must not be a nuisance to you."

"You will not be a nuisance," Martin said.

As Dick had been given the use of the library, it was only right that Susannah should enjoy the same privilege; but brother and sister were careful to use it only when Martin was not there; and Susannah, who read more quickly than Dick, was scrupulous in leaving a note of the books she had taken.

"Dear Mr Cox," she wrote once:

"I have returned *Idylls of the King* and taken volume one of *Barchester Towers*. Dick is still reading Scudamore's work based on Renard's translation of Welcker's investigation into early Greek sources on the life of Homer. He is sadly determined to be a scholar, I'm afraid; quite different in every way from —

"Yours truly, Susannah Yuart.

"P.S.: If you are free at four o'clock today, would you care to join us for schoolroom tea?"

Schoolroom tea, as Martin knew, was an old tradition at Newton Railes, and the invitation pleased him. Although his rôle was now greatly changed, the occasion itself was much the same as in early days, and brought back many memories. Katharine's children were encouraged to discuss whatever interested them, just as the twins had been, and Dick broached a subject that was prominent in the news just then.

"What are your views, sir, on this question of the slavery of Negroes in America? Are you an abolitionist?"

"Yes. I am against slavery on the cotton plantations just as I am against it here in England, in the mills and factories and coal-mines, especially where young children are concerned."

"But surely, sir, it is hardly the same thing, now that working hours have been improved here?"

"The improvements have not gone far enough. Thousands of men, women, and children still work in appalling conditions that maim, kill, and cause disease. But yes, the matter of the Negro slaves is atrocious. – That certain men should buy and sell their fellow human beings is utterly unspeakable."

"It would seem from recent news that war is certain to develop. Do you think, sir, that Great Britain will offer its support to the North?"

"So far our Government has been content merely to censure the Confederate States. I have not knowledge enough, I'm afraid, to speculate on its future policy."

"Our papa's in America," Susannah said unexpectedly.

"We don't know that! Not for sure!" Dick said, rounding on her; and he pushed his empty plate across the table towards her. "Will you be so good, Susannah, as to give me another slice of cake?"

Plainly the boy did not think it right that their absent father should be discussed in Martin's presence and he scowled at his sister for her lack of reticence. But then, on one of those impulses that make human behaviour so contrary at times, he suddenly burst out in a way that laid his own feelings bare to the bone.

"We've no means of knowing *where* he is, seeing that he never writes to us!"

And, suffering yet another reversal of mood, he turned his face away in shame, to stare out of the nearest window.

Katharine, pale but composed, spoke quietly to her children.

"No, we have no means of knowing where your papa may

be, but wherever he is, let us hope and pray that he is well in mind and body and that we shall soon have news of him." She turned towards Martin. "If my husband *is* in America, Martin, could he be in any danger, do you think, if the North and the South do go to war?"

"It is very unlikely," Martin said. "America is such a vast country that anyone travelling there could easily avoid all those areas where the conflict is likely to become active."

Katharine, he perceived, instead of avoiding the painful subject of her husband's whereabouts, was trying to speak of it as naturally as possible, and he took his cue from her.

"Certainly at present the country must be in a terrible turmoil, but even so, from what one hears, it is still a land of immense opportunities, and just the place where a man of ambition might well repair his broken fortunes. Only recently I heard of two brothers – Worcestershire men, apparently, – who had just returned from South Carolina … "

Martin's story eased the constraint. He already had Susannah's attention; soon he had Dick's as well; and when the story came to an end it was Dick who enquired whether Martin had ever been to America himself.

"No, never," Martin said. "My own travels have always been to the old world rather than the new. France. Turkey. Greece … Always, indeed, and for obvious reasons, I have been drawn to those places where, from ancient times onward, men have built their cities in stone."

"Notre Dame?" Dick said. "Chartres? Reims? Caen? Cologne?" His eagerness grew. "Athens?" he said. "The Parthenon?"

"Excepting Cologne, I have been to all those. Also, nearer home, to Salisbury, Exeter, Bath and Wells. And of course to St Paul's in London."

"Oh, yes, we've been there, too," Susannah said. "St Paul's, I mean."

"Then it may interest you to know that some of the stone used in its building came from our own Cotswold Hills."

"I didn't know that," Dick said.

"Neither did I," said Susannah. "Did it come from Scurr, Mr Cox?"

"No. Quarrying at Scurr only began about seventy years ago."

"Some Scurr stone has been used on this house, hasn't it? The end of the kitchen wing, for instance, and the new wing built the year I was born."

"Yes, and part of the coach-house," Martin said. "Also part of the stable-block, where some inferior stone had crumbled."

"How is it," Dick asked, "that the stone can vary in quality, even though it's all limestone?"

"That is due to a number of things. The make-up of the molten clay laid down thousands of years ago … The degree of pressure it was subjected to while it hardened … The thickness of the layer of stone … Then, in more recent times, whether the site has been wet or dry. I have some books that will tell you more, if you're interested, and perhaps one day you might like to come with me to Scurr and see the stone being cut at the quarry."

"Yes, I should like that very much."

"So should I," Susannah said.

That evening, when Martin sat alone in the drawing-room, reading, there came a knock at the door and Katharine entered.

"I wondered if I might speak to you."

"Yes, of course." He rose and ushered her to a seat by the fire. "Will you take a glass of wine?"

"No, thank you."

"Is anything wrong?"

"No, not exactly. But I feel it is high time that I made, as it were, a confession to you, because when you called on me in Cryer's Row and offered me the post of housekeeper here, it was to be until such time – those were your words, I think; – until such time as my husband returned. Martin, I have to tell you that I do not think he will *ever* return."

There was a silence. She looked up at him. Her face,

though calm, was extremely pale.

"I should have told you this before but ... I lacked the courage."

"Yes. I see." Martin sat down opposite her. "How long have you had this fear?"

"I think, perhaps, from the very beginning, when I read the letter he left for me. But he did not say so, in definite terms, and I told myself I might well be mistaken. I waited to see if we should have news. But now, when so many weeks have passed, it seems that my first thought was correct after all. I've read his letter again and again and the more I read it the more certain I am that in it he was saying goodbye forever."

"Would he be capable of that? – Going off, never to return?"

"I think, in the circumstances, yes. Some harsh things were said between us that day and it may be that he cannot forgive them. I haven't spoken of this to the children, of course, though sometimes I think they have doubts of their own, and after what Dick said in the schoolroom today—"

She broke off and drew a deep breath. After a while she spoke again.

"It is possible that my fears are groundless even now. There could be other reasons why he does not write to us. He may be ill ... He could even have died. And if that happened, in a distant land, there may not have been anyone who knew about us, to let us know." Again she paused, and again she went on; and although she spoke firmly enough, there was a note of strain in her voice. "It's a very peculiar situation to be in – not knowing if I am a wife or a widow – but no doubt I shall get used to it in time."

"You could, perhaps, try to trace your husband."

"How?"

"I don't know. I think you would need to seek legal advice."

Katharine, having considered this, shook her head.

"No. If Charles is alive and well, he must come back of his

own free choice. I will not importune him. If he means to stay away forever … well, then, I accept his decision. But that brings me round at last to my reason for speaking about it now, because we cannot stay here indefinitely, my children and I. That much is obvious."

"It is not obvious to me," Martin said. "So long as the arrangement continues to suit both parties concerned, I can see no reason for changing it."

"Well, not just at present, perhaps—"

"Then why not allow a definite term? Say six months. Better still, a year. And then, if your husband has still not returned, let us review the matter again."

"A year. Are you sure? Then my answer is yes. And oh, I can't tell you how grateful I am to be spared the necessity of making decisions! To be granted such a respite as this, here, in safety and peacefulness. If you only knew what it's meant to me—"

"I think I do know."

"Of course you do. That is why you gave it to us. You knew what we needed. You understood."

She looked at him in silence a while: a look that said more than words could do; and then she rose.

"I will leave you now to read your book. Oh, yes, I nearly forgot. My daughter asked me to give you this."

"This" was a tiny folded letter, sealed with red wax, and Martin, when Katharine had left him, opened it and read the following:

"Dear Mr Cox,

"I would like to say how much we enjoyed your company in the schoolroom this afternoon, and although I know you to be a very busy Person, I hope you will join us for schoolroom tea whenever you can spare the time.

"Yours sincerely, Susannah Yuart."

After the cold, wet summer, autumn so far had been open and mild, and Dick, still attending school in the town, walked

there and back every day, a distance of four miles in all.
Recently, he had been troubled with asthma, just as his uncle
Hugh had been, and although his condition was not serious,
Dr Whiteside advised caution. Fresh air and exercise were
beneficial, he said, but the boy should avoid getting cold and
wet.

When late November brought rain, therefore, Martin
gave orders that Jack Sherard was to take and collect Dick in
the closed carriage; and although Katharine had at the
outset been firmly resolved that neither she nor her children
should receive privileged treatment, she could not but yield
in such a matter and be grateful for Martin's consideration.

But this was only one of a number of occasions when she
found herself yielding, for Martin had his own ideas on how
she and her children should live, and went his own way to
bring it about, beginning with the purchase of two ponies for
the children to ride. Katharine, in private with Martin,
protested most vehemently, but to no avail.

"It is very important that my children should learn to live
according to their circumstances. We are not as we formerly
were. Nor shall we ever be again. They must accept that and
prepare for a future in which they will both have to earn their
living and go without what they cannot afford."

"I agree, of course. But that time has not yet come and I
think it would be an unnecessary hardship to deny them
those simple pleasures which I can so easily provide."

"Martin, I am your housekeeper. A paid employee. And it
is quite unheard of that a housekeeper's children should
enjoy such luxuries as you in your kindness would bestow on
them."

"You may be a paid employee but you are still Mrs Charles
Yuart, formerly Miss Tarrant, and here in this house, which
was once your own, you can never be *just* a housekeeper. It
is not possible. The whole of your past life is against it. It is
therefore necessary to arrive at some sort of compromise – a
balance, let us say, between your life as it was and your life as
it is now."

"And the terms of this compromise, of course, will be defined and laid down by you?"

"They will be defined," Martin said, "by a process of rational discussion culminating in mutual assent."

"I don't want my children to be spoilt, Martin."

"They will not become so. I am sure of that."

Thus, on the following Saturday morning, which was fine and sunny, Katharine went down to the stable-court to watch the children mount their ponies. They were helped by Jack Sherard, who, as in the old days, would accompany them on their ride, mounted on the Irish gelding, Pat. Nearby stood another horse, a sorrel mare, Gipsy by name, with a lady's saddle on her back. Sherard, meeting Katharine's gaze, touched his cap with his riding-crop.

"The mare needs exercising, ma'am. The master hoped you would oblige."

Katharine's lips came together in a little gesture of stubbornness. To accept favours on behalf of her children was one thing; to accept those favours herself was another; and on this point at least she meant to be firm. But there was a gleam in Sherard's eye; the mare was nuzzling Katharine's sleeve; and the two children were growing impatient.

"Look sharp, mama! You must go and change. You're keeping us waiting!" Dick exclaimed.

Katharine's firmness evaporated. The day was fine and the green hills called. With a little laugh she picked up her skirts and went hurrying back to the house to change.

Martin spent Christmas with Nan and Edward and their family, newly returned from travelling abroad. Katharine and her children spent it at Chacelands. Susannah hoped that the Christmas season would bring news from her father, but there was nothing.

"Oh, it's monstrous!" Ginny said. "Charles has been gone now for twelve weeks. Why does he keep silent like this when he knows how anxious you must be? Has he no feelings left at all? He will assume that you're living with us, so any letter is bound to come here."

George, however, on Christmas Eve, went into the town, to the Post Office, to make enquiries on Katharine's behalf, "in case of misunderstandings," he said. But his journey proved fruitless.

"I told them, if any letter comes, it is to be sent to you at Railes."

"Thank you, George. You are very kind."

The new year brought snow and for some days the roads were impassable. Newton Railes was cut off and Dick was unable to go to school. He and Susannah were delighted; they studied together in the morning and were allowed out in the afternoon, to romp in the grounds, which, for the most part, were free of drifts. Often Katharine joined them and they tramped together as far as the lake, with the two spaniels, Snug and Quince, who rolled in the snow and snapped at it and chased the snowballs the children threw.

Sometimes, from a window, Martin would see them return; would hear them in the back porch, where they stamped the snow from their boots on the mat, hung up their coats and mufflers and hats, and laughed at the antics of the dogs, who tried to escape a brisk towelling. And Martin would smile to himself, glad of these indications that life here at Railes brought some joy to them.

The snow lay for almost a week and was then washed away by heavy rain. February filled the dykes, sometimes to overflowing, until March winds came, keen from the east, to scarify the land and dry it out. Still there was no letter from Charles Yuart, and it was now almost six months since he had disappeared. The children seldom mentioned him now, and when they did it was with resignation. Their life at Railes was quiet and, on the whole, untroubled. Martin made sure of that. But still they kept too much to themselves and he resolved to do something about it.

Always, when he entertained friends, Katharine, though making all the arrangements and supervising work in the kitchen, remained strictly in the background, in accordance with her position. But now Martin planned a small informal supper party and wanted her to preside as hostess. Katharine demurred at once. It would not be fitting, she said. The circumstances were against it.

"You have not heard me out," he said. "The party I am proposing is, you might say, a family affair. Just your sister and her husband; my own sister and brother-in-law, together with their four young sons; and, of course, Dick and Susannah. Now, surely you must consent to join such a gathering as that, if only for your children's sake?"

"You make it very hard to refuse."

"I hope I have made it impossible."

The party was held on a March evening when, although the wind still blew cold, there was a hint of spring in the air. Supper was begun at half past five, and after it there were games and charades in the drawing-room, interspersed with music and singing. Susannah plainly enjoyed the distinction of being the only girl among so many boys, and the adults were amused to observe with what care she divided her favours among the young Claytons. She was filled with extreme elation, too, at being allowed to play duets, first with her mother, then with her aunt, on the magnificent Broadwood piano.

During a lull in the entertainments, George Winter stood talking to Nan.

"You have a fine quartet of sons, Mrs Clayton. I congratulate you on their looks and on their excellent behaviour."

"Thank you, Mr Winter. They are not always so well-behaved as they are this evening but I must say, by and large, they give little cause for anxiety."

Martin now came and joined them, glad of the chance of talking to George, with whom, over supper, he had exchanged only a few brief remarks. George had a somewhat formal manner but responded affably enough to Martin's attempt at friendliness.

"This is the first time I've set foot in this house for something over a twelvemonth," he said. "My relations with Charles Yuart were not very cordial latterly, so naturally I stayed away. You don't seem to have made any changes here and I must say I'm glad of that. Everything looks exactly the same as it always did in the old days and of course with your having Katharine here—" George broke off somewhat awkwardly and began talking instead of the grounds. "I hear you've improved the trout stream here. I'd like to do the same with mine and I should be glad of your advice if it isn't asking too much of you."

Martin was answering this when Ginny came and took his arm.

"I'm sorry to interrupt you, George, when you're talking about your favourite sport, but we're going to sing 'Don Sinnuendo' and we want Martin to be the Don."

Martin excused himself and George was left alone with Nan.

"Do you not sing, Mr Winter?"

"Not if my wife can help it. She says I keep changing key all the time. I daresay she's in the right of it. I haven't a good enough ear to know."

During the singing of "Don Sinnuendo", where Ginny, in the rôle of Pepita, flirted with Martin as the Don, finally laying her fair head gently upon his bosom, she acted her part, Nan thought, with rather more feeling than was strictly necessary. Her husband obviously thought so, too, but hid his feelings well enough by applauding loudly at the end. Nan observed, also, that Martin, as soon as the piece ended, made a point of returning to George, to resume his conversation with him.

After the Spanish interlude, there were musical games. Katharine played "hidden tunes", one after another, in a rapid medley, while her listeners sought to identify them. Then it was Nan's turn at the piano and she played "La Bande Militaire", while all the children stood in a row and played on imaginary instruments: drums, flute, bagpipes, etc., her own two eldest boys reducing the company to helpless laughter by the ferocious faces they made, pretending to puff on horn and trombone.

The evening was a merry one and it was almost twelve o'clock when the two groups of visitors took their leave. Indeed, Martin and Katharine, Dick and Susannah, were standing talking in the great hall when the tall clock on the half-landing began striking the midnight hour. Susannah was delighted at this and held up her hand, beseeching silence. Then, when the last chime had sounded, she whirled herself round and round very fast and, coming to a stop in front of Martin, sank in a deep curtsey, amidst her still billowing skirts.

"Sir, I would like to thank you for a truly delightful evening. I have not been so well entertained for many a long day past. What is more, it's the first time in my life I have ever stayed up till the following morning!"

"So it is for me," Dick said, "and I am older than you, my girl."

When, having lingered as long as they dared, they had said good night and gone up to bed, Katharine turned and spoke to Martin.

"Seeing my children so happy this evening makes me realize how selfish I've been. I've cut myself off too much from the world and my poor children have suffered for it. Susannah in particular, for she sees no young people but Dick. I've pleaded the change in my position, but part of that was just an excuse to hide myself away here, like an animal nursing its wounds. I lacked the courage to face the world in my new identity as deserted wife."

"You needed time," Martin said.

"Yes, I did. But now I need, as you told me once, to reach some degree of compromise between the old life and the new. And due to your help, as in so many things, I think I am close to that compromise. Now I must go up and see the children into bed. Good night, Martin, and again my thanks – for being such a good friend to us."

*

Spring came early that year and on the first Monday in April Jobe the gardener came to Katharine to say he thought it warm enough to fetch the bee-skeps out of the garth and stand them about the gardens. Where, he asked, would she like them put?

"That is a matter for Mr Cox to decide."

"Master's busy just now, ma'am. He said I should ask you."

"Very well. I'll come and see."

Another day Jobe came to consult her about transplanting the melon plants; later it was a question of bedding out the geraniums; of thinning the fruit on the vines in the greenhouse; of picking the first crop of strawberries. In this way she was kept busy, doing the things she loved best. She no longer shut herself away in her room as soon as her household tasks were done, but came and went, indoors and out, almost as freely as of old. It was the same with the children; they had accepted Martin's friendship and were perfectly at ease with him. Susannah, especially, was quite without shyness in this respect and always had some story to tell him; some discovery to impart; some accomplishment to display.

"Would you like to hear my new piece? It's a sonata by Johann Hummel."

"Yes, I would like that very much. But if you are to do yourself justice, you must play it for me on the Broadwood."

"Oh, Martin, I *hoped* you'd say that! It seems you must have read my mind."

"My daughter," Katharine said, alone with Martin afterwards, "is taking advantage of your goodwill."

"Surely that is what goodwill is for?"

"Furthermore, just recently, she has taken to using your first name. I'm not sure it should be allowed."

"May I not be the judge of that?"

"You are too lenient a judge, I fear. But my children are not the only ones who take advantage of you. I do it myself

and have done from the very beginning. Accepting asylum
under your roof, and all your many kindnesses, I have taken
you too much at your word, and as a result I find that time
is slipping past almost unnoticed."

"And what harm can there be," Martin said, "in living as
Scripture bids us do?"

Katharine smiled.

" 'Take therefore no thought for the morrow, for the
morrow shall take thought for the things of itself.'"

It was easy enough for Katharine to leave the future to take
care of itself because inclination favoured it. Her children
were happy and secure and this alone was quite enough to
make her happy too. Her sister Ginny, so often at Railes,
noted the improvement in her and gave credit where it was
due.

"I thought coming back here would be too painful for you,
but it seems Martin knew best after all. Seeing you smiling
and laughing again, I think I could almost forgive him for
taking Railes away from us."

The two sisters were alone together because Martin had
taken Dick and Susannah to see Scurr Quarry. Katharine sat
doing some needlework; she was smocking the bodice of a
frock for Susannah; and Ginny, in reflective mood, was
studying her intently.

"Kate," she said eventually, "have you ever thought what
you would do if Charles never returned at all?"

"Yes, I've thought about it often and long, but there is
nothing I *can* do."

"No, that is the awful thing, because George made enquiries
on your behalf when he saw Mr Godwin recently. He asked
about your position in law and it seems you cannot divorce
Charles for desertion unless he has been unfaithful as well.
But Mr Godwin said that after a period of seven years you
could apply to the court for a legal presumption of your
husband's death."

Katharine, who had lowered her needlework into her lap,

stared at her sister in angry surprise.

"*George* made enquiries?"

"Yes," Ginny said. "He does have his uses, occasionally. But if you're offended, you mustn't blame him, for he did it only at my request."

"Ginny, you had no right to do that, and if you had asked me first, I should have forbidden it utterly."

"Surely you wish to know how you stand? *I* should wish it if I were you."

"Why should I? What use is the knowledge now that I have it? Charles has divorced himself from *me*, though not by process of law, so why should I need to divorce him, even if it were possible? As for the alternative, what woman, in God's name, would wish to presume her husband dead?"

"Because, my dear Kate, in years to come, she might perhaps wish to marry again."

"I shall never wish such a thing."

"You cannot know," Ginny said. "You feel that now at this moment, of course, but it may be a very different matter when a number of years have gone by."

"I shall have grown old by then."

"Oh, no, you won't! You must *not* grow old! You must stay young for your children's sake and to make up to yourself somehow for the hurt and unhappiness Charles has caused you. Surely you feel some anger against him for abandoning you and the children like this? Of course you do! And so you should. Wasn't that partly why you accepted Martin's offer of employment here? Because it was just the opposite of what Charles assumed you would do? Oh, I know you wanted your independence. – You've always been obstinate about that. – But if you are honest I'm sure you'll admit that it was also a kind of revenge, because you knew how Charles would hate the idea of your coming back here to Newton Railes to work for Martin of all people."

"As by now it appears certain that Charles does not intend to come back, he will never know what I've done. But yes, Ginny, you are quite right. – I did feel a certain satisfaction in doing something I knew he would hate ... Rather an ignoble motive, I'm afraid, and certainly not my chief one, but—"

"Oh, my dear! You can't expect always to live up to your own high principles. And indeed it's a great comfort to me to find that my high-minded sister is guilty of mean thoughts sometimes. It restores my faith in human nature."

With the coming of spring and the warm weather, Ginny was at Railes more and more, sometimes two or three days a week. She never sent word of her intentions; she came when the impulse moved her; and she liked to take them by surprise.

"I'm really quite grateful to Martin now for employing you as his housekeeper. It gives me such a good excuse for coming back to the old place. Not to mention making it easy for me to see *you*, my dears."

It was an afternoon at the end of May and the two sisters, with Susannah, were strolling about the gardens. Underfoot, in the green walk, the calamint yielded up its scent, while, out on the open parterre, as they emerged into full sunshine, they were met by the warm heady sweetness of the wall-flowers – crimson, yellow, and claret-brown – that filled the border beneath the terrace. From the parterre they walked down to the lower lawn and sat together on the stone bench that gave a fine view of the parkland. There, among the limes and the sycamores, only now beginning to leaf, the chestnut trees were in full glory, their pyramids of creamy white blossom standing erect among the bright green leaves, tier upon tier on the undulent branches.

"Railes in the springtime is beautiful. Everything is just at its best. It's so beautiful, it actually hurts, and as I was driving up through the park, I couldn't help thinking that if only I had married Martin, I should have been mistress here now, and all this loveliness would be mine. Just think of that, my dears! – Mistress in my old home."

Susannah's eyes had opened wide.

"Did Martin propose to you, then, aunt Ginny, long ago when you were young?"

"No, he never did propose. But he would have done, I daresay, if I had ever encouraged him."

"Do you wish you were married to him?"

"Sometimes, my dear Susannah, I could wish myself married to any man, so long as it wasn't your uncle George."

"Oh, dear!" Susannah said. "Have you and he been quarrelling again?"

"Quarrelling, I very much fear, is the only thing that keeps us alive."

A little while later, when Susannah, at her aunt's request, had gone into the house to "rout Martin out of his study", Katharine took up the subject of George.

"These quarrels you have so frequently – I trust they're not really serious."

"No, no! We do but quarrel in jest, that's all."

"Sometimes it seems, from what you say, that you go out of your way to provoke him."

"Well, I have to do something to pass the time."

"And I can't help feeling it is less than wise to come here so often as you do, now that this is Martin's home."

"I come to see you, and my nephew and niece, not Martin," Ginny said.

"Does George believe that?"

"Probably not. He is suspicious of everything. But I'm not giving up my visits here, whatever George may think or feel. Why, this is the one bright spot in my life! The one haven where I can be safe from the aura of George's disapproval."

Ginny's haven, however, was not so safe as she supposed, and scarcely had she spoken these words when there was a sound of voices and, turning, she beheld her niece coming tripping across the lawn, bringing not only Martin but her uncle George as well.

"What on earth are you doing here?" Ginny demanded, with frank displeasure.

"I am here by invitation," George replied equably. "You

may remember, at the party in March, that Mr Cox very civilly offered to show me the work he's had done on the trout stream."

"You didn't tell me you were coming today."

"Nor did you tell me that you were."

"How ridiculous."

"Yes. I agree. We could have come together."

There was a cold silence. Ginny looked away in disdain. George spoke to Katharine; Martin offered a few remarks; and then the two men went off together, down across the lawn to the nearest gate that would let them out into the park.

"There! You see! That is typical. He must always be spoiling things. And why Martin should ask him here, knowing what I have to bear from him, is more than I can well comprehend."

"I think Martin, very sensibly, is anxious to avoid being the cause of any misunderstanding between you. Plainly he means to be friends with George."

"Well, I wish him joy of it!" Ginny suddenly stood up. "And now, my dears, I will take my leave of you. No, no, I won't stay to tea. My pleasure in the day is quite spoilt. You may tell my lord and master that I am gone to my dressmaker. Perhaps he would like to follow me there!"

Susannah, when her aunt had gone, was eager to question her mother on a subject mentioned earlier.

"Aunt Ginny seems to think that Martin was once in love with her. Do you think he was, mama?"

"A great many young men were in love with your aunt in earlier days."

"Including Martin?"

"I cannot say."

"If it's true that he loved her … that may be why he has never married."

"Possibly, yes. But Martin is still a young man and I have no doubt whatsoever that he *will* marry one of these days, when the right young woman comes along."

"Oh, I hope he does not, mama, for what would become of us if he did?"

Soon, now, the English papers were full of news from America, where, in April, the attack on Fort Sumter had brought North and South into active conflict. Katharine discussed the war with her children, just as she did all current events, and together they studied a map in the newspaper, showing where the main events had occurred. During these discussions, their absent father was rarely mentioned, and then only by Katharine herself. Dick, with his stubborn reserve, would not be drawn on the subject at all. As far as he was concerned, his father no long existed, but since he could not say this to his mother, he remained silent. Alone with his sister, however, he was outspoken.

"Father's been gone now for more than eight months and we've heard nothing. He's not coming back, obviously, and I'm sure mama herself is resigned to that, although she still speaks of him as she does."

"But you do still pray for him, don't you, Dick?"

"No, I do not."

"Even though he might be in danger in the fighting between the states?"

"He didn't have to go there. And if he is there, he needn't stay. And as it is perfectly plain that he doesn't care about us any more, I don't see why we should care about him."

CHAPTER
—10—

Although Katharine, in her changed situation, could take no great part in social affairs, she was at least beginning to go about more freely now, within her own small circle of family and friends. There were visits to Ginny and George at Chacelands; to the Claytons at Town End; and, during the midsummer days, long excursions by wagonette, when all three families travelled together to Malvern, or Bath, or the Forest of Dean, where they picnicked together, happy and relaxed.

At home, too, a great deal of time was spent out of doors. Martin had introduced croquet at Railes and croquet parties were all the go. Ginny, especially, developed a passion for the game and would play it all day long if she could. She always insisted that Martin should be her partner, and she played according to her own rules, often cheating outrageously, especially when playing against George. Her behaviour became so blatant that even Dick and Susannah were sometimes out of patience with her.

"Aunt Ginny is very foolish these days. I do wish you'd speak to her, mama."

Katharine agreed with them, but speaking to Ginny brought no good result.

"If George doesn't like my behaviour, he had better stay at home."

"If you will not consider George's feelings, you might at least consider Martin's. He always behaves with great correctness but it must be very difficult for him when you flirt with him so openly."

Ginny merely smiled at this and gave a little careless shrug. Her behaviour, if anything, grew worse, and one afternoon, at the end of a visit, when George was ready to depart, and the Denbigh carriage stood in the courtyard, Ginny herself was not to be found.

"I've reminded her at least three times that we are dining at Parke House but she is determined to make us late."

George was kept fuming for twenty minutes. Then at last Ginny appeared, strolling to the carriage in a languid way, a shallow basket on her arm, containing peaches and nectarines.

"I suddenly had a yearning for them, so I went to the greenhouse and helped myself. You don't mind, do you, Martin? I've only taken a few, as you see. Now, before bidding each other goodbye, we must fix a date for our visit to Tintern— "

"Not now," Martin said, taking her firmly by the arm. "You have kept your husband waiting quite long enough for one day and I will not take part in causing him further annoyance."

George, his face like a thundercloud, handed her into the Denbigh and climbed in beside her without a word. He took the reins into his hands and drove away without more ado, nodding to Martin as he passed.

"You didn't ask if I wanted to drive."

"No. I did not."

"I might well remind you, George, that this carriage and pair are mine."

"And I might remind *you*, madam, that it was I who paid for them."

George, leaning forward slightly, touched the horses with his whip. When he leant back again, Ginny dug him in the ribs.

"Don't take your spite out on those poor brutes. They haven't done you any harm."

"I am not doing anything of the kind."

"Oh, and you're not in a temper, I suppose? That black

scowl is just for fun!"

"I *am* in a temper. I admit that. Furthermore, I have good cause."

"Yes. You lost at croquet again."

"You kept me waiting a full twenty minutes, even though you know quite well that we're dining with the Robertsons."

"Oh, goodness, is that all? What a mountain you make of everything."

"No, madam, it is *not* all. It is your conduct as a whole, especially during the past few weeks."

"You'll have to be more specific than that."

"Very well. Since you insist. It's the way you behave with Martin Cox."

"Ah, yes. I thought it might be."

"I suppose it has never occurred to you that he might find it embarrassing?"

"George, dear, you're being a cat."

"I know you assume he's in love with you but my own impression is very different and if you had any sense you would see—"

"Yes, George? What should I see?"

"Oh, never mind! It's all of a piece. The plain truth of the matter is that you flirt with him, as with other men, on purpose to enrage *me*."

"I have no wish to see you enraged. It is not an amusing spectacle."

"And you, of course, take it for granted that my chief function in life is merely to keep you amused."

"And what is *my* chief function, pray?"

"A married woman of your age should not need to ask such a question."

"But I do ask it. I should like to know."

"You could take more interest in your home for a start, and the running of your own household."

"My household runs itself. Which is to say, the staff run it for me. So if that is my one and only function, you really don't need a wife at all."

"I didn't say it was your *only* function."

"What others do I have, I wonder? You expect me to provide wifely comforts, of course, especially in the marriage bed. Well, as to that, I do my best."

"I have no complaint on that score," George replied, in a prim voice, "except that I should be happier if I thought it meant something to you."

"Why, what should it mean, precisely?"

"Love, for one thing," George said, and stared ahead, woodenly, narrowing his eyes against the dust rising in a cloud from the horses' hooves.

"And what else besides?"

"Most women, if they be worthy of the name, would naturally desire to have children."

"Ah, now we come to it!" Ginny exclaimed. "The crux of the matter! The festering gall! I've always known that I was a disappointment to you in this respect. You have made that quite plain over the years. But I never can quite understand why every man always assumes it must be the woman who is at fault."

"You can't pretend that you wanted children."

"What has wanting to do with it? Surely you are not suggesting that simply by not wanting a child a woman can stop it from happening? Because if you are, *that*, my dear George, is nothing but rank superstition."

"I am suggesting no such thing. But women do, so I've heard, have their own secret ways of … of preventing it if they so choose."

"*Do* they? Good gracious me!" Ginny, turning, stared at him, lifting the folds of her travelling-veil to obtain a better view of his face. "Well, this is the first I've heard of it and I've no idea what you're talking about."

"Haven't you?" He met her gaze.

"No. I have not."

Her look and her tone were quite enough to convince him that she was speaking the truth. She, in turn, was able to see that his surprise was as great as hers.

"D'you mean to tell me that all these years we have been married, you thought I was interfering with the course of nature?"

"Well ... yes."

"Then I think you owe me an apology. Admittedly, the sad fact remains that I have not given you a child, but even so, it still doesn't follow that I am inevitably to blame. The fault could just as easily be yours."

George was now facing forward again, his gaze fixed on the horses' ears.

"I am quite confident it is not."

"Men always say that, of course. But the facts don't always bear them out. Think of Squire Barnaby over at Sharveston Court. Eight years married and no child. But when he died and his widow remarried, she had four children all in a row. And that is not the only instance. I can think of two others at least where the circumstances proved—"

"Yes, there are instances enough. But I'm sure it is not the case with me."

"How can you be sure?" Ginny demanded.

"I wish you would please allow, just this once, that there are some things a man may know without being able to explain why."

"I will allow no such thing. Indeed, I insist that you should explain. Otherwise I shall be obliged to assume the worst of you, my dear George. After all, there is only one way you can be sure of what you assert, and that is if you had fathered a child elsewhere."

George was silent, still staring ahead. His broad face, with its strong jaw, was finely coated with dust from the road, but underneath this coating of dust she could see the colour flushing his skin. She could also see a little nerve pulsing at the side of his mouth.

"George," she said, "will you look at me?"

"What for?"

"You know what for."

He turned his head and looked at her, doing his best to

present an expression of sternest equanimity. The task proved beyond him; the challenge of her bright gaze was too strong; and his own gaze soon fell away.

"So," she said softly, drawing out the word. "So, my dear George, that's how it is ... And you have the barefaced impudence to criticize me simply for flirting with Martin Cox."

Disliking the dust on her own face, she let her veil down again, but she continued to study him as they drove for a while in silence.

"Well, well," she said at last, giving a little chuckling laugh. "Who would have thought of such a thing? It seems to me that when we get home, you will have some explaining to do, my dear."

Alone with him in their bedroom, having sent her maid away, Ginny questioned him closely.

"Is it a son or a daughter?" she asked.

"A son," George said. He cleared his throat.

"How old is he?"

"He is almost nine."

"Do you see him?"

"Yes, of course."

"What is his name?"

"Anthony."

"Where is his mother?"

"She is dead. She died of pneumonia six years ago."

"Oh, poor girl! How old was she? What was her name? Did you love her, George?"

"Really, Ginny, I cannot see that there is anything to be gained by going into the matter like this—"

"I think I should be the judge of that, seeing that I am the injured party." She looked at him consideringly. "I am not shocked, you know."

"No," he said, "it appears not."

"Would you prefer it if I were?"

"I don't know how to answer that."

"Tell me about the boy's mother. How and where did you meet her?"

"It was back in 1851. You were being very cold to me at that time and then you went off to London with Katharine and Charles, to visit the Great Exhibition, and you stayed up there for more than six weeks."

"Oh, dear! Poor George, poor George! Obviously, then, it was all my fault for going and leaving you by yourself. I might have known you would find some way of laying the blame for it all on me."

"I did not intend to do that."

"Of course you did. You always do. But on one count you are right to blame me, for you have a child and I have not, which means that I have indeed failed you."

"Almost, you sound as though you were sorry."

"Well, no woman likes to find she is barren. It seems you had better divorce me."

"Don't be ridiculous."

"Well, I'm not likely to conceive now, unless I should be like Sarah, that is, in which case I'll laugh as Sarah did and be scolded for my naughty doubts. But let us return to Anthony. Where are you hiding him?"

"He is with his grandparents, but I'm not going to tell you where that is."

"Oh, yes, you are," Ginny said, "because otherwise I shall go about rousing the whole countryside until I find him."

"With what object?"

"Because I want to see him, of course, Do you expect me to be indifferent to the fact that you have a son?"

"I don't know what I expected. I didn't intend you should find out. But if you are really serious—"

"I am perfectly serious. You can take me today."

"We are dining with the Robertsons."

"Oh, never mind the Robertsons! Send word to them that I am not well and that you are too worried to leave me alone. Please, George, you really must, for I am in such an excitement of nerves, I should probably blurt something out to them. Go down now and write them a note. Don't cancel the carriage, however. We'll go and see Anthony straight away."

They drove out to Sharveston; to a tailor's shop in Easton Street; and there, in the room behind the shop, Ginny met the tailor and his wife, a respectable couple in their fifties, Mr and Mrs Jeffery by name. At first they were somewhat dismayed when George introduced Ginny to them, but recovered themselves soon enough and spoke to her in a way that was civil and deferential, without any trace of obsequiousness. After a while they withdrew. Ginny and George remained in the room and Anthony was sent in to them, having been fetched down from his bedroom, where he had been doing school prep.

The boy was tall for his nine years, and was sturdily built. He had a smooth pelt of chestnut-brown hair, eyes of a light hazel colour, and a broad, handsome, freckled face. He was, in a word, the image of George, and Ginny, as she gave him her hand, looked from one face to the other in laughing amazement.

"So you are Anthony Jeffery."

"Yes, ma'am."

"Do you know who this gentleman is?"

"Yes, he's my uncle Winter, ma'am."

"And do you know who I am?"

"You are my uncle Winter's wife."

"How do you know that?"

"Because he once described you to me."

"It was a fair description, then?"

"Yes, ma'am, it was fair enough. And I would like to say, ma'am, how pleased I am to make your acquaintance."

"That is very pretty, sir. I am equally well pleased. My one and only regret is that it didn't happen sooner than this. Never mind. We have plenty of time to make amends. Would you like to come for a drive with us?"

"Yes, ma'am. Indeed I should."

"Go and find your grandparents, then, and we will ask them for their consent."

It so happened that Sharveston was holding its annual summer fair, down on the great town meadow between the two rivers, the Leame and the Cullen. Anthony asked to be taken there; was given a few coppers to spend; and went on a tour of the booths and stalls; – the coconut shy; the menagerie; – and watched a blackamoor swallowing fire; – while George and Ginny strolled behind. They then returned to the carriage and drove down to the bank of the Leame, well away from the noise of the fair, to a place where there were willows, and ducks, and coot, and sand-martins nesting under the bank. Anthony went to feed the ducks, throwing them pieces of gingerbread, while Ginny and George sat in the carriage watching him.

"Oh, George, he's quite beautiful!"

"Is he?" George said, in a husky voice.

"You know perfectly well he is."

"Well, he is quite a fine-looking lad, I agree. And he has a kindly nature, too."

"To think you have kept him hid all this time. How very sly and secretive you've been. I never had any suspicion at all." She looked at him with arch mockery. " 'Uncle' Winter," she said with a laugh. "I think from now on I shall call you Pope George." Then, after a while, she said: "He must come and live with us, of course."

"Good God! Are you serious?"

"Yes, of course. But why do you look so doubtful? Do you think the Jefferys would object?"

"No, I'm sure they will not. They have been very good to the boy, but they are no longer young, and I've no doubt they will be glad to be relieved of the responsibility. The problem lies in the fact that the boy bears a resemblance to me. If we have him at Chacelands, it is bound to cause talk."

"Yes, it will, most certainly."

"Won't you find that embarrassing?"

"Not in the slightest," Ginny said. "*You* will find it embarrassing and I shall enjoy watching it. But the most important thing is that you *ought* to have your son with you, seeing he's the only one you've got. And surely you are proud of him?"

"Of the boy, yes. Very proud. But of the liaison that gave him being … well, my feelings there are quite the reverse."

"Yes, and so they should be, indeed. It is only right and proper that you should feel guilty and ashamed, and you'll have to be very kind and indulgent to me, for some years to come, if you are ever to atone for it."

"Are you never serious?"

"You would prefer me in tears, I suppose, asking how you could have deceived me so. Well, that is not what I feel. Anyway, just look at that boy! How could I, or anyone else, wish that he had never been born?"

"You are being very good about it."

"Yes, on the whole, I think I am."

"Indeed, I would go so far as to say that you seem to be enjoying the situation."

"Yes. You have succeeded in surprising me and I didn't think that was possible. You are not nearly so staid as I thought. Nor so tiresomely virtuous."

Sitting together in the Denbigh, husband and wife regarded each other. Ginny had removed her veil and was studying him with a bright-eyed stare, attending to him with an interest she had not shown for years. George, for his own part, though he still questioned her complaisance, and doubted the propriety of it, could not resist the tide of warmth that so pleasurably flooded his veins in response to this change in her. With a cautious glance around him, to make sure they were not overheard, he spoke to her in a low voice.

"Must I, then, be unfaithful to you, to renew your interest at intervals?"

"Oh, dear me, no! Certainly not! It is *my* turn to be unfaithful next. That, surely, is only fair."

"Ginny, I wish you would not joke about such things."

"There! Now you're all solemn again. But why should it be so different for me to do as you have done?"

"Because I love you so very much that if such a thing were ever to happen, it would be more than I could bear."

"Well, don't be upset. You needn't worry. I would keep it a secret, I promise you." Still teasing, but smiling, too, she laid a hand upon his knee. "Surely," she said, softly, "loving me is not such a very terrible thing, is it?"

"Sometimes it is, most certainly. Whenever you flout me and say hurtful things … it is terrible enough."

"And at other times?" Ginny asked, with a beguiling tilt of her chin. "How is it then?"

"At other times it is – tolerable."

Ginny laughed. She liked her husband in this new mood. And who would have dreamt, this afternoon, that two hours later he and she would be sitting together so intimately, flirting with one another like this? After thirteen years of marriage, too! It really was quite absurd.

"That reminds me of something," she said. "What were you going to say to me when we were quarrelling earlier, and you were scolding me about Martin? You implied there was something I didn't know and didn't have the sense to see. Those were your words, I believe, and I would like to know what you meant."

"It was nothing," George said. "I was in a temper, as you said at the time."

"It's no good being evasive, George, for I'll get it out of you in the end. You may be quite sure of that. However, just for the present I'll leave well alone. We have more important things on hand. I think now we should take Anthony home to his grandparents and discuss the boy's future with them. It's high time he was given his rightful place in your home. It must be settled without more ado."

During the following week, however, refusing to wait while "arrangements" were made, she was seeing the boy every day and taking him with her wherever she went.

"This is Anthony, my adopted son," she said, introducing him at Railes. "As it is quite clear by now that I cannot have children myself, we are adopting him, George and I, and he will soon be living with us. Anthony, this is your aunt Katharine, and this is your cousin Susannah. Say how do you do to them and sit on that stool where they can see you."

She enjoyed the stir her announcement caused and she sat for a while in complete silence, watching and listening carefully while her sister and her niece spoke to the boy and did their best to hide their surprise. As such silence was foreign to her, she very quickly grew tired of it and suggested that Susannah should take Anthony for a walk, to meet Dick coming home from school. The two children being out of the way, she immediately fixed her sister with a mischievous, laughing stare.

"Well, and what do you think of him?"

"Why," Katharine said, cautiously, "he is a very fine-looking boy and, allowing for youthful shyness, has the makings of good manners, I think."

"Is that all you have to say?"

"Well, naturally I am wondering where he's come from, if that's what you mean."

"Surely you, as a wife and mother, must know the answer to that, my dear Kate, for where do children ever come from, whether born in wedlock or not? And if you are thinking he looks like George, why, then, perdee, and so he does. And with very good reason, I assure you." Then, as her sister stayed silent, she said: "Poor Kate, are you scandalized?"

"I don't know if I am or not. It is quite certain, I suppose?"

"Quite certain. Cross my heart. George has confessed everything and spoken suitable words of shame. So now you see, my dear sister, that you are not the only wronged wife in the family. But there's no need to look at me like that. I am not in the least upset. On the contrary, I think it's quite the drollest thing that has happened in years, and I fully intend to squeeze every ounce of enjoyment from it. I also intend to exact my revenge, for I shall tease George without mercy, and never again, for the rest of our lives, will he be allowed to scold or upbraid me for *my* conduct."

Martin was not at home that day, but was introduced to Anthony on Ginny's next visit, the following week. By that time he had already heard about the boy, first from Susannah, then from Kate, and Ginny was thus robbed of the pleasure of witnessing his initial surprise.

"That is half the fun, you know, – watching the way people respond when I take Anthony anywhere. But you have cheated me out of that, so instead you must tell me what you thought and felt when you heard. Aren't you indignant on my behalf, knowing that George has been unfaithful to me?"

"No, why should I be," Martin said, "when plainly you're not indignant yourself?"

"That has got nothing to do with it. It would still have been pleasant to feel that there was some gallantry left in the world, and I can't help thinking that if you had ever felt any real tenderness for me, you would be wanting to knock George down."

"Gallantry, as you well know, was never one of my virtues."

"At least you will perhaps allow that I am behaving very well, being so kind to George's son and having him to live with us?"

"Yes. I think you are being most sensible."

"You approve, then, it seems."

"Yes, I do. It will give you something to think about – at least so long as the novelty lasts."

"Oh, you wretch!" Ginny exclaimed; but she eyed him without any trace of rancour. "Plainly George is quite right. You don't care a button for me, which means I have been twice deceived."

Soon, arrangements for Anthony's adoption were completed and he was living with Ginny and George. He no longer went to school in Sharveston but had a private tutor at home. There had been talk of sending him to Rugby, George's old school, but Ginny had protested vehemently.

"He has no sooner come to us than you would send him away again. The poor boy is only nine. He won't know whether he's on his head or his heels."

George found it easy enough to yield, so Anthony, it was decided, would go to Rugby the following year. Meantime, when not with his tutor, he accompanied Ginny everywhere. She was enchanted with this new toy; heaped a great many presents upon him; and, as Katharine said to Martin, was in great danger of spoiling him.

"But I dare say she will get over that. And George, I think, will be firm enough. It seems they intend telling him that George is his father, not his uncle, but are giving him time to settle down. It has caused a stir in the neighbourhood, Ginny says, but she is quite frankly revelling in it. It is certainly an unusual situation."

"Unusual, but not unique," Martin said, "and in early days, from what we are told, it was even commonplace."

"In noble houses, yes, of course, and especially in royal ones. But I never expected to see such a thing within my own family. However, I can't help feeling that it may be productive of good, because now, for the first time in years, Ginny and George have a common interest. Indeed, I hardly like to be too sanguine, but I think it has done the marriage good." Katharine, meeting Martin's gaze, gave a smile and added: "Though she still cheats just as shamelessly when playing against him at croquet!"

But the croquet summer was nearing its end. Soon the hoops were removed from the lawn and put away with the mallets and balls, into the box with rope handles, which was stored in one of Jobe's garden sheds. There was a nip in the morning air; the dewy grass was silver with cobwebs; and the first bonfires were lit in the grounds, burning the first of the fallen leaves.

Soon, from the little birch grove outside one wall of the Tudor garden, came the sound of axes biting into wood. The trees were diseased and had to be felled; each stump was being grubbed up; and the timber burnt immediately on a fire in the space already cleared. One misty afternoon, Dick, Susannah, and Anthony were helping to heap the wood on the fire, while nearby the adults stood watching them. Katharine stood talking to George. Ginny and Martin stood some way behind.

"It makes me sad to see those birches go," Ginny said. "They've been there ever since I can remember. We used to play in them, Hugh and I, when we were children together. The trunks were much more silvery then … and the leaves in spring had a sweet rough scent … Hugh always loved these birch trees, especially when a breeze was blowing, and we used to swing up and down on the branches, with the leaves all whispering about our heads."

Ginny turned and looked up at Martin.

"Oh, for the days that are gone!" she said, and suddenly there were tears in her eyes. "Sweet happy days when life lay before us and I thought the world would be young forever. Tell me, Martin, do you ever have the feeling that you are still waiting for life to begin? No, no, of course you don't! You are like Katharine in that respect. You both always do what you *mean* to do. But it is rather strange, is it not, that I, who always live for the moment, should feel the moment has passed me by, while you and Kate on the other hand – Oh, I don't know! I can't explain. I don't even know what I'm trying to say."

Still looking at him, she laughed through her tears, and her face had a sweetly vulnerable look that he had seen there only rarely. He began speaking to her but she silenced him with sudden brusqueness.

"No, don't encourage my foolishness. Let us talk of practical things. Tell me what you will do with this ground. Shall you replant it with new birch trees?"

"No. Jobe thinks it's wiser not, in case they take the same disease. But your sister has an excellent plan and I think, when you have spoken to her, you'll find it more than compensates for the loss of this little grove here."

*

The grove of birches now being felled grew outside the north wall of the Tudor garden, always known as the "blind" wall because there was no gateway in it. Katharine's plan was that a gateway should be made in this wall, to correspond with all the others, and that outside this gateway, the approach should be planted with a double row of laburnum trees, interspersed with wisteria, which, when they grew and were pleached overhead, would form an arbour some thirty feet long. The surrounding area would be newly turfed and planted in semi-wild fashion with daffodils and fritillaries, bluebells and quamassias, all the way to the little stream that fed the round pool and the bog-garden.

Later that afternoon, while the men and the children were still out of doors, Ginny and her sister sat together in the drawing-room. Katharine was looking through some music that Ginny had brought, and Ginny was looking through Katharine's sketchbook, which contained her designs for the new arbour and the wrought-iron gates.

"Well?" Katharine said, glancing up. "What do you think of them?"

"I think the whole scheme is beautiful. We always wished for a gate in that wall and *you* always wished you could find space for planting your laburnum arbour. Now it is all coming to pass. – As many things do, given time. You know, Kate, I was just thinking – and that not for the first time – how strangely things have worked out for you … and, in the end, how agreeably, too … because, except for Charles being gone, your life in this house is just as it was in the days when you were mistress here."

Katharine frowned. It was a while before she answered.

"I don't quite understand you, Ginny. You speak as though Charles being gone were a matter of small consequence. Almost it seems as if you forget that it is my husband you're speaking of."

"No, I am not forgetting it, Kate. But since you take me up

so gravely, I feel bound to say that in my own humble opinion you are better off without him. And surely the hurt of it has grown less in the twelve months that have passed since then?"

"Yes. Much less."

"Of course it has! One has only to look at you! And Railes can be thanked for much of that. Railes and Martin between them. But what I referred to in the first instance related to your position here. You are a paid housekeeper, yes, but any stranger coming into the room would think you were the lady of the house. And to all intents and purposes, so you are. You enjoy the same freedom and comfort. Even the same influence. – Witness these sketches of yours for alterations in the garden."

"Yes," Katharine said, "you are right, of course." She closed the double sheet of music and laid it aside. "What I feared would happen has happened in truth. I have become too settled here ... Too much inclined to impose on Martin's kindness and forget what my position really is. I am grateful to you for pointing it out."

"Oh, what nonsense!" Ginny exclaimed. "I was doing nothing of the kind, as I'm sure you must know. Whatever security and contentment you are enjoying now is only what you deserve, after all the worry and shame you endured while Charles was landing himself in Queer Street, ending with the shock of his disappearance, and I am thankful it should be so. As for your imposing on Martin, you needn't be worried on that score, when plainly he is not worried himself. The situation is of his own making, remember, and obviously he is well pleased with it. Indeed I would go so far as to say—"

At that moment the door opened, and Martin came into the room, alone.

"There, now, the very man!" Ginny said. "Were your ears on fire, Martin? And were you listening at the door? If so, you will be aware that we were just speaking of you."

"Rest assured. I heard nothing."

"In that case, I'll repeat it to you. I had been saying how

comfortably settled Kate is these days, since coming to you as
your housekeeper. Unfortunately she misunderstood and
began to speak of imposing on you. So now I am trying to
persuade her that you are quite as happy with the arrangement
as she is. As happy as any man can be, that is, when he is in
love with another man's wife. And *no*, my dear Kate, I do *not*
mean myself."

Ginny rose and went to the door, but paused for a moment,
close to Martin, looking at him with her head on one side.

"Though I must confess that all these years, until recently,
I was foolish enough to imagine that I was the object of your
devotion. What a blow to my self-esteem! I ought to be sick
with jealousy but Kate is the one person in the world that I
could never be jealous of. Now I will leave you alone, my
dears, while I go in search of George and the children. I will
do my best to keep them out of the house for at least half an
hour, but as it is almost tea-time, I warn you I may not be
successful."

Martin, having closed the door on her, turned and looked
across at Katharine, who sat erect, very still and pale, staring
absently before her. As he approached, she looked up at him,
forcing herself to meet his gaze.

"Martin—"

"Yes, it is true. I've loved you for years. Right from the time
when I was a boy and came into this house as your pupil.
Possibly even before – I can't be sure of the exact moment –
but certainly from that day onwards I loved you and knew it
beyond any doubt."

"So long ago? Yet you gave no sign."

"No. I made sure of that. For how could I dare show what
I felt when I was an ignorant lout of fifteen and you were
already a young woman, turned eighteen, and a lady what's
more, as far removed from me as the moon?"

"I still find it hard to comprehend. I was so sure – we
were all so sure – papa and Hugh as well as myself – that
you had fallen in love with Ginny. She used to flirt with

you even then. She set out to cast her spell over you and we all thought she had succeeded."

Martin, smiling, shook his head.

"It was Railes that cast its spell over me and Ginny, of course, was part of that spell. Oh, it was very flattering for a boy of my sort, that she should flirt with me as she did, and I was only too glad to respond. But it was always you I loved, from that first day in the music-room, when we sat at the table and talked together, and you said you knew I had it in me to make something of myself. Oh, if you knew what that meant to me! You made me feel I could do such things—! And yet you made me feel, too, that even if I failed in my efforts, it wouldn't really matter because – I should still be myself. From that day on I was your slave. I would have given my life for you, if I had been called upon to do so."

"Martin, I don't know what to say."

"I think, perhaps, it would be better if we were to – to leave the matter just at present. I would not have spoken of it … not at this time, nor in this way … if Ginny had not said what she did."

"No. I am sure you would not."

"You are upset."

"Yes. For you."

"Please don't be. There is no need. I wish I could persuade you of that but … your sister may return at any moment and—"

"Yes. You are right." Katharine rose. "I think I had better go to the kitchen and speak to Cook about serving tea."

Before she could leave the room, however, the three children came bursting in, followed soon by Ginny and George. The two boys were keen to describe how the last silver birch had been felled and how its stump had been torn from the ground.

"It was bigger than all the rest and took a lot of fetching out—"

"But it's gone on the fire now, along with the rest—"

"We both helped to drag it there—"

"Heave-ho! Stamp and go!"

"I think it's a shame," Susannah said, "that all those lovely trees are gone."

"Yes, but they were all *dust* inside."

"May I show Anthony your sketches for the new garden, mama? We have all washed our hands."

"Oh, what a lovely lot of new music. Did you bring it for us, aunt Ginny?"

"Yes. And next time I come I shall expect to hear you play two new pieces at least."

"Oh, I must tell you what Dorrie said when I showed her my new metronome. I set it ticking for her, you see, and when she had watched it for a while she said, 'Yes, it's very nice, miss, but it don't play much of a tune, does it?'"

"You should try her instead with the tuning-fork—"

"Or, better still, the plectroquill—"

"Is it nearly supper-time? I'm starving!" Anthony said. "I hope there will be one of Cook's special hams ... "

Martin smiled at his youngest guest and crossed the room to ring for the maid.

Some hours later, at half past nine, Martin sat in that room alone. The visitors had departed at half past seven; Dick and Susannah had gone to bed soon afterwards; and Katharine, having gone with them to hear their prayers, had not yet returned. Martin, unable to read, rose and walked about the room; but after a while he stood on the hearth, schooling himself into patient stillness. Soon the door opened and Katharine came in. He saw her into a chair and sat down opposite her.

"I am much relieved to see you," he said. "I feared you might be avoiding me."

"No, not exactly. But I felt I needed time to think and I could only do that when alone. Now I feel I need to talk."

"Yes."

"I still cannot get over what you told me earlier today. I always felt we were good friends, of course, and I knew I had your respect and goodwill, but I never dreamt there was anything more and it grieves me very much indeed that I should have been the means of causing you unhappiness."

"I did not say that my love for you made me unhappy. It never has. Please believe that."

"But you've never married. And you ought to have done. I thought it was because of Ginny, but whatever your reason, it is wrong to set yourself against marrying, as though there were no other woman in the world."

Martin smiled. "It was never a conscious decision. There was no solemn vow on my part, by which I embraced the celibate life. In earlier days I always assumed that I should meet some nice girl, of a background closer to my own, and that I should fall in love with her. It would, I thought, be love of a kind quite different from what I felt for you. A love more suited to everyday life. But years went by and it didn't happen. And now, after these past twelve months, I know without doubt it never will."

"Martin, no! You must not say that. A young man like you, with so much to give! You have no right to deny yourself the happiness marriage could bring you. And to do so puts a great burden on me."

"But I *am* happy. That's the whole point. And although I have no right to love you – so the world would say if it knew – I feel quite sure that I was meant to play an important part in your life. This may seem presumptuous of me but let me explain.

"When your husband's business failed and as a result this house became mine, I felt that fate had ordained it so, though I couldn't quite understand why. I thought perhaps it was because of the love I had for it and for you, and that I had been chosen, so to speak, to keep Railes unchanged, for your sake. But I felt a certain guilt, too, at playing the part of usurper, and I wondered if you hated me for it. I hoped and prayed that you did not, and sure enough you gave me a sign, for when I arrived and came into this room, I found you had left the piano open and a piece of music on the stand. Do you remember doing that?"

"Yes, of course. The Chopin study. I knew it was a favourite of yours."

"And was I right in thinking that you meant it to show you forgave me for taking your home away from you?"

"It was not a question of forgiveness, because you had done nothing wrong. But yes, it was meant as a sign of some kind … I'm not sure what … To show I was still your friend, I suppose, and to let you know that I *understood*. But it seems I didn't understand after all, because I thought you wanted Railes for Ginny's sake, and now you tell me it was for mine."

"Yes. I regarded it as a special trust, though I still didn't know why it had fallen to me to fulfil that trust. Then, when I heard that your husband had gone and that you and your children were left alone, I thought I understood more precisely why God had entrusted Railes to me. It was so that I could, as it were, give it back to you … to be a sanctuary for you and your children, for just as long as you needed it. And if God further wills that you and they should need that sanctuary for another two or three years, – or five – or ten – then I shall know with certainty that my life and yours were meant to be linked."

Martin paused and drew a long breath. He was watching her face very carefully, trying to read every thought and feeling expressed there. And, as she remained silent, he spoke again.

"Katharine, I know I have no right to ask anything of you, but if in the course of time something of what I feel for you could perhaps be reflected back, in however small a measure, for whatever possible reason—"

"No, Martin. It cannot be. I am not free to love you."

"You are not free to marry me – not yet at least – but the law can't dictate what you think or feel."

"*I* can dictate it," Katharine said, "and I am still married to Charles."

"Do you still love him?"

"Yes, of course."

"Even though he's deserted you?"

"He is still my husband, Martin, and my marriage vows were not taken lightly."

"But if, as you fear, he should never return, what then?" Martin asked. "I know there can be no question of divorce—"

"No, there cannot."

"But I know too that the law grants freedom to a deserted wife seven years after the date of desertion. I learnt that from Mr Godwin. I presume you know that your brother-in-law consulted him on your behalf."

"Yes, Ginny told me. But it was not done at my request."

"Mr Godwin assumed it was. He was deeply anxious for you and that was his only reason for discussing the matter with me. I hope you will believe that and not be offended by it."

"I am not offended, Martin. Mr Godwin is an old friend and whatever he might do or say, I know him too well to doubt his motives."

"I'm glad to hear you say that. And I'd like to think that you might have said the same of me. But now that you know what I feel for you, you will of course understand that my own interest in your legal position had a selfish element in it. Katharine, is it possible, do you think, that in another six years' time, if your husband has still not returned, you might consider taking that course by which the law sets you free? And is it possible that *then* you might consider marrying me? Even if only to give me the right to look after you and your children and provide for their future as they grow up?"

"I cannot answer that, Martin. I don't know how I shall feel in six years' time. But I do know it is all wrong that you should be thinking in this way. I'm not a young girl. I'm thirty-five. And you must *not* waste your life waiting for me."

"The time would be nothing," Martin said, "for I should be like Jacob, you know, who served seven years for his Rachel … and they seemed unto him but a few days, because of the love he had for her."

"Martin, dear, it is not well done of you to play upon my feelings like this."

"Katharine, I'm sorry. I did not mean to make you cry. I only wished you to understand that whatever you felt towards me, it would be enough, and that so long as I had you close to me, as I have these twelve months past—"

"No, Martin, it will not do. If I had known from the beginning what you felt for me, I would never have come here. And now that I do know, I cannot stay."

"Surely," he said, with a chill at his heart; "surely you would not leave here simply because I've put into words what I have felt for seventeen years?"

"Yes, I must. It is for the best."

"Best for whom? For yourself, do you mean?"

"I think," she said, "for both of us, but most especially for you."

"Will you please tell me this – is my love an insult to you?"

"Martin, it grieves me very much that you should ask such a question as that, and I can't understand what your motive might be."

"You *are* much above me, remember, in what the world calls rank."

"Rank has nothing to do with it. We both know that. Any woman, whoever she was, could not be anything but honoured by such a love as yours. But now that I know how you feel towards me ... now it's been spoken of between us ... we can never be as we were before. It will be too difficult. People might easily sense something and if they did it would lead to talk."

"If you were to leave suddenly, don't you think that would lead to talk? And what about Dick and Susannah? How would you explain to them your sudden decision to leave? Then there are the servants here. At present they accept the situation, but if you were to leave suddenly they would be puzzled and suspicious, and suspicion would surely fall on me. They would think me guilty of some offence—"

"Indeed they would not!" Katharine said. "They know you too well. And I would make sure there was no such risk, by remaining on terms of friendship and goodwill with you, for the world to see."

"Is that what you feel for me? Friendship? Goodwill?"

"Yes, and a great debt of gratitude."

"If you feel these three things, then I think you owe it to me to remain in this house as I ask you to. If, as you say, you owe me a debt, this is your chance of repaying it. – By putting your trust in me. – By showing you think me a man of honour. I have loved you for seventeen years and it has been a secret till now. It is still a secret from the world and will be, I swear, for as long as ever it needs to be. Till the day I die, if you will it so. That I promise most faithfully."

"It is not a secret from my sister Ginny and you know how indiscreet she can be."

"Yes. But I cannot see how your leaving here will make her any the less so."

For a while they stared at one another and in spite of all that had gone before, now, suddenly, in the space of a moment, there was a change of mood between them. Katharine's grey eyes, although they still held a hint of tears, surveyed him with a glimmering humour, and when at length she answered him, her voice had a challenging ring to it.

"It seems there is no confuting you. You argue like a trained advocate. But in one sense you are right, of course, for whether I go or stay, it will not stop Ginny's quick tongue."

"I think there is one thing that will stop it – the sisterly feeling she has for you. You are the one person above all others that she loves and respects without reservation. And, I may say, without selfishness. Provoking she may be – mischievous, too, – but Ginny would never do or say anything that she knew might cause you real distress. For that reason, I am sure, you need have no misgivings in continuing here."

"Martin, I feel I must ask to postpone any further discussion until I have clarified my thoughts."

"Won't discussion help to do that?"

"Not as you conduct it," she said, "for you lead me too much where I want to go."

"We human beings are apt to think that the only correct decision must be the one that gives us pain. But this is not so, because just as often the heart knows best. And in the present instance I urge you to think how many of those closest to you would be made sad if you left this house."

"You are playing upon my feelings again. Therefore, I will bid you good night. What I need is more time alone to think matters over in my own way."

"Very well. Just as you wish."

They both rose, and Martin accompanied her to the door.

"At least you do not need to hurry in coming to your decision," he said. "Indeed, if only you take long enough, the question will determine itself."

"Now you are laughing at me," Katharine said, and her look, although there was shyness in it, showed she could still be easy with him; showed she was taking him at his word, accepting that she need not pity him. "You think because I am a woman, and have just confessed to some lack of firmness, that I am incapable of making any decision at all."

"No. I think you are incapable of making any but the *right* decision. And in that certainty I place my trust."

One last glance and she turned away. "Good night, Martin," and she was gone. He closed the door after her and faced the emptiness of the room.

CHAPTER
11

He had loved her so long, and hidden it so long, that concealment had become second nature to him, and often during the past seventeen years he had congratulated himself on his ability to act a part. But his complacence had been ill-founded; Katharine now knew what he felt for her; and he, in a moment of folly, had betrayed his most secret hopes and aspirations. He reproached himself bitterly for this and was fiercely determined to make amends. He had been guilty of weakness. Now he must demonstrate his strength. Katharine must be made to feel that Railes was still a safe refuge for her; that never again, by word or look, would he cause her distress or embarrassment. This was his sworn resolution, and in keeping to it he had his reward.

The last days of October passed, and Katharine was still there. The laburnum arbour was planted on the north side of the Tudor garden; the new gateway was made in the wall; and she was there to see it done. Mulberries ripened on the old tree – an extra good crop that year – and still she was there, to pick the fruit, and to help Cook in making the jam.

"I feel it is wrong of me to stay, yet I stay all the same," she said once, alone with him.

"And what of the future?"

"It is in God's hands."

She found the decision easy to make because Martin had proved as good as his word. His demeanour to her, even in private, was just as it always had been: correct in the formal observances, yet always so warmly considerate that she rarely experienced awkwardness even of a trivial kind. She had feared that her own powers of dissimulation might not match up to his; that, being a woman, *she* might betray the secret *he* had kept so long; but in fact there was little difficulty, partly because of his example, partly because in this at least her will proved equal to the task.

She was always extra vigilant whenever her sister was present but although, every now and again, she would find Ginny watching her with a conspiratorial smile, there was nothing overt to cause her unease. All in all, Ginny's behaviour at this time was perfectly normal. She flirted with Martin as usual, teased her husband when he was with her, and grumbled about him when he was not. As for George Winter himself, whatever part he had played in divining, and betraying, Martin's secret, he now kept his own counsel. The nature of that secret was thus confined to four people, all of whom were equally anxious that it should remain so.

It was very strange, Katharine thought, how easily the human mind could absorb new knowledge, even when, initially, that knowledge had caused such astonishment. But here, paradoxically, circumstances played their part: being obliged, for safety's sake, to banish this particular knowledge to the back of her mind, she soon found it had lodged itself there and quietly made itself at home. Thus, in a matter of weeks, Martin's love had become part of her life; something she took so for granted that often, during their day-by-day encounters, she scarcely thought of it at all. Almost it seemed as though in time she could even forget it altogether.

But in this she lied, and knew that she lied, for she found, unexpectedly, that she did not want to forget it. Nor, even, to take it for granted. And as the time passed, and her confidence grew, she would sometimes look at him – while he was talking to the children, perhaps, or showing them a new book he had bought – and allow herself the indulgence of thinking: "This man loves me. He has loved me for seventeen years"; and although she still felt sad for him, the thought of his love was a comfort to her; a source of strength; Balm Gentle to her woman's pride, wounded by her husband's desertion.

She reproved herself for this indulgence, charging herself with vanity. It was wrong to think of Martin's love when she was not free to accept it. She knew that perfectly well. But how, *how*, could she not accept it, when she knew it was there and felt its warmth, just as she felt the sun on her face and was grateful for it when she walked out of doors on these mellow-sweet autumn days? Even if she had left Railes, he would still think of her with love, and whenever she thought of him it would be with this same warm gratitude. She would remember the look in his eyes, that evening when he confessed his love. The way he had spoken. His voice, his tone. And it needed a stronger heart than hers not to be moved by the knowledge that she was the object of such tenderness. Must she pretend it wasn't there? Or that it meant nothing to her? What virtue was there in such a pretence? Martin loved her and she was glad. No self-reproof would change that.

For Martin himself, now that he knew Katharine would stay, it was a time of joyous relief. Only one thing could have given him greater happiness and that was if she had returned his love. This, he knew, was impossible. She loved her husband and wanted him back. Therefore, as a man of honour, he must force himself to hope and pray that Charles Yuart would return. Even while he told himself this, however, there was a serpent voice that whispered, "Yes, but what if he doesn't return? What if she should hear he was dead?" And although he experienced some guilt at this, he did not allow it to burden him, for whatever his own thoughts and feelings were, they would not influence events. *Their* course was governed by another power and could not be foreseen. Better to live by the hour, the day. And, if providence granted it, the months, the years. It was a philosophy that accorded well with the season. Autumn was beautiful that year and yielded days of such perfection that it was all too easy to hope that their peacefulness might last forever.

They spent Christmas at Newton Railes and were joined by the Claytons and the Winters, which made a party of thirteen altogether, seven of them children.

"Considering you are a bachelor," Nan remarked to her brother, "you seem to have a way of collecting a good many children about you."

"It's something to do with this house, I think. It likes having young people in it."

After a short, easy winter, there came a moist warm spring, followed by a summer which, although fine on the whole, brought a number of heavy thunderstorms, so that the rivers and streams of the Cullen Valley ran brim-full even in June and July. Such a plenitude of water would normally have been welcomed by the woollen mill owners but that was the summer of 1862 and England, along with the rest of Europe, was affected by events in America, where war between the states had worsened and spread. The stringent American tariff had reduced English trade most seriously, including the textile trade, of course, and all along the Cullen Valley, mills were reducing their output. In Chardwell it was said that the Hurnes now regretted buying Hainault Mill and would gladly have sold it again if only a buyer could be found. Needless to say there was no hope of that during the present state of stagnation.

But although the woollen trade might be in the doldrums, its sufferings were nothing compared with those of the cotton trade in the north. There, as the year progressed, conditions became grave indeed until, by August and September, the plight of the Lancashire cotton mill workers was a matter of concern throughout the country. When a national distress fund was set up, nowhere was the response so great as in the towns of the Cullen Valley. Chardwell, naturally, led the way, and as most of the schemes for raising money involved organized entertainment, the general atmosphere of the town was such as to provide a welcome antidote to the gloom hanging over its own chief industry.

Throughout the winter, concerts and balls; throughout the following spring and summer, an endless round of fêtes and bazaars. The larger houses of the district competed with one another in inventing new entertainments and one of the most popular was the Robin Hood Pageant held in May at Newton Railes, where young bloods could try their skill in shooting with the longbow; in sword-fighting (with wooden swords); and – a great favourite, this, – in combat by quarterstaff on a plank bridge over a stream.

In addition to the various social events taking place at Railes, there were more private matters demanding attention, and the most important of these was the subject of Dick's future career. He would soon be sixteen and he talked of leaving school at the end of term to begin work of some kind. The question was, what kind? He discussed it first with Martin.

"As my father has abandoned us, it is essential that I should begin earning a wage as soon as possible, so that in due course I shall be able to support my mother and sister."

"With your exceptional skill in drawing, and your interest in architecture, I had thought you would choose that as your career."

"Yes. It is what I should most like to do. But learning it would take too long."

"I was hoping," Martin said, "that out of the friendship existing between us, you would be willing to let me sponsor you during your apprenticeship."

"That is very good of you, sir, but I really feel— "

"Before giving me your answer, I suggest you take time to consider the matter. As a qualified architect you will be much better able to support your mother and sister than you would as a counting-house clerk or a cloth salesman. True, it will take longer to achieve, but meanwhile your mother's position as housekeeper here ensures security for you all."

Dick was much moved by Martin's offer; he talked it over with his mother.

"What ought I to do, mama? Would it be wrong for me to accept?"

"I think the decision must be your own."

"At least tell me what you feel. You are such an independent person yourself, I thought you would say that I must refuse."

"No, I do not say that. Martin is our very good friend, and the nature of his friendship is such that if you were to accept his help, I know it would please him very much indeed. And, I may say, it would also please me."

Within a short time, decisions were taken and arrangements made. On leaving school, Dick, after a holiday away with friends, would enter the office of William Bonnamy, of Wyatt House, Chardwell, there to be trained in the principles and practice of architecture for a term of five years. Martin would pay the premium and would make Dick a monthly allowance to cover all his personal needs until such time as he qualified in the said profession and was able to support himself. Dick's cup was brim-full. He admired William Bonnamy enormously. And he could not thank Martin enough for securing the interest of such a man and giving him such a good start in life.

"I promise I shall do my best always to be a credit to you. And to my mother and sister as well. Certainly I intend to make sure that no one has cause to be ashamed of me."

This conversation took place in June. Dick was to begin his apprenticeship in September. But on a date between these events, without any warning whatever, Charles Yuart returned to the district and presented himself at Newton Railes. He had been gone almost three years, the greater part of which time he had spent in the gold-fields of California.

It was just after four in the afternoon and Susannah, having finished her lessons, had gone off into the park to meet Dick coming home from school. Martin had gone to Culverstone on business concerning the gravel pits and was not expected back until later. Katharine, therefore, was all alone, sitting on a window-seat in the drawing-room, smiling to herself as she read and corrected an essay Susannah had written on the subject of the crinoline, asking "how much larger will it become?" While Katharine sat doing this the maid, Dorrie, came into the room in a state of agitation and said:

"Please, ma'am, the master is here."

"The master?" Katharine said, puzzled. "Is he back already?"

"Not Mr Cox, ma'am. It's the master that *was*. Mr Yuart. – Your husband, ma'am."

Katharine stared, feeling her face grow stiff and cold. Numbly, she put Susannah's essay aside, and rose to her feet. At that moment Charles walked into the room. The maid withdrew, closing the door. Husband and wife faced each other. Katharine drew a difficult breath.

"Charles," she said, almost voicelessly, and was lost for a moment in disbelief.

He came to her and kissed her cheek. His hand rested briefly on her arm. Katharine, trembling, sat down again on the window-seat, but he, ignoring the gesture by which she invited him to join her, stood very stiff and erect before her.

"You look at me as if I were a ghost. But I'm real enough, I assure you."

"I'm sorry, Charles, but it is a shock, seeing you so suddenly like this after such a long time."

It was not only the suddenness: it was the change she saw in him. In three years he had lost flesh, and his body now had a spare, muscular hardness. His face, too, was much thinner, so that jaw and cheekbones were more pronounced. But, most striking of all, his skin was burnt a deep red-brown, against which his blue eyes appeared almost supernaturally bright.

"I too have received a shock, for I went first to Chacelands, expecting to find you living there. Your sister and her husband were not at home and I had to learn of your whereabouts from a rather impertinent servant-girl. I hardly expected this, Katharine, – that you should have come back here to Railes to keep house for Martin Cox. You could have made your home at Chacelands. Your sister spoke of it often enough."

"I preferred to keep my independence. Coming here enabled me to do so."

"I beg your pardon, Katharine, but to me it seems you made that choice out of wilful perversity, and without even the slightest regard for the gossip it would cause in the district."

"I would remind you," Katharine said, speaking very quietly, "that as a woman whose husband had left her, I was already the subject of gossip in this district, and of pity, too, and *that* was certainly not from choice, wilful or otherwise. But surely you have not come back after all this time merely to upbraid me and quarrel with me?"

"It was not what I intended, nor what I hoped for, but finding you here in this house— "

"Yes, Charles, I know how you feel. And obviously there is much to be said between us before – before we can hope to reach an understanding. But will you not sit down? And will you not let me ring for tea?"

"Thank you, but no tea for me."

He did however sit down and, after a short pause, made an effort to speak peaceably.

"I hope you are in good health. Certainly you appear to be."

"Yes, I am thankful to say that the children and I are very well."

"Where are the children? Are they here?"

"Susannah has gone to meet Dick coming home from school. They should be back fairly soon, but on a fine day like this, they sometimes linger in the park."

"What about Cox? When will he be back?"

"Not yet, I think. He had business in Culverstone."

The first shock had passed away; Katharine now had command of herself. Nevertheless, as they talked together, she was many times overcome by a sense of unreality. This was her husband; the man she loved; the father of her children. Every day for almost three years she had prayed for his safe return, yet now that he sat before her, it seemed like a dream. So strange was her sense of his presence there that parts of his story went unheard. She gazed at him; she listened to him; yet half her mind remained disengaged.

On arriving in America, he had travelled first to Perry Springs, in Virginia, where a large consignment of his cloth had been burnt during the disturbances earlier that year. On the strength of the documents he carried with him, the local trading committee had paid him the nominal sum of four hundred pounds in compensation for his loss. With this money he had travelled by sea along the coast to California, then across country to the gold-fields, to a tinpot town called Moses; and there he had purchased a "ticket" allowing him to dig for gold in an area of the Polk Horn Hills.

He had not made a fortune, he said. No lucky strike of the kind reported sometimes in the English papers. But, by dint of grinding hard work, knee-deep in icy cold water, his back bent under a burning hot sun, he had, day by day, slowly and surely, won a fair share of the precious grains; sometimes a nugget the size of an acorn; once a "scob" weighing fourteen pounds: always enough to encourage him to work all the hours God gave, while weather and light permitted it. At the end of twenty-eight months he had sold his claim and travelled to San Francisco. There he had banked fifty-two thousand dollars, which, in English money, meant something in excess of ten thousand pounds.

"Not a fortune, as I say, but quite enough for me to set myself up in business and to buy a house. I have not yet decided what my business there shall be, but the opportunities are immense for a man like myself, who is willing to work. It is an incredible country, Katharine, and San Francisco is a town like no other in the world. It is new and it's growing fast. It's a place that will take your breath away."

"You mean you intend," Katharine said, "that we should come to America with you and settle there for the rest of our lives?"

"Yes. That is why I am here. At first I was going to send for you, but then I decided it would be better if I came and fetched you, so that I can look after you on the voyage out. But why do you look at me like that? Is there something amiss with my plan?"

"Yes, Charles, I'm afraid there is. It makes no allowance whatever for my feelings in the matter."

"As we are husband and wife I naturally take it for granted that your feelings and wishes will coincide with mine."

"They ought to, I know. But as we have lived apart for so long, the habit of wifely compliance has fallen somewhat into disuse. I do not wish to go to America, Charles. I cannot think why you should ask it of us. After deserting us for three years, now to demand we should travel half way round the world, to a country totally strange to us ... A country which is at war with itself—"

"The war is nothing," Charles said. "It has scarcely touched the west. And I did not desert you. I went because my life here had become insupportable to me. To speak of desertion is absurd."

"How else should I speak of it when for three years we had no news of your whereabouts? No means of knowing, even, whether you meant to come back to us?"

"Of course I meant to come back to you! But first I had to find a way of regaining my self-respect. That was not done in a day, Katharine, and if you only knew the conditions in which I lived and worked—"

"But we *didn't* know," Katharine said. "We were not *allowed* to know. And what if you had not succeeded in regaining your self-respect? Would you have come back to us then?"

"The question doesn't arise," he said.

"It does for me, because I don't think you *would* have come back, and we'd have been left, the children and I, waiting for news that never came. Wondering, year in, year out, whether you were alive or dead."

"Seeing that I am now here, sitting with you in this room, all this is irrelevant. And it seems to me that after three years I could have expected a welcome somewhat different from the one I've received."

"I'm sorry, Charles, but after three years of silence between us it is difficult to behave quite normally. I am still in some confusion and all this talk of America has come as an extra shock."

"Are you refusing to come with me?"

"I am asking that you should consider my wishes in the matter. The children's, too. We need to talk it over with them. We need to consider what it will mean."

"It is not their business to take part in making decisions over such things. Nor, precisely, is it a wife's."

"I would remind you yet again that during the past three years I have been obliged to make decisions myself and as a result—"

"I need no reminding of that!" he exclaimed. "I can see the result plainly enough!" As he spoke, he looked round the room, gesturing angrily with his hand. "*This* is one result of it! Your presence here in this house!"

He got up and walked about, stood at the window a moment or two, then turned and stood looking down at her.

"Obviously, during that time, you acquired a taste for making decisions. Perhaps that is why my return has inspired you with something less than joy. Perhaps, to put it more bluntly still, you'd be happier if I had never returned at all!"

There was a silence during which his words hung between them like an unresolved chord. Then the door opened and the children came in.

They knew their father was there, of course; the servants had made sure of that; so they were, in some measure at least, prepared for the strange and difficult meeting. Even so, they were under constraint, and stood awkwardly in the doorway until Katharine, who had risen at once, went and drew them into the room, doing her best, by voice and touch, to give them what assurance she could.

"Well, now, is it not wonderful, that here's your papa come back to us? You cannot believe your own eyes, which is just how I felt when he first came in. And, like me, you are lost for words."

"Yes," Susannah said, nervously, and curtseyed to him. "How do you do, papa?"

Charles kissed his daughter's cheek; shook hands with his son; and observed, in genuine wonder, how much they had grown – *and* grown up – since he had seen them last.

"I expected to find you changed, of course. Three years is a long time. But I went away leaving two children and I return to find you are almost adults."

The children did not respond, and Katharine, to fill an uncomfortable pause, made much of the simple business of getting them all seated together. Still the two children were silent, sitting together on the settee, and although they regarded their father with open curiosity, their bearing towards him remained aloof.

"Come, now," Charles said impatiently, "am I such a stranger as all that?"

"Yes, papa," Susannah said. "It isn't only we who have changed. *You* have grown much older too."

"Yes, I know. It's the hot Californian sun has done that. It ages people rapidly, especially those who work in its glare."

"Is that where you've been? California?" Dick said, speaking now for the first time. "What were you doing there? Looking for gold?"

"Yes. But if you are expecting to hear that I am now a millionaire, I'm afraid I must disappoint you. Still, my time in the gold-fields was certainly not wasted, and I'm glad to be able to tell you that I am in much better case now than I was before leaving England."

"Why did you never write to us?"

"At first because I was on the move, travelling the breadth of America. Next because I was waiting until I had good news to impart. Then, later, when time had passed, and I was on my way home, I decided to make it a surprise."

Here something flickered in Dick's face, and Charles recognized it as scorn.

"However," he said, in a changed tone, "judging by the reception accorded me, the surprise has not been much to your liking."

"What reception did you expect? A fatted calf?"

"Dick!" Katharine said, in sharp reproof; but before she could say any more, Charles had rounded fiercely on her.

"Evidently, in my absence, madam, you have been very busy turning my children against me."

"That is not true," Dick said. "Never once in three years has my mother spoken a word against you. But we have minds of our own, Sue and I, and what we both feel is— "

"I do not need to be told what you feel. It is already perfectly plain." Charles, though still extremely angry, now made an effort to bring his temper under control. "I can see," he said carefully, "that in your eyes I have done wrong, and if I have I am sorry for it. But one thing I promise you – whatever injury I may have done you by my absence, I fully intend to make up for it."

There followed a long silence, during which Charles and his children eyed one another, still with impatience on his side and doubt on theirs. Eventually, Katharine spoke, addressing herself to the children.

"We have been talking in such a way that we have all upset one another. The most important thing is that your papa has come home to us. Obviously, that means change in our lives, especially as he has certain plans for us, which we shall need to discuss. But before we begin I think we should have some tea. It is well past our usual time. Dick, will you please ring the bell?"

Dick got up and did as she asked. Then he returned to his seat on the couch and looked at each of his parents in turn.

"What plans?" he asked suspiciously.

Martin, also, on coming home, heard immediately of Yuart's return, first from Jack Sherard the groom, then from Cook, who led him into the still-room, where they could talk privately. She, like the rest of the staff, was in a state of great perturbation.

"I had made up my mind, after all this time, that Mr Yuart must be dead. Drowned at sea in a shipwreck, I thought, though I never said that to Miss Katharine, of course. But here he is back again, all just as sudden as when he went, and I wish I knew what to think of it, and whether it's for the best or not, because I simply cannot understand how he could behave in such a way."

"How long has he been here?"

"Best part of an hour. Tea was sent in a while ago, just after the children came in."

"In that case I'll join them," Martin said, "as soon as I am presentable."

He went upstairs to freshen himself, which gave him a little time to think; a little time, in privacy, in which to absorb the shock of the news and all its many implications. This was no easy task but when, in a while, he joined the company in the drawing-room, and Yuart rose to meet him, Martin by then was confident that his face and manner were well controlled.

"Mr Yuart. Your servant, sir. Please accept my felicitations on being thus reunited with your family."

"Mr Cox. I'm obliged to you. I apologize for my intrusion here while you were absent, but I'm sure you will agree that the circumstances constitute a valid excuse."

"Indeed, the circumstances are such that it cannot be termed an intrusion at all."

Martin, still very formal, turned and nodded to Katharine and smiled across at Dick and Susannah. He then turned to Yuart again, inviting him to resume his seat; but this invitation Yuart declined, saying he had matters of business to attend to in the town.

"I have taken a room at The Post House and will stay there a few days while making certain arrangements regarding my wife and family. What these arrangements are, she will tell you herself. I think it suffices if I say that as soon as they are completed she will be leaving your employ. You will, I'm sure, agree to waive the usual quarter's notice."

Yuart spoke in a crisp, perfunctory way, making it clear that Martin was not required to answer.

"Meanwhile, it will of course be necessary for me to see my wife occasionally, but I will do my best to ensure that my visits here do not inconvenience you. The situation, I promise you, will be of the shortest possible duration."

A few last courtesies and he was on his way to the door. Katharine got up and followed him, intimating by a glance to the children that they too should accompany him. While they were all out of the room, the maid came in, bringing fresh tea for Martin, and a moment later, when she had gone, Katharine and the children returned. Katharine, to busy herself, poured Martin's tea and gave it to him. Fleetingly, her glance met his, and she gave him the token of a smile. She and Susannah sat down on the couch; Dick sat perched on one of its arms. Martin stood, sipping his tea, looking at each of them in turn. All three faces were strained and pale. Eventually Susannah spoke.

"Papa has been in America. He intends taking us back there with him. We're to be ready in three or four days. A week at the outside, he says. Then we're to travel to Liverpool, and take ship from there."

"I see," Martin said, in a flat voice. "All very sudden for everybody."

"I think it's monstrous!" Dick exclaimed. "First he runs off and abandons us! Now he would tear us up by the roots! He says we have no choice, Sue and I, being both of us under age, but what about mama? – Has she no rights at all, where such decisions are concerned? Even if she has no rights in law, wouldn't you think that my father should at least have enough decency—"

"Dick!" Katharine said, interrupting him. "You mustn't expect Martin to answer questions of that kind. You place him in a difficult position."

"You mean he is bound to take our part?"

"There can be no question of taking parts. I, being your papa's wife, and you his children, we owe him the duty of obedience. Nothing in the world can alter that."

"I know, I know! But surely papa has some duty, too. – To consider our wishes in such a matter? Instead of which, I am to forego my chance of a place in Mr Bonnamy's office, to do God knows what in San Francisco!"

"Yes, and just think!" Susannah said. "Whatever will aunt Ginny say when she comes back from travelling abroad and finds us gone from here forever, without having seen her to say goodbye? I think papa is very cruel. He thinks of no one but himself."

Katharine, having had time to reflect; having, while talking to Charles, seen how set he was on his chosen course, now made some attempt to conciliate her children on his behalf.

"You must understand, both of you, that during the past three years your papa has had a very hard life. A dangerous life. And a lonely one. We, in those years, have had one another. We've had aunt Ginny and uncle George. And Martin. And Railes. But papa has been in a strange land, labouring incessantly, suffering all manner of hardships and— "

"That's not our fault," Dick said. "He didn't *have* to go out there."

"It was a sacrifice, nevertheless, and one that was made in part for our sakes, so as to build a new life for us. Now papa has every right to expect that we should do our best to make up to him for those three years."

Dick and Susannah remained silent. Katharine then spoke again.

"Come, now," she said, in gentle reproach. "This is no way for us to behave, when we have so much to be thankful for. Papa has come back, safe and sound, and we're a complete family again. That should make it a day of rejoicing. A day for giving thanks to God."

Still the young faces were obdurate. Dick's, especially, was set in grim lines.

"If I could see *you* rejoicing, mama, then I might rejoice myself."

*

Martin, throughout this interchange, had said not one word, because such was the nature of his relationship with this family that his deeper feelings had to be hidden. Katharine knew what those feelings were; the children did not; the love he had for her, and for them, could only be conveyed in terms of friendship. Still, because of the circumstances, that friendship had been a special one. He had been able to help them; had become an important part of their lives. But now, at a stroke, he was nothing at all. His friendship carried no privileges, now that Charles Yuart was back. He could not intercede for them; he had to stand by while events took their course. In practical terms, his friendship was worthless. He was just a man of straw who had won their trust with promises of future help which he was now powerless to fulfil. And the knowledge of this, together with the prospect of imminent parting, was almost more than he could bear.

The children, however, understood, and he soon found, on talking to them, that they both saw him as one of themselves: a fellow victim of circumstance; and although they did not comprehend the exact nature of his love for their mother, they accepted without question that she, and they, were important to him. They took it for granted, therefore, that his sense of loss was akin to theirs, and Susannah once, turning to him, suddenly said in a voice of tears:

"Oh, *Martin*! I wish you could hide us away somewhere, in some secret place, so that we could stay here with you and never, never leave Railes at all!"

"Yes," Martin said, "I wish it too."

But there was no hiding-place, or escape, as the children knew only too well. Once before they had left Railes; now fate decreed they must leave it again; and although they continued to argue the matter, passionately, as children will, all they achieved at the end of it was a kind of angry acceptance and a fierce resolve to make the most of the few days that were left to them.

In the light of this resolve, everything they did, however trivial, had a special significance. They and their mother, always close, were drawn even closer at this time; they attended her everywhere, and every quiet word they spoke, as they went about the house and garden, was recorded forever in their hearts, together with the sights, sounds, and scents of the place, and all that made it so dear to them.

"'Eyes, look your last!
Arms, take your last embrace!'"

"Surely, when we left before, it wasn't as bad as it is this time? Why is that?" Susannah asked.

"Because that was then, and this is now, and we were not going so far," Dick said.

Railes that evening was beautiful and brother and sister were both determined to absorb its essence into their souls so that, however far they went, they would carry that essence away with them. Determined, too, instinctively, to leave something of themselves behind; something of what they thought and felt, which would always, they hoped, be part of Railes, just as Railes would always be part of them.

There came a moment later that evening when, the children having gone to the stables to talk to Sherard, Martin and Katharine were alone, walking together on the sunny parterre.

"America," he said, in a hollow voice. "Somehow I never envisaged that."

"No, nor did I."

"I've often thought about losing you. I have forced myself to think of it, so that I should be prepared. But never for an instant did I think that I could lose you so utterly. It is, I suppose, a judgment on me."

"A judgment? Why?"

"Because two years ago, when we talked about your husband, and you told me you still loved him, I made a vow to myself, that I would pray for his return. That vow has not been well kept. I felt he had made you unhappy enough. I feared he might make you unhappy again. Also, I had my

own selfish reasons, as you know ... so whatever prayer my
lips formed, it was nothing but empty words. And although
I often told myself that I was prepared for his coming
home ... in my heart I felt sure it would never happen. That's
why I say it's a judgment on me – that I am paid out for my
falseness."

He paused and Katharine glanced at him: a soft upwards
glance, quickly withdrawn; but a glance of such sort indeed
that if Martin had not already loved her, – if this had been his
first meeting with her – he would certainly have loved her
from that moment on, and thought the world well lost for it,
because of what that glance conveyed.

"God, how we delude ourselves where our own wishes are
concerned!" he said. "Of course Charles has come back to
you! What man would not?"

Katharine made no reply; her face was turned away now;
and they walked for a while in silence, across the parterre and
down the steps, onto the sloping lawn below. Then Martin
spoke again.

"If by some miraculous means the clock were turned back
a few hours, and you found his return had been only a
dream, would you be glad or sorry?" he asked.

"Martin," she said, in a low voice, "you know you do wrong
in asking me that."

"No doubt I do wrong in loving you, but I do love you all
the same, and always will till the day I die."

"You mustn't," she said. "You must try to forget."

"Even if that were possible, would you really wish to be
forgotten?"

"I would wish to spare you pain."

"Will *you* be able to forget what you're leaving here?"

"No, of course not. This is my home. I've lived here the
greater part of my life. When I am gone far away, all my
memories will be of this house."

"Yes. Quite so. And in just the same way the house itself will
always hold its memories of you. Can you imagine how it will
be when you are gone from here? Have you any idea how

much you'll be missed? Why, the very stones will ache for
you!"

"Martin, don't!" Katharine said. "I beg you will not speak
like that. Do you think I feel less than the stones?"

"Katharine, I'm sorry. I'm a selfish brute. That I should
add to your distress—"

"You wouldn't, I know, deliberately. But just at present,
with things as they are, what I need from you is your strength."

"Strength," he repeated, hopelessly, and made a gesture
with his hand. But in a moment, when he spoke again, it was
with greater firmness. "Yes. Very well. Such strength as I
have – it shall be yours. Command me any service to the
world's end ... even to the very Antipodes."

"At least we're not going so far as that." Glancing at him,
she managed a smile. "There! I have found some comfort in
our destination – that it is only six thousand miles away, when
it might have been twelve. Perhaps if I try hard enough, I
may find other things to be thankful for. But one task at least
I would charge you with. That when you know our
whereabouts there, – and we shall send word as soon as we
can – you will write to us regularly, giving all possible news
of home, down to the last detail."

"That will be no task to me. But will you write to me in
return?"

"Of course. I'll send you news from the New World."

"With your permission," Martin said, "I will in due course
visit you there."

"You would travel so far?" she said, marvelling.

"Yes. Why not?" Meeting her glance, he smiled at her. "It
is, as you say, only six thousand miles."

Later that evening, however, when he had spent some hours
alone, he found himself, for the first time, questioning the
inevitability of it. And, seeking Katharine's company again,
he broached the subject differently.

"I wonder if we are making a mistake in accepting it so
fatalistically."

"I have no choice but to accept it."

"So long as your husband sticks by his intention, no, you have not. But what if he could be dissuaded? I have given the matter much thought and I think if I were to speak to him and put certain propositions to him—"

"It will be useless," Katharine said. "He will not accept help from you. You offered it when Hainault failed and he rejected it out of hand."

"That was more than three years ago. The situation is different now. He may be open to suggestions."

"I don't think he will. His mind is set on America."

"Then why has he come back here like this, when he could so easily have written instead, asking you and the children to join him there?"

"I wondered about that myself. I think perhaps it is because he wanted Chardwell to see that he has done well for himself and that he can hold up his head again."

"Exactly so."

"It is only natural, Martin, dear."

"Perfectly natural, I agree. Any man would feel the same. That's why I think it may be worthwhile speaking to him. Three years ago he was penniless. Now he's a man of some substance again. Which means, if any proposition were put to him, he could discuss it on equal terms. Will you not allow me to try? If he refuses, nothing is lost. He can do no worse than he plans at present."

"No, that's true."

"Then I have your permission to speak to him?"

"Let me sleep on it," Katharine said, "and we'll talk of it again in the morning."

In the morning, Martin's resolve was firmer than ever, and Katharine now gave her consent. He therefore sent word to the stables, requesting his horse for half past eight, but then, just as he was crossing the hall, Charles Yuart himself appeared, letting himself in from the kitchen court. Speaking curtly, as always with Martin, he apologized for his early call.

He was anxious, he said, to see his wife.

"As it happens," Martin said, "I was on my way to call on you."

"With what object, Mr Cox?"

"Firstly to say how much I regret your decision to return to America." Martin, as he spoke, motioned Yuart to one of the chairs at the fire-place, but Yuart, with a gesture, declined. "That regret, I am quite sure, will be felt throughout the whole district, and with good reason. Your family has been connected with the Cullen Valley for many generations. Your cloth was sold on three continents. Sadly, in the past three years, that tradition has been broken, but I think it would be a thousand pities if it were to be broken forever."

"Perhaps I should thank you, Mr Cox, but I don't quite grasp your motive in speaking to me in this way, and frankly I am suspicious of it."

"If you will only bear with me, and give me a little of your time, I would like to explain myself and put certain proposals before you which I'm sure—"

"I'm sorry, Mr Cox, but I'm in some hurry to see my wife. I would ask you not to detain me."

"May I speak to you afterwards?"

"I'm afraid not. I have considerable business on hand and it will take most of the day."

"What about tomorrow? Can I see you then?"

"It seems I shall have to be blunt," Yuart said. "The plain truth is, Mr Cox, that there is nothing you could say to me that would be of any interest whatever. Now I really must insist that you allow me to see my wife."

Martin perforce had to comply.

"Very well. If you will wait in the morning-room, I'll ask Mrs Yuart to come to you."

Yuart gave a nod and turned away. He went into the morning-room and after a while Katharine joined him there. She kissed him and sat down on the couch, but he chose to remain standing.

"I have just had some talk with your friend Cox. He was good enough to express an interest in my plans for the future and to say what a pity it is that I should think of severing my connection with Chardwell so decisively. He shows the same stubborn inclination to concern himself in my affairs that he has shown in the past and seems unable to understand that his opinions are a matter of indifference to me. However, it happens, coincidentally, that in this particular instance, his views and mine are the same for once. I have come here this morning, Katharine, to tell you that I have changed my mind. I am *not* going back to America."

"Not?" Katharine said. She caught her breath.

"No. I've decided to stay in England. In the Cullen Valley, where I belong. I came to tell you without delay because I know, from what you said yesterday, that it will be a relief to you."

"Oh, Charles! A relief, yes. If you only knew—"

"I can see for myself what it means to you. Your look tells me that, without any words." He came now and sat down with her, taking her hands into his own. "Indeed, your manner does much to compensate for your cold reception yesterday."

"Whatever my manner yesterday, I hope you will make allowances, Charles. It was a shock to the children and me, that you should come back without warning like that, when we had thought you were lost to us. And the news that we were to leave England—" Pausing, she collected herself. When she spoke again, her voice was calm. "Tell me why you have changed your mind."

"Yesterday, when I left you, my mind was in something of a turmoil. I kept thinking of what you'd said – how upset you were on hearing my plans – so before dining at the inn I went for a walk round the town, to get my thoughts into some sort of order. Then I walked out along the valley, beside the Cullen as far as Craye, then along the bank of the Leame and round by Holsey and Cresswater.

"It was not intended to be a sentimental journey. I had thought, in the past three years, that Chardwell meant less than nothing to me. I even thought I hated it. But as I walked about the town – even more when I walked in the valley – I knew I'd been wrong. Passing the mills, especially ... John Jervers' and Daisy Bank ... Unity Mill and Brink End ... Hainault, too, though I didn't go close ... I began to think what a fool I was. Hearing the clack of the looms again and the thud of the stocks ... seeing the mill-folk at work in the yards ... the smoke going up from the chimneys ... even the *reech* from Burley's Dye House ... all these things made me think, 'Damn it, this is where I belong! Cloth is my trade. It's in my blood. For good or ill, my place is here!' I suddenly felt, with certainty, that I was ready to start again. In spite of what's happened in the past, I knew I could still be a clothier, and win back something of what I had lost. Be part of the life of this district again. And that is what I intend to do."

There was a silence. He looked at her. And she, responding to that look, leant forward and kissed his mouth. Her hands pressed his in thankfulness.

"Oh, Charles, I'm so glad! Not only for myself and the children but for you as well. It's the right decision. I'm *sure* it is."

"Oh, yes, there's no doubt about that, because last evening, after my walk, I called on Alec Stevenson and talked matters over with him, and Alec tells me that Tom Maynard of Loxe Mill has been advertising for a working partner. Loxe is a fair-sized mill at Obank, which specializes in the cheaper suitings; but at least Maynard's cloth is good of its kind, not like the rubbish they make at Kendall's. Maynard, it seems, is a sick man and needs someone to run things for him. Anyway, Alec thinks it worth a try, so I called at Loxe before coming here and left a note for Maynard, asking to see him at ten o'clock."

Charles rose, somewhat abruptly, and stood looking down at her.

"Alec told me something else. It seems the Hurnes over-reckoned themselves when they bought Hainault and for some months past it's been let to Robert Cornelius who pays scarcely more than a peppercorn rent. Alec thinks when the lease runs out there's a good chance of my getting it."

"Charles, that would be wonderful."

"Yes. But that as yet lies in the future. My immediate business is at Loxe Mill and I think it is time I was on my way there."

Katharine rose and accompanied him out to the great hall. He stood pulling on his riding-gloves.

"Are the children here?"

"Dick's gone to school. At this moment, probably, he will be telling the headmaster that we're leaving England in a few days. Susannah is upstairs in her room. We were sorting her clothes, ready for packing, when Amy came to say you were here."

"You will still need to pack your clothes," Charles said, "for I shall be taking you out of this house as soon as I've found suitable accommodation."

In another moment he was gone. She heard him riding out of the yard. Behind her, from the stairs, Susannah spoke.

"What did papa want, mama? Did he come to hurry us up?"

"No, my darling, he brought good news." Quickly, Katharine crossed the hall. "We are not to leave England after all. He has changed his mind. We're to stay here in Gloucestershire. – In the Cullen Valley. There, now, what do you say to that?"

"Oh, mama! That is wonderful news!" A flutter of white organdie skirts, and Susannah was in her mother's arms. "Oh, I was thinking so badly of him! But now – dear papa! How good he is! I wish Dick was here to share the good news. Can I go to Petty's and tell him, mama? And where is Martin? We *must* tell *him*!"

From across the great hall, unnoticed till now, Martin stood watching them. He had come in from the stable-court.

"What is it that I must be told?" he asked.

But Katharine, turning to meet his gaze, could see that he had already heard.

CHAPTER
12

Thomas Maynard was a stoutly built man in his early fifties, with a broad, blunt-chinned face, cheeks somewhat red-veined above a growth of greyish-brown whisker, and a pair of piercing blue eyes, good-humoured but shrewd, under jutting grey brows. He and Charles were barely acquainted; in earlier days, at meetings of the Clothiers' Association, they had sometimes exchanged a few words together; but that was all. So today, in the office at Loxe Mill, they met virtually as strangers, as Maynard himself remarked when, after a formal handshake, the two men sat down, facing each other across the big shabby desk, littered with bills and order-books, samples of wool and snippets of cloth.

"We have lived very different lives, Mr Yuart. You were always prominent in the town's affairs, whereas I played no part in them at all, which means that although we are almost strangers, I know quite a lot about you."

"In other words, Mr Maynard, you know that I failed at Hainault Mill and as a result was made bankrupt. There cannot be any soul in the Cullen Valley who does not know that."

"I also know that you then vanished from the district completely, leaving your wife and children behind. There was plenty of talk about that, most of it to your discredit, I fear."

"Yes. I can well imagine that. And no doubt there will be plenty of talk again now that I'm back."

"Does it not worry you?" Maynard asked.

"I shall try not to let it," Charles said.

Maynard looked at him steadily. Then he consulted a letter which lay before him on the desk. It was the one Charles had written, asking for this interview.

"You've been in America, prospecting, you say. And profited by it, obviously. Which brings me to the point of your visit. Mr Stevenson referred you to me so presumably you know what it is I'm looking for."

"Yes. He gave me a copy of *The Gazette*, containing your advertisement. In it you ask for a working partner, with a thorough knowledge of the cloth trade, willing and able to take responsibility, and with twenty thousand pounds to invest in your mill."

"Do you have that much money, Mr Yuart?"

"No, I do not. But knowing you for a sound businessman, I judge that you don't really need the money, except as an earnest of my conscientious commitment to the mill. Well, I have ten thousand pounds to invest, but as it is all I've got in the world, save what I need for immediate expenses, my commitment could not be more complete."

"Any applicant could say that."

"According to what Stevenson told me, you've been looking for a partner these three months or more, so far without success."

"Yes, that's true. Those men I have seen so far have shown more optimism than sense. If they had all been knocked into one, they would not have made what I'm looking for." Maynard paused. His eyes searched the younger man's face. "What I want is a man who knows every aspect of the trade. A man with energy and enterprise. A man who will run this mill for me as I have run it myself in the past."

Speaking with some vehemence, Maynard leant forward and thumped with his fist upon the desk. But the action made him red in the face and he leant back, breathing hard, pressing his hand against his chest. After a while he spoke again.

"In the past two years I've been subject to attacks of bronchitis and they've weakened my heart. My doctor says I must take things easy. Do half a day's work instead of a whole. Keep out of the loom-shops because of the dust. In other words, Mr Yuart, this mill, which has been my whole life, must now be only *half* my life! Still, with the right kind of man to help me, at least the mill need not suffer. The question is, are you the right man? You know the trade – none better – but you failed at Hainault nevertheless. You took too many risks, Mr Yuart. That won't do for me here at Loxe. I am a cautious man myself and in this trade caution pays."

"I made mistakes and I paid for them. That experience, you may be sure, left me a wiser man."

"It left your creditors wiser, too, since your debts were never paid in full."

"I lost every single thing I possessed. They could scarcely have had more from me."

"Mr Yuart, I will speak frankly. I have no sympathy to spare for men who take the risks you took and run up debts they know they can't pay. If, as you say, you lost everything, it was only what you deserved. However, you are not the only clothier to have failed in this district. Nor are you the only one who couldn't pay his debts in full. And there was one thing at least in the sorry affair that redounded entirely to your credit."

"Indeed," Charles said, somewhat stiffly.

"Yes. According to what I heard at the time, your creditors were prepared to accept whatever payment came to them from the sale of your business assets alone, and would not have pressed for the sale of your home. Presumably you knew that, and it says much for your rectitude that you chose to sell it all the same."

Charles, white-lipped, met Maynard's gaze.

"It was, as I'm sure you'll agree, the only course open to a gentleman."

"I'm sorry, Mr Yuart. I can see the subject distresses you."

"Certainly it is one that I prefer not to discuss."

"Then I will return to the subject in hand. You say you have ten thousand pounds to invest. Where is it?"

"It is in San Francisco. I have already written to the bank there asking for a draft to be sent to me immediately. It will take perhaps six or seven weeks to come."

"Why didn't you bring it with you?"

"Because I intended returning there. But I changed my mind. For one thing, my wife was upset at the idea. For another, my own roots are here, and they proved stronger than I had thought."

"Well, I'm certainly prepared to consider you as a partner, Mr Yuart. Subject to further discussion, of course. But one point must be clear from the start. I want a man who will make up for my own deficiencies, and I am willing to pay him well, but he – you – must understand that I intend to remain master. Nothing is to be done without my approval. All decisions will rest with me."

"I understand perfectly. I would feel the same myself. You need have no fear, Mr Maynard, that I wish to take Loxe Mill from you. In fact it is only right to tell you that in time, as my position improves, I intend to set up again for myself, in a mill of my own. However, as it can only be in a small way at first, I shall be perfectly well able to manage both mills, without any detriment to either."

"H'mm." Maynard's blue-eyed gaze was keen and there was a hint of amusement in it. "With ten thousand pounds at your disposal, you could set up in business by yourself just as soon as your draft arrives. There are plenty of mills to let in this district. You could even afford to buy one so long as you were prepared to start small."

"I am aware of that. But after what happened at Hainault, beginning again by myself would present a great many problems."

"Quite so. Problems indeed. Whereas, in partnership with me, in a business that's known to be steady and sound, you can ease yourself back into the trade, quietly, by the back door, as it were. Put plainly, Mr Yuart, I am to provide you with my protection while you find your feet again."

"Yes, if you choose to see it that way."

"I like to see things the way they are. But don't misunderstand me – I have nothing against the arrangement. It suits me right well. You, as my managing partner, will give this mill the time and energy that I can no longer give it. In return I will pay you eight hundred pounds per annum, plus a share of the overall profits commensurate with the value of your capital investment. I will also provide the protection already mentioned – my good reputation in the trade. That seems fair enough to me. Indeed, I think it's a good enough basis for us to get down to details, don't you? I can then get Mr Stevenson to draw up the deed of partnership so that when your draft arrives from San Francisco he'll have it ready for us to sign. Are you agreed?"

"Yes."

"Right. I'll get Anstey, my clerk, to come in and bring my ledgers for you to see. You'll want to know what fettle we're in. Not so good as it might be, I'm afraid. Our profits were fifteen per cent last year but I'm hoping soon to improve on that. In fact I'll go so far as to say that it's up to you to see that we do."

"I will certainly do my best."

An hour and a half later, the two men again shook hands. They had reached an agreement. And although the terms of the partnership were not entirely to Yuart's liking, he was on the whole well satisfied. The financial rewards of his new position were reasonably good. Good enough, anyway, to provide the basis for future enlargement.

As Maynard's manager, Charles began work at once, acquainting himself with every detail of the mill's capacity and performance, and making notes for improvements. By the end of a month he knew every man, woman, and child employed there; the work each did and how well it was done. He knew every loom and spinning-machine and the idiosyncrasies of each; and of course he knew all the types of cloth; what orders there were on the books and who the mill's best customers were.

During these early weeks he drew a monthly salary, but as

soon as his banker's draft arrived from San Francisco and was paid into the Loxe Mill account he became, officially, Maynard's partner. The deed of partnership was signed and sealed and the ten thousand pounds thus invested began earning its share of the profits. The duration of the partnership was set at three years only, but if these early days were anything to go by, his future at Loxe looked secure enough. The mill was already efficiently run but Charles, energetic, ambitious, determined, brought new ideas; a new impetus; and Maynard was soon offering a few cautious words of approval.

"You've got the same drive that I once had. But something seems to be driving *you*. You should think of your wife and children sometimes. A man's work is worth more if he takes some recreation sometimes, especially with his family."

Charles, though he smiled, made no reply. Maynard, the elder by ten years, was inclined to speak in this fatherly way, though Charles did his best to discourage it. He liked his partner well enough but had no desire whatsoever to allow any personal element into their relationship. Maynard himself was a widower, and his only living relatives were a widowed daughter and her infant son, who lived with him at Patesbridge. Maynard might hint – and sometimes did – that he and Rose would enjoy meeting Mrs Yuart, the former Miss Tarrant of Newton Railes, but these hints fell on deaf ears. Obviously, Maynard thought that because Charles had fallen from his former position as an independent clothier, and now occupied a subordinate one at Loxe, it placed the two men on an equal footing. In this he was mistaken; their partnership was purely a business one; and Charles intended to keep it so.

Charles and his family, after spending some weeks in furnished rooms, had moved into a rented house at Grove End, on the outskirts of Chardwell. It was a pleasant stone-built house called Rose Villa, with a small garden surrounding it, and a fine view out over the lower town. Neither the house nor its locality was quite what Charles would have chosen for his wife and children; nor did the domestic staff, acquired with the house, come up to his expectations; but—

"At least it is all a great deal better than being a paid domestic yourself, as you were with Cox at Newton Railes, and just for the present I think it will do."

"Of course it will do! It's a beautiful house!" Katharine said warmly. "So sunny and bright and comfortable, and with such pleasant neighbours nearby, what more could we ask?"

Here Susannah, following her own thoughts, answered what her father had said.

"Mama was not *treated* like a paid domestic while we were at Railes, papa. Martin always treated us with the utmost kindness and consideration, and we lived there, all three of us, almost as if it were still our own home."

"I know that perfectly well. I saw it myself when I came there on my return from America. But however comfortable you and your mother may have been, in my own view the situation was one that can only be deplored."

Nothing more was said then but later, when Katharine was alone with the children, she counselled her daughter in discretion.

"I think it would be better to avoid speaking of Martin and Railes when papa is here. I'm afraid it's something that vexes him."

"But papa spoke of it first, mama. I merely answered him."

"Yes, but you need not have done, for papa was speaking to me, not to you."

"I think it is very unfair, mama, that we should not mention Martin's name when he has been so good to us."

"So do I," Dick said. "And I for one will soon be forced to speak about Martin to my father because of Martin sponsoring me when I enter Mr Bonnamy's office."

Dick had only just returned from spending a fortnight's holiday with a school friend who lived in Somerset, and the date on which he was due to begin his architect's apprenticeship was only another fortnight away.

"I think, if you agree," Katharine said, "I will approach your papa first and put the whole matter to him; but as he is so busy just now, I am waiting for a suitable moment."

"And when will that be, I wonder?" Dick said.

He and Susannah exchanged a glance of youthful disillusionment, tinged on his side, as Katharine saw, with more than a hint of anxiety. She resolved to speak to Charles with the minimum delay.

It happened, however, the very next day, that the subject of Dick's future was broached by Charles himself when, in the latter part of the evening, he left his work in the study and joined his family for a while.

"Dick, I forgot to mention it before, but I was talking to Mr Maynard about you, and he was good enough to say that a place could be found for you at Loxe."

His words were followed by a cold silence, during which three faces were turned blankly towards him. Then, pale but resolute, Dick replied.

"I'm sorry, father, but I have no wish for a place in the mill. I want to be an architect and it is already arranged that I should go into Mr Bonnamy's office in two weeks' time, to begin my apprenticeship."

Charles turned towards his wife.

"Why was I not told of this till now?"

"Because you have been so very busy and we were waiting until you had time to discuss the matter thoroughly."

"Apprenticeship with an architect will mean paying a premium. Probably fifty pounds at least. I am not willing to pay such a sum."

"The indenture has already been drawn up and the premium paid. Martin Cox paid it. It was his birthday present to Dick."

"I see."

"Charles, I know you will be displeased at this, but it was done before you came back."

"Then it's just as well I came back when I did – in time to

have this transaction revoked."

"Surely you will not do that? Dick's heart is set on it."

"Dick's place is in the woollen trade. His future is cloth. At present I work in another man's mill but as soon as the opportunity occurs I intend taking a mill of my own. – Most probably Hainault. Is it so unreasonable that I should expect my only son to come into the trade with me? To learn how to run a mill and take over from me when I am gone? Surely any father is entitled to expect that? And I do expect it, I assure you both."

"No! I won't go!" Dick exclaimed. "I hate the cloth trade and everything about it. The smell of the mills makes me feel sick!" He rose suddenly from his chair and took a few paces about the room, turning at last towards his father and facing him defiantly. "If you should try to force me, papa, I'll do what you did three years ago. – I'll run away."

For a moment it seemed as though Charles would reach out and strike the boy. Katharine feared it and so did Susannah and each, quite involuntarily, betrayed her fear in a different way; Katharine by a protective gesture, Susannah by giving a little cry. Dick himself, though his face twitched, held his ground stubbornly, until his father, with an effort, found his voice and answered him.

"You, sir, had better go to your room. Susannah, too. And don't come down, either of you, until you have my permission."

In silence, the boy and the girl obeyed. Charles then turned to his wife.

"No doubt I have Martin Cox to thank for this show of rebelliousness. I am unwilling to suppose that you alone are responsible for it."

"Charles, you must not put Dick into the mill. He is asthmatic. The wool-dust would be very bad for him, just as it is for Mr Maynard. His future health would be endangered. Possibly even his life."

"The boy never used to suffer from asthma."

"No, it began about three years ago. Soon after you had left us."

"You will tell me next that I am to blame for it."

"No. But asthma subjects, the doctor says, are often affected by shock and distress. Also, it runs in families. My brother Hugh suffered from it and *that* was first brought on by shock."

Charles was visibly abashed. He stared at her in silence a while. His anger, however, had not diminished: it had merely found another cause, since fate seemed against him at every turn.

"And will my son suffer less, working as an architect, breathing stone-dust on building sites?"

"That will be out of doors," Katharine said, "and will not be very long at one time."

"I suppose I must be thankful that he does not wish to work as a mason-cum-quarryman. Because obviously his choice of profession is due to Cox's influence. You will not deny that, I suppose?"

"No. But I would remind you, Charles, that during the past three years, at a crucial time in Dick's life, *your* influence was missing."

"You need say no more, madam, to make me fully aware that I have been away too long. The consequences of my being absent are only too evident and now that I am back I must be extra vigilant with my son to be sure of preventing further infringements of my authority. As for the question of his career, it seems from what you tell me that I must set aside my own wishes and allow him to have his way. Regarding the boy's apprenticeship fee, it is of course out of the question that Martin Cox should pay it. I want charity from no man, least of all him."

"I understand that, of course."

"Thank you. It is gratifying to find that on this one point at least we are in agreement. Now, if you will excuse me, I still have work lying on my desk."

"Won't you go up and speak to Dick? He would be so delighted if you did."

"No, I think not. I have been forced into this concession,

Katharine, and my son's delight, as you must know, raises no corresponding joy in me. Furthermore, I have not forgotten that his manner to me a moment ago was insolent in the extreme. Perhaps it escaped your attention. Perhaps, during my absence, you have failed to perceive the growth of recalcitrance in that young man. Perhaps—"

"Dick never behaves like that as a rule, and I'm quite sure that by now he is bitterly regretting what he said."

"Then you may tell him, if you will, that when he is ready to apologize, he may come to me in my study. No doubt the apology will come easily enough once he knows he has got his own way. No doubt, too, he has already discovered that this asthma of his has certain advantages attaching to it. But let him beware of assuming that because I have yielded this once, it will set a pattern for the future, for he will find himself mistaken."

Charles left the room. The door clicked shut. Katharine, for a while, remained where she was, sitting upright in her chair. Outwardly, she had been calm till now, but Charles's anger had affected her, and she needed time to recover herself. She took deep, steadying breaths, and when the inward tremors ceased, she rose and went upstairs to the children.

If, as Charles had predicted, his return had caused gossip in the town, he himself heard little of it. For one thing, he was too busy at Loxe, often working twelve hours a day. For another, it was his policy to keep himself in the background until such time as the townspeople, having grown used to his presence there, accepted it without much thought. Living out at Grove End, this was easy enough to achieve. His visits to the town centre were few; his meetings with fellow townsmen brief; and when he was invited to give a public talk on the war in America and his adventures in the gold-fields, he firmly declined, although he was offered a handsome fee.

Katharine and the children, of course, had no social life at this time. They knew their nearest neighbours by sight and sometimes exchanged a few words with them, but Charles had made it quite clear that anything more was out of the question. The children resented this bitterly but spoke of it only to Katharine.

"If we're not allowed to make new friends, nor to see our old ones, then it seems to me," Susannah said, "that we might just as well have gone to America after all."

Soon, however, the gloom was lightened by a visit from their aunt Ginny, newly returned from the Continent. She drove out to Grove End at once, having heard from the servants at Chacelands that her brother-in-law had returned from the dead and had whisked his family away from Railes.

"The things that happen when I turn my back! And where is the prodigal, I'd like to know? What, still at the mill at this late hour? Well, perhaps that is all for the best, otherwise I should have wanted to ask what he means by putting you to live in a place like this. Oh, it's better than Tack House Lane, I agree. Nothing could be so bad as that! But Grove End! I do declare! It's really too genteel for words. And the houses are all so exactly alike, they might have come out of a box of toys. Now sit down, all of you, and tell me the whole story, beginning with Charles coming back to you."

When, after many interruptions, they had told her all she wanted to know, she sat for a moment in silence; and although her blue gaze was as bright as ever, there was something else in it, too.

"Well!" she said then, in a brisk tone. "We must give thanks, of course, that Charles has been safely restored to the bosom of his family. But I still don't understand why he kept silent all that time and frankly I cannot forgive him for it."

"Neither can we," Dick said, speaking for himself and Susannah. "And I'm sure mama feels the same, though she won't admit it to us of course."

"Oh, aunt Ginny, I'm so glad you're home!" Susannah said ecstatically. "We've been in this house for weeks and weeks and scarcely been out or seen anyone. It's not so bad for Dick, going to his office every day, but mama and I get so dull sometimes ... Papa has bought only one horse, you see, and of course he uses that himself. So we can never go out in the trap by ourselves, and although we take a walk every day, there's nobody we can call on because all our friends are too far away."

"Then, tomorrow, my dears, I shall come for you at half past one and take you back to Chacelands for tea. What do you say to that?"

"Oh, that will be wonderful! Won't it, mama? Papa can't possibly object to that, now, can he?"

"I wish I could come," Dick said.

"And so you shall," Ginny said. "Tell me what time you leave your office and I will come and fetch you."

"I'll ask permission to leave at four."

"Very well. It is arranged. But now I really must go home, for I have been travelling for days, you know, and am quite exhausted. I came because I couldn't wait to hear all about Charles but now – *à bientôt*, my dears. Give me a kiss. There! Now I'm gone!"

The following day was close and warm, with a sky that threatened thunder storms. When Ginny came to Rose Villa, therefore, it was in the closed carriage, with the coachman, Cobbold, driving. Because of this, and because she had so much to say, they had travelled some distance before Katharine observed that they had turned off the main turnpike by the left fork instead of the right.

"Ginny, you said you were taking us to Chacelands."

"Yes, so I am. But we are going to Railes first."

"Oh, aunt Ginny!" Susannah exclaimed, and turned to her mother with glowing face. "Railes!" she said, with a rippling laugh. "Whatever would papa say?"

"Your aunt Ginny is well aware that your papa would not approve."

"Then we must take care," Ginny said, "not to let papa know."

"Supposing Martin is not at home?"

"Oh, but he will be. I made sure of that by sending him a message last night, telling him to expect us for tea. And he sent back to say that he would."

Katharine, though with a heightened colour, laughed at her sister's stratagem, and Susannah, relieved, clapped her hands.

"Oh, aunt Ginny, I do love you so! – You always make things *happen*!" she said.

"What a nice thing to say. And how true it is. But I wish I had some control over the day's weather, for I fear we're going to be caught in it."

Sure enough, the storm broke as they drove through the gateway into the park, so that by the time they were drawing up outside the main front door, the rain was fairly tippling down. Martin, however, was watching for them and came out at once with a huge umbrella, to escort them into the entrance hall. From there, having shed their cloaks, they passed into the great hall, Ginny still twitching her skirts to be rid of the last few glistening raindrops.

"Well, Martin, how formal we are, coming in by the front door! Almost, we might be strangers here."

But in fact there was nothing formal in this reunion of old friends: in the bustle and laughter of their arrival as they hurried in out of the rain; in the way Susannah, still a child, suddenly flung herself at Martin and gave him a hug; in the noisy exuberance of the spaniels, lolloping forward to welcome them; in the pleasure the three visitors felt at seeing the old familiar objects that furnished and adorned the great hall; in the way they and Martin then gathered at the great bay window, looking out at the storm sweeping across the parkland.

The rain was a heavy downpour now, slanting like white rods of glass from clouds the colour of indigo. Thunder cracked overhead and the sky was splintered by lightning. For a short time the rain was a torrent; then, within seconds, it eased and stopped, leaving a hushed silence behind it. Garden and parkland were seen again, but with colours muted, the leaves of the trees, especially, so blanched by the rain and its drifting vapour that all the many shades of green were dimmed, softly, as in pale glaucous jade. Inside the bay window, too, vapour now formed on the small leaded panes, making it difficult to see out. The party therefore moved to the hearth where, true to established custom, a good log fire burned, although it was only early September.

"Oh, I'm all gooseflesh!" Ginny exclaimed. "Why do storms make us feel like that?" And she spread her hands to the fire's red glow. "How lucky it didn't break earlier, or Cobbold would have been soaked to the skin."

She drew up a stool and sat down on it, extending her legs to their full length so that her feet, poking out from her skirts, were in the very hearth itself. She looked up at Martin, who stood nearby.

"Well, sir, are you pleased, I wonder, at having three ladies to visit you?"

"Indeed, I am delighted," he said.

"And which of our trio, pray, are you most delighted to see?"

"That is a truly impossible question. Paris himself could not answer it."

"Then I shall be Aphrodite and we'll see what bribery can do. And when you have given me the golden apple I will reward you, as she did Paris, by helping you to carry off the fairest, most beautiful woman of all."

"Oh, but aunt Ginny," Susannah said, "that means Helen of Troy and you know what trouble *that* caused."

"You are quite right, my child. I have taken the parallel far enough." Ginny flicked a speck of dust from her sleeve and looked up at Martin again. "Speaking of abductions, however, neither my sister nor my niece knew I was bringing them here today until we were well on the road, and Katharine, I'm afraid, is still angry with me."

"What nonsense you talk," Katharine said. She was stooping, fondling the dogs. "I am not angry with anyone."

"Then why are you so silent with us?"

Katharine looked up with a smile. Her face was flushed from the warmth of the fire.

"If I have been silent, Ginny, *you* have more than made up for it."

"Well, I'm only just back from abroad, remember, and have travelled through six different countries since seeing you last, which means I have a lot to tell. But, you know, it's a very strange thing – I'm never homesick while I'm abroad but the moment I set sail for England I simply cannot wait to be there! Oh, it is so good to be back, especially here in our old home. It's really very good of you, Martin, to let us come in on you like this, but no doubt you feel it's the least you can do, having taken the house away from us. Tell me, have you got a new housekeeper yet?"

"No. I have interviewed a number of women but none was really suitable."

"You are hard to please, having had Kate here. But if you think to find another such as she, you will only seek in vain, I fear."

"I'm afraid you are right," Martin said.

"How very inconsiderate of Charles to come back and take her away from you. I suppose you make do with Cook again and expect her to do everything. How is the old body nowadays?"

"She is very well," Martin said, "and if you were to visit her in the kitchen, she would be overjoyed."

"So I shall. But not now." Ginny glanced at the clock on the stairs. "I think, while the rain holds off, this is a good time to send for Dick, so that poor old Cobbold may not be drenched. Shall you and I go with him, Susannah, and give your brother a surprise?"

"Oh, yes, I should like that! Are you coming, too, mama?"

"No, your mama cannot come," Ginny said. "She must stay with our host, for civility's sake."

Martin and Katharine returned to the window, clear now of vapour, and in a while saw the carriage making its way down the drive. The storm clouds had passed over now and were heaped up darkly over Holm Hill. The sun shone in a warm golden surge, lighting the misty parkland in such a way that the carriage, rounding a bend in the drive, appeared to be vanishing into a rainbow. And behold, when the two watchers craned their necks, a rainbow could be seen in the southern sky, its colours bright against the livid clouds.

> "'Who sees the rainbow in the sky
> Knows the storm has passed him by.
> Who sees the rainbow touch the ground
> Knows where good fortune may be found.'"

Martin turned towards Katharine.

"My sister Nan told me that rhyme when we were children at Scurr," he said. "She believed it had a meaning different from the obvious one – that seeing the rainbow was riches enough without going to the rainbow's foot to dig in search of a crock of gold."

"What did you believe, yourself?"

"I was disappointed, I think. I wanted the rainbow *and* the gold. But now I'm older I think Nan was right. The crock of gold is not only a myth – it is *meant* as a myth. It represents what we can't have. Or, perhaps, what we ought not to want."

Sunshine was flooding in at the great window now, filling the bay with its light and warmth, bringing to life the rich greens and golds in the Polonaise carpet, and casting over all, inevitably, the criss-cross reticulations of shade created by the many hundreds of small rectangular window panes. Some chairs had been set in the window-bay, ready for the visitors, and Martin and Katharine now sat down, choosing positions where they faced each other, without the sun's glare being in their eyes.

"How quiet it is," Katharine said, "now that my sister and daughter are gone."

"Your sister is in an excitable mood."

"She's amusing herself at our expense."

"Does it trouble you?"

"A little, yes. The things she says in front of Susannah – I shall speak to her privately when I can. But otherwise, apart from that, it does not worry me at all."

"You are not angry with her, then, for bringing you here today?"

"No, I'm not angry," Katharine said.

"Nor for leaving you here with me?"

"No. Of course not. I could have gone with them – if I had wished."

"But you did not," Martin said. "You stayed with me – for civility's sake."

They smiled at each other and were silent a while. Then Martin spoke again.

"There are so many questions I want to ask that I hardly know where to begin. I receive news of you sometimes … but never what I want to hear. I know you live at Grove End but it could just as well be Antartica, so severed has your life been from mine since you left this house. I hear more about your husband than I do of you. He is gone into partnership with Maynard at Loxe Mill, I believe."

"Yes, and he is doing very well. He is determined to recover his old position and is working hard towards that end. He and Mr Maynard are on very good terms."

"So much for Yuart the clothier. But what of Yuart the man at home? I have seen Dick twice and I know all is not well between him and his father since the argument over his career."

"Dick is rebellious. That angers Charles. But I hope in time they will come to a better understanding together."

"And what of your own understanding with Charles? *You* were rebellious too, I hear, when pleading Dick's case with him. And I have seen enough of your husband's temper to feel anxiety on your behalf."

"There is no need for anxiety."

"As a loyal wife, you'd be bound to say that. But I am anxious all the same because under your composure you look … "

"Yes?" Katharine said. "How do I look?"

"Rather less than your whole self."

"Oh, Martin, you must try to understand! Charles was away nearly three years. That is a long time for two people to be apart and it is no easy matter learning to be husband and wife again. Charles is changed. I can't quite say how. But Charles says *I* have changed and I think that's true. Certainly there are grievances between us. Wounds, as it were, that are not yet healed. Charles says I cannot forgive him for leaving the children and me for three years. But Charles in turn cannot forgive *me* for coming back here while he was away. Perhaps if I showed some sign of repentance, it would be a different matter. But I feel no repentance and never shall ... because the sanctuary you gave the children and me, and your kindness to us in those three years ... well, you know what that meant to us. We speak of you often, when we're alone, and it's always such a comfort to us, to know that we have you as our friend."

"Even though the friendship between us is such a thorn in your husband's flesh? – Another source of grievance between you and him?"

"Yes, even in spite of that."

"Will the grievances heal in time, d'you think?"

"I don't know. I hope they will. But let us not talk any more in this vein. We have only a short time together and every moment of it is precious. Oh, Martin, my dear friend, if you only knew what it means to me to be here in this house with you again. To be sitting alone with you like this, so quiet together, and so *comfortable*. I don't know which warms me the most – this sunshine streaming in on us both or the pleasure of your company. But one thing I know for sure – together, they are blessing and balm."

Ginny's advice, on the way to Railes, that the visit should be kept secret from Charles was not such as Katharine could follow. For one thing, deception was hateful to her. For another, the burden of secrecy was bound to prove hard for

the children to bear. Reserved though they were in their
father's presence, some hint of the visit was sure to slip out.
Katharine decided, therefore, that they should speak of it
openly, but without dwelling on it in any way that might
cause him irritation.

It happened that Charles was late home that evening,
which meant that he and she were alone when, on asking
about her visit to Chacelands, he learnt that she had first
gone to Railes.

"You went to Railes? Why was that?"

"Ginny took us, as a surprise."

"And no doubt it was a pleasant surprise."

"Yes, very pleasant indeed," Katharine said.

Briefly, he stood looking at her. Then he turned and left
the room and she heard him go into his study. He was still
there when she went to bed.

It was nothing new for Charles to work late at the mill; nor
for him to continue at home; and because of this, during the
week, he and the children rarely met. Only on Sunday was
he with them for any length of time and on these occasions,
although he took some interest in Susannah, enquiring
about her week's lessons, his remarks to Dick were brief, cool,
and impersonal.

"My father means to punish me because I wouldn't go into
Loxe Mill," the boy said to Katharine once. "I've been with
Mr Bonnamy for more than ten weeks now and never once
has my father asked me how I am getting on."

Katharine knew this was true, and it worried her. At the
same time, Dick's manner to his father left much to be
desired, and when she taxed him with this he said he found
it difficult to be himself when his father was present.

"If you could just make an effort," she said. "For instance,
if you were to show him some of your work ... "

"No, mama. I couldn't do that."

"Not even if I were to suggest it when you are together next
time?"

"Well, I don't know ... "

"Let me try," Katharine said.

On the following Sunday, therefore, with Dick's consent, Katharine duly raised the matter.

"Charles, Dick has been showing us the drawings he's done for Mr Bonnamy, and I'm sure if you have time to spare you will find them very interesting."

"Indeed? What sort of drawings?" Charles asked. Seated, he looked across at his son.

"Drawings to do with my work, papa. Some are sketches and some are designs, all illustrating aspects of our local architectural styles." Dick went to the side-table and fetched his portfolio. "Would you like to see them, papa?"

What it cost the boy to say this was very plain to his mother and sister but not, it seemed, to his father; for Charles, though he glanced at the portfolio, made no attempt to take it.

"Has Mr Bonnamy seen your drawings?"

"Yes. He was kind enough to say they were excellent."

"And what about Martin Cox? He is often at Bonnamy's office, I gather, so presumably you have shown them to him?"

"Yes. He, too, thought they were good."

"Well, since these two men, by virtue of their calling, are well qualified to judge and pronounce, I hardly think my opinion is needed. I know little of architecture. My comments would be useless to you."

Dick turned and left the room, taking his drawings with him. The door had scarcely closed on him when Susannah, rounding on her father, spoke out indignantly.

"Papa, I don't understand you! Why are you so unkind to him?"

Without waiting for an answer, she went out after her brother. Katharine sat facing Charles.

"I can only echo Susannah. – Why do your treat him so?"

"I only spoke the truth. That boy has no interest in anything I might say to him. He has shown his drawings to all and sundry before condescending to show them to me and now it is only at your instigation."

"He would not approach you before because he feared your indifference. Now his fears have proved justified. You are not only indifferent but hostile to him – all because he has chosen a profession which you connect with Martin Cox."

"Cox has certainly played a more prominent part in my affairs than I would have chosen."

"And because you dislike him so much you wish us to end our friendship with him."

"I wish it had never existed at all."

"Well, I cannot undo the past, Charles. And, as far as Martin is concerned, I would not do so even if I could."

"In that case there is nothing more to be said."

"I could find much to say if I thought you would listen sympathetically. And I would be willing to *do* much, to create a better understanding between us. But this thing you ask of me, that I should reject a friend and his friendship—"

"I have asked nothing. I have merely made my feelings clear. For most women, a husband's wishes would be enough, but you would have me forbid you outright, thus exposing myself to the charge of being a harsh, domineering husband. Perhaps that is how you see me. It is certainly not how I see myself. But you have always had a gift for putting me in the wrong and it is not, I suppose, surprising that I now find myself arraigned by my two children as well as by my wife. Dick, in particular, from the day I returned, has been sulky and churlish in the extreme. Yet now, over these drawings of his, he would have me pat his head and say what a clever fellow he is."

"Charles, he is young. He is sixteen. Surely you, as a grown man, can make some allowances for him. You are his father, the most important person in his life. Of course he wants commendation from you. It is only natural. He is a boy, with a boy's feelings—"

"Do you think, because I am a man, that I don't have feelings of my own?"

"I know what your feelings are. You are bitterly disappointed because he has chosen a profession different from yours. But can you not forgive him for that? Can you not find it in your heart to take some interest in his work?"

"It is absurd to speak of forgiveness. You make too much of the boy's concerns. However, I am prepared, as you suggest, to make some allowances for him, bearing in mind that during my absence he came under doubtful influences."

Charles rose and went to the door.

"I am going to my study. You may tell the boy, if you choose, that I am willing to receive him there and will look at these precious drawings of his. Possibly, if I see him alone, we shall do better, he and I, than when you and his sister are present."

But Dick, on receiving the substance of this message, rejected it with passionate scorn.

"Never, never, *never* again shall I seek to interest him in my work, or in anything else whatsoever. He deliberately sought to humiliate me and would do it again if he had the chance. But he shall not have the chance again. I will make quite certain of that. It is no good, mama, speaking to me of love and respect between father and son, because in my case they no longer exist. My father cares nothing for me. But what of that? I did without his love all the time he was away. I shall do without it now that he's home."

Nothing Katharine could say would move her son from this avowal. The wound had gone too deep. And although she still hoped that time and its kindlier hours would bring a better understanding, in her heart she feared that the signs were against it.

Charles, determined to re-establish himself in his native trade, applied himself to it with such single-mindedness that Ginny, on one of her visits to Rose Villa, scolded him roundly for cutting himself off from the world.

"The Yeomanry Ball last week, Ginotti's recital the week before, and the Yuarts were not present at either! Explain yourself, Charles, if you please."

"I will not attend public functions until I can do so on equal terms with those people I am likely to meet."

"And what about private functions? Will you accept invitations from friends?"

"No. Not until such time as I can return their hospitality and that is impossible in this house."

"Surely you can come to Chacelands, just for an informal family meal?"

"You forget, my dear sister-in-law, that your husband and I are not on good terms."

"Oh, how ridiculous men are! To keep up a quarrel all these years! I don't know who's worse – you or George. But if you yourself will not come, at least you will not object if Katharine and the children do? I will send the carriage for them, of course."

"I have no objection," Charles said. "They are free to do as they please."

At regular intervals, therefore, Katharine and the children were invited to Chacelands; sometimes to tea, sometimes to supper; and always on these occasions Martin was invited too.

"Is it not kind of me;" Ginny said once, seated alone with Katharine while the two men and the young people were gathered around the billiard-table; "is it not *angelic* of me to bring you and Martin together like this? I always send him a note, you see, the moment I know for sure you're coming. Oh, don't worry, it's always discreet. I simply say, 'The family will be here at such-and-such a time. I hope you'll be able to join us.' And somehow – it's the oddest thing – he always seems to manage it."

Katharine, unravelling a skein of silk thread, glanced at her sister but made no reply.

"There!" Ginny said. "I've made you blush! And it is only right that you should. For who would have thought, in earlier days, that time would cast me as go-between for my virtuous, high-minded elder sister and her *cavaliere servente*?

It really is too amusing for words except that you're so *pudique*, both of you, that sometimes I despair of you. It is such a waste, I could weep salt tears. For here I have been, these two years or more, simply longing to be unfaithful to George, in revenge for Anthony, and Martin, who could have been my *amoureux*, prefers playing Aucassin to your Nicolette. How unfair it all is! I can't think of any other man who might do, which means I have no choice, perdee, but to be faithful to George after all."

Ginny paused, looking archly at Katharine, her head on one side.

"I suppose it is no use asking what Nicolette feels for her Aucassin? She wouldn't tell me, anyway. Oh, well! *N'importe! N'importe!* It means I can use my imagination, which is more diverting than fact as a rule, don't you agree, Kate?"

"In your case, yes, undoubtedly." Katharine, having finished her work on the skein, wound it into a neat coil and laid it in her sister's lap. "There is your silk, all tidy again."

"Ah! Would that all knots could be undone so easily as that!" Ginny said.

The little party at the billiard-table, having finished their game, now came to the fireside.

"Martin, come and sit here by me," Ginny said, and, as he complied: "Tell us how things are at Railes, now that Christmas is drawing near. Will you be spending it at home?"

"Yes. Nan and her family are coming and will stay for three days or so. On Boxing Day I intend giving a small supper party and I very much hope that you and George and Anthony will be able to come."

"We'll be delighted. Won't we, George? We have not seen the Claytons these many months past. And what of the Yuarts? Will they be there?"

"As yet I don't know, but I hope they will." Martin looked directly at Katharine. "I thought if I sent a written invitation, addressed to your husband and yourself, he might perhaps, at such a season, find it possible to accept."

Before Katharine could answer him, her daughter and sister broke in together.

"Oh, mama! Surely he will?" Susannah cried, while Ginny, fiercely indignant, exclaimed: "Of course Charles must accept! It would be too churlish for words if he didn't and I would very soon tell him so!"

"Well, we shall see," Katharine said.

But Charles, when Martin's invitation arrived, treated it with angry contempt.

"Does this man seriously think that I would accept hospitality from him? If so, he mistakes me entirely, and his skin must be thicker than I had supposed. Either that or he is obtuse, for surely I have made it plain just what I feel about him?"

"Martin is neither obtuse nor thick-skinned but, being a friend of myself and the children, he wishes, out of courtesy, to extend his friendship to you as well."

"Courtesy!" Charles said, scoffing. "The man is an ill-bred parvenu and what you see as courtesy is merely the vulgarian's desire to display the importance he thinks he's attained. You may be taken in by it but I am not. As for my going to Newton Railes ... I will not set foot in that house again until the day comes when I am reinstated as its owner."

Katharine stared. It was some time before she could speak.

"And how will such a thing come about?"

"There is only one way. I shall buy it back. Oh, it will take time, of course. But perhaps not so long as you think. At present I'm running another man's mill but in another two or three years I shall be renting Hainault. I've already seen Sidney Hurne and he has promised me a three-year lease with an option to purchase it when I can. After that, when I have my own mill again, it will not be long before I am in a position to buy back Newton Railes.

"You may remember, when Hainault failed and I was obliged to compound my debts, there was a chance that the house might be spared. But you set to work and persuaded me that it must be sacrificed with the rest. It seemed to me at the time that you were determined to martyr yourself, perhaps as a means of punishing me. Be that as it may, I will not recriminate with you now, but the one indisputable fact is that Railes was sold to pay my debts. Obviously, then, it is my duty to do everything within my power to get it back. You will understand that, I'm sure."

"No, Charles, I do not understand. Railes belongs to Martin now. Even if you had means enough to buy it back from him tomorrow, what possible reason can you have for expecting him to part with it?"

"From what I have been led to believe, Cox has always regarded you and your family with respect amounting to veneration. It seems to me only right, therefore, that when in time the occasion arises, he should be prepared to relinquish his tenure in favour of those who, in every moral sense, are its only rightful heritors."

"In other words," Katharine said, "you would appeal to these finer feelings which, just a moment ago, you declared were utterly lacking in him."

"Oh, I think he would give way to us, if only because of public opinion. Your self-made man cannot endure being the object of disapproval. But why are we arguing in this way, as though Newton Railes meant nothing to you? You returned there promptly enough to keep house for Cox while I was away. Surely, then, you must wish to go back, reinstated as its mistress?"

"It is not a question of what I wish, but of what I expect. And I do not expect to go back."

There was a moment of silence between them, broken suddenly when Charles, who held Martin's note in his hand, turned and flung it into the fire.

"In that case, coming back to the present, it will be no great disappointment to you if we do *not* dine there on Boxing Day. Perhaps, as I'm a busy man, you will write declining his invitation yourself."

"Yes," Katharine said, "I will write to him."

CHAPTER
13

B y the end of 1863, profits at Loxe Mill had already risen by one per cent. By the following spring they had risen again. More gratifying still, the state of its order-books was such that in the course of that same year a further increase could be expected, bringing the mill's estimated profits up to a clear twenty per cent. This satisfactory state of affairs was due in some measure to improved trade in Europe, but chiefly it was due to Charles Yuart's energy, acumen, and experience. Also to his imagination, for, although still contemptuous of the fancy suitings made at Loxe, he was full of ideas for new designs, and these had found favour everywhere. His partner, Maynard, was delighted, and gave credit where it was due.

"That brown and fawn check is doing well. So is this blue-grey herringbone. We've got repeat orders for both and it's only a few weeks since they went out. Altogether, it strikes me that we make a good team, you and I. Let's hope it continues so."

Maynard, in the previous months, had enjoyed an improvement in his health, due, plainly, to the fact that with Yuart in charge of the mill, he was relieved of anxiety. He could spend a short day in his office now without any undue strain, though in winter, when the cold wet weather came, he was often forced to stay at home, nursed by his widowed daughter, Rose. On these occasions, Charles would ride out to Patesbridge two or three times a week with letters and cheques for Maynard to sign, and a list of items to discuss. Maynard by now was glad to give Charles a free hand, but

lways with the proviso that he was kept well informed, down
o the last detail.

"I may not be much use at the moment, but I still want to
now what's going on."

And when, with the weather, his health improved, so that
e could return to his office, there was, as he freely admitted,
ittle for him to find fault with there.

"You're certainly making things hum," he said. "There
sn't an idle loom in the place. Almost every piece of cloth is
espoke and that is how I like it to be. And *you* are reaping the
enefit, too. Your investment is turning over nicely and
ou're in a fair way to becoming warm. If *I've* got nothing to
grumble about, we can say the same for *you*, eh?"

This, of course, was true enough, and Charles on the
whole was well pleased. The profit accruing from his
investment, being added each month to the capital sum,
together with the major part of his salary, the investment
accordingly grew, thus yielding still larger profits which, in
turn, were invested again. Thus, by the end of his first year
at Loxe, his share in the mill's capital was just over twelve
thousand pounds. And it was roughly at this time that Robert
Cornelius, who rented Hainault Mill from the Hurnes,
suffered a series of strokes and died.

Charles, on hearing this news, went at once to his friend
and solicitor, Alec Stevenson, to discuss taking over the mill,
and within a week or two it was done. Sidney Hurne, eager
to secure a tenant who would buy the mill just as soon as he
could, was only too glad to let it to Charles at a mere two
hundred pounds per annum. The option of buying, needless
to say, was written into the terms of the lease.

Maynard, when he heard of his partner's doings, was more
than a little put out at first. Admittedly, Charles had warned
him that he would be renting a mill of his own, but it was all
happening a great deal sooner than expected, and Charles,
to finance his own enterprise, was asking to withdraw the
bulk of the sum he had invested in Loxe; namely ten
thousand pounds. Yes, Charles agreed, defending himself,

his plans had certainly ripened prematurely, but this was
entirely due to an unforeseeable circumstance, namely the
death of Cornelius. As for the question of his investment,
Maynard had admitted asking for this merely as a guarantee
of commitment, and Charles now argued that his achievement
at Loxe was surely guarantee enough that he would be
equally conscientious throughout the term of their
partnership.

"Furthermore, as you yourself said, my chances of
succeeding as an independent clothier will be greatly
improved by the fact that I am also in business with you.
Plainly, then, it is in my own best interest, not only to preserve
good relations with you, but to make sure that my remaining
investment continues to earn the maximum profit."

"Yes, yes, that's true enough."

"Of course, you are entitled to refuse me this favour, in
which case I will still rent Hainault but shall be obliged to
leave it standing idle until my investment with you is such
that I may remove a substantial sum and still leave the
original ten thousand pounds intact. But I don't need to tell
you that to leave Hainault idle—"

"Yes, well," Maynard said gruffly. "I shall have to give in
to you, I can see. I only hope you are capable of running both
mills without one of them suffering for it. Namely, mine."

"Loxe Mill will not suffer. I give you my word."

In due course, and with little delay, Charles withdrew ten
thousand pounds from the Loxe Mill account at the District
Bank and with it opened an account for Hainault at Coulson's
Bank in Trinity Square. This was where he had banked in the
past; his private account was already there; and the manager,
Mr Harriman, after a number of searching questions, and a
few words counselling caution, agreed that Charles, when his
business required it, should have the use of an "occasional"
overdraft to a sum not exceeding two thousand pounds,
chargeable at six per cent. The high rate of interest, as
Charles well knew, was to discourage any ill-considered use
of this concession. These limits and these terms, together

with Harriman's advice, were extremely disagreeable to Charles, but thus, he reflected bitterly, did a man's past history cast its shadow over present endeavour.

Further difficulties were to come and chief among these was the problem of obtaining credit from local tradesmen. In particular, Pirrie and Son, the Cullen Valley wool merchants, having lost money to Charles in the past, now refused to trade with him unless he could promise to pay on the nail. This of course was out of the question, for credit was the life-blood of successful commerce, and just as Charles, when selling his cloth, gave the cloth-merchant three months to pay, so he in turn, and because of this, required the same terms when buying the raw materials of his trade. But this was a problem that he had foreseen and again Maynard was willing to help by allowing Charles to buy his wool under cover of the Loxe Mill account.

"No doubt they will wonder at my buying top quality merino all of a sudden and they may well twig the reason for it. But my credit has always been good in the trade and so long as they have my signed acceptance they won't worry over-much. Just as, when I have yours, I hope I needn't worry, either, because what it boils down to, Yuart, is that I am acting as surety for you and there is a great deal of money involved."

"I know that and I'm grateful to you."

"You'll have to arrange your own haulage, of course, shifting the bales from my place to yours. Or did you have it in mind, perhaps, that I'd lend you a loan of my carts as well?"

Charles, aware that a joke was intended, did his best to smile. Enduring raillery of this kind was one of the penalties he had to pay for being Maynard's obligee. It was something he detested, especially when, as now, it occurred in the hearing of Maynard's clerk, a man who, Charles felt, was already inclined to treat him with much the same familiarity. George Anstey had been at Loxe Mill for fifteen years; he was fussy and self-important and he liked, in a sly way, to score off Charles whenever he could. Sure enough, in the course of time, when Charles's consignment of wool had arrived and been removed to Hainault, here was Anstey, in Maynard's presence, reminding him that his note for the cost was almost a week overdue.

Charles, in a temper, went to his desk and wrote out the promissory note, under the previous Friday's date. He thrust it into the clerk's hands and watched as the man, with finicking care, entered the details into his ledger and filed the note in the slotted box labelled "bills receivable".

"You mustn't mind Anstey," Maynard said, when he and Charles were alone, later. "He has my best interests at heart, you know, and he likes to keep a tidy bill-box."

"I need hardly remind you, Mr Maynard, that as your partner I too have your interests at heart."

"Ah, but you've got another string to your bow, now that you've taken Hainault, and perhaps Anstey fears that certain things here may possibly slip your mind."

"Perhaps you share that fear yourself."

"Yuart, you should know by now that if I have anything to say, I speak out in plain terms, without beating about the bush. I always will, be sure of that."

"I am glad to hear it," Charles said.

It was a strange experience, being back at Hainault Mill, especially as, in the first few days, all his memories were of that period four years earlier, when he had left it, a failure and a bankrupt. But he had no time to dwell on the past. There was too much to do. And as he threw himself into the task of managing the mill as it already was, while, simultaneously, implementing plans for expansion, the excitement he felt was so great that it banished past suffering from his mind.

He was back where he belonged, in the mill which had been in his family for more than two hundred years and which he himself had helped to develop, by the addition of modern buildings and by being the first man in the valley to purchase the new power-looms. He was making his own cloth again and it was only a question of time before he would regain his old position as one of the leading clothiers in the district. A man who, having married into one of the oldest families in the county, had a duty to that family which he was determined to discharge.

Hainault first. Then Newton Railes. Quite clearly it was intended that he should regain possession of both. To this end he was committed and nothing, he vowed, would stand in his way. There was a mountain of work to be done but the thought of it did not dismay him. On the contrary, the magnitude of his task acted as a stimulus, so that he felt himself imbued with superhuman energy. What had to be done, he would do, even if it took twenty years. But it would not take half that time. Nor even a quarter of it. On that he was fiercely resolved.

At present the cloth he made at Hainault was mostly worsteds and cassinettes and there were orders enough on the books to keep these in production for three or four months at least. But too many looms were standing idle and this was a state of affairs that Charles meant to alter without delay. First he had to judge – in some cases, re-judge – the calibre of his mill-hands. Many of these were known to him, having worked at Hainault since early days; others had been brought in by the Hurnes; but, old hands or new, so relieved were they at finding their employment secure, that he had their allegiance immediately.

Soon the idle looms were uncovered and the best of the weavers were set to work producing cloth of the quality that had made Hainault's name in the past: superfine broadcloth in the traditional plain colours, which, in the right market, commanded high prices and won esteem. Admittedly that market had shrunk but so too had the competition, partly because many mills had closed, partly because those that remained had changed over to the cheaper cloths. Francus Warde, the London merchant, seeing the dark blue Hainault

Pastello coming off the looms again, undertook to purchase the lot just as soon as it was ready, and talked of ordering more later.

"It is good to see you back, Mr Yuart, especially here where you really belong. The woollen trade has suffered badly over the past few years and many good clothiers have been forced out of business. Still, it's an ill wind, as they say, and those few who are still making good quality cloth now have the market to themselves. We've come through the worst of our troubles, and the future, I am glad to say, looks a good deal rosier. We shall still have our ups and downs, no doubt, but one thing is certain – quality always wins in the end."

Charles had no doubts on that score, but Warde's assurance was welcome all the same, and the practical aspect of his faith – namely, the size of the orders he placed – was even more welcome still. His purchases encouraged Charles to increase his output by a third, while the relevant trade bills, signed by Warde, although they would not be paid for three months, were discounted readily by the bank, which made their value – less one per cent – available to Charles immediately. Together with other acceptances, from the sale of the cheaper cloths, turnover was very healthy. Mostly, these sales were made through local merchants, or through travelling salesmen dealing directly with tailoring firms; but his biggest buyer was Francus Warde, one of the best-known merchants in the country.

And just as money begat money – which of course it was meant to do – so faith begat faith, which meant that in a few short months Charles was already expanding his range to include three more quality fabrics: doeskin, fields, and Hainault rib. One of these, only just on the market, won awards at the International Exhibition that year. As a result, orders came flooding in, and Charles, increasing production to meet demand, needed more capital to cover his costs.

Once again he applied to the bank and this time Mr Harriman, impressed by what Charles had achieved so far, agreed to extend his overdraft from two to four thousand pounds, at the same time reducing the rate of interest to a reasonable five per cent. To Charles, this agreement was doubly welcome: first, because it met his immediate needs; second, because it signified that he had regained the bank's trust. Obviously he was making some progress in eradicating the past. He had also begun to climb the ladder that would raise him to his former status.

Reviewing the situation so far, he was well pleased. Quietly, without any show, he had re-established himself as a man of business. Now he felt the time had come to do the same on a social level. Accordingly, during the summer and autumn of 1864, he and his family were occasionally seen in public: first at the annual Hospital Fête, held in the grounds of Hackford Hall; next at a gala performance of *Dido and Aeneas*, given in West's Concert Rooms; and, in mid October, at a ball held in the newly refurbished ball-room of The Commercial Hotel.

This was Susannah's first ball. It was also her birthday, and she was fifteen. She danced the first dance with her uncle George; the second with her cousin Anthony; and the third, a quadrille, she danced with Martin. But first they stood talking together, sipping glasses of iced grenadine.

"You see I am wearing your birthday gift." She touched her necklace with one white-gloved hand. "Do you think it looks well on me?"

"It looks just as I hoped it would."

The necklace was a fine gold chain, set at intervals with tiny white opals, each scarcely bigger than a grain of rice; and from the chain hung a larger opal, also white, but with a delicate play of colours in it, set off by its gentle convexity and by its thin fine rim of gold.

"Did you choose it yourself?" she asked.

"Yes. I bought it in London recently. I liked it the moment I saw it and when it turned out that opal was your birthstone I felt I'd been guided in my choice."

"Perhaps you knew I was to wear a white dress."

"Perhaps I did."

"The truth is, I wanted mauve, but mama would not hear of it."

"Be grateful to her. She was quite right."

"Oh, but mauve is so pretty ... Also, it's all the fashion, you know."

"Yes. I have only to look round this room to see that."

"White is so dull. And commonplace."

"You only think that because you are young. But your youth is the very reason white becomes you. It signifies purity, innocence, honesty. Also hope, another youthful attribute."

"But I don't wish to be innocent always. I should prefer to be ... a mature woman of the world."

"In that case you had better wear mauve."

"I suppose you think I'm still a child."

"At the age of fifteen," Martin said, "you are child, girl, and woman all in one."

Susannah, sipping her grenadine, looked at him over the rim of her glass, in a manner learnt, whether consciously or not, by studying her aunt Ginny.

"And at what age, precisely, shall I put away the first two conditions, and enter wholly into the third?"

"Don't be in too much of a hurry to put the first two behind you, for the woman who is really mature is one who has lived each phase to the full. That is what makes her mature – she retains the wisdom of *all* her years, not merely of the later ones."

"Is it the same for a man?"

"Yes. Hence the saying – young men think old men are fools while old men *know* that young men are fools."

"Then what we retain is not wisdom at all. It is merely the knowledge of our past folly."

"If we recognize it as folly, we have learnt wisdom."

"Why is it," Susannah asked, "that older people always want us young ones to stay young?"

"If you could see yourself this evening, you would not need to ask that."

"But I *cannot* see myself," she said. "Oh, I looked in the mirror at home, of course. Probably for a good half-hour. But I saw nothing that gave me joy. All I saw was a white dress, which I wished was mauve."

"In that case," Martin said, "I will be your mirror now, and try to show you to yourself; but to do so I shall be obliged to borrow another man's words." And he quoted:

"'No fairer maid was ever seen,
Nor any fairer clad than she:
Walking the lily launds between,
She fairer was than they, to me.

"'Her gowne was of white sendille made
And no adornment did she wear
Save a girdle, gold embraid,
And eke a tresslet in her hair.

"'Fairer than the lily-lea;
Fairer than all maidens, she,
Cloth'd in her white simplicity.'"

"Oh, Martin! Is that me?"

"Well, those lines could never have been written of any young woman wearing mauve."

"No, they could not! – They are mine!" she said. She looked at him with glowing face, and all her attempts at worldliness were, for the present at least, forgotten. "You have quite changed my feelings about this dress and I shall wear it again and again. And when it can't be worn any more, I shall keep it in a safe place, wrapped in layers of fine muslin, spread with dried southernwood. And years later, when I am old—"

Here Susannah was interrupted because, the interval between dances having ended, the orchestra now struck up the introductory bars of their quadrille. Martin took her empty glass and set it aside, with his own. Formally, he bowed to her, and formally she gave him her hand; and he, as he led her into the dance, saw how many pairs of eyes were turned upon the face of his young partner.

*

Later he danced with Ginny who said:

"What *have* you been saying to my niece, to induce such a state of rapture in her? I have never seen her so radiant. She is over the moon."

"I'm sorry, but the compliments paid to one lady should never be divulged to another, I feel."

"Even when the first is a child and the other her aunt?"

"Especially not then," he said.

"Very well. I shall not press. But now it is my turn, if you please, to be sent into a state of rapture by means of your gallantry."

"That, I feel, is less easily achieved when the lady has reached mature years."

"Nonsense. I am no age at all."

"You are the same age as myself."

"A woman is *never* the same age as a man. Surely you must know that? But obviously your gallantry is reserved for young creatures of fifteen."

"One such only."

"And that because she is her mother's daughter. Speaking of Kate, it seems you have not danced with her yet. Why do you practise such austere self-denial? It seems you are something of an ascetic."

"Far from it, I assure you. If I were, I should not be dancing with *you*."

"Come, now, that's better. It makes some amends for your earlier slight. And in return I have a message for you from Kate. She says she has reserved the supper-dance for you and has written your name into her card. Make the most of her, Martin, my friend, for George and I are going up to London soon and will probably stay two months at least, which means no meetings for you at Chacelands."

The supper-dance was a waltz by Rüschler; a pretty tune called *Weinrose*, which Katharine, as a young girl, had played on the schoolroom piano at Railes when

Martin, in borrowed pumps, had received his first dancing lessons, tutored by Ginny and her twin.

"What a long time ago that seems," Katharine said. "And yet, in some ways, only yesterday. You were nervous of dancing the waltz then, I remember, but you outgrew your fears eventually."

"It is lucky for me that I did, for how else should a man have licence to hold a woman in his arms, in a public place, for all to see? To move with her in close unison? To smile at her and look into her eyes, all without exciting comment?"

"Don't be too sure of that last," Katharine said.

"Oh, I shall be discretion itself. For instance, I will now glance up at the ceiling and you, if you please, will do the same. And any interested observer will see that I'm drawing your attention to the new chandelier, made by John Daniell of Bristol."

"Indeed," Katharine said, "it is very fine."

"Now, note the walls, which are newly papered, and tell me how you'd describe the colour. Cornelian, do you think, or cinnamon?"

"It is difficult to say … "

"At least you'll agree that the dado is white?"

"Yes, and embossed with fantastical urns."

"Now, having done my duty as far as appearances are concerned, perhaps I may ask if you will allow me to take you in to supper?"

"Of course," Katharine said, meeting his gaze. "It is why I saved this dance for you."

Following the October ball, he did not see her again for some weeks, and then it happened purely by chance.

He was at Newton Childe, engaged in a survey of the church, the stone-work of which was so badly eroded in places that extensive repairs were needed. He had been there almost an hour, making detailed notes of the damage, assessing the amount of new stone required, and collecting some of the loose chips, so that the colour could be matched at the quarry. He was taking a last look at the tower when he heard the sound of the churchyard gate and turned to see Katharine come in.

"Martin! What a happy surprise!" She came to him and gave him her hand, and such was the warmth of her greeting, – of the pleasure expressed in her look and her smile – that the grey December day was transformed. "What are you doing here?"

He explained his errand and showed her his notes, and they talked for a while of the church and its needs. Katharine herself, as he could see, had come to visit the family graves. She carried a few sprigs of evergreen and a bunch of wild sweet violets picked from the hedgerow on her way.

"Susannah is spending a fortnight with Ginny and George in London, so I am alone during the day, and this morning I took it into my head to walk out here. I felt I wanted to get out of the house … out of the town … into the hills."

"It's a long way from Grove End."

"Not if you come up by the fields, and take the short cut across Railes, as I did."

"It's a good three miles even then."

"The distance was nothing. I enjoyed the walk. And with your company on the way back, I shall enjoy it even more. Will you wait for me? I shan't be long."

"Yes," he said, "I will wait for you."

It had been a mild winter up till now, and most of the trees in the parkland at Railes still bore their leaves, in their autumn colours. The crimson maples, especially, glowed like fire; and even the great horse-chestnuts, their lower branches sweeping the ground, still wore their rusty brown-and-yellow habit, rather, as Katharine said, like monks of a tatterdemalion order. Everywhere, on all sides, the Manor Farm cattle grazed the lush grass, together with a few fallow deer that had strayed in from Chacelands. There were a number of pheasants about, especially under the beech trees, where they pecked for grubs among the fallen beechmast. And high up in the walnut trees, rooks squabbled over the nuts.

Martin and Katharine walked slowly. They had plenty to

ay to each other, and Katharine, as always, was full of questions, eager for every bit of news relating to the household at Railes. On her own home life she was somewhat evasive, and Martin did not enquire too closely. He knew from his meetings with Dick that the boy's relationship with his father was strained, and so, to avoid distressing Katharine, he did not refer to Dick at all. Instead he spoke of Charles Yuart and his rapid achievement in re-establishing himself as a clothier.

"I hear he's doing amazingly well, not only at Loxe but at Hainault, too."

"Yes, and I thank God for it. He works so very hard, you know, running the two mills together, that he deserves to succeed at last. The only thing is, I fear for his health. He has such a powerful will and drives himself so relentlessly ... Even at home he works and works ... He says, after the gold-fields, his work now is nothing at all, and it's true he never seems to tire. Almost, he seems indestructible. It means so very much to him, to be running his own mill again ... though he won't be really satisfied until he has actually bought it back. That is the goal he has set himself. That is what spurs him on. And if hard work can achieve it – combined with the present improvement in trade – it seems he will likely have his wish."

"Yes, so I believe," Martin said. "In fact, from what I hear in the town, he should reach his goal in two or three years." Then, choosing his words with care, to avoid any hint of irony, he said: "No doubt, too, in the fullness of time, he hopes to do the same with Railes."

Katharine came to a sudden halt and faced him almost angrily.

"Martin, how can you *know* he hopes such a thing when it is so *unreasonable*?"

"Simply because, if I were Charles and had been to blame, as he was, for losing my wife's family home, I should hope the same thing myself. And it's not so very unreasonable. Not as far as I am concerned. Because if and when the time comes—"

"Martin, *no*! I won't hear of it. Railes is yours, in every possible sense of the word, and there is no question of your giving it up."

"It would be a sacrifice, I admit, but one I would make in all happiness, for your sake."

"I will not allow you to."

"Forgive me," Martin said with a smile, "but if your husband should one day be in a position to approach me on this matter, the outcome will rest between him and me."

"You would disregard my wishes, then?"

"In this one instance, yes. Because your own wishes would be compromised by your close concern for mine. But before you say any more, I would like to tell you that even if your husband's hopes should not be realized, Newton Railes will still return to your family, in time, because in my will I have left it to Dick."

"But that too is wrong," Katharine said, still speaking with strong feeling. "For one thing, I'm sure you will marry one day. Oh, yes, you may smile at me, but you are still a young man and cannot know what the future holds. Also, you have four nephews to think of."

"My nephews are remembered in my will, I assure you. And my brother-in-law, as you know, is heir to a flourishing building business, which means that his sons are more than adequately provided for. But Newton Railes is another matter and will come to Dick. Edward Clayton knows that. He will be one of the trustees, if I should die before Dick comes of age. Dr Whiteside is another. And both men fully approve. Not that it would have made any difference whether they did or not. I would not have changed my mind. I would merely have changed my trustees."

"Argument, then, is useless, it seems."

"Quite useless," Martin said.

"I have no choice but to yield."

"Let us say, rather, to accept."

For a while longer she looked at him. Then, in silence, she turned away, and they walked on together as before.

"Very well," she said at last. "That you should leave Railes to Dick – if and so long as you do not marry – I am willing to accept. And on his behalf, and my own, I thank you from the bottom of my heart. Words can't express what I feel about it, but I think you know without being told. But for you to talk of parting with Railes during your own lifetime – that I cannot and will not accept."

"Well, as it is only a hypothetical question at present, I suggest we leave it until such time as it takes concrete form. If it ever does."

"You are just trying to silence me but I am not done yet. I still have much to say on the subject and will not be put off so easily."

"Very well," Martin said. "I am all ears, as Cook would say."

"Now you are making fun of me, and I take it amiss. I am only too well aware that as a woman I have no rights when it comes to making decisions, even in matters such as this, which are of the closest concern to me. But I thought that you of all people would at least give me a hearing, without making light of my opinions and subjecting me to male condescension."

"God forbid I should do such a thing—"

"God forbid it indeed," Katharine said.

"—for although you may have no rights in law, you know that as far as I am concerned, you have rights and privileges above those of anyone else in the world."

"But what use are they, these rights of mine, when what I say has no influence with you? There! You cannot answer that! And it is as well, for I need time to think. I therefore request that you remain silent while I prepare my argument."

"My lips shall be sealed," Martin said.

So again they walked on together and in a while came to the place where the carriage-road divided. From here they could see the house, some two hundred yards away, its grey stone-work merging so well into the greyness of the day that a stranger approaching for the first time might easily fail to perceive it there. A slight movement of the mist, however, and it stood revealed, betrayed first by its dominant feature: the square-bayed window of the great hall, its small rectangular panes of glass all glinting unevenly, some with a dark deliquescence, as of oil-and-water, others with the cold pallid sheen of pewter. Between the bay window and the porch, creepers glowed a dark fiery red, while, all along the main wall, between its double row of casements, the foliage of the Chinese wisteria was a pale, relucent yellow-gold, trailing from the convolute vine. Somewhere in the grounds at the side of the house, garden rubbish was being burnt, and its smoke drifted across the park, spreading out very slowly to lie flat and still in the damp hollows. The smell of the smoke was the smell of autumn: of damp dead leaves burning, and old lichened wood, and moss raked from the lawn and parterres.

"Look at this place," Katharine said. "That house. The grounds. The way everything lies together, as though God himself ordered it so. I have no clever arguments, Martin. I will leave Railes to speak for itself. Why in God's name should you give it up when it is yours beyond all question? Not only because you bought it but because it means so much to you."

"I can't deny what it means to me. I have loved that house more than twenty years. Every acre of land that goes with it. Every tree that grows in its soil. When it first became mine, it seemed nothing short of a miracle, and I still feel exactly the same now. It has been such a *privilege* to me, Katharine, to have lived here these four years past, and my pride in owning it is great indeed. But the miracle of it is due to something that ought never to have happened, and I have felt all along that in one sense I was here merely as a steward, entrusted with its care until such time as the rightful owners could claim it again. But that too is a source of pride to me, – that fate should have chosen me for the task – and when the time comes for me to give it up, whether to your husband during my lifetime, or to Dick on my death, I hope it may be found that I have discharged my duties as a good steward should.

"Oh, Martin!" Katharine exclaimed, and, looking at him with tear-filled eyes, she shook her head over his words, in a kind of tender exasperation. "What am I to say to you, when you are so loving and so unselfish?"

"There is no need to say anything, except perhaps 'so be it'."

"And that I'm resolved *not* to say, for I can be stubborn, too, you know! But I am willing to call a truce, for, as you said a moment ago, the situation may never arise . . . in which case I shall merely have wasted my breath and *you* will have made me cry for nothing. There! Now I am done with it! No more arguments. No more tears. We see each other too seldom to spend our brief time in disagreements, whatever their cause. Suffice it to say that just for the present, and I hope for long years to come, you remain lord and owner of Railes whether you like it or not."

"As it happens, I like it very well, and so long as I remain here, I mean to enjoy it to the full. Furthermore, as its lord and owner, I beg that you will do me the honour of taking luncheon with me today. It would make a number of people happy ... not just myself but Cook and Jobe and Jack Sherard and all the rest of your old staff ... to see you in your old home again."

"I shall come, of course," Katharine said, "and it will make me happy, too."

She slipped her hand into his arm.

CHAPTER
14

1865 was a good year for trade in England. Europe for onc
was at peace with itself; the war in America had come t
an end; and everywhere it was felt that a new prosperit
lay ahead. The Cullen Valley was no exception; its fore
most trade was enjoying a boost; and Charles Yuart
running two mills simultaneously, was achieving miracles a
both.

Business at Hainault was so good that the manager a
Coulson's Bank had extended the mill's overdraft yet again
Charles had also, through his solicitor, Alec Stevenson, bee
able to borrow a further two thousand pounds from Josep
Samms, the former ironmonger, who, having retired fron
business to live in some style at Fordover House, now mad
use of his capital by putting part of it out on loan at a high rat
of interest. Charles had to pay seven per cent, but, Hainaul
profits having risen to a clear twenty-one per cent, th
arrangement was well worth while. Throughout this period
therefore, he was increasing production steadily to meet th
growing demand for quality broadcloth. As a result, he wa
buying ever-increasing quantities of the most expensiv
wools, still under the aegis of his partner at Loxe. One da
Maynard remarked on it. He had three invoices in his hand
relating to Yuart's purchases, and was frowning over the siz
of the orders.

"I should have thought John Pirrie would allow you credi
in your own name by now, seeing you're doing so well a
Hainault."

"Possibly he might," Charles said, "but I don't want to risk is saying no."

"H'mm. Well, don't be too rash, man. Your orders this quarter alone amount to nearly two thousand pounds. That's a lot of money for a man in a small way of business like ourself."

"If my business is to grow – and it *is* growing rapidly – I must have wool in these quantities or I can't make enough cloth to meet my orders. As for the money involved, you have my promissories for that, and so far, as you well know, every one has been paid on the nail."

"I should hope so indeed!" Maynard said, with a sharp look. "We'd have had words on the subject sooner than this if they had *not* been so paid!"

Charles reddened but said nothing. Luckily, the clerk, Anstey, was not in the office at that moment. After a while Maynard spoke again.

"You are ambitious, Mr Yuart, which is natural in a man of your age. You're impatient to make Hainault Mill what it was before. But – *festina lente*, Mr Yuart. *Festina lente*. That's a motto I learnt at school and I'm sure you did too. I would commend its wisdom to you."

"There is another motto which says 'Strike while the iron is hot.' That is what I am doing, Mr Maynard, – not only at Hainault but here, too, – and the result as you yourself have said—"

"Yes, yes," Maynard agreed. "You've worked wonders, I grant you that, and you mustn't think I'm not grateful for it." He laid the invoices down on his desk and sat back in his armed chair, his hands clasped across his middle. For a while he looked at Charles in silence. Then he gave a little grunt. "Well, I've done lecturing you for today. Now it's your turn to lecture me. You can tell me about this idea of yours for credit-capping with Francus Warde."

All in all, Maynard was pleased, and, as Charles said, had good reason to be. During the greater part of that year, Loxe

was working to capacity, and its new designs, which Charle
had created, were selling well at home and abroad. Th
order-books were well filled and the ledgers, when auditee
showed that profits had risen to a record twenty-five pe
cent. All this, as Maynard acknowledged, was due to Yuart
efficiency.

"You've certainly done what I asked you to do. You'v
pulled this mill up again to what it was in earlier days, befor
this dammed illness of mine reduced me to the poor hal
man I am now."

This was said at the onset of winter, when the first fog
came down on the valley, and Maynard, with his chroni
bronchitis, was obliged to remain in his own home. Durin
the fine summer that year, he had been at the mill almos
every day, arriving after ten in the morning, as his docto
advised, and leaving at four in the afternoon. But no
already the weather was such that he dared not venture ou
of doors, let alone go to the mill, and the strict confinemen
fretted him. As in the previous two winters, however, Charle
now visited him at home, taking cheques and trade bills fo
him to sign, and acceptances for him to endorse, togethe
with other "receivables". If Charles was too busy, Anste
went instead, but once a week without fail Charles took "th
books" for Maynard to see, and on these occasions would sta
perhaps an hour or more, giving detailed news of the mi
and answering Maynard's eager questions.

"Oh, if you knew how it vexes me to sit here playing th
invalid while another man does my work for me! Still, I mus
count my blessings, I know, because I have got two good mer
in you and Anstey. You and he are my eyes and ears. An
what *you* don't tell me, be sure *he* does!"

Maynard cocked an eyebrow at Charles, for the animosit
that existed between his partner and his clerk was a source o
some amusement to him. But Charles, as always, was not t
be drawn.

"I admit I don't report every petty squabble that flares u
in the loom-shops, nor every bit of vulgar gossip bandiee

about among the pickers. I have neither the time nor the inclination. I'm much too busy making sure that the mill is kept running smoothly and efficiently. And, I might add, profitably."

"Yes, and in that you've succeeded right well. Nobody could argue with that. It's been a good year, thanks to you. Let's hope for another one like it, eh?"

1866, however, although it began well enough, soon brought problems, due to the sudden collapse of a prominent firm of London financiers, Overend, Gurney, and Company, who, after some years of highly doubtful business practice, had now gone into liquidation with debts, it was said, amounting to many millions of pounds. To Charles, reading about it in the papers, the news was of small significance. He dismissed it as one of those convulsions that seized the City periodically, only to die down in a while, its cause and outcome alike unknown to most of the country's population.

The first indication he had that others felt differently was when Joseph Samms sent him a note calling in his loan, which he wanted paid in three days. Charles, though worried, was certainly not going to plead for time with a jumped-up ironmonger. He therefore sat down at once and wrote the man a cheque, comforting himself with the thought that his overdraft at the bank cost two per cent less than his loan from Samms had done. Soon, however, came an urgent message from the bank's manager, Mr Harriman, asking Charles to call on him. The Hainault account was now overdrawn to the sum of seven thousand, four hundred, and twenty-one pounds, far in excess of the six thousand pound limit agreed between them the year before. The bank had honoured Mr Yuart's cheque to Mr Samms on the assumption that the situation thus created would be of the shortest possible duration. Could he have Mr Yuart's assurance that this was indeed the case? Yes, certainly, Charles replied. It would be corrected without delay.

Unfortunately, just at this time, incomings at Hainault Mill were quickly cancelled by its outgoings, and Charles began to regret his haste in paying his debt to Joseph Samms. At Loxe Mill, one morning in June, there was fresh cause for anxiety, for among the papers on his partner's desk were three or four receivables, now mature and due for payment, which Anstey had placed there ready for Maynard to endorse. And among them, as Charles could see, was a promissory note of his own, written three months previously, in payment for wool, for a sum close upon nine hundred pounds. After his interview with Mr Harriman, it was certain this note would not be honoured.

The time was just after eight o'clock. Maynard, of course, had not yet arrived, and George Anstey was out in the yard, checking deliveries of coal. Charles, after a moment's hesitation, removed his promissory note from the pile and put it into his breast pocket. He sat down at his own desk and began looking through his own correspondence, though his mind still dwelt on what he had done. There was, of course, always the risk that the watchful clerk, when he returned, might discover the loss of the note, in which case Charles would arrange that it should be "found" elsewhere in the office. – At the back of the bill-box, perhaps, or between the pages of the relevant ledger.

In the event, all was well, and his action went undetected. As for the nine hundred pounds, he would pay that debt later on, perhaps when his next wool bill fell due, by writing a freshly dated note that covered both amounts together. He had no doubt whatever that by then his present difficulties would be resolved, because all this year Hainault cloth had been going out in large quantities, the value of which, when the trade bills returned, was enough to cover his present debts two or three times over. The bulk of this cloth, especially of the superfines, had gone to Francus Warde of London, and one of Charles's bills of exchange, sent to Warde the previous week, was expected back imminently.

Three days later the bill arrived, duly signed by Francus Warde, and Charles, with relief and satisfaction, took it at

once to Coulson's Bank, where he laid it before the manager.
The bill, payable in London, was made out in the sum of nine
thousand, five hundred pounds; it would not only pay off his
overdraft but would leave him in credit to an amount slightly
exceeding two thousand pounds. Mr Harriman, having looked
at the bill, laid it down again on his desk. His face became very
stiff. His voice, though controlled, conveyed anger.

"Mr Yuart, this bill, as you well know, is not payable until
three months from now, and *that*, in your present situation
with us, simply is not good enough. I pointed out, when last
we met, that your overdraft is now far in excess of the limit
agreed, and asked you to remedy the situation without delay.
That you promised to do but instead you bring me this
acceptance of Francus Warde's—"

"I don't understand you," Charles said. "That acceptance
is worth a substantial amount of money. Francus Warde, as
you know, is one of the largest and most highly respected
cloth merchants in London. I have done business with him
for years. So have a score of other clothiers in this district.
You must have discounted *hundreds* of Warde's acceptances
during your time in this bank. Certainly you've discounted
a large number for me, two of them in recent weeks."

"Quite so, Mr Yuart. And those acceptances of yours which
I already hold do nothing to mitigate the extent by which you
have exceeded your credit with us. At present, in fact, they
merely add to the risks imposed on this bank by your recent
business transactions, which is why I must insist – yet again
– that something of a more concrete nature be done to
reduce those risks without further delay."

"I would remind you, sir, that this bank earns its quarterly
one per cent on all my acceptances and a further annual five
per cent on the sum of my overdraft."

"I would remind *you*, Mr Yuart, that if, as is rumoured at
present, the Bank Rate should rise to ten per cent, your
overdraft and your acceptances will be costing you
accordingly. It is therefore in your own best interests, as well
as the bank's, that you should take steps to remedy your

present position before it becomes critical. Furthermore, I would remind you that as you do not *own* Hainault Mill, the only security you offer in return for our loan is the business you carry on there."

"Yes! And yet *you* would jeopardize that business by making unreasonable demands!" Charles, leaning forward, jabbed his finger at the trade-bill lying on the manager's desk. "*That* represents the business I do. *That* is part of its hard-earnt profits. *That* is value for value received."

"Not until three months from now, Mr Yuart, and in the present financial situation, three months is a long time. I have here an urgent memorandum from my Head Office directing me to stop all further extensions of credit, except on the soundest security, and to call in all outstanding debts *instanter*. I can make no exceptions to this ruling, as I'm sure you will appreciate."

"Is that your last word?" Charles asked.

"I'm sorry, Mr Yuart, but you must have read the papers, I'm sure. This affair of Overend and Gurney has caused panic in the City and it's already spreading to the provinces." Mr Harriman picked up the bill and looked at it for a moment or two. "You could try your luck with the brokers, of course, but … there's a run on the discount houses at present, just as there is on the banks, so I can't pretend to any great optimism." He laid the bill down on the desk again and pushed it gently towards Charles. "Perhaps, if you have no other resources at your disposal, your partner at Loxe would be willing to help. Presumably you have a substantial investment there which would form the required security if Mr Maynard *were* so disposed and would discount this acceptance for you."

Charles did not answer this suggestion. For one thing, he thought it presumptuous. For another, his present investment at Loxe was a mere two thousand pounds, since the greater part had been withdrawn to finance his business at Hainault. But there was no reason why Harriman should be told that, for it was, as Charles saw it, nobody's business but his own.

"The matter will be dealt with. You may rest assured." He put the bill into his pocket and rose to his feet. "But that you should refuse a perfectly good acceptance drawn on the account of a firm with the solid reputation of Francus Warde is something beyond my comprehension. And I take it amiss, sir. – I will tell you that!"

From the bank he went straight back to Hainault, there to peruse the mill's books, together with his clerk, Preston, to see which of his customers could, with justification, be called upon to settle their accounts. But the total value of the sums due was not nearly enough to meet his needs and calling them in would take time. Also, he ran the risk of offending those customers forever, a risk he could ill-afford to take. It seemed the only course open to him was to do as Harriman suggested and ask Maynard to help him out. On arriving at Loxe, however, he found that his partner had gone home. It was after four o'clock, later than Charles had realized, and, going about Loxe Mill affairs, mostly in the loom-shops, he put Hainault out of his mind until, at half past seven that evening, sitting at his desk, alone in the office, he applied himself to the problem anew.

If he *was* going to ask Maynard's help, it would be better to go to his home, where they could be private together, safe from the possibility that the clerk might be listening at the door. But Charles, even now, still had his doubts, and somehow, alone in Maynard's office, those doubts were magnified. To reveal the state of his business affairs, which he had guarded so jealously; then to endure Maynard's questioning, followed by his homilies: the prospect was more than Charles could stomach, especially when, at the end of it all, Maynard might very well refuse!

He, too, had been made nervous by the present financial situation and had left a memorandum for Charles, which lay before him, on his desk.

"No long credit to new customers. Ditto, no sale above £400. A note to be sent out with <u>all</u> trade bills, requesting their

<u>prompt</u> return. Old, established customers to receive their usual
commutations but beware of orders exceeding their norm".

And so on, for a page and a half.

But Charles, long before he reached the end, was not reading
the words for their sense: he was studying Maynard's
handwriting; and, familiar though it was to him, he saw it now
in a different way, as though the neatly formed characters stood
out, each in turn, from the white page, in response to some
thought not yet fully formed in his mind. Moving his chair
backwards a little, to catch the full light from the window, he
read the whole memorandum again. After this, having laid it
aside, he leant back and lit a cigarette. But smoking it took too
long and, rising, he threw it into the hearth.

He went over to Maynard's desk and brought back
Maynard's pen. He sat down again at his own desk, some
clean sheets of paper in front of him, and, consulting the
memorandum, began copying Maynard's script, paying
particular attention to the heavy strokes crossing the t's, and
the flourishes adorning certain capitals, especially the T and
the M in the signature on the second page. Within a few
minutes he had covered a whole sheet with extracts copied
from the memorandum, after which, on a second sheet, he
wrote out the whole of the alphabet, first in capitals, then in
small letters, all in Maynard's own style.

After studying these for a while, he copied Maynard's
signature, again and again, all down the page. Then he
practised a number of phrases, together with certain
abbreviations, habitually used by Maynard when endorsing
cheques or acceptances. It was really very easy to do, Charles
thought, and he viewed the results with some surprise. But
now, having reached this point, he became aware of his
quickened pulse; of the tight constriction in his chest. He got
up and lit another cigarette but this time he smoked it right
to the end, walking to and fro all the time, slowly, with
measured pace, intended to allay his nerves.

The cigarette finished, he returned to his desk and, with
the same deliberate movements, took his notecase out of his

pocket and removed from it the trade bill refused by the manager of his bank. He laid it on his blotter and smoothed it out. Written and signed by himself, requiring payment in ninety days, it was cross-signed by Francus Warde, accepting it as payable by the London bankers, Collet and Bown. It was worth nine thousand, five hundred pounds, and yet, Charles thought bitterly, his own bank in Chardwell had refused point-blank to discount it for him, thereby placing him in a position of the utmost gravity. The thought served to harden his resolve and, with a sudden angry briskness, he turned the trade bill over and round so that it lay blank side up, in a position convenient for him to write across it, narrow-ways. Thus, in his own elegant hand, and using his own fountain-pen, he inscribed the following endorsement: "On maturity pay Mr Maynard of Loxe Mill the full value of this acceptance in return for value discounted as pledged in the following." Under this he signed his own name.

A pause while he re-consulted his crib and then, using Maynard's pen this time, he inscribed a second endorsement, immediately below the first, in a slow, painstaking imitation of Maynard's script and turn of phrase.

"To Jarret and Son, Bnkrs. Chardwell:
On demand pay Mr Yuart the value embodied in this bill less discount of one per cent, the said bill, when minuted, to be retd. to me at Loxe Mill, as holder payable in due course."

Underneath this false endorsement Charles then wrote the false signature: "Thos. Maynard of Loxe Mill." Lastly, to complete the false transaction, he endorsed the bill yet again, in his own name, as current payee.

His task ended, he sat back and lit a third cigarette. His hands were shaking badly; there was sweat on his upper lip; and the tightness in his chest was now severe. To calm himself, he inhaled the smoke deep down into his lungs and let it out very slowly, eyeing his handiwork all the while. He had committed a forgery but had not yet uttered it. There was still time for him to draw back. But even while he sat and

smoked and weighed the alternatives, this way and that, he
knew he would not draw back now. For one thing, it meant
destroying the bill, with all the complications involved in
informing Francus Warde of its loss. No, the act must be
completed, otherwise production at Hainault would soon come
to a standstill, and his future there would be imperilled. All
because of some scare in the City which would, no doubt, be all
over in a week or two, like so many others that he could recall.

Furthermore, this forgery was merely the means of effecting
a loan, but without the lender's cognizance. Maynard would
have his money back as soon as Warde's acceptance matured
and that would be in ninety days. The chance of his ever
discovering the deception was so remote that it could easily
be dismissed. He rarely visited the bank now. If he wished to
know how his credit stood, he asked Charles to obtain a note
of it when he was there on the mill's business, and, Loxe Mill
credit being always in a highly satisfactory state, the requests
were few and far between. As for the mill's official audit, that
was still a long way off.

Charles, all in all, was pleased with himself. A man whose
livelihood was seriously threatened must use whatever means
came to hand if that livelihood was to be protected. He was
reasonably calm now. He had done what he knew he had to
do and this had brought a sense of relief. He stubbed out his
cigarette and dealt with the papers on his desk. The Warde
acceptance he returned to his notecase, and this he returned
to his breast pocket. He took up the sheets of paper on which
he had practised his forgeries and burnt them in the fire-
place; also the top page of his blotter and the contents of his
ash-tray. By now it was nine o'clock; he lit the gas and turned
it up; returned Maynard's pen to its proper place, and sat
down again at his own desk. He took the mill's order-books
from a drawer, together with the day's correspondence, and
applied himself to the day's business. There was nothing
unusual in his staying so late at the office. Running two mills
meant a great deal of work and often he was at one or the
other until ten or eleven o'clock.

*

The following morning, at Coulson's Bank, he sat again in the manager's office, and again the Francus Warde acceptance lay on the desk between them.

"If you will turn it over, Mr Harriman, you will see that I have taken your advice and applied to my partner for assistance. He has agreed to discount that bill for me with a draft on the Loxe Mill account at Jarret's."

"Ah, yes. Yes, indeed." Mr Harriman, having read the endorsements on the back of the bill, laid it down again, well pleased. "How very satisfactory," he said. "The brotherhood of the trade, eh? One clothier helping another. I am delighted, Mr Yuart, as I'm sure you must be. Mr Maynard is a sound man. No one could hope for a better business associate, as I'm sure you'll agree, and it is obvious from *this* that he in turn must have come to value you very highly during your three years of partnership."

"I think I can safely say that we have a good understanding, he and I, based on mutual respect and interdependence."

"Quite so. And what better basis could there be on which to found such an understanding?"

"Do you wish me to wait while you send across to Jarret's?"

"That will not be necessary. Mr Maynard's signature is guarantee enough for me."

"In that case, as my balance with you is now in credit, I assume that I may have the use of it without any further delay. For one thing, while I am here, I will draw cash for the Hainault wages, which will save me coming in again tomorrow."

Mr Harriman, far from demurring, accompanied Charles out to the public area of the bank; chatted to him while he drew his cash; and instructed a runner to carry the bags of coin out to Mr Yuart's horse. He and Charles then shook hands. The *status quo ante* had been restored.

Driving away from the town, Charles congratulated himself. His stratagem had worked well. Hainault was safe. He could

breathe again. His only remaining anxiety lay in watching for
the Warde acceptance when it arrived at Loxe Mill. As it
transpired, he had not long to wait, and luckily, when the
post came, he was alone in the office. The envelope, bearing
the Jarret insignia, was easy to identify. He extracted it from
the pile of letters and put it into his pocket, where it remained
until late that night, when, alone in his office at Hainault, he
could safely open it. The trade bill, duly minuted, with the
second endorsement officially marked "Paid As Directed"
had in addition, pinned to it, a separate docket with the
written instruction: "Return to Mr Thos. Maynard at Loxe
Mill, near Patesbridge, as holder payable in due course."

Charles put the bill and docket together into his notecase,
which he always carried everywhere, safe in his inner breast
pocket. Just how he would deal with the bill so that, on
maturity, it would repay Maynard's "loan", Charles had not
yet decided; but as Maynard himself also did business with
Francus Warde, and had acceptances in his name lodged at
Jarret's, it should be easy enough to arrange. Anyway, he told
himself, he had almost ninety days in which to solve that
small problem. At present he had more urgent matters on
hand: two busy mills to manage and a so-called crisis
threatening the country's trade. He had sailed in these
troubled waters before; he must steer a more careful course
this time if Hainault was to weather the storm.

He had paid off his overdraft and was in credit to the tune
of two thousand pounds, and Coulson's now, he was confident,
would discount future acceptances for him without any
quibble. They would not, however, allow him the use of any
further overdraft; nor could he hope to borrow elsewhere;
and this just at a crucial time when Hainault cloth was in such
demand! All of which meant that he and his clerk would have
to put their heads together to ensure that Hainault's limited
resources were put to the best possible use.

The crisis, he found, was real enough; and soon, with the Bank
Rate fixed at ten per cent, its effects were felt throughout the

country. All along the Cullen Valley, frightened clothiers were reducing production, and Thomas Maynard was one of them.

"I've been reading the London papers and I don't like the look of it. It's even causing trouble in Europe and it seems we're in for a rough ride."

Charles, though he knew that Loxe Mill finances were founded as though on solid rock, agreed to Maynard's proposed reductions without question, because less work at Loxe meant more time for him to spend on his own affairs at Hainault. There, for the time being at least, production went on as usual, for Charles, taking advantage of his fellow clothiers' nervousness, had bought their "surplus" stocks of wool, some of it the finest merino, which they let him have at bargain prices. Furthermore, these clothiers – Sidney Hurne was one of them – had agreed to issue trade bills giving him credit of six months, thereby showing, he thought with contempt, that they trusted his handling of the present crisis but not their own.

So, the Hainault looms were as busy as ever, and his cloth, both worsteds and superfines, was leaving the mill as soon as it was ready. True, his buyers, such as Francus Warde, were also asking for long credit, but this he could well afford to give. "Whatever you make, I will take," Warde had said to him, earlier; and his trade bills came back, signed in acceptance, as promptly as they had ever done. Altogether, the present situation, so alarming to the timid, was turning out pretty well for Charles; but this fact he kept to himself and, following the wisdom of the prophet, told it not in Gath nor in Askelon. Whenever Maynard asked him how he was faring at Hainault these days, Charles always made the same reply: "Oh, we are just marking time, that's all, like everyone else just at present."

"Very wise," Maynard said. "You can't be too careful at times like this."

Within another few weeks, it appeared that the worst of the crisis was past. The newspaper pundits predicted that the Bank Rate would soon return to normal, and with it, little by little, the life-blood of the country's commerce would begin flowing freely again.

Charles, as he read, smiled to himself. Not only had he weathered the storm but the ill wind had blown him some good; all because he had kept his head and maintained a firm grip of the wheel. This was what he said to himself, sitting at his desk in the Hainault Mill office, as he laid the newspaper aside and turned his attention to the morning's post. The pile of letters, opened by his clerk, lay ready for him to read; all except one on top of the pile, which remained sealed in its envelope, this being very clearly inscribed: Private and Confidential.

This letter, Charles found, was from the office of Francus Warde and Son, cloth merchants of Brigg Street, London, but was written by a firm of accountants, informing all who might be concerned that the said Francus Warde and Son, having found themselves unable to meet their financial obligations, had declared their condition to the Court of Equity, and that the said court had appointed Messrs Smith and Gray, accountants, of 12, Market Row, London, to act as Receivers.

Mr Yuart, as a creditor of the firm of Francus Warde and Son, was invited to submit details of all transactions he had had with the said firm, stating the value thereof, and to state the value of any trade bills held by him against payment in the name of the said firm. The writer added that it was his duty further to inform Mr Yuart that Messrs Netherton and Phillips, solicitors and Notaries Public, had issued a statement to the effect that trade bills and all other acceptances signed by Francus Warde in recent months were invalidated and would not now be honoured, etc., etc..

Charles stared at the letter in disbelief and for some seconds was utterly numb, divorced from thought, feeling, and consciousness, as though by the effects of ether. When the letter slid from his grasp, the sudden movement startled him, for his nerveless fingers had loosened their hold without the knowledge of his brain. At the same time he became aware that his clerk, Preston, across the room, was looking at him in concern.

"Is anything wrong, Mr Yuart, sir? Have you had bad news?"

"Yes, I have had bad news," Charles said, and it took all his self-control to utter these words without choking. Abruptly he rose from his desk. He picked up the letter again, folded it quickly and noisily, and thrust it into his pocket. "News that means I have to go out."

"Shall I send word to the stables, sir?"

"No, no. I'll go myself."

His one idea was to get away; to be alone in some quiet place, where he could recover himself, safe from inquisitive eyes; where he could think without interruption and weigh the gravity of his position in the light of this disaster. Within a short time, therefore, he was well away from Hainault, riding along the narrow lanes between Brisby and Cowle, ascending gradually until he came out on to the open slopes of Brisby Common. There he dismounted and sat down on a slab of rock. He took out the letter and read it again, though its words and their meaning were clear enough, and were already incised upon his mind.

No amount of close study could alter the facts contained therein, nor reduce their significance. The Francus Warde acceptance, by means of which he had "borrowed" nine thousand, five hundred pounds from the Loxe Mill account at Jarret's Bank, was now worthless. Worthless, too, were a number of other Warde bills discounted for him by his own bank in sums totalling another four thousand pounds at least. Together with the wool-bill which he had delayed paying at Loxe, and other bills from local tradesmen, his debts at Hainault were now immense. Furthermore, there was a risk that the method by which he had transferred money from Maynard's account to his own might now be exposed, bringing his probity in question, since his motives were bound to be misunderstood.

*

Rack his brains how he might, there were only two possible solutions to his problem: one, if he could borrow enough money to make good his peculations; the other, to throw himself on Maynard's mercy, requesting time to pay his debts, little by little, out of Hainault's future profits. Either way, he needed to act; it was no earthly use his skulking here; and so, still sick in the stomach, he re-mounted his horse and rode back down the lanes till he reached the main road to Chardwell.

Throughout the morning, and for part of the afternoon, he went from one place to another, desperately seeking a loan; and everywhere he received the same answer, couched always in the same brusque terms used by his friend and solicitor, the first of those on whom he called.

"Yuart, I don't understand you. To expect a loan at a time like this, when the country is only now emerging from one of the worst financial crises of the century! I don't know what trouble you're in, but whatever it is I cannot help. No, I will not listen to you! You may promise what interest you like but promises are not security and without security, as you surely must know, you cannot possibly hope to borrow such a considerable sum. You will only be wasting your time if you try."

And so it proved, with every money-lender in Chardwell itself and with three more in Sharveston. Charles endured insolence and impertinence; even derision; but still he returned to Hainault empty-handed. Only one course remained: he would have to see Maynard; but still he delayed doing this, telling himself that first he would write to the bankrupt Warde's receivers, demanding that all stocks of Hainault cloth be returned to him immediately, so that he could sell it elsewhere.

But he had barely crossed the threshold when his clerk handed him a copy of *The Chardwell Gazette*, which carried, on the front page, a full report of Warde's collapse. Therein it was stated that Warde's warehouse at Friary, London, had been found to be completely empty; that Warde had, some weeks before, sold all the cloth in his possession at knock-down prices and had used the money thus quickly raised to dabble in risky speculations. Almost all of it had been lost and it was feared that Warde's creditors "would be lucky to receive two pence in the pound".

In addition to the newspaper, Preston handed Charles two notes, both of which had been delivered by hand. The first was from Maynard, asking Charles, in a terse sentence, to come at once to Loxe Mill. The second was from Mr Harriman, asking him to come to the bank. Obviously, both men had read about Warde in the newspapers; and Maynard, having done business with Warde, would that morning have received a letter from the accountants, as Charles had done.

Charles sat down and scribbled an answer to Maynard: "Busy at present. Will come when I can." He wrote in similar vein to the bank. He then wrote a brief note to his wife, saying that, as he would be working extra late that night, he would probably sleep at the mill. Having sent these three notes off by messenger, he asked for a fresh horse to be saddled for him, and immediately went out again, chiefly because he was afraid that Maynard might come looking for him. There was nothing he could do; only postpone all confrontations for as long as possible, in the desperate, irrational hope that something miraculous would intervene to save him from ruin.

Katharine, receiving her husband's message, found nothing in it to make her anxious. He quite often slept at the mill and always kept a change of clothes there. Dick, however, when he got home, found his father's message disquieting, for he had seen the day's papers and knew of Francus Warde's collapse. Mr Bonnamy had drawn his attention to the news item, asking if his father would suffer by it. Dick thought it only too probable and had asked permission to leave the office early that day. His chief concern was for his mother and it was some relief to him that as yet she knew nothing about it.

"You are home early today," she said. "Why is that?"

"I have an important errand to do, over at one of our building-sites. I came to tell you I should be late and not to keep supper for me."

On this pretext he left the house and walked over to Newton Railes, to discuss his anxieties with Martin. Martin, as it happened, had been in Chardwell that afternoon and had found the whole town alive with talk concerning the Warde débâcle.

"I went to see you at Bonnamy's but you had already left. Does your mother know about Warde's collapse?"

"No, not yet. My father sent word to say that he was busy and wouldn't be home tonight, but she sees nothing untoward in that. And so far she has heard nothing of it from the neighbours." Dick paused. His young face was pale with worry. "I wish I knew what was happening. Warde was my father's biggest buyer. He's bound to have been affected by this."

"Yes, I'm afraid there's no doubt about that."

"If you know something that I don't know, I would rather you told me at once."

"I know nothing concrete but according to what I've heard, your father was in the town all morning trying to raise a substantial loan."

"Did he succeed?"

"I don't know. But I think it very unlikely."

"Of course it's unlikely!" Dick exclaimed. "With the banks still as nervous as they are – he must be insane to expect such a thing!"

"Not insane. But desperate, yes."

"Martin, what am I to do?"

"As it is a question of money, there is nothing you can possibly do. And in all probability there's nothing *I* can do, either, since your father feels as he does towards me. Still, I intend to try all the same … Perhaps, if he is desperate *enough*, he will accept my help this time."

"I suppose I shouldn't have come to you. If I had an ounce of pride in me—"

"Some things are more important than pride. And one of them is friendship."

"I came for my mother's sake, not his. If it weren't for her—"

"Yes, I know."

"When are you going to see him?"

"I'm going at once," Martin said. "You can come with me in the trap and I'll set you down at the foot of the Burr."

"No. I'm on my way to Chacelands now, to see aunt Ginny and uncle George. It's Anthony's birthday party tomorrow, remember, and I want to tell them not to mention the Warde business in front of mama. Uncle George is sure to have seen the newspapers and – well, I know we can't keep it secret forever, but if you are able to help somehow—"

"Then your mother may never need to know at all. But whatever happens when I see your father, – whether good news or bad – I will tell you of it at Chacelands tomorrow, when we meet there for Anthony's birthday. Meanwhile, try not to worry. We must hope for the best – and pray for it."

When Martin arrived at Hainault and called at the office, he was informed that the master was out; that no one knew where he was, nor what time he would be back.

"In that case I will wait for him."

He declined a seat in the office and chose to wait outside. For a while he walked on the river-bank; then he returned to the mill-yard and passed another half-hour walking slowly to and fro, watching two packers at work, and looking in at some of the buildings. The mill clock had struck eight and Martin was checking his watch by it when Yuart at last rode into the yard. He was making his way towards the stables when he saw Martin and came to a halt.

"What are you doing here?"

"I want to talk to you on a business matter. Will you step aside, where we can be private?"

Yuart dismounted, and a man came and took his horse. Martin stood waiting for an answer, during which time Yuart looked at him long and hard.

"Very well. If you insist."

They left the mill yard together and walked out into the open. Once away from the noise of the mill, they came to a halt and faced each other.

"Whatever your business," Yuart said, "I shall be glad if you make it brief."

"I'm here because I've heard the news about Francus Warde. I know you must be hard hit by it because you have been trying to raise a loan. If you've succeeded, I will take my leave. But if, as I fear, you have not—"

"You may take your leave, either way, and the sooner the better," Yuart said. His handsome face was slightly flushed and his breath confirmed that he had been drinking. Still, he was well in command of himself, his speech just as precise as ever, even when conveying anger. "Do you think I would borrow from you? *You*, who have taken so much from me? – Stood in my way so many times? – Come between me and my son—"

"I have taken nothing from you except what you've lost through your own folly. But since it cannot be denied that we have changed places, you and I, and that your losses have been my gain, surely the present situation is one where your grievances might be redressed."

"I am not deceived by you, Mr Cox, as my wife and her sister have always been, and my children are now. I recognize you for what you are. You come to me with offers of help because it gives you a sense of importance. You think, when you try to patronize me, that it makes us equals. And you risk nothing! Not a penny piece! For you already know I will not accept it."

"If I could convince you that my offer is perfectly genuine—"

"My answer would still be exactly the same."

"You may dislike me as much as you wish – it is nothing to me – but can't you for once set that aside and do what is best for your family? I am offering you a loan—"

"Without even knowing how much I need?"

"Well, we should need to go into the matter, of course."

"And there would, no doubt, be conditions attached,

giving you power to interfere in my affairs."

"I have no desire to take your business away from you. Quite the reverse, for as well as a loan to settle your debts, I am willing to advance further sums so that you can buy this mill outright and continue to run it."

There was a pause. Yuart, it seemed, was taken by surprise. Martin, encouraged, went on.

"But I should certainly wish for some arrangement that would safeguard your business from the kind of trading that brought you to ruin six years ago and seems about to do so again. And before you dismiss that stipulation, let me remind you, Mr Yuart, that if you come into the bankruptcy court you will, with your past history, find yourself under restrictions far more severe than any I should impose on you. That is, if you're allowed to continue trading at all. You could find yourself awarded with a dead certificate."

Once again Yuart was silent, though what he was thinking could not be guessed, for his face had now a withdrawn look, as though he had turned in on himself.

"Yes, well," he said at last. "You have stated your business and I've heard you out. Now, Mr Cox, I will bid you good night."

"You mean you refuse?"

"Certainly."

For a moment longer they looked at each other, Martin seeking even now to penetrate Yuart's stubborn reserve. He wanted to ask about Thomas Maynard and the state of the Loxe Mill partnership but knew that his question would go unanswered. Suddenly Yuart turned away and Martin was obliged to follow him. They returned to the mill yard, and Martin, angry, climbed into the trap. Still, with the reins held loose in his hands, he made one final attempt.

"If you should change your mind, – and I hope to God you will – you have only to send for me."

Receiving no answer, he drove out of the yard and on to the road. His mission had been utterly fruitless. Yuart, he knew, would not change his mind. And this was the news he would have to impart when he met Dick at Chacelands the following afternoon for Anthony's birthday celebrations.

Early the following morning, even as the first mill-hands arrived for work, Charles, after a few hours sleep in the little apartment adjoining his office, was already up and about, watching them from the window, where he stood drinking a cup of coffee. By the time the mill came alive and the clack-clack of the looms was heard, he had washed and shaved and was fully dressed, in clean linen and neck-cloth, his outer clothes most carefully brushed.

Briskly he strode into his office and sat down at his desk. The first few remarks he addressed to his clerk had all been prepared beforehand and conveyed the impression of a man who, though burdened with serious problems, had the solutions well in hand. He read through the first delivery of post as though each letter were of vital importance; looked through the order-books, making notes; and spent a good twenty minutes examining some samples of wool which the sorter had sent in to him. The clerk, Preston, meanwhile, went about his own routine tasks and, taking his cue from Charles, tried to behave as if yesterday's news had receded to the back of his mind.

Shortly after half past nine a messenger came, bringing a second note from Maynard, demanding Yuart's presence at Loxe Mill *without any further delay*. And this time Charles went.

As soon as he entered the Loxe Mill office, George Anstey rose and withdrew, leaving the partners alone together. Maynard, grim-faced, sat at his desk. He motioned Charles to sit opposite.

"You know, of course, what I have to say. It stems from this Francus Warde affair."

"Yes."

"I have, myself, done business with Warde, and yesterday, when the news broke, I received a request to call at my bank as soon as I could. Mr Hollis was anxious to speak to me about certain acceptances, drawn on Warde, which the bank had discounted for me. Luckily, they are of small value, though the loss of some four hundred pounds is quite bad enough, God knows. But there was another matter that Hollis wished to discuss with me – a bill drawn on Warde in *your* name, which *you* had endorsed in my favour, and which I, it seems, re-endorsed, authorizing a draft to you of nine thousand, five hundred pounds."

Here Maynard consulted some notes which lay before him on the desk.

"Yes, sir! Nine thousand, five hundred pounds! I still can't believe it even now." He drew a deep, painful breath, and looked directly at Charles again. "I don't need to tell you that I know nothing about such a bill. It never even passed through my hands. But the details were there, in the bank's ledgers. I saw them with my own two eyes and Hollis's clerk wrote them down for me."

Maynard waved the paper aloft; then slapped it down again on the desk.

"I sent for Anstey to join me at the bank, but he could throw no light on the matter. On perusing Hollis's ledger, however, he uncovered a second mystery. This time something that *should* have been there but was not. – To wit, a prom note of yours, payable on the fourth of June, for wool from Pirrie's, which Anstey put out for me to endorse on that date and which *you* should have paid into the bank. When we got back here, we looked it up in our own ledger. That note was worth almost nine hundred pounds. So, altogether, it appears you have swindled me out of a total of some ten thousand, four hundred pounds. Unless, that is, there are further sums that have not yet come to light."

"There are no further sums," Charles said, "and I had no intention of swindling you."

"Perhaps you would like to explain yourself, then, though I have to warn you, here and now, that there can be no explanation that is likely to win my sympathy."

"It was when this banking crisis began. Samms, the money-

lender, called in his loan. I paid it, of course, immediately
and as a result got a balance against me at Coulson's. The
insisted I clear it at once but refused to take up the Ward
acceptance. I was desperate. You must see that. I would
never have done it otherwise. And if Francus Warde hadn'
defaulted, you would have had your money back withou
knowing it had ever been borrowed."

"And what about the prom note for wool, which yo
purloined from this desk? That's got nothing to do wit
Warde but it still hasn't been paid all the same. And quite
frankly, I can't help feeling that the longer its loss remaine
undiscovered, the less likely it was to be paid."

"That is not so," Charles said. He reached into his breas
pocket and took out his notecase. From it he removed tw
papers: the Warde acceptance and his own promissory not
for wool. He laid them down in front of Maynard. "As yo
see, I have kept them both very carefully. I would scarcel
have done that if I had *not* meant to pay you back. Also, th
total sum is such that its loss could not possibly have gon
undetected forever, and I'm not such a fool – or such
scoundrel – as to think it would."

"So you say! So you say! But whether you *would* have
repaid me or not, the inescapable fact is that *now* you ar
quite unable to."

"At present, yes. But given time I can and will. And you do
have two thousand pounds of mine invested in this mill."

"That still leaves almost eight and a half thousand owin
to me. And no doubt by now you have other debts besides."

"Yes. I do."

"To what amount?"

"I cannot say precisely – not to the nearest penny."

"H'mph!" Maynard said, scornfully. "I doubt very much
you could say, even to the nearest thousand pounds! You ar
ruined, man, and must face the fact. You have done as yo
did six years ago – taken risks with other men's money an
thrown it away down the drain. When you first came to m
and offered yourself as my partner, you told me you ha

learnt your lesson, and I was fool enough to believe you. Then, two years ago, you asked to withdraw ten thousand pounds from your investment, and again I was foolish enough to say yes. I *trusted* you, Mr Yuart, and you have betrayed me at every turn."

Maynard was breathing heavily; his face was darkly congested; but when Charles expressed concern, it was dismissed with angry impatience. After a while, as his breathing improved, Maynard reached out and picked up the Warde acceptance. He read what was written on the face of it; then turned it over and read the reverse, with its three endorsements, one apparently in his hand and carrying his signature. Although he already knew what he would find there, the sight of it affected him deeply. He laid the acceptance down again and placed the prom note on top of it.

"So," he said, meeting Yuart's gaze. "Forgery. Theft. Embezzlement. I know little about the law, Mr Yuart, but I would say that conviction for these three things together would carry a heavy penalty."

"Is that what you want? To see me indicted as a criminal?"

"It is more a question of what you deserve."

Charles sat silent a while. He badly wanted to light a cigarette but this was forbidden in Maynard's presence because the smoke made him cough. Instead he took out his snuff-box and inhaled a pinch at each nostril. He closed the box and held it tight-clenched in his hand.

"Supposing I could repay what I owe … immediately, in a matter of days … what would you say to me then?"

"What possible chance can you have of doing that?"

"A definite chance – by means of a loan."

"Surely you cannot be serious. Even if you have found some Isaac willing to accommodate you—"

"The loan would come from a private source."

"A friend, do you mean?"

"No, I would not call him a friend. Nor do I wish to divulge his name. Suffice it to say that he is a man who knows of my present difficulties and has offered to lend me what money I need."

"Well, all I can say is that this mysterious benefactor is an even greater fool than I myself have been. If indeed he exists at all."

"He exists. I swear to that."

"And yet there is no friendship between you."

"No. None."

"Then why should he make such a generous offer?"

"I cannot say."

"Yuart, I don't understand you. Are you telling me that you have accepted a loan from a man who, to judge by your look and your tone, is someone you dislike exceedingly?"

"No, I have *not* accepted it," Charles replied angrily. "I have no *wish* to accept it and I made that plain to him last night. But if, as it now appears, there is no other way of saving my honour, then I am forced to think again. I'm forced to consider accepting his offer, however distasteful it may be."

"Whether you accept it or not, your honour will not be saved, Mr Yuart. – Only the outward appearance of it. Which raises another important question concerning this nameless benefactor. You say he knows of your difficulties but does he also know, I wonder, that you have been guilty of theft, forgery, and embezzlement?"

"No."

"Well, obviously he would have to be told. Any man lending so large a sum of money would need to know the risks involved. And I should feel it my bounden duty to make sure that he did know."

"Even though it might mean losing your chance of full reparation?"

"No decent man would wish reparation if it meant another man's loss, Mr Yuart, and by suggesting such a thing to me you reveal yourself yet again as an unprincipled scoundrel."

Charles, white-faced, made no reply. Maynard, now merciless, went sternly on.

"Perhaps it's as well that you do so reveal yourself, for i

helps me to see matters clearly, and hardens me in my decision. I asked you to come here so that you might have a fair hearing, but nothing you have said inspires any hope that you will ever change your spots. I must tell you, therefore, that I do not feel inclined to be lenient. Your misdemeanours have been too grave and they must be made public. Men must know once and for all, Mr Yuart, that you are not safe to have dealings with."

"Is that your final word?"

"It is."

"I don't ask for mercy on my own behalf – I can see it would be useless – but have you thought how it will be for my wife and family when all this is known?"

"I know precisely how it will be for them and it grieves me deeply. They have already suffered in the past and now they are to suffer again. But still I cannot be party to any attempt at concealing your dishonesty. It is of too serious a nature. I feel, therefore, that I have no choice but to see Alec Stevenson and put the whole matter before him. As he is your solicitor as well as mine, that will mean complications, but he will soon tell me if I'm to seek advice elsewhere. No doubt the legal dissolution of our partnership will involve certain formalities, but as far as I am concerned, it is terminated here and now. The same applies to your position as manager. You will please hand over your keys. I have no more to say to you, Mr Yuart, except to bid you good day."

Charles took the Loxe Mill keys from his pocket, unfastened them from his fob-strap, and laid them down on the desk. He got up and went to the door. There he paused and looked back.

"I will not ask you to reconsider your decision—"

"It would be useless if you did."

"—but I would ask you to believe that I never *intended* to cheat you."

"But you *have* cheated me," Maynard said, and his sharp upward gaze showed that for him the matter was perfectly simple. "You have cheated me grossly. And others, too."

Charles left the office without another word.

*

From Loxe he rode to the inn at Patesbridge, where he ate an early luncheon, and drank three glasses of brandy. He sat long over his third glass, glad of the brandy's comfort and warmth, which, as it spread through his veins, gradually quelled the rigor that had seized his stomach in its chill spasms. He found, too, now he knew the worst, that while one part of his mind remained darkly clouded, the other was working well enough. He was able to think; to accept, at last, the inevitable; even to plan accordingly. It was not, after all, the first time that events in his life had been such as to make it unbearable to him. And the remedy now was as before.

On leaving Patesbridge, he returned to Hainault, where his clerk sat eating his lunch in the office. Charles, with a word of apology, sent him on an errand to the spinning-shop. He then emptied the cashbox, tipping the coin into two linen bags, which were easily stowed away in his pockets. Almost as soon as the clerk returned he again left the mill "on a matter of business" and rode home to Grove End. He had a well-prepared excuse for returning at this unusual time, but to his surprise it was not needed, for his wife and daughter were away from home. They had gone to Chacelands, the maid said, for Master Anthony's birthday party. Mrs Winter had called for them in the carriage soon after luncheon. Master Dick would be there too. Mrs Winter intended collecting him from his office in town.

"Didn't you know about the party, sir?"

"Yes, but I had forgotten it."

He went into his study and removed what money there was in his private cash-box. He then went upstairs and packed a bag. Downstairs again, he spoke to the maid.

"Will you tell Mrs Yuart when she returns that I have been called away on business."

"Yes, sir. Certainly, sir." She opened the front door for him. "Will you be gone long, sir?"

"Just give her my message," Charles said.

He left no note for Katharine this time. He would write later, saying goodbye to her and the children, perhaps when he reached Liverpool. Perhaps later still, aboard ship, on his way to America.

Now, by a roundabout route, he made his way to Pibblecombe Halt, where he would board a train that would take him on the first stage of his journey. Six years before, he had done this same thing; had slipped away from his native district in just this furtive, inglorious manner, with the sick sense of failure heavy upon him. But this time there could be no return, for it meant facing criminal charges; possibly even imprisonment; and he could not bear the thought of that. Even if the court were lenient with him, he could never hold up his head again; not here in this place where he was known. Nor could he bear the thought of facing his wife and children again, once they knew the nature of his offences.

It was difficult to believe that fate had twice singled him out in this way; twice brought him to ruin and ill-repute; but so it was, and he must accept it. Life in England was finished for him. Almost he felt, at this moment, that life was finished for him altogether; and across his mind's eye there flashed a picture of a man falling from a great ship, to vanish into the waters below, which closed above him, in the ship's wake. Would he end it that way? Perhaps. Perhaps not. But if so, he told himself grimly, he could do it with much less trouble in the waters of the Cullen, down below. But no, he thought, in sudden revulsion: at least he would spare his family *that*. And there would be time enough to decide, one way or the other, on the long voyage to America.

He was now on the road to Newton Ashkey, which skirted the grounds of Newton Railes. Occasionally, through a gap in the trees, he would catch a brief glimpse of the house; but after a while he schooled himself to keep his gaze fixed on the road. The sight of the place was too painful to him; too closely connected with all he had lost. Soon, however, he had forded the stream that marked the end of Newton Railes land. Now the road ran with the Chacelands estate, but nothing could be seen of the house itself because of the high boundary wall surrounding the park.

From the church at Newton Childe came the sound of the clock striking four. Presumably, by this time, Anthony's birthday celebrations would be in progress. Certainly his guests should be there by now. And, the September day being warm and sunny, with a pleasant south-easterly breeze blowing, they might very well be out in the gardens, playing croquet, perhaps, or taking a stroll before tea. Charles, passing so close to the place where his wife and children now were, was overcome by a sudden longing to see them once more, for the last time, and to bid them goodbye, from a distance, without their knowledge.

Confident that this could be achieved, he turned in at the first bridle-gate he came to and rode across the park, keeping to the higher ground, most of which was covered in trees. Thus hidden, he rode slowly on, until in a while he came to a place that afforded him a view of the house. A little further, descending now, and in another moment or two he was looking across at the south front, with its orangery flanked by loggias, and its lawn sloping down to the sunken garden, where fountains played over bronze nymphs sporting with dolphins in the lilied pool. And there on the lawn, as he expected, the small family party was gathered: Ginny and George, with Katharine between them; Dick a little way behind; and Susannah talking to Anthony.

A table and chairs had been set out, and three servants came and went, bringing the paraphernalia needed for taking tea out of doors. A maid began unfolding a cloth to spread on the table but while she was flipping it open there came a strong guest of wind that carried it clean out of her hands and sent it billowing over the lawn. The maid ran after it; Susannah and Anthony went to help; but then, just as they stooped to retrieve it, Anthony's white terrier puppy came bounding swiftly across the lawn and flung himself bodily onto the cloth, snapping and yapping at those parts that continued to ripple in the wind.

Charles, sitting his horse in the distant beech grove, could see his family quite clearly: Susannah in her seersucker frock, striped in different shades of green; Katharine in white, a straw hat on her head; and Dick, standing a little apart, his hands in the pockets of his white flannel jacket. The voices of the group came only faintly across the distance and he could not hear what was said. But their laughter came clearly enough and the sound of it, especially Susannah's, was almost more than he could bear.

God! What a fool he had been, risking so much and losing it all! His living. His honour. His family. In one way, as he well knew, he was already a stranger to his wife and children and had been for years. But somehow he had assumed that once he regained his old position, understanding would be restored, bringing back the love and respect which he, as husband and father, had every right to expect from them. Now that would never be; they were lost to him irrecusably now; and if he was already a stranger to them, a stranger he would remain forever, remembered only with shame and distress. Katharine, perhaps, would pity him, but his children would not. And what was pity, anyway, compared with all he had forfeited?

Emerging from these sombre reflections, he felt that a great deal of time had elapsed, though he knew it could only have been a few minutes. But now, as he looked across at the little group gathered on the Chacelands lawn, the people seemed further off than before, as though the tenor of his thoughts, by moving forward into the future, had already increased the distance between him and them. They had the appearance of a group captured in a picture, and he suddenly knew that, whatever the length of his life would be, this was how he would remember them: his wife and children, in company, laughing together in a sunlit garden.

He turned and rode away from them, but instead of returning the way he had come, he struck off in a direction that brought him round to the front of the house and so down to the main carriage-road. He would save himself three miles this way, and if the lodge-keeper saw him pass, well, what did that matter now?

At roughly the moment when Charles reached the road, Martin, driving a pony-trap, was turning in at the main gates. Beside him, on the seat, lay a wooden box containing a new, "improved" magic lantern, made by John Betty of Birmingham, complete with a set of fifty slides: his birthday gift to Anthony. Also in the trap was a large basket filled with fruit from the mulberry tree at Railes, which had plimmed and ripened early that year, together with some bunches of grapes from the greenhouse vines which Katharine, in other days, had tended with such loving care.

Although he saw the rider ahead, coming towards him at a hand-gallop, he could not at first believe who it was, for Yuart, as he knew, had not visited Chacelands since his quarrel with George six years before. But Yuart it was, sure enough, and Martin, in surprise, drew rein and stopped. Yuart now drew near and almost it seemed, when he recognized Martin, that he too intended to stop. Martin saw the look on his face, – saw his hands pull on the reins – but then, as quickly, the man changed his mind and, giving the reins a sudden twitch, he put spur to his startled horse and rode swiftly past, going full gallop towards the gates. Martin, looking back, called after him, – "Yuart! Wait!" – but got no response; and in another few seconds, Yuart, with scarcely a check, had ridden clattering through the gateway, to vanish from sight into the lane.

Martin faced forward again. The encounter had taken him by surprise and he wondered what it could signify. Then, a flick of the reins and he moved off, still puzzled and faintly anxious, but telling himself that in a short while the mystery would be resolved. So, as Charles rode swiftly away, leaving his family behind him forever, Martin drove on towards Chacelands House, where they were waiting for him.